Grow Old With Me

Grow Old With Me

Melinda Evaul

Winding Road Ink
Soddy Daisy, TN

Grow Old With Me
Novel #1 in the Quilt Trail Series

Copyright © 2010 by Melinda Evaul

To learn more about Melinda and the Quilt Trail Novels visit, www.melindaevaul.com

Winding Road Ink
P.O. Box 1465
Soddy Daisy, TN 37384
windingroadink@att.net

All rights reserved. No part of this book may be reproduced or transmitted in any form or by any means, electronic or mechanical, including photo-copying, recording, or by any information storage and retrieval system, without written permission from the author, except for the inclusion of brief quotations in a review.

ISBN- 9780983124900
LCCN- 2010940236

Cover and interior graphic designs: Lynn Dean- lynndean@hot.rr.com
Cover formatting: James Shelley- www.shelleysphoto@photorelflect.com
Horses photo: Amanda Writesman- www.belmomentophotography.com
Author photo and house photo: Philip Evaul- www.melindaevaul.com

This book is a work of fiction. Names, characters, places, and incidents either are the product of the author's imagination or are used fictitiously. Any other resemblance to actual events, locales, organizations, or persons living or dead is entirely coincidental and beyond the intent of either the author or the publisher.

Scripture quotations are from The Holy Bible: King James Version (KJV)
Printed and bound by Snowfall Press- www.snowfallpress.com
Printed in the United States of America

DEDICATION

For my husband, Phil.
You shouldered many tasks while allowing me to write.
Thanks for helping make a dream come true.
Growing old with you is a special gift from God.

ACKNOWLEDGEMENTS

This novel is set in Love Valley, NC—located in Iredell County. Andy and Ellenora Barker founded the cowboy town in 1954. I chose to honor them in this book, and appreciate the information they shared about their unique town. They gave me permission to use their names in my novel.

I owe a huge thanks to Beth and Charlie Nance. They welcomed me into their home and fed me on several occasions. Via tours of the town, introductions to local proprietors, and e-mail correspondences, Beth and Charlie provided information about Love Valley. I mention them in the book to honor their hospitality and the friendship we developed during the writing of this novel. They granted permission for the use of their names.
   www.lovevalleyarena.com

The owners of Love Valley stores provided tours and allowed me to take pictures. They granted permission to use their store names in my novel. I fictionalized descriptions and locations to suit the needs of the book.
   www.townoflovevalley.com

A huge debt of gratitude goes to my exceptional critique partner and friend, Lynn Dean. She proofread and assisted with character, plot, and story details. Lynn kept me on track and encouraged me through every step of writing from idea to creating the layout. I'm grateful for the beautiful cover and interior quilt images she created. This book would not be a reality without her.
   lynndean@hot.rr.com   www.aNOVELwritingsite.com

Amanda Evaul Writesman of Bel Momento Photography provided the horse picture for the cover. She fostered my interest in the preservation of rural American architecture through the quilt barn trails.
   www.belmomentophotography.com

While following the Appalachian Quilt Trail through Tennessee, I found the home I'd imagined as I wrote about Mosey Inn. The Unicoi County Heritage Museum in Erwin, TN, at the Erwin National Fish Hatchery is that house. Martha Erwin, museum curator, became a promoter of my novels. She obtained permission to use the photograph of the museum on the cover.
  www.vacationaqt.com

James and Kathy Shelley formatted the cover and interior graphic layouts.   www.shelleysphoto.photoreflect.com

Amanda Kirby McCaw set up my author Facebook page.
  www.herbsspiceeverythingnice.blogspot.com

Mark Davis gave me information about search and rescue procedures. I appreciate his willingness to share his experiences and read those sections for accuracy. Any errors in details are mine, not his.

Many people from American Christian Fiction Writers taught online classes and provided writing and marketing advice. Those writing and prayer supporters are too numerous to name.
  www.acfw.com

Lee Marsh listened to my ideas and encouraged me during our weekly coffee meetings.

My friend, Shelia Berry, provided help with marketing and introduced me to the Blue Ridge Mountains Christian Writers Conference.

Attendance at the Blue Ridge Mountains Christian Writers Conference brought valuable classes from many authors. In my opinion, it's one of the best places to learn the craft of writing and to network with fellow Christian authors. I send a thank you to the leaders and teachers.
www.brmcwc.com

My final word of thanks goes to Anne Hutson who proofread my last draft.

CHAPTER ONE

A monster reached the top step of Mosey Inn's porch and extended his hand for an introductory shake. Wide-eyed, Sarah stifled the intake of breath before it became an audible gasp. She grasped a calloused hand—grotesque, missing its little finger, and marred with shriveled rope-like tendons. Hideous scars etched his face. The man's lips twitched a fleeting smile. His gaze dropped to the porch slats between their feet.

Taking a deep breath, she corrected her facial expression. They were only scars, and he was a guest—one whose money could mean survival once the tourist season ended. She blinked away her image of the handsome, well-mannered carpenter who'd called to reserve a room for several months and shifted her focus to the truth facing her. Sarah adopted her most welcoming tone and a cheery smile. "Afternoon, Mr. Pruitt. I'm Sarah Campbell."

"Benjamin, please."

She forced herself to maintain eye contact rather than allow her gaze to wander around his repulsive features. "Then call me Sarah. We're informal here."

He dropped her hand and smiled.

A smile after her reaction? She swallowed the bitter taste of shame.

He checked his watch. "Sorry I'm late. The horse trailers and trucks made it like rush hour in Charlotte."

"Friday's a mess as visitors come into town. Got back late myself. Made the mistake of driving to Statesville for groceries." She laughed and rubbed her lower back. "Cut across a friend's pasture to escape the snarl. Rattled my bones." She glanced at her dusty jeans and faded T-shirt. "Had to coax a horse away from the gate. Barely had time to tidy your room." She ran the back of her hand across her damp forehead.

He scanned the yard where beds of roses and four-o-clocks nodded in the emerging sunshine. "I wouldn't want to rush you." Benjamin gestured toward a rocking chair. "I can wait if—"

"No. I'm finished."

A breeze stirred the fragrances of a summer day. He closed his eyes and inhaled.

What was that look on his face when he opened his eyes? Uncertain how to respond she said, "I love the smell after a summer rain." Each shrub and flower appeared refreshed after the brief shower.

He combed his fingers through the hair above his right ear. "Yeah ... um, special."

The gesture seemed to indicate embarrassment, so she shook away the urge to continue the small talk. "Well, look at me keeping you standing in the heat. Forgive my manners. You must be thirsty."

"Cold water sounds good."

He followed her into the dining room where she opened a small refrigerator and handed him bottled water. "Put your name on food items and store them here. I keep it stocked with drinks. Otherwise, it's seldom used. Microwave's on the shelf at the end of the room."

"Perfect. Thanks."

Sarah concentrated on his features again, attempting to keep her appraisal hidden and nonjudgmental. Unruly locks framed his face. Mid-fifties. About her age. Did his long-sleeved blue work shirt hide disfigured arms? Its open neck exposed scars cascading to his chest like melted wax.

For an instant, their eyes met again. She caught the subtle change. Any previous humor faded. Shutters seemed to close over luminous brown eyes. Benjamin set the half-empty bottle on the table and returned to the front door. "I'll get my things and have a look at my room. Does it face the mountain or the valley?"

"Both. I gave you the balcony since you'll be here longer. Other guests use the front porch."

"Adequate, I'm sure."

No doubt about it, she'd goofed. His demeanor and tone of voice were stiff and distant. She'd created a bad first impression. Her questioning glances had offended, but it was hard not to stare and wonder how he'd received the flaws. Her occupation demanded propriety and good manners. He'd require attentiveness and respect.

He gathered his bags while she stood inside the doorway and pondered her next conciliatory move.

When he returned she asked, "What's your preference, straight to your room or a tour of the house?"

"Orient me on the way." He downed the remaining water and

tossed the container in the trash. After hefting his two suitcases, he fell in step behind her.

"Remind me to give you a front door key. You may need it if I'm not here." She snatched a dust rag from the hallway table and shoved it in her back pocket. A glance in the mirror startled her. She seldom greeted a guest when she looked so disheveled. Too late. She slowed her pace at each room. "The public sitting area is on your right. Dining room to the left. Music media and a large screen TV are back here."

He gave the rooms a cursory glance. "Your brochure mentioned a rare book collection."

"Ah, my grandfather collected books. The library is beside the sitting room."

"Is it quiet and private?"

She stopped outside the door. "Very. You'll be alone. Most people go horseback riding during the day. They'll attend the rodeo and then the concerts at the saloon."

"Those things don't interest me. Nice room. I'll browse the books once I'm settled."

Sarah's knees throbbed when they climbed the stairway to the second floor—a reminder to stop the last minute bursts of activity. She grimaced and gripped the rail for support. Had he noticed? She detected empathy in his eyes when she paused at the top. "We're at the back of the house. Your room's up front on the right. Mom named the rooms for their quilts' patterns."

Sarah motioned toward the door on their left. "Bear Paws is Ella Baxter's room. Another long-term visitor. She coordinates volunteers who help find missing people. Working on a case down in Statesville. You hear about it?"

"Saw something on TV about a missing teenager."

"That's the one. Girl's been gone a couple days. I hope Ella gets some rest today. Almost my age but acts like a youngster. Dedication will kill her." Sarah moved to the next door. "Our office area with a phone, fax, and computer."

Benjamin followed along the broad hall, their footsteps echoing on the polished oak floors, as she mentioned his fellow guests in Pine Tree, Maple Leaf, and North Carolina Lily. She gave her brain a mental shake. Babbling about people he'd meet at breakfast wouldn't help his impression of her. "Sorry to talk so much. Get's lonely around here." She unlocked his door and tossed the key on the writing desk.

Benjamin set down his suitcases and examined the molding over the doorway with keen eyes, caressing the scrolled carving with his undamaged hand. "Beautiful work. Your house has been well cared for." A slight twitch of his lips, which she interpreted as a small smile, tilted up the left side of his mouth. His face didn't move as freely on the right.

"Thanks. My grandfather built it years ago. He modeled it after the home of the fish hatchery superintendent in Erwin, TN."

Moments ago, Benjamin seemed offended. Now he complimented her home and examined the architectural details. Questions about him swirled through her head, but if she asked, it would imply permission to ask questions about her. Maybe she'd ignore him.

ೞ ❈ ೡ

The jangle of the phone stopped Benjamin's requirement to converse. "I better get that," his hostess said. "Might be a reservation. Make yourself at home." Fine workmanship drew his eye to the exposed wooden beams supporting the roof. Strategically located lamps cast a glow the color of warm honey on pine-paneled walls. Simple furnishings: writing desk, recliner, chest of drawers, bedside tables, and a black iron bed. Even with a vase of bachelor's buttons on the desk, it wasn't overly feminine. He noted a woman's touch in the blue and white quilt and pillow shams. The plaque on the door read Carpenter's Wheel. The shades of blue formed a star within a block-like pattern. If she'd purposely placed him in this room, it was a nice sentiment. A braided rag rug, matching the quilt colors, warmed the oak floor.

He plucked a chocolate from the pillow and savored its richness. Sarah's cozy home offered seclusion and comfort. A cookie-cutter hotel didn't appeal. He could relax in his room or the library after work. He'd chosen the perfect retreat to make important decisions about his future.

Benjamin stepped onto the balcony, leaving the door ajar. Heat sucked the air from his lungs. Sarah's yellow frame house stood on a slope that dropped into a broad valley. Wildflowers filled the meadows with color. Cedars scented the humid air from their windbreak along the right. An apple orchard occupied the left half of what he assumed was her land. Clouds hanging low on the horizon threatened more rain. Perhaps a storm would drop the humidity.

Sarah's laughter reached him from the office. He smiled at the sound. How many years since he'd enjoyed a woman's laughter? He'd startled her when he stepped onto the porch. He was used to that reaction—had come to expect it. However, she'd made graceful attempts to hide her dismay. Most women stammered and found a reason to avoid eye contact and further conversation. Women didn't take second looks at him, at least not with interest. Second looks were more like gawking at the aftermath of a car wreck.

He placed his palms on the balcony railing. He shouldn't think about Sarah Campbell or her laughter, but she hadn't treated him like most women. She wavered only a second before accepting his handshake, locking eyes as they talked. Her attempt to show respect must be why her laughter appealed.

Benjamin sank into the rocking chair to kick off his shoes and socks. The breeze felt cool against his bare feet when he propped them on the rail. The chair creaked with a soothing rhythm. This sure beat traffic noises and loud neighbors who disrupted his solitude.

Solitude. He smiled and shook his head. He'd known little but solitude for many years. After the accident, he didn't encourage relationships—easier to work and live alone. Too hard to deal with the loss when an acquaintance shied away. He understood their reluctance since he drew stares and whispers with each public appearance. No, he shouldn't think about Sarah.

Sarah hesitated outside Benjamin's door. He sat, scarred feet propped on the balcony railing. The wind ruffled silver streaked hair. Life had not treated him kindly. A loner by nature, she'd guess. Why had she let him see her brief revulsion? She hadn't meant to be cruel. She'd find ways to make him welcome, if he'd let her get close enough to become an ally.

Benjamin's chair creaked out some mournful tune. Did his soul moan with similar agony? Sarah stepped forward, and a floorboard popped beneath her step. He dropped his feet to the rough planks and turned. "Come on out. I'm admiring the view."

"Sorry to disturb you. It's Ella. She's bringing Chinese takeout. Do you have dinner plans?"

"I've driven enough for one day. I like sesame chicken and stir-fried vegetables. Tell her I'll eat anything. A single man doesn't complain when someone brings food."

"I hear you. It's always nice when someone else does the cooking. I'll place your order."

The caw of a crow drew Benjamin's gaze along a stone path to a terrace near the top of the hillside. A picnic table, sheltered by a rocky outcropping, invited guests to eat and rest. He'd earned a rest after spending most of his life helping older people keep roofs over their gray heads. A house in some North Carolina mountain cove away from people who stared and never offered him the time of day would accommodate his twilight years.

If such seclusion was what he wanted, why did the vision of Sarah in her faded jeans and T-shirt bring a long forgotten ache to his heart? He didn't want to admit he'd seen a shapely, beautiful woman. Her short brown hair streaked with gold and silver gleamed in the sunlight. He closed his eyes to picture her smooth skin. It glowed like the pools of warm lamplight. She'd been cleaning when he arrived, so the dirt smeared on her forehead seemed normal and somewhat endearing. That whiff of her perfume had ignited a forgotten sensation—part of him he'd buried and ignored. At least she'd thought he'd inhaled the fragrance of rain.

Benjamin shivered. His mind seldom took a wild tour of a woman's attributes. It wasn't good to allow such ideas to creep in at his age. With scars like his it added insult to the torture.

He'd seen Sarah grimace when she climbed the stairs. Did she live with pain, or was it her jaunt across the pasture? Why wonder? Thinking about the woman who provided shelter and breakfast wasn't smart.

He bolted to his feet and propped against the railing. Had he agreed to share a meal with her? How would Ella react to him? No. He couldn't eat with them. A cold sweat broke out on his forehead. His belly wanted food, but he'd come up with an excuse to dine alone.

༂ ✠ ༃

Several hours later, Sarah heard the crunch of tires and recognized the motor of Ella's Pathfinder. She peeped into the library where Benjamin lay on the couch. The open volume on his chest rose and fell with each breath. Hoping he'd remain asleep, she tiptoed to the stairway, set the laundry basket on the bottom step, and crept out the front door.

She scurried to halt Ella at her vehicle. "Welcome home. Any luck finding the girl?"

The two women turned to lean against the Pathfinder. "The sheriff let me go along while he interviewed her friends again. I'm thinking this girl skipped town. The parents believe something terrible happened, but I'm not getting that feeling."

"I hope you're right."

Ella shoved dainty hands into her jeans pockets and rocked back on her heels. "The kid's been gone three days. She could be in deep trouble even if she left by her choice. It's hard to know what a high school girl is thinking or doing. Some friends believe she went with a boyfriend. We'll keep looking. Leads will surface."

Sarah shuffled from one foot to the other, uncertain how to broach the subject of Benjamin. "So you'll be staying a while?" She squeezed her eyes shut, braced for the expected no. How was she supposed to act around the unusual man who would be there for weeks? How would other guests react around him? Could his presence affect her business? Sarah couldn't talk about such concerns with church folks, the only semblance of family she had left. She needed Ella—a friend much closer than family.

"I'll stay. The family needs moral support. I'll hustle up some public attention to help find her. Someone knows something." Ella narrowed her eyes and tilted her head. "You look nervous, Sarah. We usually have this conversation over dinner or at least sitting on the porch. Why the clandestine meeting in the driveway?"

Sarah let out the breath she held and eyed the takeout bags on the car seat. Ella would be hungry after a long emotionally charged day, but she didn't want another awkward introduction for Benjamin. "I wanted to talk privately about the new tenant."

Ella swaggered over to his truck, thumbs hooked through her rear belt loops. "Okay. But I want a look at his nice ride first."

"Leave it to you to admire a man's truck." After a worried glance at the house, Sarah tagged behind. They shouldn't snoop, but Ella sleuthed discreetly most of the time.

Ella raised her petite five-foot frame on tiptoes and hung over the edge for a look at the truck bed. "Hmm, the man does some heavy-duty work."

The huge blue truck dwarfed Sarah's Subaru. "I didn't pay attention to his vehicle. I'm not into cars and trucks. The driver interested me more."

Ella cocked up an eyebrow and chuckled. "Why Sarah Campbell, I do believe Mr. Tall, Dark and Handsome caught your eye."

Sarah set her jaw and glared at Ella. "No, that's not what happened." She cringed as Ella placed a booted foot on a rear tire. "Don't climb up there. Get down. He might see you hanging over the side of his truck."

"What's wrong with you? You act like there's some big secret with this man."

"I wouldn't exactly call it a secret."

Ella glared over her shoulder. "He drives a Ford F-350, and you don't notice. You're nervous. You want to talk in the driveway. This man has you rattled. What's wrong?"

"Oh, finish your spying first." Sarah chewed on her lip while Ella cupped her hands to peer through the cab window then ran a finger along the rear wheel rim. Sarah gave her a chance to sniff the collected residue and rub it between her thumb and fingers.

"Okay, Ms. Brilliant Clue Finder. You've taken long enough." She grabbed Ella's arm and dragged her back to the Pathfinder. "Game's over. This isn't one of your investigations."

"He's got you rattled and cranky on top of it. You don't usually get huffy when I check out someone's car. I get a free night for listening to this one."

"You're not worth that much."

"You know I'm worth it. Hey, I brought dinner, and I clean my own room. Time for you to see my value and pay up." Despite her teasing grin, Sarah couldn't discount the words.

Ella tilted her head to one side and announced, "He's hauled stone, bricks, and lumber. I say he does construction work." She held up a palm. "If I'm wrong, don't tell me. I haven't had a look at him yet. I get to guess what he does."

Sarah put her hands on her hips and gaped at the truck. "How do you do that?"

"The evidence is obvious. There's brick and rock dust in the truck bed. He's tracked sawdust to the mats inside the cab, and there's sawdust around the wheel rims. Oh," she said, holding up a finger for emphasis, "and a pair of worn leather gloves on the seat in August. He'll have muscular arms and callused hands."

"You're amazing. I would never notice those things."

"That's why I'm good at my job." She tapped a finger against her head. "Observation can tell you a great deal about a person."

"I made some observations of my own. He's ... well ... different. I don't want you to act shocked and hurt his feelings."

"What on earth are you talking about?" Ella's voice rose. "I don't shock easily, you know. I've seen about everything. You're the one who spent a lifetime secluded in this house."

Sarah grabbed one of the bags and led the way to the porch. "Sit. We're talking out here. Food can wait a few more minutes."

Ella dropped the banter. "What gives?" Worry lines formed around her unwavering blue eyes. "I've never seen you like this."

Sarah lowered her voice so Benjamin wouldn't overhear. "He has terrible scars, probably from a fire. He looks like something from a horror movie. When he shook my hand, it felt more like rough ropes than skin. I'm not sure what to do. I'm concerned about the way other guests will react."

"You make him sound sinister. I doubt he's dangerous."

"Oh, I didn't mean to imply any danger. It's just ... well, his appearance is rather startling."

"You deal with all kinds in this bed and breakfast. You're overreacting."

"Maybe, but he seemed sensitive about the scars. I'm afraid my initial reaction betrayed my shock. I doubt he would ever say anything about the look I had on my face, but I wanted to warn you before you met him."

"Consider me duly warned. I'm sorry to come home and play around. It helps me unload after a stressful day." She reached over and patted Sarah's arm. "I promise to be a good girl and not react negatively. There isn't much you can do about the way others treat him. Are the scars recent?"

Sarah's brows drew together as she nibbled a fingernail. "I don't think so. I'd say he's had them for years. Sad eyes. I think he's been hurt many times."

"I don't suppose you asked him?"

"Are you listening to me? It's none of our business, so don't poke your nose in and start asking questions."

"Sarah, you're too tender hearted and evasive. Get things out in the open. He might respect you more if you showed concern and asked. I find most people prefer honesty. Apologize if you think you offended him. Be his friend. He could probably use one."

"That might work for you, but I'm not used to meddling. I show people to their rooms, and set out breakfast. I give my guests privacy if they want it."

"You're worrying needlessly. I bet he's used to folks staring."

"I'm not so sure. Does a man ever get used to being so different?"

"Some do, and others get bitter and resent folks. Why does it matter anyway? He'll only be here a couple days."

"He's come to repair the church and other buildings in Love Valley. Mosey Inn will be his home for a while. We'll have a different relationship—see more of each other."

Ella shifted in her chair and grasped Sarah's hands. "Do you remember when my search team couldn't find the man from the nursing home in time to save him?"

"You came home crying. We talked."

"You recognized my despair. You listened with true concern. I can share the darkest aspects of my job and know you'll pray about them and offer support. God gave you a compassionate heart. Did it ever occur to you that Mr. Not-So-Handsome might be here to receive a touch of your compassion?"

"Not really. I suppose I don't consider myself a listener or nurturer."

"Maybe it's time you took a better look at yourself. God gave you a special gift, my friend. People feel at ease around you. They open up and talk because you care. I can tell you're itching to know the truth. Could be he's itching to share it, and no one ever cared enough to ask."

༄ ✠ ༅

Benjamin awoke to the sound of clattering dishes and female voices chatting in the kitchen. By the time he donned his shoes, the aroma of chicken beckoned.

He wandered into the dining room prepared to pay for his food and make an excuse to eat in his room. China plates and silverware replaced takeout boxes. The long wooden table, set for three, held a vase of fresh daisies flanked by two silver candlesticks. Definitely too late for excuses. A petite, middle-aged blonde clad in jeans, a green polo shirt, and clunky hiking boots emerged from the kitchen carrying three glasses of iced tea. He jumped, then took several deep breaths to calm his pounding heart. Strangers. He'd never get used to interacting with them.

She flashed a cheery smile. "Well, he's awake. We thought the smell of good food might bring you out of your slumber." After depositing the tea, she approached with an outstretched hand.

He shook it automatically.

"Ella Baxter. You must be Benjamin Pruitt." She didn't bat an eye or glance at his hand. "I'm glad you can join us. It's not often Sarah and I enjoy a man's company at dinner."

Had Sarah warned her about his scars? Of course she had. Ella wouldn't be so jovial on a first encounter otherwise. "I appreciate the invitation." What else could he say? He could kick himself for falling asleep in the library.

Sarah backed through the swinging wooden door and placed a bowl of rice on the table. "You didn't get much reading done. I hope you had a nice nap. You've met Ella?"

He nodded, concentrating on Ella's bobbing ponytail as she nodded too.

☯ ✠ ☧

Sarah asked, "I made iced tea. Is that okay?"

"Sounds refreshing." He glanced out the window as a jagged bolt of lightning sliced across a black sky. "A big storm's coming." How had he managed to stumble into a situation where two women would expect him to carry on a conversation? A sudden chill hit him like a blast of Arctic wind. "I should check the window in my room. I think I left it open. Wouldn't want it to rain in."

Thunder rumbled in the distance. Lightning lit up the sky.

"No need. Sarah closed it. Temperature's dropped considerably."

Sarah lit the candles. "We took care of some little details while you napped. If the power goes off, I have oil lamps. We'll build a little fire in the fireplace if we get chilly."

"Need wood?" He might manage to get dirty enough to escape.

Sarah shook her head, "Thanks, but there's enough. You can restock the box tomorrow if we use it. Besides, dinner is ready."

He needed a breather. "Then if you'll excuse me I'll go wash up. Start without me."

"We'll wait," Sarah said. "I'll check the oil lamps while you're gone."

Benjamin made a quick retreat and took the stairs two at a time. Splashing cold water on his face calmed his burning cheeks. Could he control his trembling hands? Why had he decided to stay here? He spoke to the freak in the mirror. "Sarah's being a kind hostess. In a few days, she'll leave you alone. Go eat dinner. It's expected."

He grabbed a navy pullover from the drawer. Thunder rolled across the valley like a rumbling groan, and rain pelted the roof. Blowing out a lung full of air, he headed back. He'd weather the storm of their hospitality. Small talk focused on them might work.

☯ ✠ ☧

Benjamin polished off his meal and leaned back in his chair. Ella loved to talk. Thankful for this favor, he listened as she expounded on her role in finding missing people.

"It's become an obsession. Been doing this for years. Some of the cases I follow are very cold. I often step in when the police or FBI give up. It's a great feeling when one of my people finds a clue that leads us to the person. The outcome isn't always what we hope for, but at least the family gets some closure."

"Volunteers do it all?" he asked.

"Yeah, people donate time and services. I organize searches, find counselors to console families, and hold fundraisers to pay for search expenses. Spend hours on the Internet. I coordinate volunteer teams along the east coast. Sarah lets me crash here when I come to western North Carolina. We've become like sisters. Especially since her mom died."

Benjamin saw the flicker of sorrow cross Sarah's face as she reached over and grasped Ella's hand. "Ella's been a wonderful companion. We've shared some good laughs and some very dark times." Obvious affection passed between the women.

"Well," Sarah said, "Ella's told you about her work. Tell her why you're here."

In a single statement, she put him on the spot. He'd keep it simple and to the point. "I'm a carpenter. I also do brick and stone work. The Love Valley Church hired me to fix some termite damage and patch the rock foundation. The boardwalk and several other buildings uptown need some repairs too."

A sheepish smile touched Sarah's lips as she dipped her chin to gaze at Ella. "I have to confess we snooped around your truck when Ella arrived. She's jealous."

Ella widened her eyes and nodded. "Sweet ride. I could use a truck like yours on searches. Sarah was worried you'd be upset, but we play a game sometimes where I guess what people do by looking at their vehicles. Hones my detective skills. I deduced from the sawdust and brick dust that you do construction work." Ella poked Sarah in the ribs and grinned. "He has muscular arms and callused hands. Just like I predicted. You owe me a free night, girl."

Benjamin watched the red creep up Sarah's neck and face. He had to smile at her embarrassment. "Well, I'd never have guessed my truck could tell you my occupation. Congratulations, Ella. I'll have to take better care of my vehicle. I didn't expect some super detective to nose around and find my dirt."

The pair had definitely talked about him. Sarah must've warned her to be polite. Ella's words suddenly registered. Did they see him as muscular? Withered, stringy flesh described the arm he saw in the mirror. Lifting bricks and lumber kept the muscles and skin from contracting, but his strength seemed to vanish with each passing year.

Ella's cell phone played "Ode to Joy" from its clip on her belt. "Baxter." A pause to listen. "Yeah, I have her files on my laptop. I'll pull them up and call you back." She flipped the phone closed and rose. "A clue came in on my Tennessee case. Nice to meet you, Benjamin. Got work to do." She turned to Sarah. "I'll let you know if I need to leave. I want to stay here, so I hope they can take care of things without me. See you tomorrow morning."

Benjamin half stood as Ella ran out of the room.

Sarah smiled and shook her head. "She's in her element. We won't see or hear from her again tonight unless they find one of these people. She'll be on the phone or combing through that case file all evening."

"She lives a busy life."

"A hard, lonely life. Ella's fifty-one. She's never had a husband or children. Not many roots when you're always on the road. She enjoys the time we have here. Gives her stability."

The statement carried undertones of hurt. Sarah had given away more than she intended. He was well acquainted with loneliness. The three people who'd shared dinner seemed to have much in common.

Sarah couldn't travel much and keep a bed and breakfast running. Did she envy Ella's freedom? Had Sarah lost a husband as well as a mother? Where did her father fit in the picture? Were there grown children she missed? He hadn't noticed any family photos around the house. Probably in her private rooms.

Lightning illuminated the room, and thunder boomed directly overhead. Sarah startled. Her hand flew to her chest. The lights blinked off and came back on. "Let's move to the sitting room and start a fire. I'll get dessert and coffee before we end up in darkness."

Minutes later, they'd placed an oil lamp for each bedroom on a table in the foyer. "Thanks. I'll stay in the sitting area until all my guests return. Feel free to do whatever you like after we enjoy dessert."

His excuse to leave, but the soft glow of the candlelight on her almost flawless skin stirred something in him. Maybe he didn't want to leave. A radiant fire on the stone hearth. Feet propped on an ottoman. Reading by lamplight. Did he want company? Strange notion. The scenario sounded infinitely better than his room upstairs where battery-powered emergency lights illuminated the exits.

"I'm not much of a talker, but reading beside the fireplace

would be nice if you don't mind company."

"I'd like that." She honored his hesitancy to converse.

The power blinked off as they finished their cake. Benjamin arranged tables and chairs so the lamps and candles provided better light for reading.

The storm rolled around all evening, rumbling across the valley and whistling around the eaves. Emergency lights over the foyer door didn't spoil the coziness beside the fireplace.

Benjamin kept his seat when Sarah greeted returning guests. Laughter rang through the house as they rushed in from the rain, shaking water off their hair. Some shivered in T-shirts and shorts. The outfits had been appropriate before the sudden weather change.

Sarah told each arrival, "You should be able to use the water since it's heated with gas. The electricity usually comes back on after a storm passes."

Several guests joked about their vacation to the old western style town becoming a more authentic visit because of the power outage. Sarah stressed the need for caution with the lamps. Most grabbed a cup of coffee and a piece of cake as they scurried up to their rooms.

Benjamin heard water filling the claw-footed tubs above them. Lamplight baths promised relaxation and warmth for some. He chose to remain by the fire.

Sarah didn't invite the other guests to sit with them. Nothing about her behavior suggested she was hiding him. Instead, he felt as if she were offering him privacy and protection from curious stares. Maybe it was because he would be a long-term visitor and the others were there for a night or two. Benjamin assumed the former since they sat in silence exchanging an occasional glance until the fire began to die and the movement of people above grew still.

She stifled a yawn around eleven o'clock. "Time for bed, but you can stay up as long as you want. I switched off the lights so they won't come on when the power returns."

"I'll finish my chapter then blow out the candles and lamps."

Sarah frowned and rubbed her knees. "Getting old isn't any fun. I sat too long."

"We're not old. Blame it on the weather. Thanks for dinner. I'll reciprocate."

"We'll let you. By the way, let me know if you need anything to make your stay comfortable. I want you to feel at home while you're living here."

"I'll keep that in mind. Goodnight, Sarah."

Carrying her lamp, she limped through the library, took a key from her pocket, and unlocked the door to her private quarters.

He didn't linger long.

Conflicting emotions collided as he slathered lotion over his taut dry skin and settled beneath the Carpenter's Wheel quilt. In the darkness, he listened to the patter of rain on the roof and thought about the day. Sarah's kindness brought unexpected complications. Worse, he'd enjoyed the evening. He'd never faced this dilemma. Avoiding personal contact outside the workplace had always been best. No. He couldn't let her change things.

CHAPTER TWO

Benjamin left Mosey Inn and pulled into the gravel lot beside the church a few minutes after seven on Saturday. He climbed into the bed of his truck to unlock the toolbox. Drawn by the beauty of the valley, he paused.

Stone steps descended from the churchyard to the meadow where a mist was just lifting. Dew glistened on buttercups coloring the pastures bordering the rodeo arena. Love Valley came to life as red-streaked clouds gave way to a pale gray sky.

After fetching the necessary tools, he planned his workday as tourists and residents began their morning routines in the serene domain below.

The aroma of bacon and coffee floated up the hill from campgrounds. His stomach growled since he hadn't taken full advantage of Sarah's breakfast.

Campfire smoke drifted with the fog. Clouds vanished from the mountaintop. The murmur of distant voices mingled with horse whinnies. Bawling calves and bellowing bulls competed with the distant tinkle of wind chimes on Main Street.

The chill of the previous night had passed well before dawn. By mid morning, steam rose from tin roofed stables as the puddles from last night's storm evaporated. A battered straw hat provided shade for his face, but rising temperatures sapped his energy.

As he tore termite-riddled planks from the side of the church, clouds of dust threatened to choke him. Dust crept around his safety goggles and mask, stinging his eyes and setting off a coughing fit. No telling what he was inhaling, but he couldn't stand the idea of breathing through a filtered respirator mask when humidity already sucked his breath away. Frequent breaks would have to suffice.

Benjamin located the outside faucet and then retrieved a garden hose and his backpack from the truck. Removing his hat, he slapped it against his leg to shake off the dirt. The water tasted like hot rubber hose. At least it would hydrate him and wash the dirt from his throat. The blast of water he directed over his head sent a shiver down his spine before bringing a welcome respite from the heat. Water traced dirty trails down his face and drenched his shirt.

He pulled a bandanna from his back pocket to wipe his face, neck, and hands. After folding it, he tied it around his head to keep wet curls out of his eyes. His long sleeved shirt clung like a second skin. He peeled it off and draped it over a bush.

The ground beneath a stately magnolia in the churchyard appeared poison ivy free. A shaded place for rest.

With his forearms propped on raised knees, he leaned against the rough bark and closed his stinging eyes. Not a whisper of air stirred the leaves. His heart slowed to a normal pace after placing a second water soaked bandanna around his neck and forcing some deep breaths.

He couldn't let a tourist visiting the historic church catch him shirtless. They'd see his scars. He forced wet arms into a T-shirt and soaked the bandanas again. If he used plenty of sunscreen, maybe he'd avoid sunburn and tolerate the heat.

Kudzu and poison ivy shrouded the surrounding forest, obscuring the natural growth of the trees. Benjamin tried not to think about the host of creatures that might lurk in the thicket. The towering vines transformed the landscape into humped giants who marched in endless succession like soldiers wearing green leafy camouflage.

Something moved in the brush behind him. Benjamin startled then scanned for the source. A rabbit hopped out of the woods to nibble on a patch of clover near the water faucet.

"You scared me, little guy. I thought you were the rattlesnake that left its skin on the front lawn." Just for fun, Benjamin let his mind travel to childhood adventures in the woods where soldiers or cowboys were his imaginary playmates. It seemed proper to ask, "Are you friend or foe?" The rabbit wiggled its ears and glanced at Benjamin. "Don't act surprised. I know the Kudzu soldiers sent you on a reconnaissance mission."

The rabbit hopped closer and selected a patch of grass beneath the magnolia tree for the second course of his meal. Benjamin sat perfectly still. He couldn't suppress a grin when the furry warrior lifted a twitchy nose as if sniffing for danger from the man encroaching on Kudzu Territory.

"You can tell your leaders I pose no threat. I won't invade. No need to send a more destructive scout." Benjamin leaned forward and whispered. "Bet you like lettuce. I'll share my sandwich. Wouldn't want you to say I was a bad host."

Benjamin fished in his backpack for the insulated lunch bag.

The rabbit twitched his nose, watching each move intently. "What? You already ate lunch."

Benjamin groaned and tapped the heel of his hand against his forehead. "Great! I left it. Clover won't work for me. I packed sandwiches and fruit and put the bag on the table. Planned to add drinks after I ate breakfast. Guess I left everything when I bolted to the library. Didn't want to converse with the folks coming down the stairs. Hmm, I can drink water from the hose, but I can't work long without eating. If I go back to Mosey Inn, though, I'll track dirt everywhere."

A trip uptown might be worse than incurring Sarah's wrath. Perhaps the crowds had thinned as tourists ventured onto the riding trails. His belly rumbled. Decision time.

"I hate stares and whispers." He shook his head but chuckled when the rabbit hopped closer to peer at him. "Not you, silly. The people. Listen to me, talking to a rabbit." He broke a twig into several pieces and tossed them aside. "Doesn't matter. If they knew how much I talk to myself they'd say I was nuts anyway. Too many thoughts. No one around to listen." Benjamin rose and shouldered his backpack. "I better go get this over with. You're braver than me, friend. Come visit again. You're good company."

Benjamin climbed the well-worn path adjacent to the embedded stone bleachers overlooking the rodeo arena. He emerged at the end of Main Street where rugged western-style buildings flanked a dirt road. His heart accelerated to a canter. A pause in the shade did little to compose him. He wiped sweaty palms on his jeans, clenched and unclenched fists, and tried to take some deep breaths. With all this tension, he might as well be heading for a gunfight at noon.

Tourists wandered from store to store. A few carried saddles, craft purchases, or camping supplies. Most sported cowboy hats and conventional western attire.

The Country Store stood outside the archway at the far end of Main Street. He pulled his hat low on his brow. Stepping out, he focused on the thud of horse hooves approaching the hitching rails and the clomping of cowboy boots along the walkway. It wouldn't do to make eye contact with anyone.

Country music twanged from the Silver Spur Saloon. The band must be practicing for the Saturday night line dance advertised on a placard. Horses stood flank to flank at the hitching rails. Some stamped restlessly while others dozed in the sun. Benjamin wrinkled his nose as barn-like smells drifted by on some unfelt air current. Maybe the odor wouldn't linger in the unpaved street when the animals left town and Main Street closed during the week.

As he expected, his first appearance in Love Valley created a stir. Heads turned as he strode toward the store. A little girl tugged on a woman's shirt and pointed. The mom stooped to whisper in her ear. Benjamin understood the "don't point and stare" routine.

Once he reached the store, Benjamin rushed to the aisle with food supplies. Several cans of tuna with pull tops and a box of crackers would work. On the next row, he grabbed an apple and a banana. He chose a couple of protein bars and snagged several bottles of Powerade from the cooler. That should satisfy him until dinner.

He saw the whispers of the family buying camp stove fuel. The lady perusing the saddles looked as if she might run when he passed the tack section.

Benjamin passed one woman on his way to the checkout who smiled and said, "Good morning."

He nodded a greeting. If more people behaved like this lady and Sarah, he might overcome his traumas.

Why would Sarah pop into his mind? Not the time to consider it. All he wanted was to get out of town and return to his solitude.

Over the years, he'd tolerated spectators. It didn't get easier. Counselors and doctors told him he'd grow accustomed to it and ignore them. Never happened. His heart raced and the fight or flight mechanism kicked into high gear every time. This wasn't normal, and he knew it. When he ventured out, people cut deep into his heart letting anger and hurt gush to the surface.

Why had he bid on this job? Folks were the same everywhere. Maybe he'd forget about moving.

The clerk gave Benjamin a guarded smile. Benjamin extended his left hand to receive his change so the clerk wouldn't pause in the middle of the transaction and stare at the deformed hand. He'd learned this simple action made public appearances tolerable for all parties concerned.

By the time he walked back to the church, his nerves had settled. The tight jaw muscles relaxed, and his heart stopped galloping. It shouldn't matter if people whispered and stared. He'd never see most of them again. But it did matter. He wasn't normal, and people had no inkling how much their actions hurt. Life hadn't been fair to him. God hadn't been fair. Bitterness and anguish ate at his soul. He couldn't let it go. He couldn't live with it, either.

Sarah saw Benjamin enter the store. She stepped forward to greet him. When he didn't see her, she hung back and watched from the shadows of the storeroom. Total strangers ceased their shopping to stare, point, and whisper. They acted as if he had no feelings. It was easy to see that their actions hurt since he strode through the store looking like a defensive bulldog.

Her anger rose toward the gawking audience he left in his wake. How could people be so cruel? Every muscle in Benjamin's body strained. His clenched jaw looked as if it might snap. Humiliation and wrath exuded from his pores.

She hated to admit that she'd reacted with similar shock during their first meeting. At least she'd tried to ease his discomfort and be polite. Ella was right: Benjamin needed a friend. He carried wounds far worse than his superficial scars.

After he departed, murmurs began as people resumed shopping. Sarah clamped her mouth shut to avoid lecturing them about their inhumane treatment. It wouldn't help Benjamin, but her plan might.

A trip to the General Store and Cafe resulted in fried chicken, mashed potatoes, and slaw. Picnic time. Benjamin would not eat alone and reflect on his awful trek to town.

Sarah pulled into the parking area beside the church ten minutes later. "Hello," she called.

Benjamin waved and crossed the gravel to meet her. "I didn't expect to see you here."

A pile of old wood lay in the yard. The framework for a portion of the south side stood exposed to the glaring sun. "Wow, what a mess."

"I tend to get rather dirty when the wood's so rotten."

Sarah turned to tell him she meant the building. Closer inspection explained his statement. The cloak of black dirt didn't hide the scars his T-shirt exposed. Patchy, discolored areas covered his right arm as if various shades of flesh colored candles had dripped down the extremity. Tendons and skin stretched tautly over the bones. His left arm—a different story—was a specimen for a body builder magazine.

Silver streaked curls escaped from a red bandanna tied like a sweatband. Her gaze landed on his right ear with a jolt. The upper portion of the ear was missing. She would not show her shock.

His eyes flashed embarrassment. He yanked off the bandanna, releasing his hair. The action spoke words he'd never utter as wet curls tumbled over the ear and onto his forehead.

Something about the gesture and his tormented eyes tore at Sarah's heart. Pity? No, the emotion surging through her wasn't pity at all. Attraction? Impossible. They didn't know each other. So why did she want to brush the wayward sunlit curls away from his face? Why did she want to caress his scars and tell him he wasn't ugly? She couldn't allow such thoughts to settle. She'd spent too much time as a caregiver. That explained her instincts.

"Well, you are filthy." She grinned and gestured toward the building. "But I meant the church is a mess."

"Termites. They devastate a place. Have you seen what they do?"

"No. I don't know much about buildings and bugs and such."

"Come look at this." Benjamin jabbed a finger against an exposed beam. It crumbled at his touch.

"No wonder you look like a dustbin." She took a closer look. "Do termites make these tunnels in the wood?"

His lips curved in his characteristic lopsided smile. "Yep. Those are where they've eaten the wood. The outer building can look normal, but it caves in because they've gnawed away the supports."

"Are you saying the whole building is like this?"

"Oh, I hope not. The exterminators told the town council there was extensive damage on the south and west walls. When I made my initial inspection the rest seemed sound."

"I should have Mosey Inn inspected. I hope it isn't riddled with termites." She poked a hole in a support beam.

"I doubt you came to learn about termites. What brings you to the church today?"

"I found your lunch on the table."

"Yeah, I missed it when I stopped for a drink. You didn't come to bring my lunch."

His eyes brightened. Was that happiness in his voice?

Sarah shrugged. "Well, sort of. I forgot to buy a tank of propane in Statesville yesterday. Got one uptown since some guests plan to cook out tonight. My brain can't seem to hold the details needed to keep the inn going these days. If it's not on my list I forget it."

He chuckled. "I can relate." He pulled a paper from his jeans pocket. "My hardware store order."

"You don't have coffee on your list by any chance."

"No," he laughed. "Want me to add it?"

"No thanks. Ella can get some on her way home."

"How do you ever know how much food to buy? Running a bed and breakfast must be a big task."

"It is, but I've done it for years." The chore of managing Mosey Inn became a greater burden every day. She wouldn't go there. Admitting her struggles wasn't in her plan for this afternoon. "Let's get back to the topic of lunch. I brought a picnic. Ready for a break?"

His eyebrows shot up. "A picnic? I'll forget lunch more often." He held up filthy hands. "Need to wash. Water's behind the church."

Sarah walked beside him from the car, swinging the bag in the crook of her arm. She relinquished it when he'd washed most of the dirt from his hands.

"Let's sit in the shade over there," he said, leading her to the magnolia near the vine-infested forest.

"I have an ulterior motive," she said with a wry grin. "Can you carry the tank up the hill when you get home? Every muscle is complaining after my trip across the pasture yesterday."

He laughed—a deep manly sound that made her heart do a strange little flutter. "I can see you dodging horses and bumping along in that station wagon. No wonder your knees hurt last night."

She wouldn't tell him the drive had nothing to do with her aches and pains. It hadn't helped, but days without pain were rare. "I only dodged one horse. Jasper likes apples. He moved away from the gate pretty easily."

"I'll load the tank in my truck and hook it up before I come in."

Trivial conversation occupied a wide stretch of time while they shared lunch. The rabbit reappeared for another meal of clover. Benjamin pointed to him and whispered, "I gained a companion this morning."

She tensed at the word companion, unsure if he meant her or the rabbit. Better to ignore the idea and follow another line of conversation. "I'll pack Peter a carrot on Monday. He'd appreciate the treat."

"Peter?"

"Your rabbit friend."

"Oh, I don't know his name. Peter doesn't fit him though."

"Maybe he'll introduce himself if I give him some slaw." She extended a forkful. The rabbit twitched his nose and gazed at Sarah. "So, you don't like mayonnaise with your cabbage, and you only talk to Benjamin. Guess your name is Harvey."

"Harvey. Like the invisible rabbit who talked to Jimmy Stewart in that old movie?"

"Yeah, I think I have a copy. We'll watch it sometime."

She leaned closer to Harvey and whispered, "Tell Benjamin what you want. I'll sneak it in his lunch bag." The rabbit wiggled its cottontail and scampered into the thicket.

"I'll ask Harvey what he likes. I won't tell you if he really speaks to me though." Benjamin grinned and tossed a chicken bone into the empty plastic bag. He grew serious. "Tasty, but I don't expect lunch and dinner."

"I know, but I have to eat lunch. I bought some supplies while I was uptown. I'll share. When you replenish the stash you can add Harvey's choices to your list."

"This is going to be a dirty job for a while. I'm better off bringing food than going uptown, so I'll take you up on the offer."

Benjamin wasn't going to mention the trip he'd made. Avoiding the memory of the encounter, no doubt. She wouldn't push. "Could I ask another favor?"

"Sure, you've earned them."

"There's a bathroom beside the kitchen. Would you come in the back door and shower so you don't track dirt all over the house? I don't normally let people use that bath or do laundry, but it would help us both."

"An easy one to oblige. You'll have to get a change of clothes from my room today. I'll take something down from now on. Leave some cleaning supplies. You'll never know I invaded your space."

"Thanks. I should get going so you can get back to work." Pain shot through her feet and knees as she stood. She gasped and sank back to the ground.

Concern flooded his face. "You are sore. Let me help you." He reached for her arm, but she waved him away.

"I can do it." She masked the discomfort and managed to rise. "Drive around back when you come home. I'll watch for you. You can tell me what you need from your room."

Sarah felt his gaze as she crossed the grass. She wouldn't let the pain make her limp. A warm bath and a nap before Benjamin arrived would take care of things. Guests were on the trails. She'd already cleaned their rooms. After they checked out tomorrow, she'd relax. Preparing for new arrivals could wait until Monday since no one would come until late afternoon.

Her knee throbbed by the time she reached the car, a reminder that the over-the-counter pain medications no longer controlled the aches. She couldn't afford to hire help. She'd keep going despite her pain. Benjamin had seen her weakness three times. Maybe being his friend wasn't a good idea after all. It might prove dangerous on several levels.

CHAPTER THREE

Sarah shoved kitchen utensils around and slammed drawers. Where was the rubber pad she used to open jars? The lid on the strawberry jelly wouldn't budge. A couple of angry whacks on the lid with a butter knife didn't loosen it. She'd prepared coffee, but other items needed to go to the dining room before the people waking above her arrived. Sure, one of the guests could open the jar, but now she was determined to overpower the lid.

Her fingers and wrists ached. In fact, everything ached. Must be a virus. She refused to believe her fingers were swollen and red.

"Come on, you stupid lid. I don't have time for this. Carrying that coffee urn was hard enough." One more attempt. No success. She banged the jar down on the countertop and flung the knife across the room. It clattered to a stop at Benjamin's feet.

Sarah gasped, a hand flying to her gaping mouth. "Are you okay? I didn't hit you, did I? What are you doing in here anyway?"

"I knocked and called your name. You didn't hear me with all the fuming going on." He grinned. "I'm thankful you weren't aiming for me with a real knife."

Sarah turned her back to him and brushed away tears before they could spill. Having a short temper was bad enough. Letting it flare in front of a tenant—not good.

"I overheard your frustration. Thought I might be able to help. And yes, I know you said the kitchen was off limits."

She faced him as he picked up the knife. Reaching for the jar he asked, "May I?"

She glared at him and growled through clenched teeth, "Don't you even consider saying, 'Let a man do it.'"

A grin tilted up the left side of his face. "That might earn me more than I could handle before my first cup of coffee." He popped the lid open and returned the jar. "Anything else?"

After placing the jar on a tray, she crossed her arms. "No. I'll manage. Coffee's in the dining room. You're early. I'll have the rest out in a few minutes."

He turned to leave.

"Wait." She backed against the table and rubbed her wrist. "Thank you. Sorry I was rude. I didn't sleep last night, and my hands don't want to cooperate this morning. I could use some help."

"Will you let a man help, or shall I get Ella?"

His charming grin and the teasing didn't sit well. He was trying to be helpful, but his offer fueled an emotional fire. Self-sufficient Sarah shouldn't need help.

She pointed an index finger at him. "Don't push me. You don't want to cross me when I'm in this sort of mood. I might throw more things and yell. That's not something I want to do."

What had gotten into her? Her eyes must be shooting sparks. Last Sunday she hadn't known him well enough to feel comfortable asking him to church. Now it would seem hypocritical after such behavior.

His eyes conveyed worry and gentleness. She had to get a grip. Losing total control of her emotions in front of him would be horrible. If he touched her, tears would fall.

Benjamin crossed to the sink. "I'm sorry I teased you. It wasn't polite if you're hurting." He turned on the tap and placed the stopper in the drain. "Warm water will help loosen your stiff fingers."

"I don't have time. Breakfast—"

His hand on her elbow interrupted the complaint. The warmth of his touch sent an odd sense of comfort and uncertainty through her. A handshake or an occasional hug at church didn't feel anything like Benjamin's hand guiding her toward the sink. She couldn't recall a time when a man's touch seemed intimate.

His tone said all teasing was over. "Soak your hands. I'm taking care of breakfast. Tell me what to do." He scanned the contents on the table and picked up two bags of bread.

She squeezed her eyes shut to hold back brimming tears.

"Should I place some slices on this tray so they can make toast?"

Sarah sat in the chair he'd scooted up to the sink and slipped her hands into the warm water. She regained enough composure to reply. "Please, but first, take the cream and sugar to the dining room. They'll want coffee while they wait. Spoons are in the dishwasher."

He returned with a cup of coffee. "No one else has come down. There's time to accomplish this. Want a cup of coffee?"

"Not yet. Preparing breakfast comes first."

Benjamin, under her direction, got breakfast out by the time the first person wandered down to eat. Sarah didn't know how to thank him. How would she cope if mornings became this difficult on a regular basis? She dried her hands and moved to the table.

The laughter and chatter died away as people finished breakfast, departed to their rooms, or left for a day of trail riding.

The kitchen door creaked, and Ella peeped inside. "Oh, excuse me. I didn't realize Benjamin was with you."

"He came down early and helped with breakfast."

"Morning, Ella. Any new developments on your cases?"

"I'm heading to Wilkesboro. Have a lead on a possible sighting. Mind if I take a couple boiled eggs and an apple, Sarah?"

"Take anything you want. No need to ask. There's meat in the refrigerator if you want a sandwich."

"Thanks, but the leftovers from breakfast will do. Need anything while I'm there?"

Benjamin grinned at Sarah. "Should she bring a squeeze bottle of strawberry jelly?"

Sarah ignored Ella's quizzical glance and glowered at Benjamin. "You're asking for it, and trust me, my aim is pretty good."

Sarah didn't bother explaining when she returned her attention to Ella. "We always need coffee. Get some pumpernickel or wheat bread from the bakery section at the grocery store if you have time."

Ella nodded and narrowed her eyes. "You okay? You look tired."

"I'll be fine. I didn't sleep well. Go on." She shooed her away with a wave. "We'll talk later. Hope you have some success. I'm praying for you."

Benjamin brought the coffee urn to the kitchen, placed it beside the sink, and poured two cups of coffee. After taking two plates from the dishwasher, he spread strawberry jelly on pieces of toast and peeled boiled eggs. "Cream and sugar?"

"Cream, please."

"Does Ella know you're in pain?" he asked, taking a seat across from Sarah at the table.

"Probably not. I really don't want to talk about it." She stared at him over the rim of the cup.

"You were limping when I arrived, and you could barely walk last Saturday when we shared the picnic. Now your hands and wrists are swollen. That isn't normal. Have you seen a doctor?"

"No, and it's nothing to worry about. I'm feeling better. Don't push the issue."

"Okay, I'll drop it for today, but I'm not going to forget about it. Anyone who looks at me should know I understand pain."

Sarah heard both empathy and anger in his voice. "Do you want to tell me what happened to you? How you got the scars?"

"Not today. We're avoiding unspeakable experiences."

Sarah caught the reprimand in his tone. Was she ready to reveal things about her life to him? Would he talk about his past?

Benjamin looked at the wall clock. "I didn't notice what you did last Sunday. Do you stay or go to church?"

"I stay. People check out during church hours. I depend on weekend tourists for survival. It's more convenient to worship in the evening. We eat dinner and have Sunday school before the service."

"Sounds reasonable. Didn't want to keep you."

"Would you like to join me tonight?"

"Thanks for asking, but I don't attend church." He ran a hand along his face. "I have a hard time worshipping someone who allowed this. God and I haven't had a relationship in many years."

The cold, steely glint in his eyes said he didn't want to discuss spiritual matters. He was simply being polite by asking about her worship habits.

Sarah understood how he might feel the need to avoid people after what she'd witnessed uptown. Holding God responsible was an entirely different matter. The little hint of attraction nudging at the back of her consciousness could go nowhere. A relationship with a non-believer would never work. Besides, friendship was all she wanted. So why had his touch stirred odd sensations?"

She prayed her performance this morning wouldn't jeopardize a chance to influence Benjamin's spiritual attitude. Expressing some gratitude would be a good start. "Breakfast would have been late without you. Thanks." She cradled the empty mug letting the last of its warmth seep into her fingers.

Benjamin reached across the table and took her cup. He'd sandwiched her hands between his before she had time to know what had occurred.

"Do you run Mosey Inn alone?"

"Sure. I don't normally need help. I'm just having some aches and pains right now."

"I won't fish for answers or tell you it's too much for one person, even though that's what I think. It isn't any of my business. Will you at least let me help you with chores today?" He turned her hands as if studying her swollen fingers.

His touch, combined with the pain and lack of sleep, began a reaction Sarah hadn't expected. She couldn't hold back the tears. Benjamin brushed away the droplets with a thumb. His callused, deformed hand conveyed a gentleness she'd never experienced. Without thinking, she leaned her head into his palm.

Benjamin rounded the table to envelop her in his arms. She yielded to his embrace and let her tears flow. "Sorry," he said. "I didn't mean to make you cry. Want to talk?"

She shook her head. "I'm embarrassed. Crying and letting you hold me ... this isn't the proper way to act." She shouldn't allow him to touch her, much less hold her.

Her need for comfort outweighed the incongruity of the situation. His solid chest brought vast security. The hand stroking her hair seemed to carry away some of the burden. Sarah couldn't deny the desire to linger within his arms. An absurd desire. Maybe a friendly hug wouldn't hurt either of them. He wasn't playing with her fragile emotions for intimate gain. Besides, he was right. Handling the chores today would be difficult. Could she let go of her need to be self-sustaining? He at least deserved a few answers since he'd rescued her by preparing breakfast.

⊛ ✠ ⊛

When Sarah's tears subsided, Benjamin eased away. "You are not going to traipse up and down those steps carrying laundry today. You can supervise. I'm doing the lifting and pulling."

"I won't let you do my duties because I didn't sleep last night."

Benjamin located a pad and pencil. He dropped them onto the table in front of her. "Make a list so I know what to do. You already confessed you're hurting. Don't try to deny it."

"I didn't ask for help."

"You're not asking. I'm telling. You brought a picnic when I forgot my lunch. We shared a nice hour in the shade. Payback time."

She scribbled some words and thrust the paper at him. "My list. The picnic was a kind gesture. You don't owe me." A defiant chin poked out as she swiped a napkin over a dollop of cream on the table.

He lifted her chin with a finger so she had to meet his gaze. "No arguments. I can change beds and do laundry. I could probably manage to put chocolates on the pillows. I didn't say 'Let a man do it,' but I am a gentleman. I won't let you do all the work when your fingers and wrists are swollen and hurting."

He waited for her to acquiesce but withdrew his hand when her chin began to quiver. Another round of tears hovered behind puffy red eyelids. Agitating her wouldn't accomplish what he wanted.

He hadn't intended to offer help around the B&B today. One look at Sarah's frustrated eyes had changed his plans. It didn't take much to see she had emotional issues along with physical pain. He couldn't let this lady who had shown him kindness suffer.

Where had such crazy notions come from? He must have inhaled something dreadful in the dust from the church. There was no other explanation for his actions. He'd embraced her without a second thought. It went totally against his nature to hold a tearful woman. The scary part was it felt right to have her warm body nestled against his chest while he'd soothed her sobs. Sarah Campbell had reached a place no other woman had touched during his lifetime.

She shrank back in her chair as if avoiding further contact with the finger he'd held under her chin. Probably just as embarrassed as he was. Sarah didn't seem like the type who would cry in front of a man she barely knew.

"Okay, I'll accept some help." Her little whine didn't seem to fit the angry woman who'd tossed a knife across the room. "We need to clean the dining room and kitchen."

"Deal. You sit. I'll clean."

"I said we, not you."

"I heard you, and yes, I know you emphasized we. I'll clean the kitchen." The woman was determined to remain in control. He could make do with that. "You're allowed one trip up the stairs to supervise people checking out. You're resting today."

She opened her mouth to protest.

He pointed a finger at her. "Don't say a word. I'm helping. I also noticed some repairs I can make. You are not going to object. And if you do, I won't listen."

Fisted hands went to her hips. "You have no right to come here and take over. I've run this place for years. I can continue doing it."

Good. She had some bark in her attitude again. This was easier to deal with than tears. He'd tune out the hint of hostility and press on. "I'll help with the chores today. You can resume your normal routine tomorrow. I won't interfere with your business. Will you agree to the home repairs? You'd have to pay someone eventually."

Sarah's furrowed brow, taut lips, and brooding eyes displayed her struggle. He understood. Admitting her home needed expensive repairs couldn't be easy. Sarah wasn't accustomed to receiving help.

Benjamin didn't think a silly jar of jelly or her lack of sleep brought the tears. She was sick and hiding some emotional turmoil. Some day, she'd be ready to tell him the truth. The tough part was he'd feel obliged to share his truths with her. He was definitely walking in strange territory.

By midday, Benjamin understood more about Sarah's mental and physical problems. Scrubbing toilets, tubs, and sinks had been just as hard as carpentry. Tugging on bed sheet corners made his hand ache. Sarah looked close to collapse, and he'd been the one who'd done the laundry, vacuuming, and mopping. He'd allowed her to dust and place the towels and soaps in bathrooms to keep her from harping about his taking over her duties. She'd tried to hide her discomfort, but her expressive eyes betrayed her weariness, and her limp had grown more pronounced as the day progressed.

They spread the quilt over the bed in Maple Leaf. Benjamin plopped into the recliner. "I say it's time for a break."

"No argument from me. Let's get something to drink and rest in my living room."

"I'm inviting you in. That's different. I need to sit, and I happen to prefer my chair. I'll finish early, thanks to you. I can rest for a while before church."

֍ ✠ ֎

Sarah downed a couple of ibuprofen with a glass of water. Fatigue sapped her energy, and the achy feeling taxed the threadlike hold on her emotions.

She'd never wanted assistance before. Autonomy and competency were her hallmarks. Having help and company had been a welcome change. Even worse, she wanted to curl up in his arms. A childish, inappropriate desire. As they'd worked, the years of loneliness had crashed down on her like a great landslide. She craved someone's touch. She craved Benjamin's touch.

None of it made sense. The moments he'd held her in the kitchen had set free some previously unknown desire that went deeper than a need for help with chores.

Their fingers had touched a few times when he let her help sort sheets and towels for the proper rooms. When they'd turned and bumped against each other while cleaning the bath in North Carolina Lily, it sent her into a tailspin. She had to keep reminding herself Benjamin wasn't a believer and she wasn't interested in a relationship. His comforting touch shouldn't linger in her thoughts.

The man who'd said he wasn't much of a talker had kept the conversation rolling with questions about the construction of the house. Sometime during their workday, she'd promised to tell him about her family.

She sank into her recliner and sipped her glass of iced tea while Benjamin slouched against the pillows on her quilt-covered daybed and downed his tea in several gulps.

The early afternoon sun filtered through the lace curtains covering the bank of three windows behind her. It enhanced the silver in Benjamin's curls. The gray gave him an air of dignity and maturity, qualities she hadn't noticed in other men at church. Those single men were his age, but none of them had captured her attention. They knew she had no male help at Mosey Inn but never offered to assist with home repairs. She no longer saw Benjamin's kind gesture as an intrusion. There was something special about him, but she couldn't put it into perspective.

Benjamin's position hid the right side of his face. He'd been handsome before some tragedy struck him. The deep furrowed scars didn't mar the strong, dominant jaw line. Could he learn to ignore people who rudely stared and scoffed? Sarah saw a man with a kind, loving heart. He needed people to love him in return.

Perhaps her honesty would touch his heart. Revealing her hurts wouldn't be easy. Sarah took a quavering breath and one last sip of tea before beginning her story. "You asked questions about my family and the house. I don't normally share these details, but I want to be honest with you."

"Hey, I was merely curious because of my construction background."

"I want to talk about it. I inherited this house when my mother passed away. My father died five years ago. He worked hard, but we always struggled."

"Are there other relatives?" Putting his glass on the table, he leaned forward and clasped his hands between his knees, offering Sarah his full attention.

She shook her head and compressed her lips into a fine line. "I'm an only child. Mom and Dad were the youngest in their families. The rest of my relatives are gone. I've carried the responsibility for this house most of my fifty-four years."

"What about your husband and children?"

"I never married." She paused to consider the impact of that simple statement. Her entire existence might be different if she'd married.

The expectations her family placed on her hadn't made dating possible. Her parents and church family encompassed her life.

As a teen, she'd dreamed of finding her perfect mate. That piece of life remained missing. It had never felt wrong—before today.

"A horse bucked my mom when I was twenty-one. Mom sustained a severe head injury and a broken pelvis. The fracture didn't heal right. She had problems walking. I dropped out of nursing school to take care of her."

Sarah gestured toward the rooms above them. "Mosey Inn was a boarding house. The apple orchard and our garden provided the rest of our income and food. It was enough in my grandfather's day, but it didn't meet our needs. Dad worked long shifts in a furniture plant so we could survive. Things never changed. He worked. I took care of Mom. She was like an eight-year-old after the accident—sweet and gentle. Never an adult again."

Sarah shifted in her chair and took a sip of tea. "Love Valley attracted groups of wannabe cowboys. Some lived at Mosey Inn while developing the town and surrounding farms. I cared for Mom and prepared meals for our boarders. I changed it to a B&B when Dad passed away. This house and its occupants have been my life."

Benjamin's intense gaze held great empathy. It spoke comfort to her warring emotions. "You gave up everything a woman dreams about to care for your family."

It wasn't a question. He'd stated something Sarah never voiced except in her spirit. Shocking how a near stranger saw more than close friends.

"It was the right thing to do." Her actions didn't need justification but for some reason they seemed to under the present circumstances. "Dad loved Mom and didn't want her in a nursing home. He needed me. I loved her. Now I'm an old maid with this place to keep up. There was never enough money. There still isn't."

"What about life insurance? Didn't you get money when your parents died?"

"It must have seemed like a lot of money to him. When he took out the policies, it was. I barely had enough to bury them. The mortgage is paid. What I earn has to cover everything else. Prices keep rising. I need to rent all the rooms every day to make it. When something breaks, I try to replace it. Often I find a way to make things work without the repair or replacement."

She rose, crossed to a window, and stared at the orchard. "In a few weeks, the sparse crop of apples will be ready for harvest. They'll rot on the ground. I can't pay workers to harvest them. Town folks pick some. Brings in some cash. I gather enough for my personal needs. My grandfather's bountiful orchard that once kept this place going will become a stand of gnarled, barren trees in a few years."

Benjamin joined her at the window. A squirrel, feasting on a fallen apple in the first row, captured Sarah's attention. She didn't ask what prompted Benjamin to stand beside her or what captured his attention outside. After a few quiet moments, she moved to the place he'd vacated on the daybed and continued.

"I spent the best years of my life shut away in this house. I gave up everything for my parents. They left me with responsibilities I'm tired of shouldering. For the first time as an adult, I have the freedom to travel. Do anything I want. I can't. I need a change but can't see a way to make it happen."

She'd never told anyone but Ella how she felt. Here she was spilling her heart to a man she barely knew—a man who was angry with God for some wrong he'd suffered years ago. Was she like him? No, she wouldn't consider it. Bitterness had no place in the heart of a Christian.

Shame and guilt rushed in. Benjamin would never believe God could love him after hearing her complaints. Besides, she should have a grateful heart. At least she had a home and friends.

Benjamin reached over and brushed a finger across her tender knuckles. "It must have been hard living in a town where horses and cowboy wannabes have the priority when a horse destroyed your life."

"I haven't ridden since my mom's accident. I don't crave the old western life like most people in Love Valley."

"I'd say that's normal. Have you thought about selling this place?"

"Occasionally, but I don't know what I'd do. At least I have a home. I don't have the education to get a job at my age."

"My repairs will save you some money."

"You can do some handyman work, but that isn't why you're here. You have a contract with the town, and I refuse to accept charity."

"It's not charity, Sarah, and don't argue about it. Consider it extra payment for the use of your laundry facilities. I'll do it in my spare time."

He scooted closer. "Come here. You could use another hug."

She should resist his embrace and insist he leave her private rooms. But she didn't. She needed his strength and comfort. His arms offered the peace she didn't feel and security she didn't possess. It wouldn't last, of course, but this afternoon it would suffice. She would let him hold her and bask in the comfort of admitting the truth. Her life had hurt.

CHAPTER FOUR

Heat waves shimmered from the tin roofs of Main Street. Sarah's energy lagged. Breathing became a chore. She glanced at the thermometer on the shaded wall at Andy's Hardware—one hundred degrees. Sweat trickled down her back. The humidity must be close to ninety percent. How could Benjamin work?

He had phoned asking her to bring Powerade when she returned from Statesville. She planned to fill a cooler with ice and a picnic before delivering the drinks. Maybe he'd agree to stop for the day, or at least take a long break in the shade.

Benjamin's saw buzzed on the hillside across the valley as she rushed toward the Country Store. The sound took her back to the evening they'd spent replacing the rickety railings on her porch. Thanks to his generosity, she no longer feared someone would take a tumble.

Working together on the project had been the highlight of the previous two weeks. Benjamin had taught her how to measure the precise lengths for the posts. She'd marked the lumber with a pencil in preparation for his saw.

The stoic exterior he displayed in front of others became wit and bantering. He'd teased her about trusting his skill with a hammer while she held the uprights. They'd laughed until tears stained her cheeks.

Sarah's musings vanished when she met Mrs. Hardin beside the ice machine. The last person Sarah wanted to see. She stifled a groan. She'd walked straight into the viper's lair.

"Sarah, dear, it's nice to see you looking better. You looked bedraggled when I saw you several weeks ago. Becky Spangler said you weren't feeling well."

"I had a houseful that weekend. Thanks for your concern."

The Hardin family had been prominent Love Valley fixtures since Sarah's youth. The officious woman held sway over both men and women. Few people had the courage to cross her. Avoidance was normally Sarah's strategy. Sarah saw no need to fuel Mrs. Hardin's tendency to lurk in the stores eavesdropping so she could go around spouting twisted versions of exaggerated tidbits for all listening ears.

Sarah turned to escape before the woman verbally assaulted her again. A shopper stood in the path of retreat. Mrs. Hardin's girth blocked the aisle in the other direction. She towered over Sarah like a gargoyle.

Sarah's hackles rose—no chance of avoiding an encounter.

Mrs. Hardin's plump, wrinkled face bent toward Sarah's ear. "Actually I'm extremely worried about you, my dear. I hear you have that beastly looking man staying at your house."

Sarah bristled like a dog meeting a cat in an alley. So, the gossip topic of the day was Benjamin. Sarah scrambled for ways to avert the woman's slander.

"I'm sorry Mrs. Hardin, but you must be mistaken. I don't have any awful looking male guests at Mosey Inn."

"Oh now, Sarah, you know who I mean. The man who's repairing the church. He's staying at Mosey Inn, isn't he? I went yesterday to see what sort of job he was doing on our beloved landmark. His face is horrid." She lowered her voice to a stage whisper, obviously hoping to attract listeners. "You must be so embarrassed when your guests see him. Why do you allow such people in your home, dear?"

"Mr. Pruitt is a wonderful gentleman. It's an honor having him in my home. He's making good progress on the church too. You and the town council should appreciate his willingness to work in this heat. He's a fine carpenter who could land many prestigious contracts."

Mrs. Hardin's hand fluttered to her chest and her voice raised an octave. "A wonderful man? You actually talk with him? Why, I heard he's a suspect in the case with the missing girl from Statesville. Aren't you afraid to be near him?"

As the insinuation flew from the woman's mouth, Sarah's blood boiled. She forced a calm tone she didn't feel. "There's no truth to that rumor. Ella Baxter is working closely with the sheriff and FBI. If Benjamin Pruitt is a suspect, she would know."

"Well, I was certain I heard that in the café yesterday. Don't you find it a bit suspicious that this Mr. Pruitt would show up here shortly after the poor girl disappeared?"

"No, that never occurred to me, and the police haven't questioned him. He had the contract on the church long before the girl went missing. Besides, he lives in Charlotte."

"That's not the way I heard it. I'm sure he was in Statesville purchasing supplies on the day she disappeared. That's the normal route from Charlotte. No one knows anything about him. You'd think he'd want to make friends with the people who are generously paying him to overcharge us. But no, he just stays up on the hill tearing out good siding and replacing it with expensive newfangled stuff."

"I've seen the termite damage, Mrs. Hardin. The building is rotten. And why would he want to make friends with people who associate him with a crime simply because he looks different? His scars don't make him a criminal."

"Admit it, Sarah, you don't know a thing about the man. Can you tell me what happened to make him so ugly?"

The temptation to deck the woman and silence her malicious tongue almost won. Sarah glanced around at others who pretended to shop while straining to hear the conversation. She spoke a bit louder for the benefit of the eavesdroppers. "I don't consider him ugly, and his appearance is not a subject we've discussed. It's not a good business practice to ask personal questions about my guests."

"Well, you should screen your guests a little more carefully, my dear. Your reputation as a resident and a business owner should concern you. We don't want his kind coming to molest our women and children."

Sarah ignored the jab at her reputation and concentrated on refuting the accusations about Benjamin. Mrs. Hardin's unbridled lips could harm Benjamin emotionally and financially.

"Benjamin Pruitt would never harm a woman or a child in Love Valley. He's doing the job the town council hired him to do. Others must think his skills are valuable since they've hired him as well. He didn't come from Charlotte to chitchat. He came to work."

Mrs. Hardin pursed her lips and scowled. "Still, I plan to see that the council keeps a close watch on that construction project to be certain he does it correctly. They didn't think about the women when they hired that outsider. I don't trust Mr. Pruitt. I'd advise people to be on their guard. He made a low bid so he could come here and hide out after he took that poor girl off and murdered her. I'm convinced that hideous man planned the whole thing."

"You're wrong, but it's pointless to argue with you." Sarah hefted a bag of ice, threw it in an ice chest, and slammed the lid. If only she could put a lid on Mrs. Hardin so easily. "Mr. Pruitt is a guest here. We should make him feel welcome. He's not involved in any way with the missing girl. Let the man do his job and keep your mouth shut for a change."

Too late to retract her words. Her explosive comments would incur consequences. At the same time, she welcomed the chance to put the meddling woman in her place. Out of the corner of her eye, she saw the clerk suppress a grin. One customer made a thumbs-up sign.

Mrs. Hardin placed fisted hands on her ample hips. "Well, no need to get snippy, my dear. Maybe you should consider how it looks to have your house open to male strangers all the time. After all, you are a spinster. We wouldn't want anyone to get the wrong idea about what goes on at Mosey Inn."

"If anyone gets the wrong idea it would be because of you and your gossip. I run a respectable business. You should be grateful for the people who stay at my home. They provide income for Love Valley."

"Make sure your renters are the sort of people we want, Miss Campbell. If something happens it will be your fault, mind you."

"Nothing bad will happen because of Mr. Pruitt's presence. I'm certain the work he is doing is satisfactory, and the town council made a wise choice."

Mrs. Hardin shook a gnarled, fat finger in Sarah's face. "Mark my words, dear. The man is no good. You'll regret the day he stepped into your house."

Despite Sarah's good intentions, she'd failed. Miserably. Benjamin would encounter the brunt of the woman's gossip. She'd handed Mrs. Hardin a tank of volatile fuel.

Mrs. Hardin turned and waddled away. She mumbled a gruff comment and elbowed her way between two teenagers. One of them poked his friend, pointed, and suppressed a laugh when her garter-rolled stocking slid down her stout leg to pool around her ankle. She ignored the fashion crisis and pasted on a charming smile when Becky Spangler entered. "Good morning, Becky. How's your lovely family?"

"Fine, thank you. Have a nice day, Mrs. Hardin." Becky held the door as Mrs. Hardin swished past her.

Sarah sighed, scrunched up her face, and moaned when Becky joined her.

She grabbed Sarah's arm and led her to the back corner. "What's wrong? Your face is beet red."

"You just passed what's wrong with me. I've sealed my doom."

"I should have known when I saw Mrs. Hardin. What's the old biddy up to now?"

"Maligning Benjamin Pruitt and the work he's doing on the church. She actually accused him of murdering that missing teenager."

Becky's eyes widened. "Is he a suspect?"

"Of course not! He probably will be since she's flapping her jaws about him because he looks different. He doesn't deserve her malicious gossip."

"Ella's gotten the lowdown on him?"

"Becky! Are you buying what Mrs. Hardin said?" It seemed incredible her friend would consider the idea. Surely, Becky wouldn't fail her.

"No, I just asked a simple question. The man arrived right after the girl went missing. I assumed Ella might check him out. You say she's efficient and finds details the FBI misses."

"Only if she has a reason to snoop. There isn't a reason to check out Benjamin. Are we supposed to investigate every man and woman who comes here as a tourist or to work? Do you screen the people who rent a horse at your stable to be certain they aren't unscrupulous people?"

"No, of course not. And I shouldn't. I didn't mean to rile you. You're right. Mrs. Hardin is a gossip and she can cause problems for the man. I didn't mean to question Mr. Pruitt's integrity."

Sarah slumped against the produce counter. "Oh Becky, I'm sorry. I didn't mean to jump on you. I cannot hold my temper around her. She knows exactly how to push my buttons. It must give her pleasure to badmouth me. You'd think I'd learn to keep my trap shut."

"No need to apologize. What'd she say about you?"

"She implied Mosey Inn is turning into a brothel. I can handle that silly notion. I'm riled because she's spreading lies about Benjamin. It isn't fair. How does she get away with such stuff?"

"Her family helped establish the area. Her husband forked over money for improvements. In her mind, the town owes her a debt of gratitude. Her husband forked over money for improvements. We all know she simply wants attention."

Sarah said, "My family helped this valley get its start too. I don't expect special treatment. She's rude. If people listen to this gossip about Benjamin ..." She sighed and crossed her arms. "He already has a rough time in public because of his scars."

You trust him, don't you?"

"I do. He's a good man. You should have seen the way people pointed and talked when he came in here a couple weeks ago. He's disfigured, not a criminal. When people act like her, I can see why he's defensive and sees himself as unlovable."

Becky grabbed a basket from the shelf. "You're a sweet woman, Sarah. Not everyone cares about people the way you do."

The compliment warmed Sarah like a balm. Mrs. Hardin's comments about her lack of a husband and the way she operated her business had hit where it hurt, though she didn't want to admit it.

Becky's exuberance lifted Sarah's spirits. "You're a good friend, Becky. I'm thankful you and Todd opened a stable. Your family helps keep me young. I'm counting on you to help me get Benjamin interested in church."

"Now how would I do that?" Becky said, eyeing the fresh fruit.

"Benjamin doesn't feel comfortable around adults, but your Noah's a sweet kid, and a little chatterbox. Bring him over one evening. I've never seen anyone who could resist Noah's charms. Maybe they'd hit it off."

"This Benjamin..." Becky said with a twinkle in her blue-gray eyes, "he seems to be occupying your mind today. Do I detect a hint of attraction?"

Sarah scowled and batted Becky's arm. "No. I want him interested in church, that's all."

"Right," Becky said with a wide grin. "I seem to recall you mentioning something about some sort of cream he gave you that helped the pain in your fingers."

"Pain goes along with aging. It'll catch you one day too. And yes, he had some cream that helped when I was hurting."

"So Benjamin is rubbing cream on your hands?"

"That is not what I said." Sarah frowned in mock anger at Becky. "Don't you go twisting my words. One Mrs. Hardin is enough."

Becky added bananas to her basket and whispered, "It wouldn't matter to me if he was rubbing cream on your hands. I'd be happy for you. How long has it been since you had a date, Sarah?"

"Years. You weren't born when I had my last date. I'm certainly not looking for a date at my age. He's a kind man who happens to be staying at my house. His generous offer to do some repairs around Mosey Inn deserves my friendship."

"Would you turn him down if he asked for a date?"

"He won't, and I probably would. Don't start matchmaking. I have enough trouble without adding a man into the mix."

"I think he sounds good for you, but I'll let you and Benjamin work out your own relationship. Want to have lunch?"

"Not today. He's working out in this heat. I'm taking cold drinks and food to the church."

"Not interested, huh?"

"No, I'm not. Remember what Christ said about giving a thirsty man a drink?"

"He said it was like we were doing it for Him."

"So, Benjamin's hot and thirsty. I'm putting Christian love into action. That may win him over when words won't. You'd do the same thing for a friend who asked for a cold drink."

"I suppose." Becky murmured under her breath, "I still think he's good for you. It's time you started looking for a man. You can have a life now, Sarah. No reason to stay at home all the time."

"I'm not staying at home. I'm taking a friend a picnic." She pointed an accusing finger at Becky. "No matchmaking. Got to run. He's waiting."

"Yeah, waiting for you. He could come get his own cold drink."

Sarah flipped the air conditioning to high before she headed toward the church. Becky's words dogged her like the plume of dust behind the Subaru. Why had Benjamin called her? Becky was right. He could go uptown to buy a drink. Did he want to share lunch again? He had appreciated their impromptu lunch. Probably feared facing the likes of Mrs. Hardin or her gawking counterparts. Who wouldn't?

Shade tree picnics might become the only safe haven for the spinster from Mosey Inn and the man Mrs. Hardin saw as ugly. Not likely. During the time it took to drive from town to the church, most of Love Valley would hear Mrs. Hardin's accusations about his heinous crime. Would they question Benjamin's integrity and believe the old woman? Sarah could ignore the scathing comments about Mosey Inn and her improper screening of guests.

Her stomach lurched at the thought of telling Benjamin about the encounter, but she might have to. Since she'd lost her temper and inadvertently set an evil plan in motion, finding ways to protect his reputation and his fragile ego wouldn't be easy. No one rebuked Mrs. Hardin. Benjamin could lose any trust he'd placed in Sarah when the town's gossip tried to link him with the missing girl.

☙ ✠ ❧

Benjamin removed the last piece of rotten wood from the exterior of the church sanctuary and tossed it on the pile. After two weeks of battling dust, he'd welcome the relief of working without the constrictive facemask and goggles. Repairing the foundation, placing insulation, and hanging new siding would seem easy now that he could take a normal breath.

He checked the time while letting the dust settle. "Where are you, Sarah?" He placed a hand on his rumbling belly.

Harvey hopped out of the kudzu and nibbled on clover near the magnolia tree. "Hey, pal. Time for lunch, huh? I can't wait much longer either. It sure is hot. Wouldn't do to let Sarah find me guzzling a cold drink, though. I'd have to admit my phone call was a ploy. That's a secret, by the way."

Benjamin tossed aside the mask and goggles, then leaned a piece of new siding against the building. "Perfect." Harvey stopped eating and glanced at the board. "Glad you agree." The rabbit moved to some clover near the church.

"Sarah packed a carrot for your dessert. We'll save it until she comes. You know, social outings are not my thing. Sarah's different, though. I trust her." He chuckled when Harvey waggled his tail as if concurring. "Admitting I have conversations with a rabbit—now that's something I wouldn't tell anyone except Sarah. You're good company, Harvey. Still, there's no way you could understand what it's like when I spend time talking with her."

Benjamin had been reluctant when she insisted on helping with the inn's porch repairs. It became an evening he would cherish. He smiled as he recalled the melody of Sarah's laughter. Maybe they could recapture that mood during lunch. Amazed by his thoughts, he shook his head. Wanting company was certainly new for him—especially female companionship.

The first night they'd met, he'd sensed her maintaining his privacy. The pattern continued. "I help Sarah prepare breakfast every morning. Gives me an excuse to hide. Haven't shared a meal with guests since I arrived. Well, except with Ella. She doesn't make me feel uneasy, but she doesn't create the same sensations Sarah does."

Hiding in the kitchen had many advantages. After they completed the early morning ritual, they'd sit on the back porch, chat over a cup of coffee, and watch the day come to life. Some days he wanted their early mornings to last forever. Going to work wasn't a desirable choice when Sarah's soft voice mingled with birdsong and the whisper of the breeze in the orchard.

They were friends. The idea astonished him. He couldn't quite decide if Sarah exhibited the same loving nature toward everyone, or if she saw something special in him. Ridiculous. He was far too ugly to attract a woman. Dating might spoil their relationship anyway.

His admiration of her doubled when she told him about her family situation. They'd bonded in a special way when she shared about the heartaches caused by many years of caring for her mother. No doubt, there were deeper pains in Sarah's heart that she hadn't shared. For some reason, he wanted to hear about those and ease them.

He felt ancient just trying to remember how long it had been since he'd held a woman. The memory of Sarah crying in his arms created a longing to cradle her head against his shoulder. It took great willpower not to embrace her each morning when they met in the kitchen.

"Sarah's the only one who could change my plans for that little home designed for solitude. It doesn't appeal when I'm around her. I should be smart and take steps to halt our friendship. She turns my brain into a muddle of wacky ideas." He shook a finger at Harvey. "Don't you dare tell her I think she's beautiful."

Benjamin closed his eyes to remember her slender face and the soft curve of her lips with the tiny laugh lines in the corners. Sarah's delicate lavender fragrance charmed him. He placed a hand against his cheek recalling the silkiness of her hair against it. An ache ran through him just thinking of touching her. A barrier in his heart had cracked the day he'd held her.

Then there was the other issue. Her faith ran deep, and her commitment to God held priority in her life.

His anger ran deep too. Sarah's so-called loving God had destroyed his life. The raging fire took everything from him. It still blazed in his soul. The brand was permanently in his brain as it was on his flesh. A God who loved him would have prevented his friend's death. A God who loved him would not have turned him into a sideshow freak. No, he wouldn't consider worshiping such a God.

God had destroyed Sarah's life too. She claimed to love God despite her dreary existence with her sick mother and a house full of strangers. On several occasions, she'd tried to tell Benjamin it was possible to love God regardless of those disappointments in her past. He'd tuned her out.

He wasn't so sure Sarah didn't harbor many of the same feelings he had toward God. Sarah's self-sacrifice went far beyond family loyalty. He hadn't made up his mind if she'd given up her desires for a husband and children willingly. A subtle undercurrent of hostility seemed to flow beneath her façade. It probably leaned more toward her father and mother. Answers would have to wait. Sarah wasn't ready to delve into those issues with him yet.

A phrase from a Bible verse he'd learned in his youth popped into his head. "Love one another. Love is of God. God is love," he murmured. It wasn't an exact quote, but even as he spoke the words, he couldn't accept them. They might give credence to

Sarah's sacrifices. She'd say it was the reason she'd altered her life.

Benjamin hefted two stones. He might as well begin repairing the foundation. "Sarah's pain is increasing. I can tell by the way she walks and carries herself. I've seen her little grimaces, and she frequently rubs some achy joint. Trying to convince her to see a doctor is useless. I'd have more luck taming these kudzu vines. Self-reliance serves her well as a businesswoman. It isn't good where her health is concerned. I'd offer to help pay her medical bills. She'd never agree."

His efforts to restore her home to its original beauty wouldn't erase her hardships. Benjamin could understand why a husband would want to keep his wife near him. He couldn't fathom a father placing his daughter in a situation where there was little chance for a husband and a family. It pained him to imagine the young woman who gave up everything for her parents. He couldn't reconstruct those lost years, but he could repay Sarah's kindness toward him.

Benjamin placed a stone in its place, and checked the time again and looked at Harvey. "This heat is unbearable. Surprised you aren't dozing in your shady forest. I'll save the carrot if you want to come back later."

The sun beat down on Benjamin's back. Noon slipped past. The bandana around his neck dried for the third time. His hat offered little protection.

A dull headache settled behind his eyes. Cramps in his legs and abdomen doubled him over. He'd been distracted by his thoughts and his need to keep working. Alone and fading, another spasm, and a wave of nausea jolted him into action. On wobbly legs, he headed toward the truck for a cold drink. He stumbled. The kudzu vines undulated, making the imaginary soldiers seem to advance toward the church. His head pounded in rhythm with his wildly racing heart.

☯ ✠ ☡

Sarah refused to consider there might be a shred of truth in Mrs. Hardin's evil words. Benjamin's kind dark eyes were not those of a murderer or kidnapper. His touch was gentle and warm. His manners were impeccable. She trusted him and considered herself a good judge of character.

Still, it wouldn't hurt if Ella checked his background to prove his innocence. The police might believe Mrs. Hardin or follow up on her story to keep her quiet.

Decades of conflict with Mrs. Hardin wouldn't change. Would Benjamin understand how Sarah's bad relationship had pulled him into the feud? As Sarah turned into the parking area, her heart sank. Allowing him to hear from another source might foster deeper consequences. Taking a deep breath to still her anxiety, she stepped out into the heat, ready to face the anger she'd deserve.

Benjamin dozed in the truck with the engine running. She called out and rapped on the window. "Benjamin!"

He startled awake. "Come in and cool off." He lolled his head toward the passenger's seat.

As Sarah climbed into the cab, her knee let her know it didn't appreciate the maneuver. She couldn't suppress a moaning breath. Benjamin would say something later. He noticed her pain levels and fatigue as intimately as she did.

"Sorry I'm late. Got tied up in town. Want to sit in the shade and have a picnic?" She sighed and leaned her head against the seat. "Oh, maybe not. It's cool in here. It's over one hundred in the shade."

"That's why I'm in the truck. Decided I'd cool off and get rid of this headache."

Sarah turned sideways to look at him. His flushed face and dull eyes indicated his pain. "You don't look so good. Are you okay?"

"Stupid me. I worked too long and almost blacked out. A picnic would have been wonderful when I used the church phone to call you. Now aspirin and a nap sound better than food."

She placed the back of her hand on his forehead. Alarm shot through her. "You're burning up. This is serious." A frantic adrenaline-fueled instinct took over.

"I brought ..." she spotted a bottle of Powerade sitting in the cup holder. "Never mind." She shoved the bottle at him while yanking the bandannas from his neck and head. "Drink. I'm going to wet these."

"Sarah, I'm—"

"Don't say it. Drink. I'll be right back."

She tossed some ice from the cooler into a pail of water and returned. He sighed as she laid the cold cloth on his forehead. With his eyes closed, he rested his head against the seat while she bathed his face, neck, and arms.

"I can do that myself, you know."

"Yes, you could, but I'm in charge right now. It's your job to drink. It's my job to cool you down."

"Too tired to argue. I've worked outside for years. Never got heat exhaustion. Glad you came."

"I'm taking you to the hospital for IV fluids."

"No, please, I'm feeling better."

Sarah gave him a doubtful appraisal. "You're at least going to rest this afternoon."

"Don't make a big fuss over this. I'll rest. No doctors."

Sarah draped a wet cloth around his neck. "Then don't badger me when I don't want to see the doctor."

He grinned and said, "You need one. This is temporary. Your problem is more complicated."

"That's your opinion, and I don't plan to discuss it today. Give me the keys. I'll lock your tools in the bin. We'll take my car."

"We're already in my truck. Why switch?"

"You are not going to drive and I shouldn't leave my car parked here. People might talk. Besides, I don't think I can handle this rig."

"Whatever you say." He waved an apathetic arm in the air. He turned off the ignition and reached for the door handle. "I'll help with the tools."

Sarah grabbed his arm. "You'll sit here and stay cool. I can put a few tools in the back of your truck."

He tossed the keys in her lap and saluted. "Yes ma'am. I'll behave until you get back. I don't want to spend the day with a headache."

Sarah stepped out and stood with her hands on her hips. "I am not a headache, Benjamin Pruitt."

"That's a matter of opinion, Sarah Campbell. I'll regret my overzealous work habits by the end of the day. You plan to mother me and pamper me, right?"

"Done it for years. I don't know how to act any other way. You should keep an open mind. A little TLC might be nice."

"I'll reserve judgment on that until later. I wanted to have a picnic. Could we have a picnic later if I'm good, Mom?"

"I'm going to pretend I didn't hear you call me Mom. But since you did we'll have to see if you're grouchy after your nap."

"I knew it. It's started already."

"I'll be right back so I can help you."

"Good idea. You should probably hold my hand so I don't fall."

"Because you're weak or because you want to hold my hand?"

"Hmm ... I think I'll keep the truth a secret."

"Okay smart aleck. Finish that drink and stop giving me lip. You'll follow my instructions this afternoon. Consider this payback for the day you forced me to rest."

His wobbly gait confirmed his need for assistance. Further teasing would be cruel, although the banter had helped assuage her initial fear. A car passed the church, raising a dust cloud behind the vehicle. They'd seen her arm around his waist, and his arm around her shoulder. If Mrs. Hardin caught that news flash, her tongue would wag for days about the Mosey Inn spinster's extracurricular activities.

CHAPTER FIVE

The doves nesting in the bushes stopped cooing when Benjamin erupted from the porch swing. "Mrs. Hardin said what?"

He glared down at Sarah but grabbed the swing to stop its swaying. Throwing his toast on the plate, he stomped across the porch.

Sarah had chosen to recount yesterday's events during their routine of breakfast on the porch. She deserved his anger and any rebuke he tossed at her. She's reacted badly when Mrs. Hardin's accusations flew.

Benjamin's knuckles turned white when he grasped the rail and leaned forward to stare at some distant place in the orchard.

Sarah cringed. Maybe he'd forgive her.

"I'm sorry she's spreading this lie about you. Mrs. Hardin runs her mouth all the time. For some reason she's chosen you as a target."

Benjamin plopped into a rocking chair and dropped his head into his hands. His whispered question wrenched Sarah's heart. "Do you believe her?"

Sarah crossed the porch and pulled a chair in front of Benjamin, knee to knee. "Look at me."

He raised his head and made tentative eye contact, then lowered his head into his hands again, but not before she caught the sheen of unshed tears. His lips compressed into an angry line, his tense jaw working from side to side.

Sarah placed a hand on his knee. "I never considered for a moment that you could be involved with the girl's disappearance. Mrs. Hardin concocted the story."

Her throat tightened as tears pushed for release. She hated the pain she'd glimpsed in Benjamin's misty eyes. No, she wouldn't cry. He might view her tears as pity rather than sorrow and remorse.

"I made her angry. It's my fault."

He wagged his head. "No, you didn't do anything wrong."

"I should have chosen better words and held my temper." Sarah eased into the sensitive subject so Benjamin would want to cooperate. "This gossip wields power. Even though you're innocent it might be a good idea to let the authorities check your background and your alibi."

His head snapped up. "Why should I make myself a suspect because this woman's telling lies?"

"Townsfolk fear her tongue but respect the Hardin name and money. She could do a great deal of harm. It's your choice, but I'd suggest you talk to the sheriff or at least let Ella tell him what's happened. He knows this woman's tactics."

Benjamin rubbed his eyes and gazed over Sarah's shoulder. "A large older woman came to the church. Made a big deal about the way I was handling things. She acted like it was her job to oversee my work. Complained I was taking unnecessary steps to repair the damage. She's the one, isn't she?"

"Uh-huh, she said the same sorts of things yesterday."

He sighed and swept his fingers through the thick curls over his ear. "I have jobs pending. I can't let her ruin my name. I've found more damage in the church than anticipated. It's going to take longer. I won't earn as much. Working in the heat yesterday could have killed me. Thought I should satisfy the town council." He inhaled deeply and exhaled a quavering breath. "You're worried."

"I am. You're innocent. I don't want to see you hurt. I've seen the excellent work you're doing with the repairs. Let Ella clear your name."

"Why is she saying these things about me? I'd never seen her until she came to the church."

"Because you're ... not a local, and you're ... different."

He swallowed hard and tapped two fingers against his taut lips. His pained eyes met hers for an instant. "Go ahead and say it. I'm ugly, so I must be a molesting murderer."

Sarah caressed his scarred cheek and tilted his chin so he had to look at her. "You are not ugly."

He snorted and shook his head, dislodging her hand from his chin. "You should have your vision checked."

"You're not a murderer, and you're not ugly. You're a gentle, kind man. I don't notice your scars anymore."

He scoffed and looked at her as if she were daft. "Don't lie to me. You see them. You can't overlook them. I've faced this problem my entire adult life. I can't change what happened to me. I avoid public appearances because I hate the way I'm treated. I'll finish the church repairs and leave. I'm obviously not wanted."

"That's not true. Others have hired you. Don't let one woman ruin your future or control what others think of you."

"It's not only her. People treat me like some sideshow freak. Come see the man with two faces; see his melted, discolored flesh. See one man with two different bodies." The tinny sound of a barker's voice seemed almost audible in morning stillness.

She couldn't tell him not to be angry. She'd witnessed the cruelty.

"These folks treat their horses better than me."

"You're right. Some do." Sarah twisted the hem of her shirt around a finger. Confession time. "I saw you in the store. I watched them. Not all people are so cruel."

"Most are."

"I know you've said you don't attend church. My church friends wouldn't treat you that way, Benjamin. And other people might change if you gave them a chance."

"Don't start on the church stuff, Sarah. I won't go. God ruined my life in a fire. I want nothing to do with Him or those who claim He's righteous and good."

"Does that include me?"

"No. But I can't worship your God."

"God didn't destroy your life. A fire damaged your body and your self-image. I'd like to know about it, but I won't ask. I respect your privacy."

"I appreciate that." He paused and stared at her, his angry eyes softening. "I trust you. You treat me like I'm a normal person. That's very rare."

"You are normal, Benjamin. You have scars, but it doesn't change the person inside. You're no different from the rest of us. You'll never be happy or able to overcome the bitterness until you develop a relationship with Christ."

"That's enough." He held up his hands, his jaw tightening again. "Don't push. Ella can delve into my background, but I won't go to church. I'll bet Mrs. Hardin sits in a pew on Sunday and claims she's a believer. People let her criticize strangers because they're ugly. It's wrong to listen to her lies and do nothing to stop her. I want no part of an institution like that."

"You're right. She's a hypocrite, and God doesn't like what she does. But we're all sinners who need forgiveness. I let my temper flare and said things that fueled her anger. That's a sin too. I tried to defend you, but ended up hurting you. Your bitterness isn't any different in God's eyes. We can't be perfect on our own."

"I know those things. I went to church. I even believed God loved me. I can't accept that anymore. I need you to be my friend, Sarah. Don't preach. Tell Ella to check my background. I'll talk to the FBI or the sheriff or anybody else who can clear this up. When I've completed this job, I'll go home. I need to maintain some dignity." He shoved his chair back and stalked off toward the orchard.

Sarah could understand why he felt angry with God. She was questioning some of the things happening to her. Life wasn't fair, yet God was in control. The two truths didn't always make sense.

☼ ✠ ☼

After lunch, Sarah collapsed on her bed and stared at the ceiling. Relief from pain and fatigue would be wonderful. She turned to glare at the pile of bills on the desk. The stack of envelopes leered at her. A not-so-subtle reminder about the reason she didn't schedule a doctor's appointment.

Sarah opened a bedside drawer and located a tube of ointment. She rubbed some into the sore swollen joints. If only her problems would vanish like the soothing cream.

She rolled to her side and propped her left knee on a pillow. The swelling was back. It started after she climbed into Benjamin's truck to stow the tools. Tears sprang to her eyes. She needed a nap before church. Not happening if the pain pills didn't kick in.

"Lord, I don't know what to do. I'm in terrible pain. I can't afford help. I'm starting to hate this place. I want out, but where would I go? I planned to travel and see the world after Mom died. I should be grateful for the things you give me, but I confess I'm angry. I'll never have the money or the time to leave. I'm stuck forever at Mosey Inn with bills I can't pay. And even worse, I think I'm attracted to a man who hates You. I know it's wrong to want more than a friendship with Benjamin. He needs someone to love him and so do I. It's nice when we sit and talk over coffee in the morning. I'm so lonely. I have no idea how to deal with this pain or these emotions. What should I do?"

The afternoon sun filtered through the lacy curtain. She turned again, unable to find a comfortable position. Benjamin hadn't helped her with chores this morning. No doubt, he'd wandered around the orchard until he'd settled down enough to work a few hours. He'd feel compelled to work since the restorations had left a hole in the side of the sanctuary. Mrs. Hardin would have the town council hot on his back if proper repairs took weeks and they had to continue meeting in the Fellowship Hall. Besides, for him Sunday was just another day.

His confession that he attended church before his burns surprised her. Apparently, he'd abandoned his faith. She was dying to know the details of what had happened and why he'd never adjusted. She'd keep waiting for Benjamin to open up. Sarah could only pray she'd be a faithful witness who might change his attitude.

Someone else needed to invest in this project. She'd talk with Becky Spangler at church tonight. Maybe Todd needed some carpentry work around the stables and could reach out to Benjamin. A man might be a better intercessor.

A walk around the room and some stretches didn't moderate her pain. Her knee hurt even more after the walk. It was too soon for more medication. She tried the recliner and distraction with a travel magazine.

She ignored the pages, her mind drifting to the past. Thirty-three years of taking care of her mother seemed like an eternity. In the early days, it hadn't been difficult. Sarah hoped it would be temporary. She'd spend a few months with her mom and return to college. Healing never came.

Her mom could help with simple household tasks like setting the table and dusting; chores a young child could manage. The rest—all on Sarah.

Age took her mom from a cane to a walker and eventually a wheelchair. When Sarah's father died, she considered placing her mom in a nursing home. Pointless with no money to provide proper care and little chance Sarah's daily life would change.

The stress of care giving and running Mosey Inn had exhausted her. By the end of some days, she curled up on the couch and cried once she'd settled her mother for the night. Her physical pain began shortly before her mother's death. Sarah blamed it on the stress and transferring her mother to the wheelchair. Now, almost eight months later, pain was unrelenting.

Sarah moved to the desk and thumbed through the stack of bills. She sorted them into pay now and pay when she had more money stacks. The pay later stack teetered.

Where were her Christian brothers and sisters when she'd needed help with her mother? Oh, they'd occasionally brought a dish of food and come to visit. The burden of life rested squarely on Sarah's shoulders, and it never lifted. When she looked at the whole ordeal now, anger rose from the pit of her soul.

It wasn't that she questioned her faith. She resented the past and the things she'd forfeited. These new emotions were unsettling. Her future looked grim and uncertain. For the first time in her life, she acknowledged anger toward her father.

Benjamin made her question things she assumed she'd willingly done. Maybe it would be best if he remained mad at her. She'd lose this weird attraction and the notion that a date would be nice. How had she ever arrived at this point?

※

Sarah turned the ignition. Silence. She leaned her head against the steering wheel, blew out a breath, and groaned. "Please, car, not today. I can't be late for church." Another turn of the key ... nothing.

"Need help?"

Sarah startled. "Oh, Benjamin, you scared me. My stupid car won't start."

"Pop the hood. I'll take a look."

Sarah joined him but was useless when it came to car repairs. She relied on her mechanic who'd babied the vehicle along for years. It had obviously been too long since he'd looked under the hood.

"The battery is corroded. I'm afraid it's history. I can jump it off, but you might have to do it again to get back home."

She cradled her forehead in her palm and heaved another sigh. "Thanks for looking." A glance at her watch told her to hustle. "I should call Todd and Becky Spangler and catch a ride to church."

"I'll take you but don't ask me to stay. Will they bring you home?"

"Sure, but I don't want to inconvenience you."

Benjamin placed a reassuring hand on her arm. "It's not a problem. I planned to finish a book. It'll wait. Get in the truck."

By the time they reached the church, Sarah had agreed to let Benjamin pick up a battery in Statesville and install it while she was away. Perhaps a dead battery wasn't a nuisance after all. Sarah sensed God's orchestration of events. An unexpected peace settled over her.

When Benjamin pulled up at the church, Becky Spangler was supervising six children chasing bubbles across the lawn.

Sarah inclined her head toward the boisterous youngsters. "That's my friend Becky with our Sunday school class. We'll have a time settling them down since they had playtime first."

Sarah rolled down her window and called to Becky, "Sorry I'm late. Had a dead battery. Be there in a minute."

Becky waved. "We got here early. Take your time. It'll take us both to get these munchkins cleaned for dinner."

Benjamin came around to retrieve the bags of construction paper, workbooks, and glue from the floor behind her seat. Sarah struggled to balance a dish of green beans, keep her purse strap on her shoulder, and her Bible under her arm while gracefully easing out of the truck. A good thing she'd worn slacks; his vehicle was not designed for women in dresses.

"Thanks for the ride. Don't go to a lot of trouble with the battery."

"Stop it. You're not creating a problem. Have a nice evening. I'll take care of your car."

"I appreciate the help. Leave the bags on the grass. The kids can carry things in."

Noah Spangler almost tackled her as he threw soapy arms around her legs in an exuberant hug. "Whoa. Careful, honey." Sarah jostled her armload and regained her footing.

"Miss Sarah, I thought you weren't coming. I got a pony. He's brown with black legs. His mane and tail are black too. Can you come see me ride him?"

"Of course I'll come. Your mom told me you were learning to ride. What's his name?"

"Kicker. He runs and kicks his legs up." Noah gave a horse-like demonstration.

"You chose a perfect name. You'll be a cowboy soon. Grab a bag, please. We need to clean those hands and get ready for dinner."

Noah scrunched up his nose while looking around. "What bags?"

"The bags on the..."

Sarah turned to follow Noah's open-mouthed gaze. Benjamin stood behind her, bags in hand. Surely, he'd drop them and bolt for the truck to escape Noah's stare.

"That man with you has some bags. Is he too old to carry them?"

"No, he's not too old, and that wasn't a polite thing to ask."

Noah hung his tawny head and stuck out his lip. Her admonition didn't injure his feelings long. Noah wove his eyebrows into a line and looked intently up at Benjamin. "Mrs. Wexler has lots of wrinkles, but hers look different. She has them all over her face. How come your wrinkles are only on part of your face?"

"Noah! We don't ask those kinds of questions. Tell Mr. Pruitt you're sorry."

Sarah diverted her face and winced. Noah's curiosity could chase Benjamin away before he met any of her friends.

"But Miss Sarah, Mrs. Wexler says she's proud of her

wrinkles. Said they came from laughing. I just asked why his look different."

Sarah set her dish on the truck floor so she could grab Noah by a grimy hand and drag him away before he ruined all hope of Benjamin ever crossing the threshold of the church.

Benjamin squatted in front of Noah and placed the sacks on the ground. "It's okay Noah. Don't be upset." He braced his elbows on his knees and held his arms open. The child stepped closer to Benjamin and hung his head. "I'm sorry."

Benjamin's eyes widened as if the apology surprised him. "Thanks, but you didn't do anything bad. Miss Sarah thought your question might hurt my feelings. She's teaching you to be nice."

"I didn't mean to hurt your feelings."

"You didn't, Noah. I'm not mad at you. Miss Sarah needs help with this stuff. Are you strong enough to carry two big bags?"

"Yes sir." He held up five filthy fingers. "I'm this many."

"How many is that?" Benjamin's lips slid into a smile.

Sarah couldn't let Benjamin see that his reaction shocked her. She pressed her lips together to suppress a joyful smile.

Noah proceeded to count each finger, one at a time. "Five."

"Well, I'm impressed. You're a smart young man. Learning to ride and count are big things. I know your mom is proud of you. Is the lady helping with the bubbles your mom?"

Noah nodded. "Hey, you have weird wrinkles on your hands too."

Benjamin extended his hands, palm down. "They're not exactly wrinkles."

Noah frowned and grasped Benjamin's hand. Sarah held her breath as Benjamin allowed him to finger the ropy tendons. Benjamin's behavior was nothing like she'd observed uptown. Noah must be a miracle worker to elicit such an opposite effect.

Benjamin smiled and rumpled Noah's hair. "When we have more time we'll talk about my wrinkles. You need to go with Miss Sarah and the other children."

"Okay, but how do you count?" Noah asked.

"Count?" Benjamin's forehead creased.

"Yeah, count. You don't have enough fingers."

Noah counted Benjamin's fingers. "One, two, three, four. You can't do five."

Benjamin held up his left hand. "I have five on this hand. I can use those. You don't have to use fingers to count anyway. You're learning to do that, aren't you?"

"Yeah, but I forget, so I use my fingers sometimes."

"Your mom and Miss Sarah will help you learn."

"Are you here to teach us a Bible story?"

"I'm not going to church. I brought Sarah because her car broke. I need to go home."

"You should stay for church. Mommy made corn, and Miss Sarah makes good green beans. Aren't you hungry?"

"I'll eat at Mosey Inn after I fix her car."

"Will you bring Miss Sarah in your big truck and come see me ride my pony?"

"I'd like that. I'll talk to her and see when we can come. Help her carry these bags and go wash up. Behave tonight."

"Yes, sir. Bye." Noah grabbed a bag, turned and ran back to Becky.

Benjamin rose, and then watched Noah join the group heading for the church. "Cute kid."

Sarah retrieved her green beans. "He's a special little boy."

Noah called from the doorway. "Come on, Miss Sarah. I need you to turn the water on. I can't reach it."

"Go with your mom. I'm coming."

Benjamin climbed into the truck. "I'll see you later."

Sarah lingered until the truck disappeared around the curve. What had she witnessed? She'd better talk with Becky and Todd. God had reached down with a gift tonight—a special child who'd charmed Benjamin with his curious questions.

CHAPTER SIX

Benjamin's day couldn't get much better—beautiful surroundings, cooler temperatures, hiking with the enthusiastic child. What a contrast to life a few weeks ago.

He inhaled the musty scent of rotting leaves and damp earth. As he and Noah tramped through the woods near the stable, late September sun dappled the forest floor creating deep shadows while illuminating goldenrods and asters. He latched on to the hand Noah extended and gave it a squeeze.

Noah flashed a toothy grin.

Benjamin's heart melted.

Seeing nature through Noah's younger eyes took him back to carefree childhood days when he'd spent hours in the woods with his grandfather—joyful times he'd forgotten until Noah came along.

Questions about Benjamin's scars took Noah out of the point-and-stare category. Curiosity fueled Noah's mouth. Some days it seemed he asked "why" a million times. Benjamin attempted to answer each inquiry, whether about his burns or some bug, in terms the boy could comprehend. Noah brought a different dimension to Benjamin's life.

Droplets glistening on a spider web caught Benjamin's attention. He pointed to the occupant. "The spider built a web in the lower branches of that tree. Those goldenrods beneath it attract bugs. Let's see if she catches anything."

Benjamin picked Noah up so he'd have a better view. A beetle flew from a blossom and buzzed into the web. The spider raced across the intricate silk to capture the hapless intruder.

Noah leaned closer to investigate. "Why's she rolling the bug up with webs?"

"So it can't get loose. She can eat when she's ready."

"Cool. Food just flies into her house."

"Yep. She made a strong web. It took planning and hard work."

"Sort of like being a carpenter."

"Or running a stable. Your mom and dad care for the horses

and take tourists on trails they'll enjoy. I nail the boards so walls will be strong." He poked Noah in the chest with a finger. "Your job is to study hard in school."

"Mommy says I can be anything I want."

"She's right. You'll have all sorts of choices when you grow up."

Benjamin lowered Noah to the ground and gave him a pat on the back. The boy scampered ahead to examine a mound of bright orange mushrooms growing beside a rotten moss-covered stump.

Benjamin shoved his hands deep into his pockets and slanted a final look at the web before ambling toward Noah. The kid had woven silky threads of love around his ailing heart. Noah's web tightened around him every day. Unlike the beetle, Benjamin was willing prey. Enticed by the affection of the boy and his family, he'd become cocooned in the warmth of their acceptance.

Their love and respect boosted his self-esteem. Perhaps Sarah was correct about her other church friends, but he wasn't ready yet to take the chance others would treat him like Sarah, Ella, and the Spanglers.

Noah plopped onto the ground and poked the rubbery mushrooms with a stick. Droopy eyelids indicated he needed a break.

"Want a ride, kid?"

Noah yawned and stretched. "Maybe a short one."

Benjamin grasped the boy's arm and swung him up for a piggyback ride. Noah settled in with his arms and legs wrapped around Benjamin, who nickered and pawed at the ground with his boot.

Noah giggled. "Giddy up." He jostled Benjamin's ribs.

Benjamin trotted a few paces before settling into a slow easy stride.

Noah grew heavier. His breathing slow and steady. Carrying a sleeping child shouldn't feel so right. How had he gotten into this situation? Life didn't include friends, much less a child.

Noah's parents had created the relationship. Simple. Todd brought Noah to the church during their daily riding practice. Their mounts grazed while Todd lounged on the lawn or assisted with his son's carpentry lessons. Todd Spangler had easily earned the title of friend—a new and wonderful concept.

Thinking about their afternoons brought a smile. Noah's skills at hammering nails or measuring a plank improved with each visit.

Harvey sometimes hopped from Kudzu Territory to observe the interaction between humans, horse, and pony. He'd venture back to report his findings then re-emerge to nibble grass.

Friends savoring a slice of life—sweet pleasures that brought Benjamin unexpected joy.

Spotting a deer nibbling on brush up ahead, Benjamin came to an abrupt halt. Noah's head popped up over his right shoulder followed by a gasping breath. Benjamin clamped a hand over the child's mouth. They froze. The six-point buck, sensing or smelling their presence, bounded away into the thick underbrush of blackberry briars and honeysuckle vines.

Noah squirmed on Benjamin's back. "Why'd he run? We weren't gonna hurt him."

"He's probably seen hunters or been frightened by people before. Not many folks get to see a big deer like him. Pretty impressive rack, huh?"

"Guess he was smart to run. My friend Tim has a deer head hanging on the wall at his house."

"A hunter would be proud of those antlers and the venison too."

Noah twisted and wriggled trying to see the deer and almost strangled Benjamin before he could lower the child to the ground. "You're getting too big to carry. Especially when you wiggle."

"We should have our horses."

"You'll be ready to ride on the trails soon. For now, we'll study animals, bugs, and plants. I learned about those when I was a kid."

"You were a kid a long time ago. How do you still remember it?"

"My granddaddy and my dad taught me just like I'm teaching you. You'll remember. Some day you'll teach your son." Taking him by the hand Benjamin said, "Take a look at this." He knelt and pulled Noah close. "See this plant with three leaves?"

Noah nodded and reached to touch it. Benjamin grabbed his arm. "Wait. Don't ever touch plants like this."

Noah, his eyes round and troubled, tucked his hand into Benjamin's palm. "Why?"

Benjamin swept a hand in a circle to indicate a twenty-foot area of vines spreading across the forest floor and climbing up the trees. "All of this is poison ivy. It'll make you itch for days."

"Then why did the deer walk through that stuff and get itchy?"

"It probably doesn't make him itch like it would us. See these broken branches? The deer made a path. If we wanted we could follow him."

"Are those deer footprints in the dirt?"

"Sure are. Maybe he went in the poison ivy so we wouldn't follow him. What do you think?"

"I ain't following him in the briars and poison itchy."

"Smart kid, but don't say ain't. Say I'm not or I won't. Stick close to me while we walk around this. And remember, look for those plants when you're in the woods."

"Do horses get poison itchy?"

Benjamin scratched his head and twisted his mouth to the left as he considered the question. "I doubt it. We'll have to check that one out."

"I hope not. We wouldn't have to be so careful if we were riding."

"We'll ask your dad or find out on the Internet. By the time you're ready for a trail ride, we'll have an answer."

Benjamin enjoyed their jaunts around the stable riding ring and nearby trails. Jasper, the Spangler's meek-spirited trail horse, had proven to be a good influence on Noah's frolicking pony, Kicker. Soon, Noah would be ready for an expedition. As a child, camping with his dad had been a special treat for Benjamin. He'd happily share the experience with Noah.

Noah skipped along beside Benjamin. "Can I call you Grandpa?"

Benjamin stopped short. "Why do you want a call me Grandpa?"

"My other grandpas live far away. I need one closer to play with."

"We can do things together. You can call me Benjamin. I wouldn't want them to be upset."

"They won't care if I have another grandpa. You're special. We do fun things."

Benjamin resumed walking, the little hand in his feeling especially gentle and kind. "Well I guess it'll be okay since I think you're a pretty special guy too."

"Miss Sarah told me we're supposed to love everybody. Do you love me, grandpa?"

"I sure do. You're my best pal."

"Do you love Miss Sarah?"

This halted him again and made his jaw drop. Had Noah's young eyes observed something to prompt such an unnerving question, or was he just asking because of Sarah's training?

"Miss Sarah is a special lady." Love didn't quite define their bond. Or did it? Since Benjamin didn't know, describing his relationship with Sarah to a child was impossible. He'd keep it simple. "She's my friend. Miss Sarah's teaching you good things about loving other people."

"She's my friend too," Noah said. "Some grownups do weird stuff when they love each other."

"Like what?"

"Kissin' and huggin'. Mommy and Daddy do that. It's yucky."

"Not really. It's a special way to show you love someone."

"Have you kissed Miss Sarah?"

This conversation was getting downright uncomfortable. He might kiss Sarah if it seemed appropriate. Not something Noah could comprehend. "We're friends, Noah. I don't love Miss Sarah the way your Mom and Dad love each other. Hugging isn't yucky. Is it yucky when I hug you?"

"No, that's nice. Do you hug Miss Sarah like you hug me?"

"Sometimes. Friends hug."

"Then I'll call you Grandpa and give you hugs."

Benjamin squatted in front of Noah. "Hugs from you would be great. I'd love being your Grandpa."

Noah threw his arms around Benjamin's neck and squeezed. "You need a boy like me to love you."

Benjamin beamed at the boy's simple logic. "You know, you're right. Thank you. Not many people tell me that."

"Why not?"

"Because I look different. My wrinkles scare some people."

"I'm not scared. Well, maybe a little scared of the bulls at the rodeo. Your wrinkles ain't nothin' to be scared of. They're just weird. Do they hurt?"

Benjamin opened his mouth to correct Noah's grammar. No, that could wait. The child's question was more important. "They hurt when I get sunburned."

"I got sunburned at the beach. It hurt." Noah fingered the scars on Benjamin's cheek. "Was getting burned by a fire like that?"

"Except it hurt a lot more. You be extra careful when Dad has a campfire or when Mom is cooking."

They walked in silence. Grandpa sounded good. He'd try to bring the title the honor it deserved.

ಌ ✠ ಆ

A gentle breeze ruffled Sarah's hair. It would carry a nip by evening. Miserably hot August had slipped into pleasant September. Since the break in the heat wave, the days invited outdoor activity. Sarah pulled a chaise lounge into the sun beside Becky.

The warmth on the deck behind the Spangler's house encouraged a nap before their picnic. She leaned back, yawned, and scanned the expanse above the treetops. The sky had cast off its hazy cloud-patched quilt. Brilliant Carolina blue announced autumn's arrival after a cleansing rain several days ago.

She loved autumn. She'd nestle under a quilt in the sitting room. Benjamin would probably kick back in the recliner and read, while other guests were away dancing at the saloon. Mosey Inn was booked solid during the days when the dense hardwoods of the Brushy Mountains displayed magnificent colors and brought riders in droves. The influx would offer hope for her pocketbook. She'd have enough money in a few weeks for a doctor's visit.

Becky glanced at her watch and searched the edge of the woods.

"Becky, stop fretting. Benjamin's taking good care of Noah."

Becky smiled despite the furrows in her brow. "I know. I'm not used to him running around in the woods without Todd or me."

"Are you having doubts since Mrs. Hardin's been talking?"

"Of course not. Benjamin's a trusted friend. It's a mom thing to worry when your child isn't at home."

"Mommy!" Noah yelled, bolting toward her from the woods bordering their property. "You should have seen the stuff we found."

Becky met her son and scooped him into a hug. She twirled him around, squatted, and set him back on his feet. "Oh, I missed you. You're my best big boy."

Noah said, "We found a spider and a big patch of poison itchy, and there was a deer with big antlers. Do horses get poison itchy when they walk through it?"

"I don't think—"

"Benjamin said I could call him Grandpa." Adoring eyes gazed up at Benjamin. A grin spread on Noah's face. "Is that okay, Mommy?"

Benjamin cleared his throat and stared at the ground. "It was his idea. I—"

"If you want to call Benjamin Grandpa I think that's fine." Becky picked a leaf out of Noah's hair.

Noah squirmed away from her grasp. "Can I ride my pony?"

"Come tell me about your adventure."

"Later. I want to ride now."

"Aren't you tired?"

"Nope. Grandpa carried me on his back. I took a nap."

"You can take a short ride if Daddy has time to help you

saddle Kicker. Tell him we'll be ready to eat soon."

Noah was the center of Becky's attention, but Sarah couldn't tear her gaze away from Benjamin. He strove to look humble. His eyes reflected great pride. Having watched Noah weave his way into Benjamin's heart over the past three weeks, Sarah couldn't be happier about Noah's proclamation that Benjamin was his Grandpa.

Noah started for the barn but ran back to tug Benjamin's arm. "Come ride with me."

"I'm tired and thirsty, buddy. I need to rest. You go ahead. I'll watch from here."

"You have to watch me too, Miss Sarah." Noah ran toward the barn yelling for his daddy.

"I'll get us a cold drink," Becky said.

Benjamin collapsed into a chaise near Sarah, stretched out his legs, and dangled his arms over the sides of the chair. "The kid never runs out of steam. I'm bushed. I'm trying to remember a time when I had so much energy."

Sarah laughed. "Years ago." She shot him a sideways smirk. "So, it sounds like you had a good time, Grandpa."

His joyous grin was unmistakable. "Sounds odd. It'll take some getting used to. I guess I'm the only older guy around who spends time with the kid. We're becoming good friends."

Ella emerged from the woods and plunked into a chair beside Benjamin. "Man, I'm beat. You two had me scrambling over rocks and fallen trees."

Benjamin straddled the foot of the chaise and sat up. "I figured you needed to have a few curves tossed in for tracking practice. People ramble if they're lost."

"That's true. My dog handlers do most of the tracking these days. Don't get much practice. I didn't appreciate the little diversion through the poison ivy. It took a few seconds to realize I was following a deer."

"I'll buy you some calamine if you get it. It's not my fault you can't tell deer tracks from human tracks."

She swatted Benjamin's arm. "Couldn't miss your big feet."

Becky came from the house with a pitcher of sugary sweet iced tea. "A reward for a hard day's work." She passed a tray of frosty glasses and filled them.

Benjamin drained his glass and held it out for a refill. "Noah had a great time, Becky. I'll take him out some more as the weather cools. He's curious. It's a good time to teach him about plants and animals."

"You can take him out anytime you want, Benjamin. He loves

being with you. Any news on the missing girl, Ella?"

Noah called from the training ring. "Mommy, look at me."

Becky waved. "I see you, sweetheart. You're looking great. Getting better every day."

Todd gave a thumb up sign as he leaned against the fence rail while supervising the riding lesson. "Mom's right. You're almost ready to hit the trails with us."

Benjamin drained his glass again, set it on the table, and shoved out of the lawn chair. "I'll leave you ladies to discuss the case and talk female stuff." He sidled over to join Todd at the fence.

Sarah's friends were working hard to make Benjamin feel wanted. For the time being, Noah seemed to hold the key to Benjamin's heart. At least someone had cracked a hole in the gigantic barrier Benjamin had erected to keep people out of his life.

Perhaps she held a tiny sliver of that key. Benjamin had developed a pattern of spending evenings in the sitting area waiting with her for tenants to return. They read or chatted about the day's events. Several weeks ago, a man returned from his evening at the saloons intoxicated. Since then, Benjamin hovered close by. He seemed to like the manly aspect of waiting with her. His presence brought security, though she'd dealt with unruly guests before.

After helping with breakfast, Benjamin usually lingered with his coffee since the days were cooler and he wasn't anxious to beat the heat. Amicable described their relationship. It should remain so until Benjamin's heart changed, but part of Sarah longed for mornings to last longer and evenings to pass more slowly.

Once Noah ended his ride, he busied himself playing with a litter of new kittens while the women prepared food for the cookout. Todd and Benjamin huddled over a table on the deck discussing renovating an out building to create living quarters for Todd's new stable hand.

After drawing up a tentative plan, Benjamin said, "Let's take another look. I'll get a crowbar and see how large that rotten area is."

"Stay out of Mom's way, son," Todd said, rising to join Benjamin.

"Can I come too?" Noah asked.

"Take the kittens back to their mamma and catch up with us," Todd said. "I'll meet you, Benjamin. I need to check on a horse that was limping earlier today. It'll only take a minute."

Noah hefted a cat in each arm. Their back legs dangled as he carried them around their chests. They mewed in protest earning a scolding from Becky. He deposited one of them in the cardboard box and followed Benjamin, still dangling the other kitten under his arm.

Sarah ignored Noah's disobedient gesture. His dad would deal with him once he reached the shed.

Becky resumed her conversation with the women. "I hate to see you leave, Ella. We're sure gonna miss you."

"I hate leaving, but duty calls elsewhere. Nothing's popping with the case here. The authorities called off the search days ago. I've stuck around to support the parents and follow some loose clues. I'll stay in touch and continue trying to get some leads. For now there's nothing for me to do here."

"We'll keep praying for the girl and her family," Becky said.

"Good. They'll need it. I'm heading to Virginia in the morning. One of my teams found a missing man. They got a lead from hikers about a grave." Her voice became a whisper. "Hurts when things end wrong."

Sarah said, "You mentioned he was missing for two months."

"Yeah. Sad time for the family. My new volunteer psychologist is talking with his wife and children. I need to meet her."

"I'm sure they'll appreciate the free counseling," Sarah said. "You amaze me the way you find people to give their time and money."

"Some people like volunteer work. Makes them feel good when they help a family during a rough time."

Sarah gave Ella an affectionate squeeze. "I always hate it when you leave. You're the sister I never had. Makes me thankful for e-mail and cell phones."

"I'll only be gone a week or two. I need to check on plans for a fund raising event in Tennessee. We're raising money for computer equipment and a command vehicle we can take to a new search site. I'll be back to check on the case here. The parents feel responsible for the girl's disappearance. Not a good family situation."

"You better keep in touch," Becky said. "You're family."

"Love Valley is starting to feel too much like home. I'm going to miss seeing Noah and Benjamin. It's been neat watching them bond. I'm anxious to see how this plays out."

Sarah said, "Todd and Becky keep coming up with ways to get Benjamin and Noah together."

"They're good for each other." Ella waggled her eyebrows at Sarah. "That could be said for you and Benjamin too if you'd admit it."

"I told you, no matchmaking."

"No need. The match is made. You might as well start dating."

Ella dodged Sarah's swat. "Tell her, Becky," Ella said. "I'm simply stating the obvious."

"I'm staying out of this war." Becky chuckled and handed Sarah a platter of raw hamburgers. "Take these and get them going."

"Thank you for not siding with Ella," Sarah said.

"I don't want to get stuck in the middle when Benjamin tries to convince you to give up your independence. I didn't say I don't agree with Ella."

"Enough, you two." She handed the platter off to Ella. "You can cook and talk about me. I'll go tell the men to come in about fifteen minutes."

"Yeah," Ella said, poking Becky. "You just want to walk back from the shed with Benjamin. See, I told you."

"Stop it, and don't burn the burgers. I'll be right back. Alone."

Sarah kicked a rock along in front of her as she strolled toward the building behind the barn. Humming as she walked, she considered how she'd react if Benjamin asked for a date. Ella was close to the truth. With Noah's influence, Benjamin was making strides toward trust. If Benjamin renewed his faith in God, then she wouldn't have to feel guilty about the emotions he evoked.

Sarah rounded the barn in time to overhear the conversation between Noah and Benjamin. It warmed her to see him treating Noah like a true grandson.

Benjamin said, "You need to take the cat back to the house, son."

"Aw, Grandpa. I don't want to."

"Watch the way you talk to me. Run on now and do what I said."

"But why can't I play with the kitten until you need help?"

He squatted to Noah's eye level and held him by the shoulders. "We can't have a cat under our feet while we're working. One of us might step on him. Either fetch tools for me or go back to the house and play with the kittens close to their mamma."

Noah stuck out his lower lip. "Okay, I'll take him back."

Benjamin eased the crowbar under a loose board and pried it free. Noah dallied behind and dangled a stick in mid-air. He laughed when the kitten lunged for it, twisting in the air like an acrobat.

"Noah, take the cat back," Benjamin said more sternly.

Noah moved on toward the house, and Benjamin tossed a board aside. A second board popped loose on one end.

Sarah called to him, "Hey, Benjamin, we're almost ready to eat."

He looked up and waved. "Todd's in the barn. I'll get him."

As Benjamin headed toward his truck with the tools, adrenaline surged through Sarah. A disaster unfolded before she could warn him.

✠

Bees! He should have heard them—should have seen evidence of a hive inside the wall. Too late, their droning filled his ears. Heart pounding, mind racing, he dropped the crowbar to flail at the swarm pouring from the hole. His arms instinctively protected his face. A dark cloud surrounded him.

Images of Noah and Sarah flashed in his peripheral vision. "Run! Get out of here." Those cries were his, but other voices and wails competed in the surreal drama. Searing pain compelled flight. No chance to rescue Noah. "Sarah, help Noah."

Her calls for help and a vague concept of Sarah running toward the house carrying the child registered.

His dash for the pond seemed eternal. Several horses in his path nickered and fled. He plunged beneath the water sending another horse skittering up the opposite bank.

The relentless bees hovered, dive-bombing his head if he bobbed to the surface for air. He popped back down until his lungs screamed for relief. A shadow fell across the pond as he came up for another breath.

Todd splashed into the watering hole with a spray canister resembling a fire extinguisher. "Benjamin, go under. I'll spray them."

Even beneath the water they persisted, stinging his chest, his back, and arms. When his air ran out, he surfaced to find that the burst of noxious smelling insecticide had dropped bees to the water's surface like downed kamikazes.

Agony snatched his breath. He struggled to the shallow edge on his hands and knees. Todd tossed the canister aside and hauled him out. Ella appeared and spread a blanket on the ground.

Sarah darted up, sat, and cradled his head in her lap. "Benjamin, talk to me. Benjamin!"

He cried out and swatted his arm as another bee found tender skin. "In my shirt." They'd see his scars, but pain wouldn't let him protest. "Hurry. Take it off."

Buttons flew when Todd ripped open the soggy garment. Benjamin slumped back into Sarah's lap after they tugged off the sleeves.

Pain consumed him.

Todd plucked several bees from his chest. "Honeybees. They leave stingers. We need to stop the venom."

Ella tucked a phone against her shoulder and rummaged in an orange canvas bag. "Multiple stings, upper body. Face and neck are swelling. Yeah, rapid shallow breathing." She thrust a plastic bottle at Sarah. "We have Lidocaine spray."

If Todd would stop scraping the credit card across the stings maybe he could catch his breath. Benjamin clutched a handful of Sarah's shirt. He buried his face in her lap. Groans came from deep in his chest and stuck in his throat. Heat and pain spread through him.

Sarah sprayed a cool, numbing mist after Todd flicked away stingers with the credit card. If only the spray would end the agony. Relief was momentary.

Sarah's whispered breath against his ear gave him the will to fight. "Help's coming. Hang on. I know you're hurting."

Todd said. "I think that's all. Do you see any more?"

Sarah ran a cool hand across his throbbing back. "Roll him over. Let's check his chest again."

Todd asked, "Any stings on your legs, Benjamin?"

"No. Legs are fine." Sarah gathered the rough saddle blanket around him and pulled him into her arms. Gentle fingers stroked his cheek and tucked wet hair behind his deformed ear.

Why did she have to uncover that too? He needed help. Letting them see his scars shouldn't matter.

Writhing and moaning, he focused on Sarah's misty eyes. Her face reflected the terror he felt, but there was strength and determination behind her frantic expression.

"Don't give up; stay awake."

He sucked in gulps of air. A noose seemed to tighten around his neck. He couldn't speak. Couldn't breathe. Clutching his throat, he searched Sarah's face. She had to see the plea for help in his eyes. Air. He needed air.

He managed to rasp. "Numb ... tingling."

"Keep breathing." Sarah yelled, "Do something. He's dying."

"Where's the epinephrine, Ella!" Todd's desperate tone made Benjamin glance at Ella. Todd dug in the bag too.

They understood but couldn't help. Another gulp of air. Focus on Sarah. Todd lifted his legs and shoved the canister beneath them.

"I heard him," Ella said. "It has to be here somewhere."

Ella barked into the phone. "Yes, of course I'm looking. He's wheezing ... going into shock. Get here fast."

Supplies scattered across the grass as she dumped the pack on the ground beside him.

Sarah grabbed his face and bent close. "Look at me. Don't listen to them. Breathe with me. That's right. In ... out."

Sarah's tears dripped onto his hot cheeks.

"The ambulance is coming. Benjamin, come on. Breathe with me." Sarah's voice grew distant. He clung to it and forced shuddering breaths. Air lessened with each effort. Sarah's face blurred.

"I found it!"

Ella's triumphant voice. Too weak to see what she'd found, he felt Ella moving, tugging at the blanket. A needle stung when she plunged it into his thigh.

CHAPTER SEVEN

Benjamin squinted against the bright sunlight glaring through the curtain in the Carpenter's Wheel room. It had to be late morning judging by the angle of light. He groaned and tried to find a better position. His body throbbed with each heartbeat. The itching was incessant. He needed more medication.

He vaguely remembered Todd helping him up to his bed after the all-night ordeal of medications and treatments in the emergency room. The sprint to the pond and the wait for the ambulance remained a foggy nightmare. Forgetting the fiery stings that seared his skin and took his breath might take some time.

His head pounded with his heart. He struggled out of bed, crossed to the bathroom and took off his pajama top. The image in the mirror reminded him of lobster fresh out of the pot. He couldn't blame the blurry labels on the medication bottles on his puffy eyelids, although they were mere slits. Had he left his reading glasses in the library or the sitting room? They'd be useless anyway since his swollen fingers couldn't open the bottles. It occurred to him that Sarah suffered daily with stiff, swollen hands. He'd be more sympathetic and work harder to get her to a doctor.

Sarah had given him a glass of apple juice and two pills, but he couldn't recall what time. The ointment he dabbed on his face and chest brought a touch of relief. He couldn't reach the terrible itch between his shoulder blades. Asking for help went against the desire to hide his flawed skin. Did it matter since Sarah had seen his repulsive body yesterday? Relief seemed more important.

Benjamin replaced his shirt, found his robe, and stumbled down the stairs.

Mosey Inn was silent. No one would see him wandering around in his pajamas since the guests were out riding. He retrieved his glasses from the table in the library and debated returning to his room since he could read the labels. No, he needed to know if it was time for more. Besides, he couldn't manipulate the childproof cap. Too bad the pharmacy hadn't considered his physical condition when they'd filled the prescription.

He paused outside Sarah's door. No noise—probably napping. He strained to reach the itchy spot on his back again. Forget it. He knocked softly.

Sarah cracked the door in a few seconds. Her eyes widened and her jaw dropped. "You look awful. Get in here." She grabbed his arm and pulled him into the room.

Benjamin sighed and grimaced. "I'm miserable. Is it time for medicine?" He pulled the bottles from the pocket of his robe, handing them to Sarah.

"Sit. I'll get some water."

"Make it cold and large."

He settled on the daybed and eased against the pile of quilt-patterned pillows. Delectable Mountains. At least he assumed that was the pattern since the plaque on her door gave her room that name.

He hadn't returned to Sarah's quarters since the day she'd cried and told him about her mother. The tall windows and colorful quilt squares made it cheery and bright. It didn't take much to imagine Sarah spending hours in her recliner or on the daybed, reading while her mother dozed in the big oak sleigh bed.

After downing several different pills, he said, "I hate to ask this. It's embarrassing for both of us. I can't reach between my shoulder blades to put on ointment. I'm itching something awful."

"Nothing to be embarrassed about. You need medical attention. Modesty and propriety aren't currently my consideration. Take off your robe and shirt."

After an instant of hesitation, he complied and turned on his stomach to expose his back to Sarah. He probably should consider the properness of the situation, but it didn't seem wrong since her gentle touch and words had sustained him during the crisis.

The coolness of her hand only emphasized the heat radiating from his wounds. She was right. Medical attention did take precedence over embarrassment or modesty.

"I feel like a fool," he said. "First I get overheated, then I didn't hear those bees in the wall. I'm not always a total klutz."

"That idea never crossed my mind. You missed the bees because Noah distracted you with the kitten, and I distracted you with my call for dinner. Am I getting the right spots?"

"Yeah, it's helping." He couldn't be sure it was the anti-itch ointment easing the pain. Sarah traced lazy circles on his back long after she'd applied medicine to every sore. He should tell her to stop, but he wanted her to continue forever. Did she realize the simple act of touching him stirred deep emotions?

"I can't believe they sent you home. You're covered in hives."

He snorted and turned his head to look at her. "I should have left the hive alone."

She chuckled and held out his shirt. "Sorry. An unintentional pun."

He turned over and slipped on the shirt. He rested his head against the pillows and closed his eyes. "I hope the pills kick in soon. It's been a while since I've hurt so much."

"Lie still. I'll be right back."

She placed a cool cloth across his neck and an ice bag over his eyes. "There, maybe that'll help get the swelling down. You can barely see, and you're feverish."

Sarah sat on the edge of the daybed and took his left hand. The soothing ointment she massaged into his swollen fingers eased the pain. He'd be content to lie there and let Sarah care for him until he recuperated. The time had come to talk about his burns.

The idea set his heart racing. He lifted a corner of the ice bag to look at her. "Sarah, we need to talk."

"Okay ... about what?"

His tone must have created her hesitancy. "I want to tell you about my burns. I know you're curious."

She took his right hand as if there was nothing odd about its missing finger and shriveled skin. While massaging the anti-histamine ointment into his tender fingers she said, "It seemed more important for you to trust me."

"I do. I wouldn't tell you if I didn't, and I certainly wouldn't let you see the scars."

"Is this the best time since you're feeling so bad? You should sleep if the medicine's easing your pain."

"I've waited long enough. Besides, it'll distract me."

Sarah pulled a quilt from the back of the day bed and spread it over him. She plumped up a pillow and settled on the opposite end. Benjamin scooted over to make room for her legs and tossed the end of the quilt over her.

He laid aside the ice bag and cloth. She didn't attempt to deter him from talking.

"I was twenty-two. Going to college to become an architect. I took a job during the summer as a carpenter's helper. We were remodeling an old factory into fancy apartments. A trendy way to revitalize an old neighborhood."

His mouth felt dry and swollen lips slurred his speech. A sip of water helped. More nerves than actual thirst. This wasn't easy.

"A friend from school was working with the contractor as part of his training. Sort of an apprenticeship. The place was a horrid mess. Old junk left everywhere. They just closed the business and walked away. We had to remove the debris before we could remodel. I was the grunt. They sent me up to the third floor to clean out a storage room."

Sarah reached out and held his hands. The comforting gesture told him she understood the anguish relating this story brought.

"I couldn't believe they'd dumped old propane cylinders in a corner. They were small but still capable of being lethal. I even went back downstairs and asked my boss if we should call a hazardous-waste company to come remove them. He sent me back with a wheelbarrow.

"My friend, Carl, came in and told me to keep my mouth shut. He said I'd get us fired. I should've walked away. That would have been preferable to what happened. I took my time loading the tanks into the wheelbarrow. Some were rusty. A valve fell off one of them."

"Was it leaking?" she asked.

"Oh yeah, you're getting the picture. I didn't smell or hear any gas. I heard Carl calling me. He wanted to know what was taking me so long. He walked in with a cigarette dangling from his mouth. That's the last thing I wanted to see with those ancient propane tanks between us. I didn't have time to complain. His cigarette ignited the fumes. Carl's clothes burst into flames. I grabbed a floor mat and tossed it over him. The blaze must have reached the wheelbarrow. There was this bright flash, and I heard an explosion. He fell on top of me. By then, I was burning too. I couldn't push him off. I woke up several days later in the hospital."

Sarah covered her mouth with one hand and brushed tears away with a knuckle of the other. "He died?"

"There wasn't any hope of saving him. Somehow, I landed with the rug against the left side of my body. Most of my burns are on the right side of my upper body. The way he fell on me, plus that flame-retardant rug, prevented more burns. My life changed that day."

"I'm so sorry. I can't imagine losing a friend in such a tragic way. I am thankful you survived."

"Some days I wish I'd died too. I mean ... look at me. I've had multiple skin grafts, surgeries for contractures, and I'm still a freak. I never went back to college. People talk and point. I'm isolated and alone. My life's pathetic."

"Life doesn't have to be that way. You've chosen to be a recluse. Look at the way Noah has taken to you. He isn't bothered by the scars and neither am I."

"I already said you need glasses, Sarah."

She tossed off the quilt and moved to sit beside him. Warm hands framed his face and stroked his cheeks. "There is more to a man than the way he looks. I do not find you ugly. I would never be ashamed to be seen with you in any public place."

"You'd be the first woman who's felt that way. I haven't had a date since the day of the accident."

"Because you never let a woman get close enough to honestly see who you are."

"No woman ever wanted to look past the scars. They run away as if I'm some monster."

"Then maybe it's time you allowed one to get a bit closer and see the man inside rather than the scars on the outside. When you get better we're taking Noah and going to town for ice cream."

"And give Mrs. Hardin a reason to gab? I don't think so. I won't humiliate you that way."

"Benjamin Pruitt, are you so self-absorbed you can't see I'm attracted to you? You're not just another houseguest. Do you think I sit here scratching the back of every man who walks in my door?"

"Of course you don't. But Mrs. Hardin might say you do. You're a God-fearing churchgoing woman. The people in your church would not want you with a man like me."

Her voice raised an octave as she ranted. "The people in my church don't know you. You haven't given them a chance to see your true nature. You're too busy feeling sorry for yourself to see the unique person you are. Forget the scars, Benjamin. Noah wanted a grandpa. He chose you. Other people could love you if you'd let them."

"You're serious aren't you?"

"I rarely joke." The determined tilt of her chin made that clear. "You suffered a terrible loss, and I'm not talking about your friend. Life-altering events either devastate us or make us stronger. It's time to move on. You're fifty-six. It happened years ago."

"I tried to move on. I got counseling and had surgeries. My scars won't go away, Sarah." He leaned forward and touched her arm.

"Maybe you won't let them go away. God could help you get past your scars and find a real life. People don't treat you right but hiding won't help."

If he didn't look at her, the tender plea in her voice wouldn't sway him. He clamped his teeth together and stared at the ceiling.

"Don't play the God card on me again. Besides, you're one to criticize. You won't admit it, but you resent the life you've led just as much as I do."

"Maybe I do."

His gaze snapped back to her. Indignation was obvious as she set her jaw and fumed. "I didn't think so until you came along. I'd never questioned what I did or why I did it. Now, I am asking questions, but I know something you don't."

Her index finger poked his chest. "God loves me even when I question His reasons." Her eyes were bright with unshed tears and glinted like polished swords ready for battle. "God loves me when I ask why I couldn't get married and have a family." The sharp finger jabbed her chest. "He loves me when I ask why I'm sick and hurting and don't have the money to see the doctor. God won't punish me for asking questions. He'll help me understand the bigger picture."

Sarah halted her tirade, marched to the window, and stared out at the orchard.

He didn't need to stand beside her to know she was crying. Her shoulders shook as she attempted to conceal the ragged breaths and sniffles.

Benjamin said, "Sarah, please come back over here."

She didn't look at him. "Why? I've been a jerk. You just told me about the most horrible things in your life, and I'm yelling at you. I think it's time for you to rest and for me to leave you alone."

"No, it's time to have an honest conversation."

She turned toward him but gazed at the ceiling, arms crossed over her chest.

"Please, Sarah. Come talk."

Plucking a tissue from a box beside her recliner, she blew her nose and returned to the end of the daybed. "I'm sorry. I have no right to question the way you act or feel. I can't begin to understand how much that accident hurt you emotionally or physically."

"It's okay. There's a lot of truth in what you said. I'm afraid of ridicule and avoid it at all costs."

She watched her hands twisting in her lap. "And I'm so tired of struggling to make ends meet. You're right. I do resent what my father did to me. I'd hoped to find a way to get out of this stinking horse valley. That won't ever happen."

He opened his arms, and she went to him. She curled up beside him and sighed. He snuggled her against his chest in the crook of his arm.

It was his turn to trace lazy circles on her back and stroke her hair. "You've pegged me pretty well. My life has been filled with anger. I don't want to fight with you. Can we come to a compromise?"

"We shouldn't talk about this today. It was a long frightening night. We've said things that hurt because we're frazzled."

"You were honest. That's a good thing."

"Not if we hurt each other."

"Hearing you say you're attracted to me is the most wonderful thing I've heard in years."

She wiped her eyes and looked up at him. Her lips twitched a smile.

She ran a finger down his left cheek. "It's true. This side of you is a handsome, kind man." She trailed a finger along the scarred right side. "This side is afraid and angry. I find both men intriguing. To be honest, it scares me."

He brushed a finger down the curve of her jaw. "And you're a beautiful woman; stubborn and independent but very attractive. I don't know how to make those two men compatible, but for you, I'll try."

She sighed again and adjusted her position in his arms. "That's a come-on line if I've ever heard one, but I'm too tired to care about it or cope with either side of you right now. I haven't slept."

"Not even a short nap?"

"Ella helped me make breakfast while Todd got you in bed. I couldn't go to sleep until my renters were out of the house."

"No wonder we're arguing. I should leave."

"You should. But ... I like the comfort of your arms. I don't want you to leave. I've never been held like this before."

"Look at me, Sarah." Those flashing eyes seemed weary when she raised her head. "I wish that simply holding you could take away the past and change the future. You're hurting today, aren't you?"

She nodded and lowered her head to his shoulder. "Running across the pasture hurt my knees. I'll be fine."

"You say that every morning. Words don't fix an illness. You want me to make changes. Are you willing to change too?"

"I've already changed because of you. I'm trying to decide if that's good or bad."

"I'm talking about seeing the doctor. I have to go back tomorrow. Make an appointment and come."

"Not tomorrow. I need a couple more weeks to save money."

"You have to stop avoiding the doctor because of money." He held her at arms' length and glared at her.

"I don't have insurance. I'm self-employed. It costs too much to pay the premiums. Tests and medicines cost money. It's been a good summer. I almost have enough."

"I'll pay. I'm not rich, but I have money to pay your medical bills."

"I won't take your money. That wouldn't be right."

"Here we go arguing again, Miss Stubborn."

Sarah yawned and pushed away from him. "Please, not now. I can't stay awake much longer, and we aren't going to fight about this. Your fever's coming down. You need rest. I'll put some more ointment on in a couple of hours. Do you want more ice for your eyes?"

"My eyes aren't the issue we need to discuss. I'll go upstairs so you can nap." He threw off the quilt and swung his legs over the edge.

Sarah placed a hand on his leg. "People are on the trails, and I don't expect a new guest today. Stay. You'll fuss later because I climbed the stairs every thirty minutes to check on you."

He opened his mouth to protest but clamped it shut in a defiant line. "Your knees are hurting, and you were up all night. You're saying you've been up those stairs checking on me all morning?"

"Every thirty minutes. Ella peeped in on you a few times. She's sleeping now."

"I thought she was leaving this morning."

"She decided to sleep for a while. She's getting up at two. She wanted to talk with you before she left. You were too drugged earlier."

"Did she get the report on my background check?"

"Maybe. There was a fax from Statesville this morning."

"Did you see it?"

"No. Do you want me to wake her?"

He wanted to say yes but couldn't disturb her sleep over some report. He'd caused enough trouble already.

☙ ✠ ☛

Sarah gave up on sleep after fighting achy joints for several hours. She contemplated the fact Benjamin had seen her pain despite preoccupation with his own misery. Their relationship was baffling, and now she'd admitted an attraction. It must be the lack of sleep making her do such weird things.

Ella would normally catch the little details that told the truth —a grimace, a moan, the rubbing of a wrist or knee. Lately, Ella juggled too many other details and wasn't as attuned to Sarah's inner workings. Sarah preferred to keep it that way.

She could blame her pain on the stress of Benjamin's accident or carrying Noah while running across the pasture. The truth was she'd been hurting longer than she wanted to remember. As she tossed in bed, Benjamin's offer to pay for a doctor's visit seemed wise, but accepting his charity was out of the question. She'd pay him back once the money came in.

The mantel clock in the library struck two. She heard running water in Ella's room. Sarah glanced at Benjamin. Still sleeping, but he'd awaken soon. During the last hour, he'd become more restless as the medications wore off. He'd need help with treating the hives on his back later.

She might as well take some pain pills and make lunch. As she stood, excruciating pain shot through her right knee. She plopped back on the bed, a hissing moan escaping.

Her gaze jerked to Benjamin. He stirred but didn't open his eyes.

Sarah fought the urge to groan as she eased up her pants leg. Alarm swept a shudder down her spine. Her knee had swelled to the size of a grapefruit and radiated heat. She gingerly tested the limb. It seemed possible to limp across the house to the kitchen, grab an ice bag, some food, and settle under a quilt in the recliner before her companions caught on.

She jumped when Ella tapped on the jamb of the open door. Sarah tucked her legs back under the quilt, hoping Ella wouldn't notice any signs of pain with the movement. No way would she allow Ella to see the dreadful knee.

"Sorry to startle you," Ella whispered.

Sarah motioned her in. Ella tiptoed across the room, sat cross-legged on the foot of Sarah's bed and nodded toward Benjamin. "I thought I heard him come down several hours ago. How's he doing?"

"Better than this morning but feeling miserable. He had a fever when he came down. I helped put ointment on his back. The pain medicines have him wiped out, which is probably a good thing. They should've kept him in the hospital."

"Once they knew he wasn't going to die he was well enough to go home. It works that way these days. You look rough, girl. Did you get some sleep?"

"A little. I woke up every time he moved."

"Sort of like those days when you slept on that daybed with one ear open so you could hear your mom."

Sarah sighed and shook her head. "I don't want to remember how tired I was. Some days I wondered how I would survive with no sleep and keep this place open. At least Benjamin will be well and working again in a couple of days."

"I'm sure he appreciates your tender care this afternoon." Ella's grin indicated her matchmaker side wanted to say something.

Sarah avoided the subject, already too aware of the closeness she'd shared with Benjamin earlier. "I'm thankful Todd had that medicine in his first aid kit. Watching Benjamin's neck swell while we pulled out stingers was awful. I was never so grateful to hear a siren."

Ella said, "I thought we were going to lose him."

"It's a good thing he wasn't alone at the church," Sarah said.

"Any problems breathing this morning?"

Sarah watched the steady rise and fall of his breaths and recalled the consoling sound of his heartbeat when she'd rested her head on his chest. She pushed that thought aside. "No, he's just hurting and itching. I talked him into sleeping here so I could rest. Knew I'd be waking up all afternoon to go check on him. He'll probably be fine in his own room by tonight."

Ella slid off the bed and grabbed Sarah's hand. "Let's go get some food while he's asleep. I'm starving."

Sarah gasped when Ella pulled her to her feet. The yank on her arm and the jarring of her knee took her breath. She wobbled but kept her footing.

"What's wrong? I thought you said you didn't get hurt?"

Benjamin sat up and rubbed a hand across his eyes. "It's her leg or maybe her wrist. She needs to see a doctor. Won't listen to me. Maybe you can talk some sense into her. This has been going on for days."

Ella moved to stand in front of him, hands on her hips. "Is that so? Sounds like I needed to have a talk with you." She crossed her arms, a scowl piercing Sarah. "Someone else is keeping secrets."

"Okay, I've had some pain. It's nothing. He's exaggerating."

Ella huffed. "You aren't a good liar, sweetie." She took Sarah's arm and studied it. "Your wrist and fingers look swollen. It hurt when I yanked you. Let me see your knee."

"Nonsense. Let's go make some sandwiches. I'm fine."

"Right. You can barely stand. Sit and let me have a look."

Benjamin said, "I'm going to get a glass of juice. I'll let you two fight this one out."

Sarah glared at him as he shuffled toward the door. She wanted to throttle him for telling Ella. "You could've kept your mouth shut," she shouted. "The jog across the pasture to save your hide made me twist my knee."

He turned at the doorway. "Maybe, but it wasn't a twisted knee several weeks ago when you couldn't open a jar and your fingers were swollen." His bare feet padded softly on the wooden floor. He disappeared into the library, headed across the hall toward the kitchen.

Ella tucked her chin and tapped a finger against her lips. Sarah felt like a specimen undergoing microscopic analysis.

Ella said, "It makes a lot of sense now that I stop to examine the facts. You haven't been your usual bouncy self. The man hasn't lied to me yet. When were you planning to tell me about this?"

"I'm a grown woman. I don't have to answer to you. We're best friends, but we don't talk about every little ache and pain."

"Yes we do. We talk about everything."

Conceding defeat wasn't natural, but she didn't have the energy to fight. Sarah sank to the bed. "Okay, you're right. I wanted to hide this from you. I've felt like a worn teddy bear that lost half of its stuffing for weeks. Actually months. It started during Mom's final weeks. I'm exhausted and can't sleep because everything hurts. Are you satisfied?"

"Why'd you keep me in the dark?"

Sarah hesitated and sheepishly raised her head. "Because I don't have the money to go for a checkup, and I knew you'd insist on helping me pay."

Ella's eyes widened and her mouth fell open. "You got that right. Money's no reason to mess around with your health. Oh, I'm getting a clear picture now, and I'm furious with you." Ella waved a hand toward the doorway, her boots stamping an angered rhythm while she strode from one side of the room to the other. "He's helping in the kitchen because you're hurting in the mornings. He's offered to pay, but you won't take it. Why wouldn't you let us help?"

Leather creaked when Benjamin settled on the couch in the library. "I hear you out there," Sarah said. "You might as well come back in here. Don't sit there and think I'll overlook this because you're sick. I can't believe you betrayed my trust."

Ella's blazing eyes flashed a warning. "Don't go there, Sarah.

No way. He should've told me long ago. Don't make him the bad guy here. This isn't about betraying anyone's trust."

Benjamin's swollen red face didn't mask his anger when he entered and walked over to her bed. Dark brooding eyes nailed her when he handed her a glass of orange juice. "I kept silent too long. You thought I was asleep. I saw you struggling to get out of bed. I saw how swollen your knee is. You won't take my money so, yes, I ratted on you. I thought Ella could talk some sense into that stubborn head of yours."

Sarah set the juice on the bedside table with a thud. "Thanks, but I'm not thirsty."

"Okay, you two. Stop arguing about her self-reliant stubbornness." Ella glanced back and forth between them. "He's right, Sarah. I'm taking his side. Show me your knee."

Benjamin and Ella glared at her like a pair of vultures circling over road kill. Sarah sat on the edge of the bed to pull up the pants leg and tried to keep a neutral face. It didn't work. The simple movement brought tears to her eyes.

She stared at the floor to avoid the angry look Ella leveled at her. "I suppose you've been taking pain pills and doing something to treat this? Your foot and ankle look swollen. Sarah this is serious. What were you thinking?"

Sarah compressed her lips and studied her knee. "It's worse today." She raised her hands in surrender. "Honest, Ella. Running yesterday and kneeling on the ground did something."

"Benjamin, is she telling me the truth?"

"She's been limping, but I haven't seen her leg until today. Her hands aren't any worse than yesterday."

Sarah waved her arms in the air. "That's enough. Stop talking about me like I'm not here. Benjamin has to go back to the doctor tomorrow. I'll go with him. Will that satisfy you two?"

"You need to go to the ER," Ella said.

"No. I'll accept a loan for an office visit, but I won't allow either of you to pay for an ER visit."

Ella slapped a hand against her forehead. Amazement flitted across her eyes. "You don't have insurance?"

Sarah shook her head and fingered a square on the quilt. "I had to drop it when Mom died. Her disability check stopped coming. I'm barely paying the bills, Ella."

"You've been hurting for weeks, giving us a discount, and you wouldn't ask for money to see the doctor?"

"You make me sound like some sort of idiot. I'm competing with the campgrounds and cabin owners for customers. I give you a discount because I love you. Please don't be angry with me. I have to keep my prices lower since I'm farther from Main Street. I don't need a lecture on finances." Sarah's face contorted as frustration and fatigue allowed tears to win. "The pain's bad enough. Don't make me feel guilty too."

Ella placed a hand on Sarah's shoulder. "It's okay. I understand your reasons. You're hurting and tired. I'll back off." She wagged a finger at her. "I am not happy with you."

"I know," Sarah said between sobs. "I'm just not used to asking for help. I've taken care of everything and everyone all of my life. I thought I could handle it alone."

Benjamin grasped her hand. "You're not alone anymore. We're here. You're going to get the help you need."

Ella lifted Sarah's leg and eased a pillow under it. Benjamin stood while she adjusted the covers and settled Sarah into a sitting position. "Have you slept, honey?"

"No, I hurt no matter which way I turned. I was heading to the bathroom for some pain pills when you came in. They're on the cabinet."

Ella returned with a bottle and dumped two pills into Sarah's palm. "Take these and drink the juice. I'll fix us a sandwich. We'll talk about this again when the pain eases and we all calm down."

Sarah couldn't calm down. They'd forced her into a position where she had to face the truth. She didn't want to see the doctor. Fear knotted her belly, and the tears poured.

Benjamin sat beside her on top of the quilt, plumped up a pillow, and lounged against the massive headboard. He opened his arms, and Sarah leaned against him. His breath brushed the top of her head. She sank deeper into his embrace.

He asked, "Are you mad at me, or were you posturing to hide the illness from Ella?"

"I should be mad. But I'm not. It was mostly posturing. I can't believe you recognized that. Truth is, I'm afraid to find out what's wrong with me."

He lifted her chin and cradled it in his hand. His gaze didn't show pity. How would she label that look? Love wasn't a word she could consider. Her rapid heart rate and the trembling were because of pain, not because of his touch. His breath against her cheek invited a kiss she wanted but must avoid. This wasn't the time or the place.

"Sarah, I spent hours alone and hurting after the fire. I understand fear and loneliness. Don't do this by yourself."

She should move away from him. A kiss seemed inevitable if one of them didn't move. His tender brown eyes riveted her in place. She focused on the quilt pattern to avoid looking at him.

He bent his head and captured her trembling lips in a soft kiss.

Sarah forgot pain and fear.

When they parted she pressed her lips together, but her fingers caressed the scars on his cheek. "What are we doing?"

Doubt filled his eyes. "I'm not sure, but I'm sorry." He edged away, but she clung to him.

"Don't Sarah. A kiss seemed like the right thing, but I took advantage—"

She placed a finger over his lips. "Don't say it. I've wanted your kiss for a long time. I'm not sure it was right, but I wanted it." She wound her fingers into his hair and traced his misshapen ear. "Something bad is happening to my body, Benjamin. I'm scared. I shouldn't let the fears sway my emotions, but I feel safe in your arms."

He leaned her head against his shoulder and stroked her hair. "Yesterday, at the pond, I thought I was going to die. Your eyes were filled with terror. Your whispers against my ear gave me the will to breathe when the swelling choked off the air. There was a bond between us. I can't identify what I felt. Can we explore those emotions when we're well and clear-headed? And I did take advantage of you in a vulnerable moment. It wasn't right to kiss you."

"We're too old to pretend nothing is happening between us."

"So you'll talk about this later and figure out where we're supposed to go from here?"

"I don't think we have any other choice. We're not exactly elementary school kids who kiss to see what it's like."

"Well God certainly knows I have no idea how to court a woman. In fact I'd almost forgotten what a kiss felt like."

She had to grin at his attempt to ease the tension. "You know, Benjamin, Old Maids isn't just a card game. I've had three dates in my entire lifetime, and I'm not a 'kiss on the first date' sort of woman."

His lips tipped into the smile that had drawn her to him from the first day they met. "You could have fooled me." He kissed each tear-stained cheek.

"I'm embarrassed," she chuckled. "I didn't exactly express it right."

"I'd say that's correct. Old Maid isn't a phrase I'd use to describe you. You're an exhausted unmarried woman."

"I meant the kissing part and you know it, but I won't argue about the exhaustion. I've felt horrible for days." She stifled a yawn. "Those pills are making me sleepy this time."

"Good, maybe you'll finally rest. The lines of pain around your eyes are fading. I suppose you'd consider it inappropriate if I held you until you fall asleep."

"Ella's going to see us if you do."

"Would that bother you?"

"It should, but I don't want to move. It might make something hurt and keep me awake."

"Then I'll stay."

The emotions she'd fought to suppress wouldn't accept denial. She needed comfort. She needed him, at least today. Later they'd decide if it was due to their mutual vulnerability. Prayer would come—long intimate talks. If she headed down this road, would God be pleased?

☙ ✠ ☕

When Ella returned with a tray of food, Benjamin lifted a finger to his lips. "She's asleep," he mouthed. He eased Sarah's head down to the pillow, adjusted the covers around her shoulders, and slid off the bed. Ella placed the tray on the desk and motioned him to follow her out to the library.

Benjamin dropped to the couch and ran a hand through his tousled curls. "I don't think we should force her to go to the ER today."

Ella paced the length of the room and back. "If this has been coming on for months, one day won't matter. I can't believe I didn't notice her pain before now."

"You've been busy looking for the missing girl."

"Still, this is something I should have seen. It's times like this when I wish I had a regular staff. I end up doing all the work in some areas. I need more volunteers in this section."

"Sarah wanted to hide the truth. Don't blame yourself."

"I'm glad you finally told me. I love Sarah, but she puts others before herself. That's not always healthy."

Benjamin scratched a welt on the back of his neck and strained to reach the middle of his back. He had wanted the fog of the medicines this morning. Now, he wanted a clear head so he could focus on Sarah's illness. He struggled for a solution to the dilemma. He'd need the medications to ease his discomfort for a couple of days.

Ella sank to the couch beside him. She rubbed the itch he'd tried to reach. "I'll put something on those stings when we're done talking. That is if you don't mind."

"You saw my scars already. I can't reach the place that's bothering me the most. I don't want to wake Sarah for any reason."

"Then let's get you taken care of. I need to make a phone call."

"I'll manage a few more minutes. Let's figure out how we're going to take care of Sarah."

"Sarah's never had anyone who gave a hoot. Always had to be independent and rely on her own pluck. Church friends helped some with food. Her mother was more like Sarah's child. Sarah's father was stuck in a bad place. Didn't know how to handle it. He loved Sarah, and he loved his wife. Poor man had no idea his actions were harming his daughter."

"She told me a bit about how hard things were. I'll make her go to the doctor and take good care of her while you're gone. Becky and Todd seem to care about Sarah. They'll pitch in if we need them."

Her look showed utter surprise. "I'm not leaving Sarah like this. I'll call that district's team leader and tell him to take over. The volunteers can handle the fundraiser they organized. Meeting the psychologist can wait. If she's any good, she'll adjust easily. She's dealt with grieving parents before."

"I'll call the doctor and make an appointment. They don't want me driving while I'm on this medicine. I'm sure Becky would take us. We'll make sure Sarah gets the care she needs. Or ... don't you trust me?"

"Why would you think I didn't trust you?"

"If you heard about my alibi today, I just thought—"

"That's ridiculous. If I didn't trust you, I'd have said so long ago. More people would care about you if you let them."

"That's what Sarah says. Noah and his family I can handle. I'm not sure about the rest of the world."

"The woman who matters never saw you as ugly or as a threat."

"Sarah."

"She's falling in love with you. I'm sure Sarah Campbell has never gone to sleep in a man's arms before. Never had a date since I've known her. You'd better find a way to deal with the world. You'd be stupid to toss her aside." Ella's phone played its ring tone. "Baxter."

She ambled toward the stairs, leaving Benjamin with questions and the painful itch she'd forgotten. He'd have to tolerate it until Ella finished her calls. Clearly, he shouldn't be alone with Sarah. He couldn't trust his heart, and Ella couldn't stay much longer. He'd have to talk with Becky.

CHAPTER EIGHT

Benjamin awoke from a dream where Sarah's fingertips stroked his sore back. The anti-itch ointment on the bedside table seemed to leer about forbidden territory. He'd itch all day rather than ask for Sarah's help again. He tossed and turned until the night creatures ceased thrumming and the birds started twittering in the orchard.

It wasn't merely the dream. He'd welcomed Sarah's touch, which wasn't rational or safe. She found him attractive. His reclusive side wanted to run and deny what he'd seen and heard. He'd seen the look of pleasure on her face, heard her say she felt safe in his arms. Since the day of the fire, Benjamin had never imagined a lovely woman, eyes filled with ... no, it couldn't be. Sarah hadn't looked at him with desire. But she had, and he'd kissed her. Guilt flooded in.

They'd promised to discuss it. Forgetting it happened would be easier. Did he want that? He understood loneliness and fear. He'd rarely accepted anyone's comfort, too easy to live with shame and fear, but maybe the changes Sarah wanted were good.

As the sky grew lighter, he contemplated the past weeks. Life had dramatically changed. Solitude was no longer his priority. The woman sleeping downstairs possessed the ability to change that notion. Love Valley offered bonuses far greater than a salary and a peaceful room.

Sarah Campbell needed him, maybe even loved him. Ella Baxter trusted him. Noah called him Grandpa, and the Spanglers practically treated him like a part of their family.

Sarah wanted him to embrace her spiritual beliefs. Noah had plainly told Benjamin church was important. Grandpas went to church, and Grandpas loved Jesus. Benjamin wouldn't change his life simply to please Noah or any of his new friends. Life might be improving; but second-rate, unaccepted, and ridiculed still described his innermost pain. Anger boiled every time he thought about the fire and the brand it had bestowed on him. Their loving attitudes were softening him, but he wasn't ready to embrace the notion that God loved him.

The clock read six. He tossed off the covers. Sarah would expect breakfast for her guests as usual. And if he knew her, she'd insist on helping despite Ella's strict orders to the contrary.

Twenty minutes later Benjamin found Ella in the kitchen boiling eggs. "Morning," he said. "How'd Sarah sleep?"

"Sporadic, but she got some rest." Ella handed him the coffee urn and regarded his face. "Swelling's down. You can see today. Feeling better?"

"Yep, I hurt less. Still itch. Think I'm gonna live. I'll take care of the coffee and breads." He backed through the swinging door.

Faint rosy hues drew him to the window. Streaks of purple and orange painted the cloud bank hovering over the ridge.

The beauty of the sunrise brought Sarah to mind. Sharing coffee in the early mornings and reading with her in the evenings were the high points of his day. He didn't want those times to end. In fact, he had to say there was more to that kiss than acting on manly emotions at a moment when Sarah was vulnerable. He'd never experienced a loving relationship with a woman. Was he falling in love with Sarah?

A crash and a pained cry sent him flying to Sarah's room.

His heart thundered against his ribs when he skidded from the library into her room. Sarah lay sprawled on the floor in a widening pool of blood.

"Sarah, what happened? Where are you hurt?" He knelt beside her among shards of glass and pink tinged water.

Ella ran into the room and headed for the bathroom. "Don't move her until we know what's wrong." She yanked a towel from the rod and tossed it to Benjamin.

"I'm okay." Sarah pushed herself up on an elbow. "It's just a cut." She moaned and cried out, "Oh, please!" She grabbed his arm. "Help me sit. My knee. Move my knee. It's twisted under me."

Benjamin pressed the towel against the redness pooling on Sarah's thigh. He didn't like the bluish cast around her lips or her panting, shuddering breaths. Clenched teeth and her grimace clearly said pain, but first aid training told him to let Ella assess Sarah before he complied with her pleas to move. "Careful, Ella. There's broken glass."

She knelt beside Sarah. "Is it just your leg?" She swiftly ran her hands along Sarah's body from head to toe.

"Yeah. A simple cut. Stop the fuss and help me sit."

"Okay, okay. I don't see any other injuries." Ella straightened the leg and scooted Sarah into a sitting position against the bed.

Sarah covered her mouth with her hand and squeezed her eyes shut. The gesture didn't hide the tears threatening to spill. "I should have called for help. I've made a huge mess." She squirmed and tried to shove Benjamin's hand away. "You're hurting me."

"I'm sorry the pressure hurts. I need to stop the bleeding."

"I'll be fine. Go make breakfast. I can handle this." She tugged at the towel he held, but he didn't back off.

"Stop arguing. Breakfast will wait. I'm not going away until we see how bad this is." Benjamin lifted the towel to assess the wound and satisfy her. "I need a better look. Cut a bigger hole in the pants leg."

Sarah said, "There's a first aid kit under my sink."

Ella's scissors snipped the pajama leg and revealed a jagged, gaping wound. Benjamin applied firm pressure again. What a way to start the day. They'd have to spend hours at the hospital sitting in a public waiting area.

Sarah lowered her head into her hands and wailed. Color drained from her face. "You're killing me." She gritted her teeth and dug her nails into his arm. "I'm going to faint."

"Then lie down. I'm not pushing hard. The swelling makes it hurt."

A sharp intake of breath hissed between her clenched teeth. "I'd be fine if you'd ease off a little."

When tears dripped off Sarah's chin and her pale lips trembled, he cringed. If only someone else could inflict the pain. He gave Ella a wide-eyed glance; hoping it said, "Please distract Sarah so I can do this."

Ella acknowledged his look by blowing out a long breath and nodding. "Easy. Scoot around this way. That's it, lie down now." Ella tucked a cushion under Sarah's head and elevated the uninjured leg on a large pillow from the bed. "That looks more comfortable. Take a deep breath." With a quick trip to the faucet, she brought a wet washcloth to bathe Sarah's face. "This cool cloth should help."

A hint of color returned to Sarah's cheeks. The panting, ragged breaths slowed as Ella coaxed her to calm down.

Benjamin lifted the towel for a peek. If he had to hurt her, at least his efforts were staunching the flow of blood.

Ella said, "Squeeze my hand, and tell me how you fell."

"I'm cold."

"Well, no wonder. You're wet." Ella pulled a blanket from the bed and tucked it around Sarah's torso. "Now, what happened?"

"I can't believe I was so dumb. I didn't think I needed help walking to the bathroom. I got water and two pain pills. My fingers were stiff so I dropped the glass. I guess I slipped in the water."

"Looks like you landed on this." Ella picked up the jagged base of a broken glass. "Are you feeling better?" She turned the wet cloth over and placed it back on Sarah's forehead.

"Yeah, the blanket helped." She lifted her head to look at her leg. "Has the bleeding stopped?"

Benjamin chanced another look at the cut. "Slowing down. It needs stitches."

Sarah covered her eyes with the back of her hand and moaned. "Great. I really wanted to hear that. Can it wait until our appointment with the doctor?"

"I'm not sure. We'll decide once you stop bleeding."

Five minutes later, he removed the towel. "Much better. Let's wrap it in gauze and an elastic bandage. That should take care of it until we get to the hospital."

Benjamin supported Sarah's leg while Ella wrapped it. "I'm sorry I had to hurt you. That wasn't on my schedule for today."

"I'm not usually a wimp. I dropped the pain pills. Can you get me some, Ella?"

Benjamin squatted, prepared to lift her. "Put your arms around my neck. I'll carry you to your car while Ella gets your medicine. We need to get this stitched up."

"Wait." Sarah shook her head and held up her hands. "I've known Doc for years. He might work me in as the first patient if we call. I don't want to go to the ER."

Benjamin rolled his eyes. "Don't start another money discussion."

"It's not the money. Doc opens at eight o'clock. His staff will be there by the time Ella gets me cleaned up and we drive to Statesville. Please set out a simple breakfast, tell my guests what's happened, and call him. I'm sure he'd stitch this in the office as soon as he arrives."

Benjamin heaved a sigh and pressed his lips together so he wouldn't say more. "Fine. I'll wash up and go call. Ella can help you get out of these wet pajamas and take care of the rest. I'm sure your guests are curious about the commotion. Where will I find Doc's phone number?"

"There's a list on my desk."

೫ ✠ ೂ

Ella's Pathfinder crunched on the gravel when she pulled into the driveway of Mosey Inn. Benjamin hopped out to open the back door. "Come on, Sleeping Beauty. Let's get you to a comfortable bed."

Sarah awakened and squinted against the sun.

He lifted her from the pillow-padded seat and started toward the house.

Noah bounced off the porch swing and raced out to meet them. "Why are you carrying Miss Sarah?"

Sarah lifted her head from Benjamin's shoulder. "I hurt my leg, sweetheart. The doctor gave me a shot. I'm sleepy."

He reached up and patted her arm. "I don't like shots. Did it hurt?"

"Not bad. It made my leg feel better, so I didn't mind too much."

Benjamin said, "Run ahead and hold the door open for me, buddy."

The screen door creaked open. "I got it." Becky called from the porch, "Noah, get out of Benjamin's way."

After he lowered Sarah to the bed, Benjamin said, "Thanks for coming, Becky. Sarah needed some x-rays and lab tests. It took longer than we anticipated."

"No problem. I washed the dishes, stored food after breakfast, and cleaned the rooms when people left. Towels are in the dryer." She bent to plant a kiss on Sarah's brow. "Your guests said they hope you feel better. The couple from Charlotte will call in a couple of days to check on you and make reservations for Thanksgiving."

Sarah yawned and covered her mouth. "Thanks, Becky. Sorry I spoiled your day. I didn't know who else to call."

"Don't worry about it. Noah had fun watching videos and exploring your yard."

Ella deposited a bag on the bathroom counter. "Come on in, Noah. Tell Miss Sarah what you found and then Benjamin can go outside with you. Your mom needs to help me get Miss Sarah settled."

"It's a huge toad." Noah tugged on Benjamin's arm. "Come see it, Grandpa. He was on the steps. Mommy wouldn't let me bring it in the house. He's on the back porch in a box."

"A toad, huh? I saw a whopper the other day. Let's go see if it's the same one." He extended a hand for Noah to hold.

"How can you tell?"

"I'll remember this guy. I almost stepped on him when I came in from work. He promised he wouldn't hop on the back steps again."

Noah wrinkled his nose and tipped his head to the side. "Grandpa, toads can't talk."

"This one could. If it is the same one, he needs to apologize for not obeying me."

"Yeah, right. You're just trying to find out if I've been good today."

"Well have you? Did you obey your mother?"

"Yes sir." There was a hint of question in the comment as if he wasn't sure what behavior Benjamin would consider good.

"I'm sure you did. Let's go check out this toad."

Benjamin swept Noah off his feet and turned him upside down. Noah's laughter rang through the room as a quarter and several rocks clattered to the floor. Benjamin returned Noah to his feet and squatted to gather the scattered treasures.

Noah, still giggling from Benjamin's playful treatment, snatched up a rubber lizard and tucked it in his pocket. "Aw shucks. I meant to put this in your bed. I forgot about it when I found the toad."

"Well, you better thank the toad and send him home. If I'd come home and found that green lizard in my bed, the tickle monster would've attacked you. Maybe I'll just do it anyway since you thought about teasing me with the lizard."

Noah laughed and darted toward the library. Benjamin grabbed him, swinging him off his feet. The boy squirmed and giggled as Benjamin tickled him breathless, then tossed him over his shoulder, holding him upside down by his legs. "Let's get out of the way. Miss Sarah needs to rest."

Noah tickled Benjamin and erupted into another fit of giggles.

"Watch it, boy. You're asking for it." Teasing Noah seemed to ease the tension and fear hanging over the adults.

Benjamin turned in the doorway, his smile broadening as he shoved Noah against the doorframe. "Oh, I forgot you were back there."

Noah wrapped his arms around Benjamin's waist. "You'll be sorry if you do that again, Grandpa."

Sarah waved. "Have fun you two."

"Bye, Miss Sarah. Feel better."

Benjamin winked at Sarah and twisted in the doorway so he squished Noah again. "Oops. Sorry. I keep forgetting you're there."

Noah laughed and tickled him. Benjamin set him on his feet and chased him out of the room.

His last glimpse of Sarah's feeble smile tore at his weary body. If she fought him over the doctor's orders, he'd have to get tough with her. Maybe she'd cooperate for a couple of days. This event seemed to have drained the last of her energy.

His fitful night and the stressful morning were catching up with him. The swelling might be better, but itching and discomfort would remain his companions a few more days. He'd need a nap and some medication once the women had Sarah settled into bed.

He stretched his legs out and rocked the porch swing after viewing Noah's toad.

Opening his eyes at the sound of the creaking screen door, he made a mental note to oil the hinges.

Ella handed him a glass of iced tea. "Need some ointment on those hard-to-reach itchy spots?"

"Yeah, but we need to talk with Becky first."

Becky joined them and asked, "Where's Noah?"

"We took his toad to the orchard. I suggested he pick up some apples for you to take home. He's filling the box." Benjamin pointed to the third row of trees where Noah waved and held up a bright red apple. Benjamin redirected his attention to Ella. "Is Sarah asleep?"

"We barely got her nightgown on. She'll sleep most of the day."

Becky and Ella pulled white rocking chairs close to the swing. Becky's eyes clouded, concern obvious. "I knew Sarah wasn't feeling well. I had no idea she was in pain or having problems walking. What's going on?"

Benjamin shook his head and scratched a red area on his arm. "Doc's not sure. He suspects arthritis. It could be an injury from running yesterday, but I don't think so. He made an appointment for her to see a rheumatologist in four days. The labs and x-rays the specialist ordered took most of the morning. After Doc stitched her leg and completed those tests, she was in agony. He gave her a pain shot and prescribed some pills."

Ella shook her head and frowned. "We tried to get her to stay in the hospital. She's a stubborn old mule sometimes. Can't blame her though. She'll sleep better in her own bed. I'd probably be the same way. This didn't happen yesterday. She's not been normal since her mom passed."

Benjamin leaned forward, hands clasped between his legs. "I need to ask a favor, Becky. Sarah can't manage this place alone right now. Would you be interested in earning some money until she's better?"

"We can always use it. What do you have in mind?"

Benjamin pulled a coffee stained napkin from his pocket. "Ella and I talked while they were running tests. We've jotted down a tentative plan. Ella needs to leave town to check on her volunteers. I can get breakfast ready before I go to work. Since I've finished repairing the church, the town asked me to replace some sagging planks in the boardwalk on Main Street. Then I'll go back to the church for some work on the Fellowship Hall. I think they'd let me work at my own pace under the circumstances. If you came to help in the mornings, I could be back in the afternoon to handle arrivals and make dinner for Sarah."

"Does Sarah know about this plan?"

"Not yet. Doc wants her in bed or the recliner until she sees the specialist. She can't follow those orders unless she has help. He gave her a cane to use, but it's not a license to walk when she pleases."

Becky hung her head and tugged on her lip with her teeth. "I'm not sure Sarah has the money to hire me. I overheard her asking one of the men in church to pick apples so she could sell them at the Country Store and at a roadside market in Statesville. She offered to pay him with apples for his own use and give him a room when his brother comes to visit."

Benjamin raised questioning eyebrows at Ella. When she nodded he said, "I'd pay you. I'm glad you mentioned the apples. I can tell her you're getting free apples so she's bartering for your help. She'd feel more like she's in control."

"I pack lunches when Todd takes groups on trail rides. I won't turn down free apples. Don't tell her about the conversation I shared. I didn't mean to—"

Ella placed a hand on Becky's knee. "We knew she didn't have money. You're not divulging anything secret. Sarah won't ask for assistance. She'll go along with bartering for apples, but it's time she learned to accept aid from her friends. You can bring Noah. She can help with his schooling. That'll sweeten the whole arrangement."

"I'll see if Todd can manage without me in the mornings. If our new stable hand will help during the week, I'll be here. When can you return to work, Benjamin? This appointment was supposed to be about you."

"Doc Hammond wants me on the antihistamine another day. Then I'll take them at night if needed. I'll watch over Sarah tomorrow and take care of things here. Would that give you enough time to decide?"

"Sure. By the way, Todd's called a beekeeper to remove the hive from the shed. We still want you to renovate it when you have time."

"I'll get on it right away. I have to shuffle my time around tourists, so I plan to work odd hours in town." He didn't want to say he dreaded being in a public place and would gladly repair their shed and the Fellowship Hall to avoid business hours.

"This thing with Sarah," Becky said, "it sounds serious."

Benjamin heaved a sigh. "I'm worried. If she has to cut back on activities, it'll be hard on her. Sarah's independent. I think it's going to be a while before she's able to handle Mosey Inn alone."

"Are you leaving when you finish your jobs here?"

"That's a question I haven't answered yet. I'd thought about retiring here. Mrs. Hardin hasn't made me feel like the most welcomed man in town. On the other hand, Sarah's my friend. I won't leave when she needs help."

Becky laid a hand on his arm. "She's not the only one who needs you. We need you. Noah would be heartbroken if you left him."

Benjamin couldn't look into her eyes. He'd blame the emotions on pain, but tears stung his eyes for a different reason. "I'd better go take some medicine. My eyes are swelling again. Call me when you decide."

ಬ ✠ ಲ

Sarah's sleigh bed had magically transformed into Santa's sleigh. In their fantasy world, Sarah and Noah reclined against piles of reindeer skins and bags of Christmas presents. She closed the book and slid it into his canvas book bag.

"Read it again, Miss Sarah."

Noah arched his arm and lobbed a wad of paper into the Nerf basketball hoop attached to the footboard. Sarah gave him a high five. He slithered off to retrieve it for what seemed like the millionth time. The kid might have pro potential. His aim had improved during the last four days.

"I'd say you're more interested in playing basketball."

"I can listen and play at the same time."

"My voice needs a rest. Get your coloring book. You're a great shot, but jiggling the bed hurts my knee."

"Do you need your medicine? I can carry a glass of water."

"It's not time. But thank you." She flipped through the coloring book to a page with a horse. "This looks like your pony. Find the right colors so he'll look like Kicker."

Noah dumped the box of crayons on the bed and fished through them until he found a brown one. "When can you get out of the bed?"

Sarah wished she knew the answer. "I'm supposed to see the doctor this afternoon. Maybe he'll let me walk more."

Sarah adjusted the pillows and stared out the window. Staying put hadn't been as hard as she'd anticipated. Short trips around the house made her knee throb. Putting pressure on the cane to take her weight off the leg caused pain in her wrist. There had to be a better solution.

Noah held up his masterpiece. "How's that?"

"Nice. You're staying in the lines. He needs a black mane and tail."

"Want me to get your computer so you can check the mail?"

"Good idea. I should check for reservations. Carry it carefully."

Noah eased her laptop from the desk and positioned it on her lap.

"Plug it in the way I showed you."

Her fingers didn't cooperate when she manipulated the mouse pad. They worked a bit better every day, but normal wouldn't describe the movements. What sort of rebellion had her body pulled on her? Doc's medicine had reduced the swelling in her knee but it was far from well. She tried to remain hopeful that the rheumatologist could prescribe something to make life normal again.

It took a while to read and reply to a message from Ella. The next e-mail made dollar signs dance in Sarah's head and her worries subside. God did answer prayers. She read it again to be certain about its intent.

"Noah, get your mom. I have a surprise to share with her."

Benjamin rapped on the doorjamb. "Becky's in the orchard picking apples. Didn't mean to eavesdrop."

Sarah's heart jumped into overdrive. A woodsy scent of after-shave and shampoo accompanied him. Fresh from the shower, wet curls fell loosely over his forehead and brushed the collar of his dark green shirt. How would it feel to run her fingers through his wet hair until it dried into gray streaked waves? Every day together lessened her control over those emotions. Not a smart thought when her life was in limbo.

"Hey." She glanced at the clock. "You're early."

"Wanted to clean up and eat before I took you to the doctor."

Benjamin rumpled Noah's hair and joined them on the bed. "Nice picture. Have you been good?"

"Yes sir." Noah looked at Sarah, his eyes big question marks.

"He's turning into a basketball pro, and before long he'll be reading. We're getting along just fine in our magical sleigh."

Benjamin said, "Why don't you show your mom your picture? Tell her I'll have lunch ready in fifteen minutes."

"Good, I'm hungry." Noah grabbed the stick horse from his toy box. Waving the coloring page over his head, he whinnied and galloped away.

"Is he wearing you out? You look tired." Benjamin arranged the crayons in the box, adjusted a pillow to lean against, and draped his arm along the pillow behind Sarah's head.

"He's a chatterbox, but it's better than being bored."

Sarah leaned her head on his shoulder. "You know I'm not happy about this whole arrangement with Becky."

"Your knee has improved, and Becky's glad to help. Be patient. You'll be up and around soon."

"Letting other people do my work isn't easy. By the way, I know she's not working for the apples. How much are you paying her?"

He brushed a finger down her arm and stroked the back of her hand. "Apples from your orchard plus a fair salary. It's worth every penny if it helps you heal."

His touch induced a ripple of pleasure. Avoiding physical or emotional encounters would be prudent for both of them, but those notions didn't get far when they were together. He brought yearnings she'd buried years ago. She wasn't young and naïve. More like old and lonely. Was it wrong to want affection?

Sarah focused on the e-mail she'd received. Using both hands to heft the laptop and guard her tender knuckles, she slid the computer over to his lap. "Read this. Tell me I'm not having a medication induced dream. If it says what I think it does, I'll be able to pay you back by Christmas."

"I don't expect payback, but I'll read it anyway."

Sarah mentally calculated the money she'd receive while Benjamin read the e-mail.

"Wow, what a great opportunity. And no, you're not dreaming."

The twinkle in his eyes increased her delight. She squeezed his arm like a giddy teenager. "So it really says they're filming a western in Love Valley and want to house the star at Mosey Inn for a month?"

"It says they'll pay you double the usual rate if you feed him dinner and give him complete privacy."

She'd have financial security for a while. Money to pay her bills and maybe enough to take that dream vacation.

"Can you believe it? Dinner isn't a problem since we have to eat anyway." Her face fell. "It will be if I can't walk or make my fingers work. You and Becky are making meals now."

"Look at me." He shifted to frame her face with his hands.

"This reservation starts in mid-October. You'll be ready in two weeks."

A sigh escaped as she dropped her head against the pillows. "I hope so. I dread this appointment. Do you realize how it makes me feel to stay in bed while other people do my job?"

"Yes, it goes against your nature. Give yourself some time, Sarah. Making dinner is the least of our worries."

"I'll be ready by the time this movie star comes. I won't ask you to take on extra work. You're doing too much as it is."

"You're not asking. I'm giving. If it puts a smile on your beautiful face, he can have my room with the private balcony for the month, and I'll make dinner every night. Send a reservation confirmation accepting their requests."

"I don't want you to change rooms unless it's absolutely necessary. How will this movie affect your work in town?"

"Mrs. Hardin hasn't mentioned it. I should be finished with the boardwalk repairs before they start filming. If the town needs me to work faster because of the movie, no one told me."

"So Mrs. Hardin's still coming around to check your progress?"

"Oh, yeah. Almost daily." He exaggerated a shudder. "I'm trying to ignore her. The woman's a menace."

"She likes to control things. I avoid town when I think she'll be there." Sarah checked the time. "I'll change into something nicer while you make lunch."

"Before you do, I have a question. Ella left before I had a chance to ask what the police said about me. Did she tell you?"

"No. I didn't see the fax or talk to her. Stop worrying." She gave his knee a reassuring pat. "If there was a reason to suspect you, the authorities would have asked you more questions by now."

"You're right. I'd be in jail or under interrogation if they believed Mrs. Hardin." He glanced at his watch. "We'd better get moving. Do you need Becky's help getting ready?"

"I think I can manage. I'll yell if I need her."

He tapped the computer screen. "Send the confirmation accepting their extra requests while I make lunch."

CHAPTER NINE

Sarah's foot tapped a rapid rhythm on the doctor's tile floor, the rubber sole of her tennis shoe sounding like a dribbled basketball. She tossed the travel magazine back on the table and checked her watch. Only twenty minutes? Her heart hammered against her ribs. Prayer didn't help. Concentration fled. Anxiety took control. She'd rather leave and ignore the inevitable. No wonder the minutes dragged.

Her hands turned to stiff blocks of ice. Every inch of her ached. Her blood pressure must be out the roof. Calm down, take a deep breath. Relax the tense muscles. Nothing to fear. Right!

Beside her, Benjamin looked equally tense. Slouched in his chair, he held his book so it blocked his face from curious stares. He'd selected seats that gave them the most privacy and exposed the less damaged side of his face. Still, sitting here put him on exhibit, not a choice he'd normally make.

Back in August, his self-aversion wouldn't have allowed him to accompany her. Since she'd fallen, he'd taken over the task of breakfast, and he came home in time to make dinner. Yesterday, he'd taken two new arrivals to their room rather than awaken her. A marked change in behavior. He'd insisted on bringing her to the doctor. Was God working in Benjamin's heart? She wasn't sure, but Benjamin's progress pleased her.

With Ella gone, Sarah relied on Benjamin's physical support. No, that lie wouldn't work. Her feelings went deeper. The attraction was real and resided deep in her heart. People like Becky or other church friends could meet her superficial needs. Being honest, she preferred having Benjamin here for this stressful wait. Figuring out how to reconcile her need with his lack of interest in Christianity was an issue she'd chosen to ignore. Dealing with it could come when her health improved.

Denying her illness wouldn't work any longer either. Aching, swollen fingers necessitated Becky's tying her shoes. Requesting help had been humiliating. She'd chosen a sweater and elastic waist jeans rather than asking for help with buttons and zippers.

Coldness crept up her arms, and her stomach knotted as a thought she'd avoided gelled. She had to depend on people's help with her daily physical needs. Would she become her mother? Examining that idea would require more courage than she possessed today.

She sighed, closed her eyes, and leaned her head against the wall.

Benjamin placed a reassuring hand on her arm. "You want a drink of water or something?"

She rolled her head sideways to glance at him. "No thanks."

He lowered the book to his lap. "Waiting is the hardest part."

She pressed her lips together and nodded. "You don't have to sit with me. I know you hate public places."

"I'll endure it. People aren't staring much. Guess they're afraid like you are."

She'd tried to mask the fear and questions. "Is it so obvious?"

His lips pulled into a smirk. "Your foot tapping is shaking the room." He marked his place in the book and set it aside.

Twisting in his chair, he clasped her hands. "You're freezing."

He picked up the jacket he'd folded over the arm of his chair, draped it around her shoulders, and reclaimed her hands. "Want to talk?"

Sarah stared at a coffee ring on one of the magazines. If she looked into his eyes, she might cry. "I'm terrified that my life is about to change. I can't deny that I'm sick. Mosey Inn is all I have. I can't keep it open if my health doesn't improve. What will I do if the doctor can't do something?"

The nurse called Sarah's name. Her heart picked up its pace. She cast a nervous look toward Benjamin before using the arms of the chair to push out of the seat.

A lightning bolt of agony shot up her leg.

Benjamin's soft brown eyes cut her a look of concern. "Need help to the door?"

She hadn't meant for him to hear the quick intake of breath or see the grimace.

Sarah looked at the nurse standing in the open doorway. The distance across the room had miraculously grown while they'd waited. She dipped her chin and looked up at Benjamin through her lashes. "Come with me. I can't do this alone."

Benjamin hooked his arm through hers. Words weren't necessary. His eyes said he understood and welcomed her request.

Determined to face this stroll with dignity, she lifted her chin and let him support her. People looked over their magazines as they crossed the room. Most of the stares focused on him. Another sacrifice for her.

The nurse said, "You can have a seat in Dr. Griffin's office." She led them to a room on the right. "He'll go over the results with you and your husband. I'll come back to get you ready for your exam."

Sarah's cheeks burned. Of course, they'd assume Benjamin was her husband. She opened her mouth to explain. The nurse was gone.

Benjamin grinned and picked a piece of lint off his navy blue sweater. "It's not important. Don't try to explain who I am. Still want me here?"

"I need another set of ears. I'm not thinking clearly. I might miss an important detail."

Ten minutes later, Sarah shrank deeper into her chair and gripped the arms. Dr. Griffin pulled off his glasses and focused on her with foreboding yet sympathetic eyes.

"I'm sorry. You have rheumatoid arthritis. You probably suspected that already and just needed confirmation."

No. Even as he'd shown her the deterioration of her knee and the damage to her wrists and fingers on the x-rays, she hadn't understood the depth of the problem. The labs told the story of an immune system running amuck. Her body destroying itself. Why was it such a shock? She'd known something awful was happening.

Denial came easier than accepting her loss of independence.

The doctor slid the x-rays in the folder. He pulled his chair closer. After offering her a box of tissues, he waited. At least he was kind enough to allow a few moments to absorb the devastating words.

Her heartbeat swooshed in her ears. The walls closed in. Benjamin asked a question but it didn't register. The doctor's reply receded to some distant place. It didn't need to be so cold in here. Her mind numbed, and her body shook. Deep breaths wouldn't control the trembling or give her enough air. Tears stung her eyes.

Benjamin's strong, callused hand covered hers on the armrest. His touch gave a bit of courage and comfort. She couldn't look at him. Tears would become sobs.

"I'd expected to hear strain from constant stair climbing. Maybe some back problem. Even plain old aging. Doc mentioned arthritis. I wasn't thinking about this kind. Rheumatoid?" She wiped her face with a tissue and blew her nose. "I don't know what to say. How do I deal with this?"

"You absorb the news first."

Visions of useless fingers and deformed joints etched fear through her. This was worse than any scenario she'd imagined.

Dr. Griffin dipped his head so he made eye contact with her. "I'll send some literature home with you. It should answer some of your questions. Give us topics to discuss. Today isn't the day for details. Do you have any questions at this point?"

Sarah shook her head. What could she ask? He hadn't examined her and had already pronounced a horrifying sentence. She'd be crippled and dependent on others—just like her mother. A nursing home loomed around the corner.

He patted her hand and launched into conversation again. "Treatments have come a long way in the last few years. Let's assess your pain and joint inflammation. I'll prescribe some pain medicine and something to help with swelling. My nurse can schedule an appointment for a physical therapy evaluation. I'm sure you know this disease can be crippling and cause deformities of the joints."

All she could do was nod.

"We'll do everything possible to keep that from happening." His gentle touch didn't soothe her worries.

Where did she go from here? How would she pay for therapy and medicines? "I have a business to run. My funds are limited. I don't have insurance."

He stood and crossed to the door. "We'll discuss that next time. Payment plans and other forms of assistance are available. I'm not going to lie to you, Sarah. You are a sick woman. I can't erase the damage. Our goal is to get this under control. Let's complete the exam and decide what's going to work best for you. I'll have my nurse get you into a room."

☙ ✠ ❧

Benjamin retrieved a tube of lip balm from his shirt pocket. "Stop nibbling that piece of dry skin on your lower lip. You'll make it sore." He rubbed the ointment across her lips.

"Oh, I didn't realize I was doing it." She snaked a hand from beneath the quilts—an obvious invitation for handholding.

"You're finally warm. Feeling less queasy?"

"Yeah. I think I could drink some hot tea."

Becky laid her book on the daybed and stood. "Stay. I'll make it."

Scooting his chair closer to Sarah's recliner, Benjamin rested the back of his hand against her forehead. "Fever's down. You've been preoccupied all afternoon. What's going on inside your head?"

She frowned. "Mulling things over. You should send Becky home. I'll be okay by myself."

"Nope. We've discussed it. The doctor said to rest your leg another day. The nausea's better, but the chills and fever might hit again. It wouldn't be right for me to sleep in your room. Noah's watching a movie with Todd tonight so Becky stays."

Benjamin adjusted the ice bag on Sarah's knee then resumed his role as hand holder. His touch seemed to calm her. "It's time for another dose of that new medicine."

"I'll wait until I have something in my stomach. I hope it won't make me sick all the time."

"Think positive thoughts. You've taken one dose. You already had pain and a fever. They're the likely culprits." He tweaked her nose. "You look better. Got some color back in your cheeks. Even dozed for a while."

"I feel better. The phone woke me earlier. Who called?"

"Hmm, Becky called her ... Mrs. Wexler."

A faint smile flitted across her face. "Church member. The older woman who prompted Noah to ask about your wrinkles. Remember?"

"Oh, yeah. She told Becky the women would bring meals over starting tomorrow evening."

Sarah rolled her eyes. "Food fixes everything. If you went to church you'd know that."

He ignored her sarcasm. "You won't hear me complaining. Mrs. Wexler also said they were praying."

"That's good. I'm going to need it."

Shrubs scratched against the windowpane. Sarah turned to stare out into the inky-blackness as if the sound required her rapt attention. Her thumb absently moved across his knuckles.

Dull eyes, lack of spunk, pessimism—not the Sarah he knew. His Sarah might have refused the doctor's prescriptions for expensive medications. She'd submitted instead, acting far too stoic and aloof. The doctor's explanation about rheumatoid arthritis had churned up fear in Benjamin's gut. Must have terrified Sarah too since she hadn't avoided the advice.

Benjamin's thoughts returned to the procedure room. Sarah's grasp had nearly crushed his hand. Good thing since he'd gotten a tad weak-kneed when the doctor removed fluid from her knee and injected medication to reduce the inflammation. The injection had decreased her pain this evening; however, the bouts of chills and nausea she'd experienced the past few days still plagued her. As the evening passed, her temperature fluctuated between normal and just enough fever to make her feel lousy. Perhaps the prescriptions they'd filled would break this pattern and bring some relief.

When they returned from the doctor, Sarah hibernated under a pile of quilts in her recliner. Benjamin took advantage of an afternoon away from work to install grab bars around her bathtub. Each time he checked on her she'd been asleep or blankly staring out her window.

By late evening, misty rain coated the cedars. Clouds veiled the ridge. Trees in the orchard moaned and twisted in the wind. Dead leaves skittered across the yard. Mood music.

Benjamin observed the emotional shock descend over Sarah with the early darkness of the autumn day. Her life seemed wedged between two difficult places. Still grieving the loss of her mother, she now faced the loss of personal autonomy, maybe even life changing joint dysfunction. Rotten timing. She'd been close to testing her freedom.

Ella's psychologist would say Sarah's behavior was a normal step in the grief process. Steps? He'd missed a few. Well, more honestly, he'd stalled along the journey. Why had he become stuck in the anger phase? By now, he should have been way past that point. Sarah had called him self-absorbed. It was true. He'd become stuck on self-pity. No one had helped him slide over that point and accept his appearance. He couldn't accomplish the feat alone.

Pushing Sarah to process the ramifications of her unfavorable diagnosis would only make her mad or place her in a position to stall out like him. He lacked experience dealing with women, but he'd learned enough from Sarah to know timing was important. They'd talk about the grief process later. Brooding would suffice tonight.

Becky came from the kitchen with tea and a piece of toast. After placing the tray on Sarah's lap, she rested a hand on Benjamin's shoulder. "It's almost eleven. You should leave so we can all sleep."

"I'll help you get Sarah to the bed first."

Sarah tossed the toast on the plate. The cup clattered in the saucer. "I am not crippled yet. I can still walk."

Her tone stung. She hadn't meant to strike out at him. She was scared. Who wouldn't be?

"Of course you can. I'll see you ladies tomorrow." He stretched. The prospect of a goodnight kiss died on his lips. Not wise in front of Becky anyway. "Sleep well."

Upstairs, he collapsed into his recliner and kicked off his shoes. Laced fingers behind his head made him aware of the missing finger. Benjamin lowered his hands to his lap and regarded the withered, four-fingered hand. He balled it into a fist. Not much strength, but it functioned. The doctors had doubted he'd regain flexibility to use it.

Would Sarah be fortunate enough to maintain the use of her hands? Awful images flashed across his brain. The soft fingers that caressed his face with tenderness transformed into stiff, gnarled appendages. If it happened ... he'd still welcome her caress.

Was a romance possible at their age? Truthfully, he had no idea. He wasn't sure where he wanted these strange stirrings to go.

Should it matter? He had no real ties to Sarah. Going home to Charlotte would take him out of the picture and allow Sarah to get on with her life. Right. A life of pain and trouble, unless the medicines placed the arthritis in remission. She needed him more than before.

A man who didn't care wouldn't think about this. He couldn't abandon her. It wouldn't be right. He had scruples. A kiss meant something. Love? Maybe. He wasn't ready to admit it.

He had to know more about rheumatoid arthritis so he could help emotionally and physically. Sleep wouldn't come until he gained insight. He eased down the stairs to retrieve the literature he'd tossed on the table in the library.

Sarah must be sleeping. Her room was dark. "Please, God. Take away her pain and spare her from deformities." A prayer? What was happening to him?

Wind whistled around the eave of the quiet house. Rafters and joists creaked as if complaining about the harsh treatment. He closed the office door and logged on to the Internet. He'd help Sarah beat this illness. Maybe he could make it to the next step in the grief process if he hung around to see how Sarah and her friends handled this.

CHAPTER TEN

Sarah lifted her face to the pale morning sun. She cradled the coffee mug to warm her hands. The morning stiffness and pain had improved during the last two weeks. She hated depending on some of the new contraptions the physical therapist suggested, but they helped her function. Regaining control of those aspects of her life improved the prospects for a normal future.

She finished her devotional reading for October 16, the day Bryce Fairmont would arrive to begin filming the western. A north wind brought a shiver and sent yellow leaves raining from the maple in the yard. Sarah placed her Bible on the table. She prayed for physical strength to handle the hectic schedule this guest would bring.

Benjamin came from the kitchen and wrapped the ragged Pine Tree quilt she kept on the back porch around her shoulders. "We could have coffee inside, you know."

"We need to take advantage of these last chances to sit outside in the swing. We'll go in when winter comes."

Benjamin propped a foot on the lower porch railing and leaned back on his elbows. "Are we ready for the movie star?"

She patted the seat beside her. Benjamin sat and shoved them into motion with the toe of his work boot. She arranged the quilt so he could share its warmth.

"The inn sparkles, thanks to you and Becky. I hated resting while you two worked."

He sipped his coffee and sent Sarah a sideways smirk. "You weren't exactly the most cooperative patient."

"Go ahead, say I'm stubborn. I can handle it."

"Nope, I won't go there this morning. You're in a good mood. I'd like to keep it that way."

His grin warmed her more than any quilt could.

He said, "Becky's coming to vacuum after folks leave. She's bringing the perishables for the menu the production assistant sent. That should take care of the last detail."

"I'm not exactly happy that you asked Becky to continue working."

"Get over it. You'd still be sick and in bed if I hadn't. The medications and therapy are working. You're not going to resume the chores and undo the progress you've made."

"Okay, I won't argue, at least not today. I do feel better, and I'll admit I like to spend time doing what I choose after my physical therapy sessions. It's been ages since I had free time and felt like doing more than napping."

"I want you to go horseback riding with me when Bryce leaves. I found a special place I want to show you."

"I don't ride. If we can't walk to it then it'll remain your secret place. I don't think horseback riding is on my approved exercise list."

"We'll see about that later."

She snatched a stack of papers as the swing passed the table. "Go over the plans for today with me again. Are you sure we haven't missed something important?"

"Stop fretting. You've listed everything we needed to do a dozen times. Treat him the way you do everyone else. He'll be happy. Need anything else before I leave?"

"No. Go finish the work uptown so you can expand the Fellowship Hall at church. Now that I'm back in shape, I'll handle Mosey Inn and Bryce Fairmont."

"I'm sure you will." His sarcastic smugness made her smile inside. She feigned an angered pout. "Don't look at me in that tone of voice."

The jest between them eased the case of nerves tightening her muscles. She felt like a rubber band about to snap. She struggled to keep her foot from tapping when the swing wasn't in motion.

He cast a wink and a grin in her direction. "I'm glad you have your 'I am in charge around here' attitude back. You were so down those first few days after the diagnosis it scared me."

"I was terrified. I still am, but at least I'm walking without a cane, and I can tie my shoes most of the time." She stuck out her foot to show off the bow she'd created.

"When those large handled utensils and the jar opener arrive, I'll be out of a job in the kitchen."

"Nah, I think I'll keep you. You make better coffee than I do."

Benjamin placed an arm across the back of the swing, not quite touching her. "Getting back to Bryce, his itinerary said someone will pick him up before lunch to take him to the set on Main Street."

Sarah put her foot down to stop the swing and placed her mug on the wicker table beside it. "Right. He films until late evening."

"Then everything is under control. Behave yourself so you stay well." Benjamin rose and placed his empty mug on the table. "I'll be home in time to help you make dinner."

He paused at the top of the steps and studied her. His furrowed brow and narrowed eyes asked if she could handle the day alone.

"Go on. I'm not in pain today so don't ask. Yes, I'm a nervous wreck because I've never had a movie star in my home. I'll be fine once he arrives, so leave." She shooed him away with a swish of her hand. "See you this afternoon."

She watched Benjamin climb into the pickup and head toward town. Another gust of wind sent leaves scurrying across the yard and a shiver down her spine.

Oh, how she wanted an embrace and a goodbye kiss. By some unspoken agreement, they'd avoided overt physical contact since the day she'd seen the doctor. Strong currents of attraction continued to flow between them despite the attempts to avoid them. Some days she wanted to let their relationship develop. If only he'd change his attitude about God. Was a loving relationship even possible at their age? It wasn't fair to saddle him with the possibility of her health deteriorating. Set in their ways didn't begin to describe them. Too many unsolved and unspoken questions to consider on such an important morning. One answer was certain. Mosey Inn would be a lonely place when Benjamin left.

She sauntered into the dining room, cleared away the breakfast remnants, and made a final check on Mr. Fairmont's room.

At ten o'clock, she watched a bright red Corvette speed up her dirt driveway, raising a cloud of dust. It slid to a halt spewing gravel and dirt across the yard. If all of Bryce Fairmont's entrances were so grand, Benjamin's hours of shoveling gravel to fill the potholes would be a total waste.

Sarah rubbed sweaty palms down her pants leg. She checked her appearance in the hallway mirror, finger combed her hair, and added a touch of lipstick. "Treat him like a normal person. He's no different." She blotted the lipstick with a tissue. "Easier said than done."

Sarah eased the curtain beside the front door back a few inches so she could stare without his noticing. Luggage protruded above the back seat of the convertible. No doubt, he had more stuffed in the car's trunk.

Bryce swung his khaki clad legs out of the car and took in his surroundings. Handsome didn't do him justice. The man was a hunk. Any woman would notice his sandy hair glistening in the sun and the muscles that strained against the body-hugging blue shirt. He probably spent hours in the gym to maintain that physique.

As he climbed the steps, Sarah opened the door to greet him.

His icy blue eyes flashed disdain. The look contradicted his external perfection. Belligerence rippled along his stern, square jaw.

"What were they thinking? There's nothing here but pastures, trees, and horses. Surely they don't expect me to stay here in the wilderness?"

Sarah's pulse quickened. Snapping back would complicate matters. She pasted on a smile. "Good morning, Mr. Fairmont. I'm Sarah Campbell. Welcome to Love Valley." She extended her hand.

He didn't shake it. He actually turned up his nose as if she'd offered him a dead skunk.

She tucked her hand behind her back. "You've arrived at a beautiful time of year. The leaves will peak this week."

"Is that a big deal?" His gaze scoured the landscape.

He could easily be the growling dog behind a "beware of the dog" signed fence. "A hick town. They hired me to act the part of a cowboy, not stay in a place that belongs in that century."

His bite might be as bad as the bark but she didn't care. Sarah jumped in to defend her home. "The Brushy Mountains aren't isolated from the world. I do have modern amenities at Mosey Inn. I got rid of the outhouse a few years ago." She cracked a smile, hoping her attempt at a joke would break his sour mood. It didn't. His stolid gaze placed her in the country bumpkin category. She clenched her hidden hand into a fist and told herself to keep things positive. Sarah cleared her throat, took a deep breath, and exhaled. "Let me show you to your room. I believe you'll be pleased with your accommodations."

He rolled his eyes, turned his back to her, and crossed his arms. "I need to call the director about my schedule. I can't reach him on my cell. Take me to a phone right away."

She wondered if smoke might flow from her ears like some cartoon character. No friendly handshake. No, "Hello, my name is..." What had she gotten into? Was the man always a jerk?

"Certainly, follow me." She turned to enter the house. "Cell phones don't work well uptown. If you call Moonshine Gifts they'll send someone to find him." Keeping her temper in check, she asked, "Would you like to bring your bags up to the room?"

He cocked his eyebrows and raised his voice. "Carry my bags to my room? Your staff does that."

"I am the staff. This is my home, and you're a welcome guest. I'd appreciated it if you assisted me by carrying your luggage."

"I'll place the call and have a snack while you find someone to assist you with my luggage. I need a few items in the small gray suitcase. You can unpack the rest while I'm filming."

She wasn't his personal servant, but she became one when he handed her his car keys and followed her into the house. She led him to the office area. "Guests use this phone. The store numbers are on the bulletin board. I'm recuperating from a recent leg injury, so I'm not physically able to carry your suitcases. You'll need to take care of any items you'll need immediately." She unlocked Bear Paws and handed over the key. "I'll prepare your tea and toast and bring it on a tray. You can eat in the privacy of your room."

She marched to the kitchen, tight lipped and seething. After throwing his keys on the table, she shoved a chair toward the middle of the room and sat. If his attitude continued, the month would be a catastrophe. No amount of money was worth such despicable behavior. Having someone like him at Mosey Inn wouldn't reduce her stress. She'd need constant prayer to control her temper.

Sarah heard Becky arrive around ten-thirty. Becky darted into the kitchen aflutter. "So, is he as gorgeous in person as he is on screen?"

"Oh yeah, but he's a royal jerk. He's had nothing nice to say since he arrived. I'm glad you're here. I need help taking his bags up the stairs."

"What?" Becky tossed her keys on the table and hung her jacket on the back of a chair.

"Yeah, the staff is supposed to take his bags up and unpack for him. Can you imagine?"

"You didn't lift them, did you?"

"No, I knew better than to attempt it when I looked at the piles of cases in his car." She told Becky about their initial encounter. "I intend to stay healthy so I can keep this well-earned money." Sarah dangled the keys in the air. "I'll let you have the honor. Just think, you can say you unpacked his clothes. I don't want to see him again until dinner. I might say or do something I'd regret."

෮ ✠ ෬

Benjamin laid his hammer aside and sat with his back against the wall near The Love Valley Mercantile. He missed the peaceful time alone at the church. There he'd shared quiet breaks with his rabbit friend, Harvey. In town, he rarely took a break and warily listened for the sound of boots on the boardwalk so he could keep his head down and avoid curious eyes.

The hustle of the film crew at the opposite end of town near the Silver Spur Saloon lent a hectic atmosphere to Main Street. Contagious excitement hummed around him as store managers hustled about, preparing for a banner business weekend.

He'd gladly move to his remodeling job back at the church and postpone further repairs to uptown buildings until the film crew and tourists left.

He recognized the sound of Mrs. Hardin's heavy tread too late to disappear or take up his hammer and return to work.

The old boards strained and creaked beneath her weight as she approached. "You'd be finished and out of our way if you didn't take so many breaks."

"Good morning, Mrs. Hardin." He patted the rough planks beside him since he saw no reason to get up and face her insults. "Won't you join me? It's such a nice day. Did you notice the colors in the trees behind Jack's Place are much brighter than yesterday?"

"The only scenery I want to see is your finished product."

"Maybe you'd be happier, Mrs. Hardin, if you stopped to take in the unique qualities of your town occasionally. Life is short. I'll have the last section finished in a couple hours. I'll be sure to have someone call you so you can return and take a gander."

"Insolence never becomes anyone, Mr. Pruitt."

"You're right. It doesn't."

Her mouth opened, but words seemed to escape her.

The soft thud of hooves on the dirt road competed with the ring of the horseshoeing hammer at the Blacksmith Shop. Todd and Noah reigned in their mounts at the hitching rail in front of him.

Benjamin noted Noah's prowess in the saddle. Pride swelled when Noah draped the reins around the rail and raced over to him.

"Grandpa!" Noah threw his arms around Benjamin's neck and climbed into his lap.

Benjamin kissed his cheek. "You're looking great on that pony."

Noah's chin dipped, and Benjamin felt him tremble. The child looked through his lashes at the imposing figure towering over him.

Benjamin whispered in his ear. "She's not going to hurt you.

She talks tough, but don't be afraid. Be nice. Tell her hello."

Noah's grip around Benjamin's neck tightened. The boy stared at the boardwalk. "Good morning, Mrs. Hardin."

"What brings you and your dad to town this morning? Shouldn't you be in school?"

"I have school at home. Mom's working at Miss Sarah's, so I'm with Dad learning men things. We came to bring lunch to Grandpa Benjamin. Dad said we'll get ice cream from the General Store and Café for dessert." Uncertainty flashing across his face, Noah glanced at Benjamin. The child drew a big breath, turned to Mrs. Hardin, and asked, "Want to come with us?"

Benjamin wanted to crawl through a crack between the boards. Here he was trying to teach the boy manners when the roles should be reversed. The lesson slapped him in the face. Noah possessed something he'd lost—courage to face life's difficulties head on. Benjamin's ugly face had stirred the boy's curiosity. He'd respected his overt questions and lack of fear. He'd grown to love Noah because of such frank honesty.

Noah prompted him to boldness. "Noah's right. Join us." As the words came out he questioned what he'd done. He'd have a hard time going into the Café with Noah and Todd for ice cream. Her presence? He'd never handle it.

"Thank you, but I have errands to run. Perhaps some other time. Tell Becky and Sarah hello." She nodded a polite goodbye and left.

Benjamin heard wistfulness in her tone. Something in her eyes touched him. Maybe Mrs. Hardin's dour moods came from some deep pain or loneliness. Were they so similar? He didn't want to compare himself to her. Unfortunately, the idea bore weight he didn't want to carry.

CHAPTER ELEVEN

Benjamin collected dinner plates and carried them to the kitchen. "A delicious meal. Fairmont's special diet isn't too bad."

Sarah tagged behind him like a glum lost puppy. "I'm glad someone enjoyed my hard work."

"Shall I put this in the freezer with his other untouched meals?"

"Sure. One of us will eat it after he's gone. They're paying. No reason to waste it."

She sank into a chair and stared at the floor, her arms crossed over her chest. Benjamin stepped behind her and rubbed tight muscles in her shoulders. "Stop moping. You're not the problem. The man's caused nothing but trouble since he arrived. Town's buzzing about how arrogant and foul-mouthed he is. You're angry. What did he do besides skip dinner again?"

Sarah reached up to hold his hand. "Follow me. We might as well talk where it's comfortable."

Benjamin lit the logs he'd laid in the fireplace and settled beside her on the couch. The rain-battered windows rattled—a home improvement project to tuck away on his mental list. The fire's warmth penetrated the public sitting area of Mosey Inn, but Sarah's chilly mood lingered.

Benjamin tossed a quilt from the back of the couch over their legs. "What's wrong?"

Sarah edged closer. "The man dumped a pile of muddy, wet laundry outside his door this morning. I assume that meant he wanted them washed. He didn't bother to ask. In fact, he didn't even speak when I carried breakfast to his room. He sat there reading his script and ignored me. He has no manners."

"He's accustomed to service. I doubt he knows how to do laundry. What'd you do?"

"Since he wasn't in a talking mood, I wrote a note telling him where to find the machines and gave a price for using my laundry facilities."

Benjamin wrapped an arm around her shoulder. "Where's the note?"

She chortled, "In the trash."

Sarah settled her head against him. Apparently, they'd stopped avoiding physical contact. Benjamin wouldn't argue since a whiff of her perfume sent his heart racing.

"So, let me guess. You washed his clothes and put them away."

She nodded. "I need this money. What else could I do?"

Benjamin shifted so his cheek rested against her fragrant, silky hair. "It's rained for three days. Mud is ankle deep on Main Street. Ask him to come in the back door and wash his clothes. I do it. Shouldn't he?"

Sarah poked his arm with a finger. "Don't get the idea I want you to pay to use the washing machine and dryer. Your situation is different."

"I'd pay, but you won't let me. You could at least let me pay the going rate for a room."

She shot him a frown complete with a "do not go there" look. "Bryce is already paying more than the normal rate. If I confront him, I'm afraid they'll move him. I'll lose the income. My medication isn't cheap, but for the first time in months the pain and stiffness is tolerable. I'll put up with the garbage he pulls."

Benjamin scowled. The same money excuses again. "You don't like accepting my money or the fact I'm paying Becky to help. I don't understand the difference."

Sarah placed a hand on his chest and locked her gaze with his. "I've learned over the years that I have to cater to people in order to pay the bills. The doctor has worked out some decent deals for me, but I'm not stupid. I'm not getting younger, and this illness won't go away. If remission doesn't happen, I'll have even more medications and treatments to worry about. I'm hanging on to every dime I can get."

"So charge him. If you're doing his laundry, his company should pay for that service like the other extras you're giving him. Want me to talk with him or one of his people?"

Sarah pulled back, her face a study in amazement. "You haven't eaten breakfast in the dining room since you arrived. One day when I was sick, you took renters to a room. Now you're saying you'd talk to him about missing meals and laundry issues?"

He gave her a self-assured nod. "I think I could handle that. I've done several things this week that will make your jaw drop."

"Yeah? Tell me." She kicked off her slippers, sat on the other end of the couch, and put her socked feet in his lap.

Benjamin massaged her feet while he continued the story.

"Noah and Todd came to town. After lunch under the trees overlooking the rodeo arena, we went to the café for ice cream. I sat in the booth while Noah smeared chocolate all over his face."

Her eyes betrayed her excitement. "That took courage. I'm proud of you."

"I enjoyed every minute of it. I love that kid more every day."

"You're going to tell me the place was empty, right?"

"Nope, and it gets better. I invited Mrs. Hardin to join us."

Sarah's eyebrows rose, and her mouth fell open. "No way! Did she?"

"No, but I think we declared a truce. I've seen her around, but she hasn't stopped to criticize my work since then."

"That's good news. She's treated you so unfairly."

"Noah actually asked her to eat with us. He puts me to shame. The kid has better manners than I do. I had to extend a genuine invitation. I'm seeing Mrs. Hardin in a different light. The woman wants attention. I asked myself why."

"And what's your opinion?"

"Her eyes are full of pain. She acts gruff and meddles, but inside she craves love." He lowered his head, staring at his misshapen hand. "I saw myself in her."

Sarah moved back beside him. Her fingers laced through his in a gesture that indicated understanding. "You hide, Mrs. Hardin gossips, and I fret."

Benjamin ran his free hand over his scarred face. "Facing our flaws hurts. Noah made me see that I have to meet this fear head on. Not an easy task."

"It's a big step forward. Dealing with fear is hard. I'm having problems too. This illness scares me and ... our relationship scares me."

"Getting too close and personal?"

She nodded and lowered her gaze to their interlaced fingers. "I backed away after we kissed. I haven't known what to say or do around you. I need and want you in my life. Those emotions are new to me. When you arrived, I wanted to be your friend. Thought it might help you overcome your reclusive nature. Now I'm wondering, are we supposed to be more than friends?"

"Guess it's time to stop ignoring our questions and talk about some personal issues. What makes you fret, Sarah?"

The front door flew open and banged against the wall. Benjamin startled and then jumped to his feet when Bryce Fairmont tottered through the door.

Fairmont staggered against the hall tree, rattling umbrellas and knocking coats to the floor.

Benjamin caught him before he hit the floor. The stench of vomit and liquor almost turned Benjamin's stomach.

Benjamin heard Sarah's gasp behind him. From the corner of his eye, he saw her tentative hand creep forward. She rested it on his back. He took that as a signal for him to take the lead in the situation.

Water dripped from Fairmont's muddy, foul-smelling clothes to puddle around their feet.

A small bespectacled man barreled across the porch to help Benjamin support the sagging drunk. Fairmont's escort, not much more than a teen, recoiled when he glanced at Benjamin but quickly recovered his composure. "Sorry you had to help with this. I should have walked him to the door. I thought he could stand on his own while I moved the car away from the steps." He helped Benjamin support Fairmont with one hand while removing fogged glasses with the other one.

A swipe of the glasses on his sleeve solved the issue. "I'm Steve Howell, a production assistant. They sent me to bring him home from the Silver Spur. The owner kicked him out. Bryce had too many. Got a bit rowdy."

The two men hefted Fairmont beneath his arms and dragged him to the stairway. After they sat him on the step, Benjamin stared down at Hollywood's heartthrob. A rude, arrogant sot. Benjamin's fists clenched and his jaw tightened as ire rose. He wanted to pity Fairmont but also wanted to punch him. The man had shone nothing but disrespect, while Sarah spent her time trying to please him. Now he showed up drunk.

Fairmont propped on an elbow. Bleary eyed and mumbling, he focused on Benjamin's face. Fairmont cried out, cursed, and held up his hands in a protective gesture. He cowered like a frightened child. Benjamin stooped to whisper in his ear, "I must look like the devil himself to your drunken eyes. If you ever lay a hand on Sarah, I'll show you the devil."

Benjamin turned to the man who'd ushered Fairmont to the door. He'd expected Howell to scamper off into the rain without further explanation. Instead, he stood dripping on the floor beside Benjamin.

Howell glanced at the mud and water. "I'm sorry to cause a commotion and make a mess."

Sarah said, "You're soaked. I'll get you a towel."

"Thanks, ma'am."

Sarah returned with a bath towel. "I saw you yesterday. You drove Bryce uptown. I'm Sarah Campbell, and this is Benjamin Pruitt."

He offered a polite nod. "Nice to meet you. I'll clean up, ma'am."

Benjamin said, "Never mind. I'll mop later. I'd rather have your help getting him cleaned up and in his bed. We'll talk afterwards."

Thirty minutes later, Sarah brought hot chocolate and set it on the table in front of the fireplace. Her hand shook when she poured Benjamin's cup. He touched her fingers, letting the caress linger until she looked at him. The pinched muscles around her lips and the blaze smoldering in the depths of her eyes told him what he suspected. Sarah was furious.

Steve thanked her for the chocolate and adjusted the sleeves on the baggy sweat clothes Benjamin had loaned him. He sipped the chocolate. "They wouldn't let me tell you the truth when I made the reservation. I'm very sorry."

Sarah said, "So complete privacy and this special diet was a veiled way of saying they needed to keep him hidden and out of the bars."

"Yes. He's supposed to be in rehab. They yanked him out of the facility for the role and decided he'd be fine if we drove him around and isolated him. I told them he wasn't ready, but my words don't go far. I suggested they needed to put another person here at the inn to keep an eye on him."

Benjamin asked, "Is he prone to violence when he gets drunk?"

"He's rude and demanding when he's sober. I've never seen him violent, but I'm not usually the one who deals with his drinking."

Sarah placed her cup on the table. "This is my home and a respected business. I don't want a repeat performance when other guests are around to observe this. Do I talk to him or someone else?"

"You're going to let him stay?" His eyebrows shot up and his glasses slid down his nose.

"Maybe. I'll need assurance this won't happen again."

"Then you better talk with someone else. Bryce doesn't understand the words 'appropriate behavior.' The bottle runs his life. He might promise you something he can't deliver."

Sarah jerked a glance toward Benjamin. The news didn't seem to come as a surprise to him either. Sarah said, "Thank you for your candor. I'll take care of things in the morning."

Steve turned to Benjamin. "Thanks for the dry clothes. I'll return them. I'd better get back and report to my boss."

"There's no need for you to come in the morning," Sarah said.

"I'll drive Bryce uptown so I can have a chat with your boss as well."

"I'll tell him you're coming. I'm not sure Fairmont will want you to drive him to the set."

"He won't be given a choice."

Benjamin held the door open until the taillights of Steve Howell's car disappeared. "I'll clean up and wash these dirty clothes."

"That is not your job." Anger tinged her voice.

"In a way it is. I'm the one who encouraged you to accept his reservation without question."

Sarah heaved a sigh and gazed around the soiled foyer. "Where should I start?"

"Welcome your guests as they return. Give them a towel and let them dry out beside the fire. You do it every night when it rains. I'll clean up the mess."

She acceded with a nod.

Benjamin returned from the laundry room to find Sarah staring at the embers on the hearth. He circled his arms around her slender waist. "Everything's in the laundry, and I mopped the foyer." She didn't turn from the fire or yield to his touch.

"Thanks."

He released her. "Sarah—"

She held up a hand. "I don't want to talk, and I don't want to be held. I'm furious and I'm confused. Now's not the time."

Benjamin backed away. "I'll stay in the morning until he's gone. Just for the record, I'd feel better if you asked them to move him."

"I've handled drunks before."

"What if he comes in drunk and hurts you or another guest?"

"I can handle it. I've always handled it, remember?"

"Self-reliance won't protect you if he's an angry drunk."

"He wasn't a mean drunk. The man was a pitiful disgrace. His manager or whatever you call him should have left him where he could get help."

"Some people don't want help. He may be one of them."

"If that's the case then it's their responsibility to keep him sober while he makes their movie and stays in Love Valley."

"You were already angry because of his attitude. Love Valley bars only open on the weekend. If he's addicted, he'll bring his own booze or be on the road from a bar in Statesville. You can't watch him every second. Do you want to bother with him for three more weeks?"

"I'll have an empty room Monday. I'll talk to his keepers about moving Steve or someone else in to watch him."

The woman's stubborn pride again. How could he convince her to toss the man on his ear and to stop worrying about her financial situation?

"It's not safe, Sarah."

Her scowl sent the message that she wouldn't back down. No sense arguing. At least not tonight.

"He's rude and haughty. I can handle that."

Benjamin decided to take one more shot at making her see reason. "What about the stress? Your condition's improving. You're supposed to relax. Tonight wasn't restful. Nothing about Fairmont is restful."

"I'm fine. I run Mosey Inn, not you."

She crossed the hall and paused in the library door. "Turn the lights off when you go to bed. I'll dry the laundry in the morning. You've done more than your share tonight."

༄ ༺ ༄

Sarah placed the breakfast tray on the bedside table and threw open the drapes. "Wake up, Mr. Fairmont. We need to talk."

He swore and covered his face with a pillow.

She yanked it away, tossing it on the bed. "I intend to set matters straight with you before you leave for filming today."

"Lady, I have a headache. You are not welcome in my room."

"Drunks aren't welcome in my house. You have five minutes to get dressed. I'll bring you some aspirin."

She emerged from Bear Paws and trudged down the stairs where Benjamin sat on the bottom step. He patted the floor. "Need help?"

Sarah slumped onto the step beside him. "Not at the moment. I'm getting him some aspirin before we talk."

"I thought you planned to talk with his boss about the problem."

She rested her chin in her hands, elbows on her knees. "Him first, then his people. They lied to me. They need to hear how I feel about those lies. Bryce is a problem, but they put him in this situation. I decided talking to him should come first. He's in bad shape this morning. Maybe he'll listen."

"Don't count on getting anywhere." Benjamin squeezed her leg.

"I won't, but I have to try. Will you go with me when I drive him to town? I don't want to be seen alone with him."

"Sure, I'll go. You know, this is what makes you special."

Her brows rose as she shot him a sideways glance. "What's that supposed to mean?"

"You look for the good in people and treat them with respect when they don't deserve it."

She let a coy smile sneak across her lips as she turned to look at him. "Sweet talk won't mollify me this morning."

Benjamin's alluring grin and the twinkle in his chocolate-colored eyes sent warmth through her. She must be blushing. Anger didn't last when his charm tugged at her heartstrings. She should thank him for coming to her rescue last night. In retrospect, it was a bad situation.

His statement broke her reverie. "Could I try some sweet talk later in the day, or are you mad at me for interfering with Mosey Inn business last night?"

She had to laugh. The man was a mind reader. "We'll see. It's too early to say what the day's going to bring."

"Fireworks would be my guess."

She grinned but lowered her head into her hands. "I'm not sure what to do. Bryce is a risk to my business and to me. You were right, so I apologize for my attitude. I couldn't have gotten him to bed alone. It would have been an embarrassing situation even with Steve Howell's help. I hope none of the guests heard the ruckus."

"Your last guest finished breakfast and left for the day while you were in Bryce's room. I didn't hear any murmuring from the dining room while I ate in the kitchen. I don't think they know."

"Good. Word will probably be all over town since he was at the Spur last night. I'll try to hold off on the fireworks until we see what his handlers have to say about the rumors."

Benjamin rose. "I'll clean the dining room and kitchen while you talk. Let me know when you're ready to leave."

"Thanks. I'll get Mr. Grumpy some aspirin."

Sarah found Bryce sitting in the recliner with the Bear Paws quilt wrapped around him. His perfect hair stood straight up, and his pale blue eyes lacked luster. Green around the gills wasn't a cliché.

"I don't want breakfast, and I'm not ready to get dressed." He held out his hand. "Give me the aspirin and go away."

She picked up the glass of juice and placed two pills in his outstretched palm. "I want to have a peaceful conversation, and you're going to cooperate. I let you sleep off your booze long enough."

He downed the aspirin with a gulp of juice. "I got drunk. I'm sure this isn't the first time you've had someone stay in your house who had a few too many. What's the big deal?"

Glaring down at him, she crossed her arms. She'd make her jaw ache if she clenched her teeth any tighter. "Another guest gave you a bath, put you to bed, washed your filthy clothes, and mopped up your mud. I'd say that's a pretty big deal."

He looked puzzled. "You mean that repulsive creature in my room last night was real? I thought I was hallucinating."

Sarah fisted her hands and placed them on her hips. "Benjamin Pruitt is not a repulsive creature. He's a kind man who has scars from burns. You should thank him, not make fun of him. Steve Howell deserves your thanks too. He could have left you lying on Main Street in horse manure and mud."

"Okay I get the point. I messed up."

He didn't sound contrite. Sarah pulled out the chair from the desk and sat in front of him. "They didn't tell me you had a drinking problem when I accepted your reservation. You need help."

"I was almost finished with rehab. I'm okay."

"You're an alcoholic. Stay out of the bar. Find someone who can help you get your life together."

"I've heard the spiel before. Why should you care?"

"I'm a Christian. I happen to believe a personal relationship with Christ is the solution to your problem, but now is not the time for a lecture about religion."

His eyes rolled toward the ceiling, and he frowned. "Thank you for small favors."

"I don't know what makes you drink, but I'd like to see you stop."

He barked a reply. "I said I was in rehab."

"You should still be there. Last night was a disaster. None of my other visitors saw you. I can't say what sort of spectacle you made of yourself in town."

A hint of remorse touched his bloodshot eyes. "I can't either. If Steve brought me home the powers that be know about the binge."

"They sent him to take care of you when the bar owner kicked you out in the street. Steve helped Benjamin get you settled."

"I'll thank Steve."

"You're due on the set in two hours. Mr. Pruitt and I will take you today. I plan to talk with the appropriate people. Don't make me sorry if I decide to give you a second chance."

His eyes flashed a moment of fright. "I don't want that man near me. He threatened me."

Sarah almost grinned. Had Benjamin said something that hinted at violence? The flattering thought seemed plausible. If he'd threatened Bryce, Benjamin wouldn't object to her taking advantage of the man's fear. "Benjamin's protective of me. He'll spoil your pretty face if you so much as hiccup. If you repeat last night's performance ... well, I think you get the idea."

The famous movie star presented a sad specimen of a man this morning. Her resolve almost faltered. No, she wouldn't send him back to bed or feel sorry for him. He needed to face his shortcoming and the consequences of his actions.

"Want hot coffee instead of your usual green tea?"

"Please. I'm going to need it."

Sarah left, rolling his "please" around in her head. He'd actually said a kind word. It was a start. She doubted he'd be capable of sustaining three weeks of sobriety. She prayed for protection and wisdom.

Times like this made her consider closing Mosey Inn. A Caribbean vacation sounded wonderful on a dreary October morning. She could almost feel the sunshine and warm water washing over her tired body.

No vacation today. She had to deal with Bryce Fairmont and the problems he'd caused. Would she regret her decision?

Her pain had worsened after last night's fiasco. She'd struggled to tie her shoes this morning. Benjamin was right about the stress. Calling the doctor to report the change might mean another medicine and higher costs. Discouragement seeped into her like the chilly wind whistling around Mosey Inn's aging windowpanes. Benjamin would notice the change in her physical condition and insist she rest today. And he'd be correct.

Why did his concern matter anyway? He'd move eventually. As far as she knew, he hadn't contacted a realtor about buying a home. Her heart sank. She'd miss his company when he left. Perhaps his relationship with Noah would tempt him to stay. If not, she'd be lonely again. She shouldn't become dependent on him. Too late.

The look Benjamin had given her earlier said he had more than sweet talk in mind, but did he care enough about her to stick around? Rational thought told her it was wrong to crave his kiss and his embrace, but her heart and her brain weren't talking to each other these days.

When was Ella coming back? They needed to talk. It wouldn't do to discuss these notions in an e-mail.

CHAPTER TWELVE

Benjamin zipped his jacket against the chill. Near the grill, a red maple, backlit by a beam of morning sunlight, blazed. The orchard displayed a contrast of yellowing leaves and red apples. Storm clouds rolled over the hillside. Shafts of sunlight disappeared as he dodged puddles on his way to the truck.

By the time he reached the town's junction, the sky opened its floodgates. There would be no outdoor work today. He'd work on remodeling the church kitchen so he could work inside. Good thing he had several options. He took the road toward the church.

As Benjamin pulled into the parking area, he spied Harvey huddled beneath a rhododendron near the graveyard. Benjamin eased the window open a crack so they could converse. "Why aren't you in your safe little hole? You get caught out here?" Rain drummed a heavy bass beat on the truck's roof. He might as well talk with Harvey while they waited for the downpour to slacken.

"Jobs keep popping up around the Valley. Guess that's good. I'm trying to decide if I should sell my house in Charlotte. Mosey Inn feels more like home than that house ever did. Even though I've never dated Sarah, we behave like a comfortable couple. Whoa, what a thought. Don't know where I got that notion. Keep it tucked inside your little rabbit brain. I should backpedal fast if I don't want a relationship. Honestly, I'm not sure what I want for my future."

Solitude? A rather cold and uninviting idea since she'd entered his life. They shared most of their free time together. Her presence communicated comfort and peacefulness. Sarah brought joy—an emotion he'd rarely experienced. So why did he feel restless and uncertain?

"Remember when I told you about kissing her? I can taste the sweetness of her lips if I concentrate hard enough. Thought I'd made a huge mistake. It wasn't. Started me thinking."

The passionate kisses of youthful dating could never compare with the moment he'd kissed Sarah. In all the years since the fire, he'd never considered demeaning a woman, or himself, by paying to satisfy fleshly desires. He'd buried those needs years ago. Sarah revived them. To hold Sarah and share the intimacy of her body would be ecstasy. More so, she stirred a longing for a deeper need. Abiding love.

His desire for genuine love hadn't faded. He'd ignored it; convinced himself he didn't need it.

"Maybe I do consider us a couple already. I've daydreamed about Sarah and me sitting in front of the fireplace on a cold winter night. She's snuggled in my arms beneath one of her quilts. The aroma of the meal we shared lingers in the air. Sarah doesn't hurt. I'm not lonely. We complete each other. An evening like that ... contentment."

What he felt for Sarah encompassed more than physical desire. Her smile, her beauty, even her stubborn will drew him. If he allowed an honest look, so did her faith. Sarah wasn't whole without God. He hadn't planned to impede her relationship with God. At least she had one. His spiritual relationship might change with time. Reading the Bible passages Todd suggested during their talks had also forced Benjamin to reconsider his attitude. After years, his roiling anger had cooled to a simmer.

His new friends had almost convinced him God didn't merit his resentment and anger. He should return to church. That much he knew. People's reactions had always been an easy excuse. He might be ready to face the challenge. He could handle the stares and questions. Next Sunday.

"Not going to get anything done if I sit here all day. Rain's not going to end. Stay warm, friend. We'll chat again later."

Benjamin hugged his coat closer and pulled the hood over his brow. Even then, he was drenched by the time he reached the entrance. Good thing he'd brought a change of clothes.

The quietness inside encouraged a continuance of his muddled thoughts. Sarah's explosive encounter with the film producer several days ago hadn't improved the Bryce Fairmont situation. Sure, they'd moved Steve Howell into North Carolina Lily to keep a closer eye on Fairmont. Big deal. Bryce possessed the escape artist abilities of Houdini.

Benjamin laid his hammer and chisel on the stone hearth to grab warmer clothes from his pack. Rain drummed on the roof. The thermostat was covered and locked. The switch said OFF. No wonder he couldn't get warm. He pulled a sweatshirt from his pack and slipped it on over the turtleneck he'd changed into. If that didn't help, he'd go ask the pastor to turn on some heat. Rain pounded harder. If these stormy days continued, he'd never finish the new contract for repairs to a storefront on Main Street.

The street uptown was a quagmire. They'd postponed filming until the sun returned. It was bad enough when Sarah allowed Fairmont to stay after his first drunken evening. Now she'd agreed to let him stay to complete filming.

Benjamin wasn't exactly angry with Sarah. Worried fit better. His mind kept chasing bad scenarios. Fairmont wasn't hanging around the inn waiting for the rain to cease. He'd wandered off to parts unknown. No one had a clue where he'd gone. Steve was combing bars in Statesville, Wilkesboro, and the surrounding areas. Others were looking for his car on the back roads.

A cold chill slithered down Benjamin's back like some slimy reptile from Kudzu Territory. In his opinion Sarah's money worries clouded her judgment.

She was supposedly at home in bed. When dampness settled over the valley, her aches and fevers began again. The strain of her encounters with Bryce hadn't helped. Knowing Sarah, she wasn't resting even though Becky was coming to clean.

Benjamin didn't want to work today. The thought of Sarah, vulnerable and alone once Becky left, didn't sit well. Money—that factor again. He had to work so he could help Sarah and meet his own obligations.

Getting the creative juices working might help. He formulated a plan for adding a decorative mantel to complement the décor once he'd repaired the stone fireplace and enlarged the fellowship hall. He returned to ripping out cabinets. A satisfying substitute for Bryce Fairmont's insides.

The emotional release didn't last long.

He dialed Sarah's phone. Why didn't she answer? Surely, Sarah wouldn't go out in this deluge. No reason to shop since the pantry was full. He'd bought groceries in Statesville.

His throat went dry at the memory. He'd braved the Food Lion to keep Sarah from going. Stares followed him, but he'd held up his head and even made eye contact with a few patrons. Sarah had been proud of that accomplishment. So had he.

A strange sense of foreboding settled over him around two in the afternoon. He packed his tools and drove the short distance to the pastor's home.

Benjamin hunched forward, burrowing into his coat to avoid the drips falling from the awning above the cement stoop. He could see the pastor through the glass storm door of the little room he used for a church office.

A light rap on the glass caught Pastor Morrison's attention. He looked up from his book-covered desk and motioned. "Come in out of the rain. Grab a seat."

Benjamin shook rain from his jacket and wiped his feet on the rug inside the door. "Actually, I came to ask if I could leave early."

"You're not on a time schedule. Come and go as you like."

"Thank you, sir. Sarah's not answering the phone. I'm concerned."

Benjamin saw worry form in the pastor's eyes. "Is Sarah worse?"

"Not exactly. She's better, but there's been another flare. She's supposed to be resting. The doctor told her it might take some time to get the right combination and doses of meds."

"Hate to see her have a setback. She didn't tell me." The man sounded genuinely concerned for her welfare. "I'll check on her in a couple days if she isn't improving. I'm thankful you hired Becky. Sarah's a plucky lady. Never has been one to complain or ask for assistance." He closed the book and placed it on a stack on the edge of the desk.

Benjamin edged toward the door. "I'll tell her you asked about her."

"Please do. I won't detain you, but I'd like to get better acquainted. How about sharing lunch tomorrow?"

Benjamin could almost hear the sermon forming in the pastor's mind, but he couldn't say no to the invitation. "Sure."

"Good." The pastor rubbed his palms together. "I'll toss some sandwiches and soup together around noon. My wife will be out tomorrow, so we'll have the place to ourselves. Go on now, and call if she needs anything."

"Will do. See you tomorrow."

His truck tires sank in the ruts of the dirt road leading past Todd and Becky's stable. Becky was home. She would have called or stayed if Sarah needed help. No reason to worry.

The wipers slapped but didn't improve visibility in the thick fog. A gust of wind rocked the truck. Benjamin checked for traffic and eased onto the road leading to Mosey Inn. His hand ached from gripping the wheel. Why did he feel so uptight?

When he rounded the last curve and started up the muddy incline to the inn, his heart revved into overdrive. Bryce's Corvette sat in the drive. Steve's Cadillac was nowhere in sight. His truck slid to a halt. Benjamin slammed the door and ran toward the house.

He should stop worrying. Bryce had every right to be at the inn. Probably in his room, playing the role of ornery actor.

The pep talk sounded fine until Benjamin mounted the steps. The front door stood open. Two sets of muddy footprints, one larger than the other, trailed across the porch.

Benjamin dashed into the house shouting Sarah's name.

"Sarah!" Benjamin spotted her sitting on the top step. He skidded to a stop in the foyer. Couldn't the woman follow doctor's orders for a few hours? He set his jaw and prepared to fuss. Then he scanned the scene. Any rebuke caught in his throat.

Mud encrusted the rug inside the doorway and continued up the hardwood staircase. Red clay caked her clothes. The rag she held dripped filthy water into a bucket.

Not stubbornness—Bryce Fairmont. Benjamin took the stairs two at a time and dropped to the step beside her. Her pinched face and clenched teeth telegraphed fury. He half expected to see smoke spew from her ears.

"Sarah, what happened?" Benjamin braced for an angry onslaught.

She tossed the cloth in the bucket. Sparks almost jumped from the eyes glaring over his left shoulder. She jabbed a pointed index finger toward the Bear Paws door. "He happened."

"Drunk?"

"An understatement. I won't excuse his behavior this time. Bryce is out of here when Steve arrives." She sliced the air with a karate chop.

Good thing he wasn't in striking range.

Sarah fished the cloth from the bucket. As she threw the rag onto the step, Benjamin ignored the water it splattered on him. "I have a renter coming at four. Noah has a cold. Becky left early." She wiped the cloth across the mud-streaked wood. "Why are you here anyway? Did Steve call you?"

Benjamin avoided the temptation to match her angry tone. "I had an uneasy feeling about things. Guess I was right." Reaching for the cloth he said, "Let me do this. You're supposed to be in bed."

"I can't rest. It'll take both of us to get this place presentable by four. Besides, I don't want to be babied."

Wrong. He'd baby her all he wanted. He wasn't about to let her do permanent damage to a wrist while scouring the floor. He'd tackle that issue later. "Is the room ready?"

"Pine Tree is clean. Becky checked out a couple other renters and started the laundry. The rest of the house ..." She waved in a broad arching gesture.

Sarah sagged against the wall. Her face twisted as tears left clean trails on her muddy cheeks. The cloth fell from her limp hand, plopping into the bucket to slosh red-tinged water across their laps.

Her emotional breakdown didn't come as a surprise. Still, watching the anger dissolve into sobs put a bitter taste in Benjamin's mouth. He should have insisted Bryce leave days ago.

Sarah gaped at her chest. Every breath came in a short gasp. Had she just noticed the mud? Impossible. She frantically rubbed her hands down the front of her shirt as if trying to remove the stains. The back of her hand repeatedly scrubbed across her lips.

This wasn't normal. Something horrible seemed to motivate her. The actions and emotions bordered on hysteria. As she swiped again and again at her shirt and mouth, revulsion clouded her eyes.

Worry grabbed Benjamin. "Sarah, what's wrong?" He grasped her shoulders and dipped his head to capture her gaze.

She didn't respond. In fact, it seemed she didn't see or hear him.

He gently shook her to gain her attention. Keep it low key. Calm. Soothing. He reached to pull her into a hug. Better not. "Sarah, look at me." His hand rested on her knee.

With wide frightened eyes, she stared over his shoulder, and wrung her hands in her lap.

"Sarah, Did Bryce hurt you?"

Sobs shook her shoulders. "Not exactly."

Every muscle in his body tightened. Her tone set his mind chasing after Bryce Fairmont infractions. "Exactly what did Bryce do?"

She retrieved the rag, wringing it out. Sarah scrubbed the stains on her chest. "I don't have time to talk about it."

Benjamin's voice rose despite efforts to remain calm. "You're not doing any good with that wet rag. Stop smearing the mud on your shirt and tell me what happened."

She ran a wet hand across her lips again. "Later!"

Seizing the filthy rag, Benjamin tossed it over the edge of the bucket. "There is way more to this than a dirty house and Bryce coming in drunk. We're talking, now."

A quivering hand eased forward and slipped into Benjamin's hand. He gave it a little squeeze. She gasped, her grimace showing pain.

"Sorry. Didn't mean to hurt you." Benjamin cradled her hand, gently turning it to check for injuries. "Your knuckles are swollen." He checked the other hand. More of the same. No blood, no overt signs of physical harm. She'd better tell him the particulars of the "not exactly" fast before he unleashed his rage on Fairmont.

Finally, she focused on his face and then collapsed into his arms. "Hold me. I'm so tired. I'm hurting. He's created this mess. I can't take much more."

Benjamin pulled her into a hug. "You'll be okay. I'll take care of things."

He soothed her with more calming words and stroked his hand along her back. After a few moments, her sobs turned to ragged breaths. He shifted her to look into her face. "You're soaking wet. Let's get you dry. I'll come back and clean."

"Wait. Check on Bryce first. He fell."

Benjamin's heart dropped into his stomach. An injury could spell problems for the inn. "Where is he? Is he hurt?"

"In his room." Sarah swiped away a tear. "He's ruined it."

"It? The room? Never mind. I'll check on him after I take care of you. Tell me again so I'm sure. You're in pain, but you're not injured, right?"

She chewed on her lower lip. Her head wagged. "Bryce didn't hurt me." Another blank stare over his shoulder.

Fear surrounded him like a fetid odor. He searched her eyes for answers. "You're not making sense, Sarah. What happened between you and Bryce?"

A violent chill seized her. Blue lips said, "Not now. I'm so cold. Help me up. I need to change clothes. Get me to my bed."

She attempted to stand, sucked in a sharp breath, and wobbled on the stairs. Benjamin steadied her.

She clung to his arm for support. "My feet." Her delicate features contorted as pain hit. "I don't think I can walk." Color drained from her face.

Benjamin scooped her up. Dampness soaked into his shirt when her arms circled his neck.

Reaching her room, he searched for a place to set her without ruining furniture or bedding. He chose the wooden chair by the desk and eased her down.

His hand cradled her cheek. "Tell me what to do. You're freezing."

She brushed a cold hand along his arm. Concern formed in her eyes. "Don't look so frightened. I'll explain later." She pointed to the dresser. "Get some dry clothes from that third drawer. I can put on sweat pants and shirts without help."

"Let me run some hot bath water. Your teeth are chattering."

"Not yet. Go check on Bryce. Be sure he's okay. The whole experience is still a bit fuzzy."

"Bryce can wait." Benjamin entered Sarah's bathroom, ran hot water over a washcloth, and returned. He placed it on the desk along with the clean clothes. Leaving her wasn't a good idea; however, propriety dictated he must. "Are you sure you can manage?"

Sarah shoved him. "Go. I'm fine. I'll wash off some mud and change."

He picked up the cloth and wiped her face. Her resolve seemed as fragile as her health. Forget propriety.

Icy fingers caressed his hand as she took the cloth. "Go. I'm worried about Bryce. I just left him there."

"Leave your clothes on the floor. I'll do laundry later."

Trepidation followed Benjamin to Bear Paws. Maybe he had the whole picture backwards. Had Sarah inadvertently injured the man?

The door creaked open at his touch. Bryce looked and smelled more like a muddy pig, straight from the sty, than a Hollywood star. Fully clothed, sprawled on his back across the bed, his snores rivaled the snorts of any hog.

Sleeping off another round of booze. Pathetic. No, he wasn't. The man had created absolute misery for Sarah during his stay. She'd catered to him and pampered him. Was this his way of saying thanks?

Benjamin leaned on the bed, supporting his weight on fisted hands. He hissed thru clenched teeth, "I warned you not to hurt her. Lay here and freeze after what you've done. Steve can rouse you and give you a bath. You'll get no help from me."

No response. Plastered.

The temptation to harm Bryce was overpowering. It wouldn't bring satisfaction if he couldn't comprehend and fear the threat hovering over him.

The Bear Paws quilt. Benjamin groaned, fingering the layer of mud. They'd never remove the red clay stains. Bryce must have fallen in a puddle. Still, it didn't explain Sarah's chest and face wiping behavior. He didn't want to consider what Bryce had done besides ruin the quilt and create extra work and pain for Sarah.

"You're out of here as soon as Steve arrives." Benjamin's tightly clenched jaw popped. He punched a fist into the pillow beside Fairmont's head. "I'd love to belt you. Oh, don't worry. You're not worth the trouble. I'd be the one in jail, and you'd be free to roam around drinking."

Benjamin composed himself with several deep breaths before returning to Sarah's room.

Tapping on her door, he asked, "May I come in?"

"Yeah, I'm dressed."

She pulled back the covers to slide into bed as he entered.

Pressing her hands on the mattress to gain a sitting position brought a wince.

He'd insist on a long soak in the tub later. Mud still smudged her face. She'd need a manicure to clean her fingernails.

She shivered and burrowed beneath the quilt. "I'll help you clean once I get warm. I should've gotten out of those wet clothes."

"Do you want an electric blanket or a heating pad?"

"No, give me a minute. Just a chill."

"Have you been feverish again?" He placed a hand on her forehead.

"I had a low-grade temp around noon."

"Did you call the doctor?"

Sarah nodded. "Right before Bryce showed up. The doctor changed a medication dose. I'm supposed to go in if I get worse or don't improve in two days." Disappointment loomed in her eyes.

She improved until Bryce disappeared for a drinking binge several days ago. Now this. His throat tightened. Sarah had to get better. Watching her deteriorate would kill him. He grabbed a quilt from the daybed and tucked it around her shivering form.

How was he supposed to act in this delicate situation? Did he offer comfort via physical contact or simply listen? This relationship was too complicated. They needed to come to some understanding about where they stood, but where that was he had no clue.

After wiping the desk chair with a sponge, he pulled it beside the bed. He took the tube of pain relief ointment from the bedside table. Holding it up, he asked, "May I?"

"Please. All my joints ache."

He squeezed an inch of ointment into his palm and worked it tenderly into her fingers and wrists. "You took a pain pill?"

She nodded and stared at the ceiling. Glistening moisture lurked in fatigue-etched eyes. Bryce should pay her medical bills. He'd worsened this flare.

Sarah didn't look at him, but asked, "I left Bryce on the bed, right?"

His brows pinched together. "He's sleeping one off. Sure you're okay? You seem a little confused."

"I'm just angry. The pain is getting to me. I'm not thinking straight."

"So, tell me what happened." He eased a wrist-protecting splint on each arm and fastened the Velcro straps.

"I heard Bryce drive up, so I went to the door. He parked by the huge puddle in the driveway. He fell getting out of his car."

Benjamin flipped back the edge of the quilts. "Your feet are like ice." As he rubbed medicine on her feet, a sharp cry made him jerk away his hands.

"Sorry. They're sore. Don't stop. It'll help."

Once he'd applied the ointment, he snagged a pair of socks from the drawer and slid them over her inflamed toes. Next, he positioned a wooden frame beneath the sheet and quilts. He'd constructed the device after her initial doctor's visit to hold the covers off her tender knee. "That should help."

"It does. Who'd ever believe bedding could hurt so much?"

"Finish the story. You went out in the storm to help Bryce."

Sarah glanced at him and blinked back tears. "I couldn't let him flounder around in the mud. He didn't harm me, Benjamin. I know that's what you're thinking."

"You're acting a bit weird. It is a logical explanation for your behavior. He did something more than create a mess."

She covered her eyes with the back of her hand. "I helped him out of the puddle and steadied him by putting an arm around his waist. We made it up the stairs to his room. Somehow, he stumbled over the rug. I tried to break his fall. In the process, he pulled me down on the bed with him. I fell against him. He must have thought I did it on purpose."

Tears coursed down her cheeks. The quivering of her chin made his heart pound. He didn't like the ugly scene Sarah's story created in his mind.

Sarah placed a hand on his arm. "Bryce kissed me."

Benjamin clamped his teeth together. Rushing back up to punch the man might quell his rage. "Are you saying he—"

"No!" She held up a hand, and then whispered, "I was furious and yelling at him. He passed out." She lowered her gaze to some spot on the quilt.

If she couldn't look into his eyes, there was more to this tale. "Bryce didn't stop with a kiss."

Shrinking deeper beneath the quilts, she tugged the covers to her chin. Her eyes revealed the truth as tears welled. "I was so scared. He groped at my shirt and kissed me again. If he hadn't blacked out ... I couldn't have stopped him."

The image sent fire through his veins. Placing elbows on the bed, Benjamin dropped his head into his hands.

He slipped out of the chair to sit on the edge of her bed. She was sobbing again, splint-encased hands covering her face.

He dared to stroke a finger across her forehead. Maybe his touch would soothe. "You're safe. I'll take care of everything.

Bryce can't hurt you now."

"Hold me, please, hold me. I can't shake the fear." She sat up, wrapping arms around his chest.

No complaints from him. If she found a safe haven in his embrace, he'd oblige.

Silence hung over them for minutes before she released him and eased back against the pillows.

The strength he admired had transformed her face to determination. Terror no longer consumed her. "Get Bryce out of here. I don't want to see him again. But don't hurt him." She placed a hand over Benjamin's tightly clenched fist.

She knew him well. His thoughts had strayed toward retaliation in those moments when he should have been comforting her.

She opened his hand to thread her fingers between his.

He lowered his head and studied their hands. "You're right. I would love to punch his pretty face."

"Don't do it." Her other hand stroked his arm, eyes wide, anger smoldering in their depths. "Mrs. Hardin's caused enough trouble with her malicious tongue. I'm flattered that you'd want to uphold my honor. You can't. Bryce would win, Benjamin."

"The police should know the sort of man he is."

"No matter how angry we are, this stays quiet. You and Steve take care of it with his people. Please, I couldn't handle a scandal. He'd find lawyers and people to back him. I sent a mixed signal with the fall. In his drunken state, he read it wrong. It's my word against his. Since he didn't harm me, it isn't worth your reputation or mine."

"It might save another woman in the future."

She pressed her lips together and squeezed her eyes shut. Shaking her head she said, "It's not a battle I can fight. I'm too tired and too sick. If I have to, I'll tell the producer the truth. But that's the end of it."

"I don't agree, but I'll follow your wishes for now. Steve and I can take care of things. I doubt this is the first time Bryce made inappropriate advances."

"I'm certain it isn't. I should have listened to you. If I'd kicked him out after his first drunken episode…" A heavy sigh expressed the rest. "Too late for regrets. My stubborn need for money almost cost me dearly."

He stroked her cheek and planted a kiss on her forehead. It felt warm—too warm. "Sorry. I probably shouldn't kiss you right now. Wouldn't want you to see my affection as inappropriate."

"There's no comparison. Your loving care is welcome. I'm

thankful you came home. I needed you this afternoon."

"Not something you readily admit."

"No. But life is different now. This disease has changed many things. I'm learning to appreciate help. Especially yours."

Benjamin asked, "Will you do something for me?"

Sleepy eyes lit up with uncertainty. "Maybe."

"Will you talk about what happened with someone like Becky or Ella? Another woman who could—"

She jabbed a pointed finger in his chest. "If you promise you won't have a personal altercation with Bryce. It happened, I'm fine, and it stays in our private circle of friends. Am I making this clear enough?"

Benjamin hesitated. "I'll let Steve handle it."

"Good. Keep us out of the fray."

Sarah turned to look at the clock. She tossed back the covers. "The new guest can't see the house looking like this. We'd better get busy cleaning."

He pushed against her shoulders, easing her back to the bed. "I'm cleaning. And I'll get Bryce out of here. Your reputation is at stake. I'm sure you don't want a new guest to see a drunk leaving the house. Like it or not, I'm in charge this afternoon. You," he poked a finger at her, "have a fever. You're staying in bed."

"I should greet her, not you."

"Why? You think she'll get scared away when she sees me, is that it?"

Sarah bit her lip. "That's not what I meant."

"It sounded that way."

"I didn't think you'd want her to see you. You normally hide from tenants."

"That's about to change. I'm ready to face some challenges."

She reached up to run her fingers through his hair. "I'm not ashamed to let people see you. I'm embarrassed by my behavior this afternoon." She hung her head and pulled the covers back under her chin like a child hiding from the bogeyman.

"What? Bryce tried to assault you. That's scary, not embarrassing."

"We've shared a dark secret. Telling you; your intimate care. Well, it seems a bit too personal."

Benjamin said, "You're scared to admit it. So am I. We're acting like a couple."

Her eyes rounded and her mouth dropped open. "We can't be a couple. We've never even dated."

"We have a date every morning over coffee. We date in the evenings when we read together. Just because we haven't been on a formal outing doesn't mean we aren't involved."

"I guess at our age those things might count as dating."

He'd better not prolong his stay. Sarah wasn't the only one feeling a bit too warm. "We'll discuss the topic of a real date later." He eyed the clock. "I have a house to clean. Or are you going to be stubborn and waste my time by insisting that you help?"

"No, I'll be a good girl and take a nap. I'll help by calling Steve. You clean; I'll make sure he comes to get Bryce out of here before four."

Benjamin brushed a kiss across her lips. Big mistake. He lingered a moment too long so her warm breath teased the skin on his cheek. Oh, how he wanted, no ... needed, true love. He had to joke about it. If not, he might admit the truth. He'd found what he wanted at Mosey Inn. Problem was she'd never want him.

He strode toward the door to put some distance between them. "Call Steve. I'll leave the door open so I can hear you. I expect you to yell if you need help. Maybe there's hope for two old folks. Think we could ever be a real couple?"

He didn't wait for an answer; too afraid to hear her say no.

CHAPTER THIRTEEN

The tenuous glow of sunlight teased Sarah awake. She opened one eye to glance at the clock. Six-forty-five. Her heart bolted. Breakfast would be late. The aroma of coffee met her next breath. She fought the urge to supervise. No reason to climb out of her warm bed; Benjamin had it under control.

Had she slept fourteen hours? She couldn't recall most of last night. Maybe Benjamin's forcing her to drink a glass of juice and the kiss with his whispered, "Sweet dreams, gorgeous," hadn't been a dream.

It sure seemed odd to have someone taking care of her. The role reversal made her mind spool off a ream of questions. She'd ponder them later. The hostess should make an appearance at the breakfast table.

Sarah unfastened the braces on her arms. Stretching, she tested each joint. Stiff fingers and wrists. The rest of her felt less achy. She slipped on her robe and slippers and lumbered to the bathroom. Chilly this morning, but no rain pelted the roof. Warm water from the tap soothed her stiff fingers.

She looked like Bryce after a bender. Dark circles under her eyes, hair standing out like porcupine quills, face pale as the porcelain sink. Nothing gorgeous about her today. Did she look so horrid last night when Benjamin treated her like a queen?

She grasped the big handle on the battery-powered toothbrush and gave the bad taste in her mouth a quick fix. Forget trying to improve the rest of her appearance before breakfast.

Sarah treaded gingerly toward the closet. The Bear Paws quilt, draped over her recliner, caught her eye. Benjamin's thoughtfulness again. A faint reddish-orange stain marred the center. He must have spent hours cleaning it while she slept. She pulled the quilt to her chest. Strong scents of laundry soap and various cleaners tickled her nostrils.

Her stomach lurched at the memory of what almost happened. Tragic, but appropriate, that some of the stain remained in the quilt. Ella would have to switch rooms when she returned. She'd understand why Sarah needed to avoid Bear Paws for a while.

If memories of yesterday lingered, Sarah would treasure one as a special gift—dear, sweet Benjamin. Her last fully cognizant thought was of Benjamin talking with the new arrival around four-thirty. Snippets of conversation about the book collection had drifted in from the library. He'd sounded at ease. She suspected he was shaking in his work boots. Benjamin had come a long way. The idea that he'd done these deeds for her made them more endearing. Without his assistance, she wouldn't have gotten her much-needed rest and freedom from severe pain.

She ran her tongue over her lips. The sensation of Benjamin's lips against hers returned. She should have been repulsed after her encounter with Bryce. She'd welcomed Benjamin's kiss; longed for his strong, safe arms. His suggestions about dating and being a couple left many questions. This hadn't been her intention when he arrived. Attracted to him, needing him, scared beyond belief, and no idea how to proceed—she'd created a disaster.

"Good morning. Feeling better?" She whirled to find him standing in the doorway.

"Don't come in. I look terrible." She shooed him with a wave of her hand.

He turned his back to her but didn't leave. "I didn't ask how you looked. Although, I've heard mudpacks work wonders for your skin. Feeling better?"

"Yes, Smarty Pants. Get back in the library. I'm not ready for visitors."

He stepped behind the door but continued to chat. "I set out breakfast. Your guests are happy. Noah's better so Becky's on her way over. I'm heading out to work soon."

"Church or town?" She scurried into the bathroom. The mirror, rarely her friend, was her worst enemy today.

"I'll work uptown since I have sunshine."

Sarah ran a brush through her hair. She sure needed a shower. She wiped a smear of mud from her cheek with a damp cloth. Must have missed that spot yesterday. A touch of blush and dab of lipstick. Better. Nicer clothes could wait. He'd come to check on her, not visit all morning. "Come on in."

He peeped around the corner of the door, a grin on his face. "You look nice this morning."

"Liar."

"It's the truth." He crossed the room and lifted a corner of the Bear Paws quilt. "Sorry about the stain. I tried the cleaning suggestions from the quilting books in the library. Nothing helped. The article on the Internet sounded promising. Didn't work."

"Thanks for trying. I've lived here long enough to know red clay is almost impossible to remove. When I was a kid Mom would get so mad." She smiled at the memory. "I spent hours climbing the muddy bank beside the pond one summer. I'll never forget the thrill of swinging on a rope to drop into the water."

"I wouldn't stick a toe in that pond. Those turtles are big enough to take off a limb."

She laughed. "They were babies when I went soaring."

His lopsided grin warmed her. "I can see you doing that. My mom hated it when I played soldier and got grass stains on my jeans. Didn't make sense at the time. I empathize now that I do my own laundry."

Sarah unfurled the quilt across her bed. Smoothing the fabric with a nostalgic touch, she folded it. The blue squares edged with red triangles resembled claws that stood out in sharp contrast against the creamy yellow background. "I should have stored it when Ella left. I hope she won't be too upset. She chose the colors. Mom made it especially for her."

"Your mother made this?" He touched a blue square.

"She made all the quilts in the house. Her head injury was strange. She could barely take care of her personal needs, yet the woman could design and sew a quilt without help. I kept her supplied with cloth. She stitched away."

Benjamin examined the tiny hand-stitched threads she had created with obvious care. "Amazing."

"Follow me." Sarah went to a closet in the library.

"There isn't another Bear Paws with the same colors. We need to select a similar scheme so I don't have to paint the room." She browsed through stacks of quilts stored with textile-preserving papers between the folds. "This North Carolina Star should work."

Benjamin lifted it from the stack and draped it over the couch while Sarah rummaged through a bag of plaques wedged beside the quilts. She laid the North Carolina Star nameplate on top of it.

Benjamin said, "Have Becky put the quilt on the bed. I'll change the label on the door tonight. That quilt on the top shelf is gorgeous. What's it called?"

Her stomach soured and her head spun. Leave it to Benjamin to notice her buried treasure. She swayed and grasped the doorframe.

Benjamin grabbed the desk chair and slid it beneath her. "Hey, what's wrong?" he asked, squatting in front of her.

She willed the tears pricking her eyes to cease. "Silly me, I'm overreacting. Mother made it before her accident. It's a Double Wedding Ring." She folded her hands to prevent their trembling. "A quilt I'll never use."

"I hit a nerve. Sorry."

"You didn't know. And you're right. It is beautiful. Mom used strips of my childhood clothes to piece it. Memories to share with a husband."

"You loved your mom."

Sarah nodded. "Life changed so drastically. She became a child. My father lost his mate. I lost the parents I knew. It hurt to watch them."

Benjamin took her arm and led her back to the day bed in her quarters. She curled her legs beside her and tucked her feet under the edge of the quilt.

He sat, wrapping an arm around her shoulder. Sarah rested her head against Benjamin's broad chest. "My parents used to work in the kitchen making meals for our boarders. I caught them kissing sometimes when I was a child." She giggled. "Grossed me out. After Mom fell, I don't recall seeing her kiss Dad." Sarah frowned as an image of her parents flitted across her brain. "Mom didn't understand that sort of affection. How was Dad supposed to respond to a wife who became a child?"

"He kept loving her. When you told me about the accident, I couldn't understand how your father could ask so much of you. I see it differently now. You loved them, so you did it willingly."

"I'm not so sure I did do it willingly. I've always assumed that was the case. Since you arrived, I've questioned several things about my life."

"Bad influence, huh?"

"No." She poked him in the ribs, causing a grunt. "You've made me think. I felt obligated to care for Mom. I didn't mind missing college events like parties and football games. I expected to care for her a few months. It lasted a lifetime. Friends married, moved away, had kids. They led normal lives. I never experienced normal."

"You lifted a burden off your dad's shoulders."

She narrowed her eyes and studied him. "Dad never expressed that to me, but you're right. I never planned to spend my life caring for a child-like mother or behaving like Daddy's wife." Her hand flew to her mouth. "Nothing physical between us, mind you."

"I understood what you meant."

She cuddled back into Benjamin's arms. "We became people caught in the same old daily grind. That accident altered every personal relationship I had. I never questioned the changes it caused until after Mom died. Then I realized what I forfeited."

"You gave love feet."

She cast him a questioning look.

"Your mundane existence—it became your purpose. Love isn't what I thought it was."

Sarah placed a hand on his chest and gazed into his eyes. "How so?"

"People don't consider me loveable. I'm grotesque or scary. I thought love was physical. Those college-aged hormones with the whole dominant male thing." He snorted a little laugh and shook his head. "The fire changed that for sure; nothing physically attractive about me. I lost my worth. Few people ever treat me as a person with value. Oh, they appreciate my skills as a carpenter, but it's because I do something that benefits them. They don't consider I need affection and kindness."

The pain in those statements wrenched her heart. "They don't know the real Benjamin Pruitt. They'd behave differently."

"You show me affection, Sarah. If more people behaved like you—"

"My affection comes from God. I'm not perfect and never will be here on earth. We can't fully love others or ourselves unless God rules our hearts. We're sinful, selfish people otherwise."

"I've thought about going to church with you. Not simple when public appearances make me physically ill."

"You handled the tenant yesterday. Church wouldn't be much different."

"Sitting in a room full of people while they stare…" A shudder ran through him, and he shifted uneasily. "It's not the same."

"God wants your love and worship. He looks at your heart. You sat in the café with tourists because you care about Noah. When you're ready to admit that you need and love God, you won't be so bothered by the way people treat you."

"I met the guest because you were too sick. I had no choice. I have a choice about stepping into church."

Sarah sent a knowing smirk his way. He had a choice about both situations, but she wouldn't force his hand. He'd acted out of … no; it wasn't true. Love for her? She wasn't prepared to apply that word to what they had. She steered the conversation back to his topic. "You're implying I had no choice when Mom got hurt."

"You took over because your mom's life couldn't be fixed. You loved your parents. Your father loved his wife. Sending her away would have taken away his soul. You gave him a chance to show his wife he could still love her even though she didn't comprehend the love he had for her."

"Very profound," she said with raised eyebrows.

"You've been patient about my phobias. You overlook the scars and treat me with dignity. I know it sounds silly, but we have something special. At least it's special to me. You care. I probably shouldn't say this..." He rubbed a hand over his freshly shaved chin and stared at his lap.

She lifted his chin with a finger. "Go ahead. What's on your mind?"

He held his breath as if drawing in courage. His exhaled words tumbled out like a babbling brook—sweet and pure, gentle and melodic. "The way you treat me is the closest thing to true love I've experienced."

She took in a short gasp of air. Her eyes had to reflect total amazement, but he continued.

"I'd like to explore a deeper relationship if you could ever consider one with a man who looks like a beast."

He'd used the "L" word. She clamped her gaping mouth shut.

Did her gestures of affection and the attraction she voiced represent love? She considered the reactions she'd witnessed when he walked through the Country Store. Trauma? Crushing. Humiliation? Absolute. Distrust? Total.

She'd tried to counteract those events with kindness. Confusion surged through her. True love? It went beyond self. It made sacrifices. It could only come ... from God. Benjamin exhibited true love toward her. Impossible. Or was it? As a child, Benjamin had gone to church and heard the truth of God's love. Had he known the love only Christ could produce in a person? If so, he'd buried his faith under an avalanche of pain and self-loathing. That was certainly plausible, considering what she'd observed. One thing was certain: God would never relinquish Benjamin's heart once He possessed it. God would whittle away every raw, painful area until Benjamin became a new person.

Until that happened, a mountain stood between them. She'd waltzed into this relationship with her eyes closed and drilled a hole the size of Texas in Benjamin's heart. Yes, she had special feelings for him. He'd helped her through a difficult period in her life. She couldn't consider a dating relationship until Benjamin changed his spiritual beliefs. If God didn't work fast, she'd have to reject Benjamin's advances. Devastation? She might as well stomp him into the mud on Main Street and grind up the pieces with her old riding boots.

Would she be equally devastated?

CHAPTER FOURTEEN

Sarah took a sip of hot tea before setting her rocking chair in motion. Languid rays of autumn sun cast long shadows across the porch at Mosey Inn. They couldn't ask for a nicer day to celebrate Ella's return. Sarah inhaled the tantalizing scent of grilled steaks the afternoon wind carried from the terrace. Her mouth watered, and she placed a hand on her growling stomach.

Becky tossed a pile of papers on the table and dropped into a chair beside her. "Only one week until Thanksgiving. Where has this year gone? I can't believe it's time to practice a Christmas program."

Benjamin's mellow laugh captured Sarah's attention. A smile threatened to escape as the sound tickled a secret place in Sarah's heart. She placed her set of papers on the wicker table and let her gaze drift up the hill to the terrace. Benjamin and Todd kept watch over the grill while Noah lobbed fallen apples into the orchard in futile attempts to knock down the few remaining apples.

When the screen door banged, Sarah jumped.

Ella said, "Sorry to startle you. Sure smells good out here. I'll carry the baked potatoes and salad. You need to finish your plans for the Christmas program later. Don't want the food to get cold."

Sarah said, "We're at a good stopping point."

Ella balanced the tray of food on the edge of the table to give Sarah a hug. "It's nice to see you looking better. Hated traveling with you sick. Things kept coming up. Hope I get to stay until the end of the year."

"I missed you too. Maybe your volunteers can keep things rolling. We'll have a girly night and catch up before bedtime."

Ella said, "You bet we will. Right now, those steaks are calling my belly. Hoof it up the hill with the rest of the food, girls."

"Wait here, Sarah," Becky said. "I'll get the pitcher of iced tea and the salad dressings."

Sarah nodded and watched Ella trudge up the path. Sarah rubbed her knees. Good today. The trek would have been hard a week ago without a strong arm to lean on.

The screen door slammed again. Becky placed her tray on the table. "You're looking up the hill as if it's Mount Everest. Need help making the climb?"

"No, I was thinking it's nice my medication is working so I can walk up without help."

"It didn't hurt to get rid of Bryce Fairmont. Now that your stress level is down, you're a new woman."

His name evoked a shudder. "It has made a difference. Benjamin says they're about to wrap up filming since the rain stopped. That's one movie I don't plan to see."

Becky said, "They're renting horses one more day. The extra money was nice, but I won't miss Bryce." She fisted her hands and placed them on her hips. "And to think, I used to believe he was so handsome. It goes to show you can't judge someone by their looks."

Oh, how Benjamin needed more experiences with people who overlooked his exterior. Sarah anchored their papers with her empty mug. "We'll finish planning the Christmas program tomorrow. I'm starving. Let's eat."

Sarah slid onto the picnic table bench. She'd made the walk from the house only slightly winded and with little pain.

Benjamin scooted in beside her. He leaned toward her so his shoulder bumped her arm. His windblown hair invited her fingers to rearrange it. She avoided the temptation. She wasn't doing so well warding off the emotional rollercoaster ride he caused.

Todd forked a sizzling slab of meat onto her plate. Benjamin picked up her utensils and cut it into bite-sized pieces. "Thanks," she whispered. "These steaks smell even better than the last ones you two grilled."

Benjamin winked. "My secret marinade." His crooked smile brightened his face.

It was next to impossible to disregard that grin. She returned it with a shy sideways glance and a little smile. "I want ranch dressing if you'd open it, please."

A look across the table found Ella with raised eyebrows and pursed lips. Full of questions, and rightly so. When Ella left, Sarah would have pitched a fit if anyone had cut her meat. And asking someone to open a jar for her?

Benjamin enlarged the fork with a padded foam sleeve before relinquishing it to Sarah. His hand lingered an instant when their fingers touched. The smile they shared spoke volumes. No, she wouldn't blush. Ella already had enough fodder to keep them up half the night. Sarah had no simple answers to the complex situation that had developed with Benjamin during Ella's absence. She had dozens of questions herself.

Todd cleared his throat, which ceased the jabbering around the table. "Want to ask the blessing, Noah?"

"It's Grandpa's turn. He hasn't prayed yet."

Todd looked across the table at Benjamin and shrugged. Sarah held her breath. Would he pray?

Benjamin's smile faded, but his face didn't show dismay. "Your Dad taught you a prayer last week when we ate lunch together. I'm not sure I know the words. You pray. Maybe I'll be ready next time."

"Okay," Noah whined. "Remember, close your eyes."

"I'm the one who told you that." He pointed at Noah and grinned. "Pray, kid. Miss Sarah's tummy is rumbling."

Noah covered his mouth and giggled. "I heard it too."

If Noah and Todd were praying during meals with Benjamin, what other sorts of conversations had they shared? She should talk with Todd about the spiritual changes she'd observed in Benjamin.

After Noah said the blessing, Becky asked, "Noah, have you invited Grandpa to Thanksgiving dinner?"

"Yes, ma'am."

Sarah halted her fork in mid-bite. Why hadn't she thought of that? They could ease him into the church through the social event. Sarah finished the bite of steak and said, "It's a local tradition. You really should come. Did Noah explain what we do?"

"Just that almost everyone in the valley attends. Sounds like it's expected." Benjamin combed his fingers through the hair covering his flawed right ear. Sarah recognized the gesture as a sign of discomfort. She hoped he wouldn't change the subject.

Ella piped up. "You should go. You've done so much work around town. People need to have a chance to say thanks."

"They're paying me. All the thanks I need."

Sarah said, "I think Ellenora Barker has cooked the turkeys on Thanksgiving ever since Love Valley was founded in 1954. It's a day we celebrate the community spirit Mr. Barker wanted when he built this place."

Noah said, "Mr. Barker's my friend. He always gives me a hug when I go with Dad to Andy's Hardware Store."

Benjamin said, "They're nice folks. She gave me glasses of iced tea when I worked uptown."

Todd said, "People would want you to come, but attendance is always optional. Andy Barker wanted Love Valley to be a place where people help each other. Everyone pitches in to provide the meal." Todd placed his fork on the edge of his plate. "The gathering reminds me of the first Thanksgiving. Like the pilgrims, we had a rough year when we moved here. Our neighbors welcomed us and taught us how to survive in a tourist-dependent setting. New friends kept us from going hungry."

Noah shoved a forkful of potato in his mouth and said, "Miss Sarah always brings apple pie. You don't want to miss that."

Benjamin frowned at him. "Don't talk with your mouth full, young man."

Sarah snaked her hand over to the tight fist she glimpsed in Benjamin's lap. His surreptitious glance said her touch gave him strength in the tense situation. No one else seemed to notice his discomfort. He wrapped cold fingers around her warm hand.

"Benjamin," she said, "the people around this table care about you. We know it might be hard to venture into a large community crowd. You're overcoming those fears. If you come, we'll stick with you."

"I'm not making any promises, but I'll think about it."

An hour later, Benjamin and Sarah passed their plates to Ella. He said, "We'll be along to help with the dishes. It's going to be a nice sunset."

Ella patted Sarah's shoulder and grabbed a tray. "Cleaning can wait. Perfect sunsets are rare."

Noah raced around the table and edged close to Benjamin. "Can I watch the sunset too, Grandpa?"

Ella set the tray down and put her hands on Noah's shoulders. "Hey, I just came home. You spend almost every day taking a walk or riding your pony with Grandpa. I heard you could read. Come read me a story. Here, carry these two bottles of dressing down to the kitchen."

"Can I have a cookie when we get to the house?"

"Catch up with your mom and ask."

Noah jogged ahead of her and ran circles around Becky.

Ella winked. "Have fun, you two."

Sarah stretched her legs out on the bench when Benjamin straddled the seat behind her and pulled her into his arms. He kissed the top of her head. "Gorgeous evening. Almost as radiant as you."

She caressed the hands he wrapped around her waist. "Flattery is always welcome."

He whispered in her ear. "I'll go to dinner if you'll face one of your fears."

She nestled her head against his chest and asked, "Which

one? I have quite a few these days."

"The horseback ride I mentioned."

"You're asking a lot."

"Likewise."

She swiveled to drape her legs over the leg Benjamin had outside the picnic bench and leaned back against his supportive arm. Much easier to judge his reaction from this angle. "Do you work on Tuesday?"

"Not if you're agreeing."

She scrunched up her nose. "Should we consider it an official date? We'd be out of the public eye, but sharing time in a different setting."

"Sounds official to me."

His lips met hers with a kiss that oozed warmth through her limbs.

When he broke the kiss, she glanced toward the house. "We shouldn't. They might see us."

His lips twitched with a "so let them" grin before he kissed her again.

Any nip in the air vanished. Her heavy sweater became excessively warm. "Please stop." She placed her hand on his chest and pushed away from him. "I'm not ready for this kind of relationship. I'm not sure it's right."

"Neither am I, but I need to know if it is." He nuzzled her hair and whispered, "That's why people date. Maybe you'll have a better idea about what you want after you have an all-night talk with Ella."

"It's only fair since you've been talking to Todd."

"We haven't talked about us."

She lowered her chin and glared at him, a smile playing at the corners of her lips. "You expect me to believe that?"

"Yeah!" Sarcasm dripped from his deep voice. He stared at her, wide-eyed, his mouth hanging open. "Do you doubt my integrity?"

She fiddled with a loose thread on the edge of his collar. "Of course not. I just figured."

"Todd listens. He's helping me make positive changes."

Positive changes sounded good.

The reddening sky etched diamonds in Benjamin's silver-streaked hair. She threaded her fingers through the thick, curly strands. Every inch of her begged for another kiss.

No. She wouldn't. Too many questions lurked between them. She needed time to see the outcome of those positive changes. Another kiss might steal her heart and break his in the process.

"I don't want you to make spiritual changes because of me."

"Wouldn't dream of it. If I tossed up a false front, you'd see through it. You are a factor though. You made me look at my life. I didn't think people could accept me. My heart's been broken a thousand times. Planned to keep living in solitude. When you introduced me to these special friends, I found a ray of hope."

He trailed his callused fingers along her cheek. "You, Sarah, are worth the risk of another crack in my heart."

Perhaps the callus on his heart was softening. *Lord, I don't want to make a mistake, and I can't do this alone. Help us show him the only Person who mends broken hearts.*

༨ ✠ ༩

Ella slouched into the pillows she piled against the footboard of Sarah's bed and crossed her arms. "Wipe the snarl off your face and stop fretting. I'm fine in North Carolina Lily. If you apologize for the quilt one more time I won't choose a new one."

Sarah plumped up several pillows and arranged them against the headboard. "Okay, okay, I'll hush." She settled into her cozy nest. "I'm so glad you're back. No one else can argue with me like you do and get away with it."

"Hey, somebody has to keep you in line." Ella grinned. "That brings us to my next point. Are you being honest about your health? You look tired."

"Of course I look tired. It's late, and we had a busy day. I'm much better. This new medication is working wonders. There is no new joint damage, less pain, the inflammation has improved, and my energy has increased."

"A succinct accounting." Ella narrowed her eyes and frowned. "Why don't I believe it? You put on a good show at dinner, but something's bothering you."

"I'm being honest."

"Right. Things are so good you're planning an exotic Christmas cruise."

"I wish. No money for that."

"Finally, an honest answer."

"Therapy and medicines are not cheap. Business gets lean in the winter. I had a good summer and fall. I'll manage. I always have."

"I'll pay you more during the winter."

"No you won't. Your help around the place is more beneficial."

"You will not go without treatment. Raise your right hand."

Sarah giggled. "You're being silly."

"Come on. Do it."

Sarah rolled her eyes but obeyed. "What am I promising?"

"You'll tell me if you need money."

Sarah lowered her hand and met Ella's steady glare. That look could squeeze orange juice from a rock. "I promise. Money isn't the real problem." Truth couldn't hide from the owner of CLUES: Continue Looking Until Ella Stops. Ella would search the world while badgering everyone until she either found her missing person or discovered a reason for the disappearance. Vagaries wouldn't appease Ella.

Sarah studied her nails intently before looking up. "I'm asking questions that never occurred to me before."

"What sorts of questions?"

"Ones that shake my faith and make me wonder about God's goodness." She pulled in a deep breath and steeled herself for the inquisition.

"Sounds normal. Look at the year you've had." Ella ticked the list off on her fingers. "You lost your mother and developed a long-term illness, that actor caused emotional trauma, and you're struggling financially. Those are huge issues. God is bigger than a few questions about difficult things."

"I've given people the pat answer before. Hard times help us grow. God is always faithful. It doesn't satisfy when I'm in that situation."

Ella hugged a pillow and inched closer. "Explain. I'll be quiet and listen."

Sarah sighed, dropping her head against the headboard to stare at the ceiling. "I'm looking back at my life. Why did Mom get hurt and prevent me from finishing my education? Why do I constantly struggle to put food on the table? Did I do the right thing by taking care of Mother instead of getting married and having a family? Will there be anyone to take care of me when I get too sick?"

Ella took Sarah's hand. "I can probably add more to that list. Where were the people in the church when I needed their help? Why did I live a lonely, dreary existence? You're talking about things you've kept bottled up for years. They stem from heartbreak, anger, and fear. I hear similar questions every day. There are no easy answers. It boils down to one question. Can we trust God to be there when the worst possible thing happens?"

"I would have said yes a few months ago. Then a man named Benjamin walked up on my porch, and my questions began."

"So he caused you to look at the realities of life and ask why." Ella shrugged. "Sometimes we get an answer, and sometimes we have to trust. God has a plan and a reason. God won't zap you because you're scared, angry, and seeking answers, Sarah. He'll deepen your faith if you turn to Him for answers."

Ella's warm grip on Sarah's hand didn't do much to reassure. "Tell me, Sarah, what's your worst fear?"

She chewed on her lip and fought tears. "Becoming my mother."

Ella pursed her lips and shook her head emphatically. "No way. You are not your mother, and you never will be. Brain damage, not the physical problems, trapped her in a child-like state."

Sarah's voice rose. "She still required physical care. If this illness turns me into a crippled old woman, I'll wind up in a nursing home. I don't have a daughter to take care of me. I could become a terrible burden. The only people in my life are friends. I can't ask them to do what I did for years."

"A friend is sometimes closer than a brother." Ella patted Sarah's arm. "I think I read that in the Bible somewhere."

"Don't joke. This is a serious concern."

"Who are you talking to? I won't be running CLUES forever. If you get worse, I'll take care of you. Besides, Benjamin will be here."

Sarah laughed and rested an arm across her forehead as she sank deeper into the pillows. "Benjamin won't be here to take care of me when I'm old."

"Wrong." Ella wagged a finger in Sarah's face. "He'd stay at Mosey Inn and take care of you the rest of your life if you'd let him. The man loves you."

Sarah furrowed her brow. "You're the one who's wrong. I'll admit we're close, but taking care of a sick old woman isn't what he wants to do the rest of his life."

"Examine the facts, girl. Who helped run this place when you couldn't walk? Who calmed your fears and stood by you when the doctor and Bryce Fairmont turned your world upside down?"

Sarah squirmed. Ella's knack for getting to the root of issues backed her into an uncomfortable corner. "Benjamin."

Ella's eyebrows rose. "Why did he bother?"

"Because ..." She didn't want to admit it to herself or to Ella. "He ... loves me."

"Ah ha, light dawns. Becoming a burden isn't your greatest fear. Falling in love with Benjamin scares you more."

Sarah's gut tightened. Profound. Was it true? She mulled it over for a while. "Okay, you're right. How did I let this happen?"

"You listened to your heart. He's never allowed anyone to love him. I knew the moment I met Benjamin that you were supposed to help shatter the wall of distrust he had built against the world. I bet he's asking some tough questions too. Your health now or in the future won't be a problem. Benjamin's doing more as a friend than some husbands do to show their wives love."

"It would be wrong to let him into my heart before he's made a commitment to God."

"Benjamin told Noah he'd gone to church before the fire. We're praying he'll return to his faith. We have to accept him where he is and leave the rest in God's hands."

"That's fine for you and the Spangler family. I'm the one falling in love with the man." She threw up her hands. "How does God want me to respond?"

"Pray. Show Benjamin you can accept his disfigurement. Show him how special he is to you as a man. No other woman has valued the sweet spirit hidden under those scars. God will strengthen your faith, and Benjamin will learn he can be loved."

"It isn't so simple. We might end up with broken hearts."

Ella leaned against the footboard. "Is Benjamin worth that chance?"

CHAPTER FIFTEEN

Sarah's mouth felt as dry as the leaves rustling beneath Jasper's plodding hooves. She tightened her grip on the reins. Her fingers cramped inside her leather gloves. Better to tolerate a bit of pain than focus on the memory threatening to suck each breath from her chest.

Behind her, Benjamin's horse shied and snorted. Sarah twisted in the saddle to see them. Topper sidestepped, sending pebbles skittering off the trail. They rattled as they slid down the steep precipice and disappeared into thickets of rhododendron and laurel.

Benjamin leaned forward and soothed his wide-eyed horse. "Easy, boy. We'll be on flatter ground soon."

Did her fear make Topper skittish? Perhaps he could smell her reluctance. If Benjamin took a spill because of her, she'd never forgive herself.

"We're okay," Benjamin said. "Don't worry." He patted the horse's neck. "You were made to run, weren't you, boy?" He slackened the reins and urged Topper up the rocky slope. "I'm helping Todd get Topper adapted to riding on steeper trails. He's improving."

"Could have fooled me." Jasper ambled forward as Topper approached from behind. "Todd should sell that one to some rancher or rodeo rider. If a tourist took a spill, it could ruin his company."

Conversation dwindled as they concentrated on the trail. Her saddle creaked when she leaned left to brush aside brown tendrils of kudzu. The vines towered above them like forgotten party streamers. Frost glistened on the dried foliage where a few rays of sunlight penetrated the forest canopy.

Eerie silence assaulted her; too quiet for comfort. No birds sang. No breeze stirred the barren limbs on this cold November morning. Shrouded in the tomb-like covering, she pulled in a deep breath. It chilled her lungs and dried her lips even more. A squirrel ratcheted its warning call from a tree on her right. She jerked her head toward the sound, gasped, and reined Jasper to an abrupt halt.

Benjamin edged Topper alongside her. "What's wrong?"

She shivered. "I'd forgotten how quiet it gets deep in the forest. The silly squirrel startled me."

"You're cold. Need to call this off?"

"Nah, I'm just nervous. Conquering a fear adds to the chill. Lead on."

He stroked a gloved hand along Jasper's withers then let his hand come to rest on Sarah's knee. "You should loosen up on the reins. You'll make your hands sore."

She tilted her head sideways, setting her mouth in a stern line. "I know how to ride." She coaxed her fingers to relax. "Sorry. Didn't mean to snap at you. These woods hold painful memories."

"Talking might help."

She cut him a sideways glance. He was right, but she'd talk when the mood struck her. A jostle of her knees urged Jasper back into motion.

The trail widened and flattened after the next switchback. Topper adopted the slow steady pace Jasper set. "Mom taught me how to ride when I was about Noah's age."

"She must have been a great coach. I heard you were a champion barrel racer in your teens."

She knit her brows together, studying him. "I don't remember telling you that."

"Small town. Word travels."

"Mrs. Hardin?"

"No. Your pastor. Your prize winning adventures came up during a lunch conversation."

Her jaw dropped. "When did you eat lunch with my pastor?"

"We shared meals several times when I was making repairs at the church. By the way, you're more beautiful than you were as a teen."

She lowered her head and sighed. "Don't tell me he pulled out those old rodeo pictures."

"He was recounting his bull riding days. I recognized you in one of the pictures. He didn't deliberately snitch on you."

"We went to school together. Our rodeo days coincide. I was a lanky tomboy. He preferred curvy cheerleaders. Polar opposites that didn't attract."

"He said you competed in the races several summers."

"Mom and I spent three summers doing the circuit. When you grow up in Love Valley, horse blood runs in your veins."

"It shows. You're no novice rider."

Sarah closed her eyes and allowed her mind to drift. "If I concentrate I can feel every twist and turn around the barrels. My horse, Phoenix, and I had a unique harmony. He responded perfectly to my shifts in the saddle or the twitch of the reins. I've tried to forget that aspect of my existence. I can't. I've been uneasy today, but I must say being in a saddle feels normal again."

"You make your relationship with Phoenix sound almost romantic."

His smile brightened her mood. "I suppose racing is a bit like two becoming one. Those are special memories from long ago. I loved everything about horses until..." The vivid memory assailed her with a wave of unexpected grief. Time to confess. "I was riding with Mom the day she fell."

The color drained from Benjamin's face. He grabbed Jasper's reins and halted the horses. "Why didn't you tell me? I had no idea you saw your mom's accident."

The horses stamped and snorted as if impatient to move on. Their breath spewed clouds of white mist into the chilled morning air.

Sarah tugged at her scarf and tucked her neck in like a turtle. "It's irrational to let a frightening memory control a part of my life I once enjoyed. Someone should have put me back in the saddle and made me ride years ago."

Sarah rested her hands on the pommel and shifted her weight. "We were on a family outing. Mom was an excellent rider. She was out of sight around a switch back. We heard her scream. Dad and I arrived in time to see her horse rearing. She fell backwards onto a pile of rocks."

Benjamin asked, "Something spooked her horse?"

Sarah nodded. "Probably. I always suspected a cougar. People had heard them in that area. We never figured out what happened."

Benjamin's warm hand rested on her thigh. "Your Mom couldn't recall the details?"

Sarah shook her head. "I watched her fall." Sarah chewed on her lip as echoes from the past haunted her. "When her head hit the ground, it sounded like someone dropped a watermelon."

The old feeling of helplessness surged through her. "Dad stayed with her. I raced back down the trail. The doctor said she wouldn't survive. Days later, when she regained consciousness ... well, you know the rest of the story." Sarah pressed the fingertips of one hand against her forehead.

Benjamin grasped the hand she rested on the saddle horn. "Let's go home. You met the challenge and rode a horse. What I wanted to show you isn't worth this kind of pain."

Sarah slipped off her glove and caressed Benjamin's scarred cheek. "I had the option of saying no."

He turned his head and kissed the palm of her hand. The cool brush of his lips against the tender skin squeezed the breath from her chest.

Maybe he'd think the cold caused the redness in her cheeks. "We promised to face difficult situations this week. Going to the community dinner will place you in an equally uncomfortable position."

"You've set a brave example. I'll try to match it."

Not wanting to see his reaction, she nudged Jasper forward then spoke over her shoulder. "Prayer got me back into a saddle. Don't look to me for courage to face the people of Love Valley."

She sensed his smirk behind her back.

"You won't let religion drop, will you?" he asked.

"Never. God is relentless when one of his children strays. I'm simply doing the job He assigned me. It comes with the relationship. Get used to it or forget dating me."

"I think I'll tolerate your job assignment." He flicked the reins to move Topper forward. "There's a stream ahead. We'll water the horses before we turn back."

"We aren't going back until I see your special place. Talking about the past helped. Horse must run in my veins after all. Saddle life might become a habit again."

"Good. I'm not sure public appearances will be so easily rectified."

Fifteen minutes later, a stream gurgled beside the tree-lined trail. Patches of ice hugged boulders along the edge. The damp cold crept into her bones. Her medication and exercise regimen made life almost normal, but riding a horse on a frosty day wasn't such a good idea. However, in this case Benjamin was wise. Once she'd voiced her painful memory, fear subsided. The joy of riding returned with each switchback. If her body would cooperate, she'd tackle another trail with Benjamin.

Her knees ached, but she wouldn't complain. Benjamin already knew. She'd watched him steal looks of concern as she'd squirmed in the saddle during their trek. One of those poignant couple-like moments stirred her soul. It no longer felt disconcerting that he aptly read her emotions and physical needs.

Sarah prepared for pain to shoot through her leg when she put pressure on it to dismount. Benjamin was at her side before she had time to swing her leg over the saddle and stand in the stirrup.

He halted her with his words. "Don't put weight on your leg."

She glowered down at him. "So how am I supposed to get down?"

He shot her a don't argue with me look. "There's no need to aggravate your knee when it isn't necessary. Take your feet out of the stirrups. I'll help you."

She complied, sliding off sideways into his outstretched arms. He lowered her to the ground while softly kissing her.

His lips took away the chill and brought life back into her stiff limbs. She could get used to moments like this. Was she ready for heartbreak if they ended this tentative relationship?

Benjamin draped the reins over a branch so the horses could drink from the stream. He pulled a tattered quilt and an insulated lunch bag from his saddlebag. "The path is over here."

He wrapped the quilt around Sarah's shoulders and took her hand. They stepped off the main trial onto a tiny path between some bushes. "I found this special place in late summer. I'm hoping the frost hasn't marred the beauty. It's a short hike if you're feeling up to it."

"A walk will do me good. I'm ready for an adventure. Lead the way."

"Watch your step. Tree roots hide under the leaves."

Benjamin veered to the left, tramping through a thicket of dried kudzu. He grasped her arm to help her over a moss-covered fallen tree. Fragrant pines and dense hardwoods obscured the sky. Pushing aside branches, they followed the narrow path—a mere rabbit trail in the brush. A tunneled grove formed overhead. Light faded, and undergrowth became sparse. The sheltering arc of trees eliminated the babble of the brook, and the stillness in the forest became absolute. Sarah wanted to stop her heartbeat to keep from breaking the quietness of the peaceful surroundings.

When the path widened into a shady glade, anticipation of some spectacular revelation gleamed in Benjamin's eyes. His face lit up with joy like a child on Christmas morning.

A bend to the left brought them to a landscape unlike any she'd ever seen. The musty smell of rotting, fallen timber and moist earth hung in the air. Damp logs and leaf-strewn soil sprouted massive mushrooms in peculiar shapes and colors. In this forest glade, seldom touched by sunlight, a thick bed of moss, six feet or more across, blanketed the ground below a stately hemlock. Sarah stood at the edge of the dense green carpet absorbing the beauty of his hidden place. Glancing around and above her, she gaped in silent awe.

Benjamin whispered, "Incredible sight, huh? I stumbled on it while following a deer."

"It belongs in a fairy tale. I've never seen such a surreal place." She laughed. "I'm waiting for the seven dwarfs to greet us." Sarah squatted to run a hand along the moss. "Amazing! It feels like a fleecy blanket. Can we sit on it to eat?"

"Sure. The moss may be a bit damp. After lunch, I'll show you the unusual mushroom and fungi growths. I took pictures and researched them on the Internet."

Sarah gingerly spread the quilt over the moss. Benjamin helped ease her down into the comfortable softness.

Benjamin said, "When I found this place, there was an imprint in the moss where the deer had slept. Maybe he won't mind if we share his private retreat. These woods won't hold heat long. I wanted to be here at midday so we'd have the most warmth."

He handed Sarah a napkin and a sandwich. They ate in silence, making hand signals to each other when an occasional rustle in the brush signaled the passage of a mouse or chipmunk. A bird's call and the reply of its mate were the only other breaks in the tranquility of Benjamin's secret place in the forest.

Sarah lay back on the blanket, hands behind her head. A few rays of November sunlight filtered through the canopy and bathed their spot with feeble light. She closed her eyes and concentrated on the quiet solitude and the softness of the moss.

When she felt him staring at her, she cracked open her eyes just enough to see. His face spoke louder than words. "What? Do I have a grape juice mustache or crumbs on my chin?" She bantered, not ready to acknowledge the way his look of adoration thrilled her.

Benjamin drained his cup and tossed it in the bag. "No, I was just thinking a kiss would be appropriate on such a nice afternoon." He propped on an elbow and wrapped an arm around her.

She couldn't contain her smile of fulfillment. Her arms encircled his neck when he bent to kiss her. The gentle warmth of his lips amazed her. A shudder ran through her when his hands moved along her back. She'd never considered such pleasure in the arms of a man before Benjamin entered her life.

He broke the embrace and sat up. "We can't do this. I wanted to share this beautiful place with you, but ... well ... temptation is a powerful thing. Forgive me. The kiss was a bad idea."

"Oh, I agree." Sarah feigned a cough, rose, and moved to the bright orange mound of mushrooms at the base of a mossy stump. "Well now, moving on to a better topic, tell me about these. This one is gorgeous. What's it called?"

He pulled a small photo album from the bag and paged through it. "The mycologist on a website gave it this name." He pointed to the label he'd added to the photo.

Sarah couldn't miss the fact that Benjamin crouched beside her yet avoided contact. Embarrassed by the desires his touch created and her own inappropriate actions, she vowed to be more cautious in the future. A future? She shouldn't consider that notion. Not when they'd come so close to forbidden territory. She pretended to study his photographs and follow his line of conversation. Her thoughts grasped a new realization. Benjamin displayed moral integrity, a characteristic few men possessed in this modern world. His choice to avoid temptation had nothing to do with his physical deformities. Oh yes, he was worth the chance.

CHAPTER SIXTEEN

Sarah's head snapped up when she heard Mrs. Hardin talking in the adjacent grocery aisle. "You actually saw them sneaking out of town into the woods? Sarah hasn't ridden since her mother's accident."

Another familiar voice said, "They rode right past my house. Didn't seem to care who saw them making eyes at each other. Up to no good, I tell you."

Mrs. Hardin said, "I knew he was trouble the moment I laid eyes on him. Still think he had something to do with that girl's disappearance in Statesville. I'd say the man isn't sleeping alone in his rented room after all this time there. Sarah had a better upbringing. She shouldn't be teaching Sunday school if she's going to live this sort of lifestyle."

Sarah gripped the handle of the grocery cart, her face hot and red. It was bad enough to know Mrs. Hardin lurked around the corner spreading lies. Worse to hear the voice of a neighbor Sarah considered a friend joining in the gossip. Their words rankled more since Sarah had conquered a huge fear during that ride and Benjamin was on the verge of breaking free from his self-imposed captivity.

When Benjamin threw a can of green beans into the cart, Sarah jumped. The stern set of his lips alarmed her.

She placed a hand on his arm. "Calm down. Ignore their lies. Forget the rest of my grocery list. I'll make something else for the dinner."

"No, we'll go teach them a lesson. We rode out of town in plain sight." His clenched teeth and stern eyes signaled trouble. "We've done nothing wrong."

Apprehension strangled her. Tomorrow's headline might read, "Two Arrested during Food Lion Brawl."

Benjamin's demeanor became composed and dignified; however, a mischievous grin twitched his lips. "Can you follow my lead?"

He'd aroused her curiosity. She nodded as he snatched the cart and maneuvered it around the corner. Sarah dogged his heels.

"Excuse me, ladies," he said. "Could you tell me where to find cinnamon? Sarah needs it for her apple pie."

Sarah forced a straight face and locked her gaze on the gossiping friend who balanced a plump toddler on her hip.

The woman seemed to consider bolting. Instead, she plastered on a smile. "Try aisle three."

The child grinned and reached for Benjamin. If adults followed his example Benjamin might have a different mindset.

Benjamin ruffled the toddler's curly brown hair. "Cute kid. You must be proud."

Her smile became genuine. She planted a kiss on the boy's chubby cheek. "My grandson."

Sarah said, turning to Benjamin, "Oh, where are my manners? You know Mrs. Hardin. Emily and Thomas Pierce are neighbors. I doubt you've met them."

"Nice to meet you. I'm Benjamin Pruitt." He nodded a greeting. "It's good to see you, Mrs. Hardin. Will you and your husband be at dinner tomorrow?"

She lifted her double chin in the air as if speaking to them was beneath her. "If I make it through this mob. I think everyone in Statesville is here shopping for Thanksgiving."

The child offered Benjamin a half-eaten animal cracker.

"Thank you," Benjamin said, accepting the gift without hesitation. He popped the cracker in his mouth. Emily froze statue still with her mouth agape. Benjamin found a replacement cracker in the circus themed box the boy extended. "Look, a monkey."

He gave it to the boy who beamed a smile and laughed. Benjamin leaned closer and whispered in the child's ear, just loud enough for the women to hear. "When you're older, someone should tell you about see no evil, hear no evil, and speak no evil."

Sarah coughed and strangled on her words. "I'll look forward to your pumpkin pie, Emily."

"Sounds delicious," Benjamin said. "Good afternoon, ladies." He placed an arm around Sarah's shoulder, grabbed the cart, and sauntered down the aisle. "Let's see, aisle three would be on the left. What else is on your list?"

When they were out of earshot, Sarah clamped a hand over her mouth to stifle a laugh. "I can't believe you stood up to Mrs. Hardin that way. Emily almost croaked when she saw me. The looks on their faces were priceless."

Benjamin stuck out his tongue and made a gagging noise. "I hope the kid didn't have a cold. If I get sick will you take care of me?"

She linked arms with him. "You know I will."

Noah bounded up, throwing his arms around Benjamin's legs. "Grandpa! Can I have a cookie too?"

Benjamin hefted Noah and said, "Hi, buddy. I don't have any cookies."

"I saw you giving Thomas a cookie."

Becky rolled her cart into place behind theirs. "We were at the far end of the aisle. I made Noah wait until you finished talking."

"Mom said it isn't nice to erupt."

"You mean interrupt," Benjamin said. "The cookies belonged to Thomas. He shared with me."

"Are you going to be his Grandpa?" Noah's pouting lips and jealous tone made Sarah keenly aware of the bond between the pair; good thing Noah didn't see her as a threat.

Benjamin winked at Becky. "Are you worried I'll forget about you, Noah?"

Noah laid his head on Benjamin's shoulder. "I don't want to share you."

Benjamin hugged Noah closer. "I said hello to the boy and ate a cookie. It doesn't mean I love him more than you."

"He doesn't have a daddy or a grandpa. You might think he needs you more than me."

Sarah caught Benjamin's questioning look and mouthed, "Later."

Benjamin said, "It's crowded, and we need to finish shopping. Miss Sarah has an apple pie to make."

Noah leaned back in Benjamin's arms, his attitude brightening. "You're coming to dinner tomorrow?"

"Of course I am. You need to introduce me to all those people at church. Hmm, do you love more than one person there?"

"Sure."

"See, I can talk to Thomas and still love you."

Noah wrinkled his nose and frowned. "Maybe, but I don't want to share you with him."

"I understand. You're my very special boy." Benjamin asked Becky, "Does Noah deserve some animal crackers?"

"He's been good." She patted Noah's back.

"Then let's find a box and let Miss Sarah talk to your mom for a minute."

"Piggy back ride." Noah beamed.

"Want to plan a walk in the woods before it gets too cold?" Benjamin asked as they disappeared.

Later that afternoon, Benjamin unpacked groceries while Sarah measured flour for a piecrust. He twisted the lids open on jars before placing them in the refrigerator. Sarah seldom mentioned the simple tasks he performed anymore. Many household chores had become routines he performed to make her life more comfortable. Easy stuff, like fetching apples he'd picked and stored in the cellar or popping lids worked without hitches. Their riding excursion? A near disaster. He'd never intended to cause trouble between them or elicit suspicion in the community. At least she'd appreciated the horseback ride. She'd enjoyed his special location, but his misstep toward intimacy could have ruined everything between them.

Figuring out this dating stuff was too complicated. A simple kiss could be deadly or divine. Maybe he should simply tell her he loved her. If she tossed him out, he'd survive. Or would he?

He chose an apple from the basket, pulled the trashcan close to his chair, and watched the peeling spiral away from his knife. If only life would proceed so smoothly.

He glanced at her when she tapped a measuring spoon against the bowl. "Sarah, you said we'd talk about Emily and Thomas later. What's their story?"

Sarah dusted flour from her hands and joined him at the table. "I didn't want to talk where people could hear. I debated whether I should tell you. Considering Noah's reaction, and the fact Emily pulled you into this via her slander, you need to hear the truth. Karla, Emily's teenaged daughter, got pregnant several years ago. Karla tried drugs, alcohol—you name it. The boyfriend left town, but she got her life straightened out. She's back in high school. Emily is helping her raise Thomas."

"What about Emily's husband? Noah said there wasn't a grandpa." He sliced the apple he'd peeled and selected another.

"Emily's husband left right after Karla was born. They had a hard life. The community and our church stood by Emily after the divorce and later during Karla's rebellion and pregnancy. She considered adoption but decided to keep Thomas. The community has welcomed him."

"No wonder you looked so hurt when we overheard Emily dragging us through the mud."

"Mrs. Hardin is never a surprise. Emily's accusations hurt. I haven't talked to her much since I've been ill. I don't know if she's fallen in with Mrs. Hardin's crowd or if she simply joined the conversation at the store."

Benjamin set the knife aside and heaved a sigh. "I owe Emily an apology. What I did was mean spirited."

"You were honest. Maybe she won't be so quick to speak next time."

"Still, I'll tell her I'm sorry when I see her again. I'm sure she's endured her share of gossip during the years. My revenge doesn't seem so sweet since I know her story."

Sarah lowered her head and reached across the table to grasp Benjamin's hand. "You're right. I laughed because it felt good to get even. I'm no better than Mrs. Hardin."

"You are not anything like Mrs. Hardin. You just praised Emily and her daughter for proper actions under bad circumstances. She didn't bother to learn the truth about us or consider how her words could harm us. I needed to know the truth so I can act appropriately around them."

Sarah returned to the counter and selected several spice containers. "I hope Emily won't ignore me now."

"Will she show up at the meal after what happened today?"

Sarah paused and adopted a thoughtful look. "I think so."

"Could she use some free carpentry work around her place?"

"I'm sure she could."

"I'll have to find a way to make Noah understand I'm not replacing him with Thomas."

Sarah added spices to the apples Benjamin had sliced. "Maybe I can get the church youth group involved in a work project. If Noah thinks he's entertaining Thomas while people work it might help."

"That's a good idea. I am obviously under scrutiny as a single man in this community. I wouldn't want to create more gossip by being alone at Emily's house."

An hour later, the scent of cinnamon, nutmeg, and apples filled the kitchen when he lifted two steaming pies from the oven. Sarah's intricately laced pastry was a work of art. No wonder people asked her to bring apple pie for the Thanksgiving meal. Tempted to sample a wedge, he placed them on a cooling rack and crossed to the refrigerator. He'd stave off hunger with a glass of milk rather than mess up Sarah's plans for dinner when Ella returned from Wilkesboro. A missing slice of pie might not sit too well with Sarah today.

Benjamin entered the public sitting area where Sarah had fallen asleep on the couch. No doubt she was sore and tired after their horseback ride the previous day.

He lit the fire and tucked a quilt around Sarah. She stirred but didn't awaken. He sank into the adjacent recliner, but racing thoughts prevented napping.

His overly zealous mouth had gotten him into trouble. Promising a public appearance, making amends with a stranger, and now a community work project; he must be nuts. The thought of people staring at him made a cold chill slither down his spine. Perhaps he could coordinate some carpentry work and feign a reason to miss the community meal. No, he wouldn't disappoint Sarah and Noah by backing out. He was a man of his word even when fear told him to run.

Sarah's Bible seemed to call to him from the table. He flipped to Hebrews chapter four to read the verses Todd had discussed with him a few days ago. Benjamin silently read, "For we have not an high priest which cannot be touched with the feeling or our infirmities; but was in all points tempted like as we are, yet without sin. Let us therefore come boldly unto the throne of grace, that we may obtain mercy and find grace to help us in time of need."

He studied his shriveled arm and deformed hand. He could comprehend infirmities. How he'd managed to work as a carpenter with the disability amazed him. Establishing relationships plagued him more. Talk about a weakness. Since the accident, he considered himself a spineless, worthless man. Not dating material in anyone's book. Was his self-appraisal honest? Todd kept reminding him that weak areas caused people to rely on God for strength, but relying on anyone besides himself seldom worked.

Tempted? A long list, as well as some obvious sins, rolled through his head. His behavior in the woods yesterday, for example. If he and Sarah had acted on the inner stirrings created by his blunder ... fleeting satisfaction. Every aspect of their—dare he call it a relationship—would have changed.

Boldness didn't exist in his vocabulary. Anger, resentment, and fear better characterized life. Approaching God hadn't crossed his mind since childhood. To approach God without doubt, knowing God cared enough to hear and assist him, seemed beyond comprehension. Yet Todd said God wanted personal relationships where people talked freely with Him.

Todd had explained that a man's only access to God came through Jesus, the high priest mentioned in the verse. Benjamin had ignored that part of the discussion since he had no plans to bring God into his life.

The phrase "in time of need" seemed to jump off the page. If he'd ever been needy, it was now. He had to face the community and behave graciously. His stomach rolled, and his palms grew damp. He'd agreed to do the impossible.

The verse said to ask for help. God had never seemed useful before. Where was God on the day of the fire? Was it merciful to alter his life forever? Sarah would say God had held Benjamin in His loving arms providing protection and mercy. Death might have been more merciful.

Sarah murmured something in her sleep. He placed the Bible on his lap to observe her. This beautiful woman treated him as if he was the most handsome man alive. She had willingly kissed him yesterday. She'd experienced the same temptation.

He wasn't daft. He might sit here scoffing at the words he'd read, but they made perfect sense. Like it or not, God had to become a part of his life if he wanted Sarah's love and devotion.

Her words on the trail flitted across his mind. "Prayer got me back into a saddle. Don't look to me for courage to face the people of Love Valley."

He was in a dark, lonely valley of his own making. "I don't know anything about prayer. It's been years since I've spoken to You. I'm terrified about this dinner. I need help. Will You even consider listening to someone like me?"

CHAPTER SEVENTEEN

Benjamin lifted the picnic basket from the rear of Sarah's Subaru. His feet seemed too heavy, and his head throbbed. Sweat formed along his hairline. That didn't fit with the smoke curling from the chimney of the church fellowship hall on this chilly Thanksgiving night. He tightened his grip on the basket handle. Could he get out of this dinner date by feigning an excuse of illness? It wouldn't be far from the truth.

Sarah took the fisted hand he held at his side and stroked soft fingers across his knuckles. "You look exactly the way you did the moment we met."

He coaxed his hand to relax beneath her touch, but the thumping in his chest didn't calm. "Nervous would be an understatement. Terrified is a more appropriate word."

Sarah gave his hand a squeeze. "Your hands are freezing."

His hands might be cold, but his face blazed. He could imagine the red and white patches of scars practically glowing in the moonlight.

He let out a quavering breath and placed the basket back in the car. "Why can't I overcome this? You'd think after all these years I wouldn't care if people see a hideous creature when they look at me."

"Don't belittle yourself. I'm proud to be your date." Sarah's hand cradled his hot cheek.

He gave Sarah a little poke in the ribs. "You're just proud because you have a date."

She scrunched up her eyes and stuck out a defiant chin with a playful smirk above it. "That was low."

"What can I say? You asked for it." He forced a smile. "Will you tell people it's a date?"

She tucked her chin and kicked at the gravel with the toe of her shoe. He'd bet she was blushing, but the moonlight wasn't bright enough to tell. "If they ask. But it won't happen. They wouldn't be so bold."

"No. They'll just talk about us tomorrow."

Her hands flew to her hips, and she tossed her head back in a laugh. "Well, the man has figured out small town life."

Her laughter soothed. His jitters settled down a notch. If only he could learn to shake off hurtful comments with a laugh.

"Why, Sarah? Why, put yourself in a position where you know they'll talk?"

"I respect you. I want you to see that others can respect you too."

"You treat everyone with respect. Well, maybe not Mrs. Hardin."

She cuffed him lightly on the chin. "Watch it," she said. "Play nice. We're supposed to be making amends for our bad behavior."

"Ah, yesterday. I think I made promises beyond my ability."

Sarah sobered and ran a hand along his cheek. "Teasing doesn't help, does it? You're scared. To be honest, the changes in my life terrify me. I'm not practicing the things I say. I've told you only God can provide the courage and strength we need to face them."

He stared off into the darkness. He'd tried praying. It hadn't worked. If God had listened, then fear wouldn't weigh his feet down like mud-caked work boots. Thanksgiving Day wasn't the right time to dash Sarah's hopes that he could make peace with God.

He nodded toward the church building. "Will they be able to look beneath the scars, Sarah?"

"I want to believe they can. There's no way I can guarantee it. Look, we agreed to overcome a fear. I rode a horse. You need to face social situations."

"I don't need you to remind me that I'm a man with no backbone."

Her head snapped up and her eyes flashed disapproval. "I do not see you that way. If I said something to imply that, it's because I don't know how a man thinks and feels. It took guts and brawn to withstand the pain and the emotional ridicule you've faced. I don't want some macho-man. I value your kind heart and tenderness. It takes great courage to show love. Let them see the Benjamin I see. They'll like him."

Her arm slipped around his waist. Its warmth against his back felt safe and reassuring. With a gentle tug, he nestled her against him.

Expectation danced in her eyes. Trembling lips and her upturned face confirmed her mutual desire for a kiss.

Just before their lips met, a car door slammed in the next row. His head jerked up. He couldn't kiss her here. He had enough worries tonight. If someone saw them, Mrs. Hardin would tell the town they were necking in the church parking lot.

He cleared his throat, released her, and backed away. Joking to cover up his emotions seemed wrong, but sullying Sarah's reputation seemed worse. "Okay, you win. I'll be brave. Besides, it's your first official date in years. It's important to you."

She chuckled and shoved him. "You're a cad. Get moving before I decide to hang out with Ella and make you walk home in the cold."

"Sarah, about the kiss ... I'm sorry. It wasn't the right time—"

She touched two fingers to his lips. "Wrong place, wrong time." She extended her hand. "We should go."

Forcing air into his lungs, Benjamin picked up the basket. "Lead on."

So much for courage. They weren't ready for a real public display of affection, but he should be brave enough to tell her how he felt about her. He couldn't even admit he'd prayed for help. Hiding those things with jokes didn't make him braver. Might as well go act like the coward he was.

They crossed the expanse of gravel and stepped into the light on the breezeway. Then, Sarah hooked her arm through his. She glanced up into his face. Confidence radiated from her eyes.

Truth hit him like a two-by-four. God had heard and answered. Sarah stood beside him—courage in bodily form. Sarah, tolerating, even laughing, at his inane cracks because she understood he was too afraid to move. Ella, Pastor Morrison, and the Spangler family waited inside. None of them would see him as weak. When he accomplished this goal, they'd rejoice with him. Friends—a word he now used but needed to incorporate into his heart.

His feet grew lighter as Sarah walked in step beside him. The basket no longer seemed as heavy as a wheelbarrow loaded with bricks. A light breeze eased his burning cheeks.

Benjamin hesitated outside the entrance. The building hadn't intimidated him during those quiet days when only he had occupied it.

Sarah whispered in his ear. "Smiles and nods work unless they stick out a hand. If so, shake it with confidence."

Sarah flung the door open.

The babble of voices, punctuated by the high-pitched laughter of children, poured into the night. A few people milling around the food laden tables near the entrance turned to see who'd let in the cool breeze.

The door slammed. A graceful retreat was no longer an option.

Sarah's wink boosted his dose of courage. She swept him into the crowd with a smile on her face and a firm grip on his elbow.

A fire burned on the hearth. With the body heat in the packed room, it only added ambiance. A touch of pride rose in Benjamin's chest. He'd repaired the stone chimney and hearth to make them useable. The dark, smooth wood of the mantel he'd added gleamed in the firelight.

Sarah leaned close so Benjamin could hear above the racket. "We'll take the green beans to the veggie table."

He spotted Ella on the far side of the room. Near the desserts of course.

As they wove among folks he'd seen uptown, the proprietors of campgrounds and stores smiled or murmured polite greetings. A few awkward stares flitted over unfamiliar faces. He chose to ignore them.

The saloon owner gave him a friendly slap on the back. "Thanks for your help with Fairmont. The man spoiled two concerts. Glad he won't be back."

"No problem," Benjamin replied.

The blacksmith bumped against Benjamin. "Hey, you're the guy who came by with Todd. How's his horse?"

"Better. New shoe helped."

"Glad to hear it. Come chat sometime."

A woman he'd never seen grabbed his arm. "The fireplace and new kitchen are beautiful."

"Thank you." Feeble words, but they must have worked. She scurried off toward the beverages.

Benjamin wasn't so inclined to flee by the time they reached Ella. "Welcomed" might eventually weasel into his description of the night.

Ella linked arms with him. "Careful. Don't make your date jealous."

"Hi, friend." He grinned down at Ella's smiling face. "They don't know Sarah's my date."

"Don't kid yourself. How often do you think she's ambled into a town dinner on the arm of a man?"

He grimaced. "Never?"

"You guessed that one right."

Ella led him to the fireplace while Sarah chatted with women who shuffled around cakes and pies to make room for hers. Ella fingered the rough-hewn stones. "The stonework is excellent, and the mantel blends perfectly with the new kitchen cabinets."

"This was easy. Tearing out the termite damage in the heat was the chore."

"They've said as much." She gestured toward the people. "Don't think your efforts went unnoticed."

The clink of metal against a glass hushed the jabbering. "Find a seat, please. We'll get started." Pastor Morrison adjusted the microphone at the far end of the dining room.

Benjamin and Ella joined the Spanglers and Sarah at their table. Sarah's thank you smile, when he held the chair to seat her, added to the warmth of the room.

Noah climbed into his lap, smelling like an odd combination of soap and freshly baked yeast rolls. "I prayed you would come, Grandpa." Noah settled in and rested his cheek against Benjamin's chest.

Pastor Morrison said, "Andy and Ellenora Barker founded this town and welcomed us as family. We're thankful for their generosity." He shifted his stance to address the couple. "We're glad God blessed you with long lives."

Noah's belly growled, making him giggle. Benjamin clamped a hand over the boy's mouth and coughed to avoid laughing. If the Pastor spoke much longer, Benjamin's stomach might join the chorus.

Pastor Morrison said, "We are honored to have Benjamin Pruitt as our guest tonight."

Benjamin's heart thudded. He stiffened. All eyes turned toward him. No chance to slink away and hide.

"Without Benjamin's hard work, we wouldn't be enjoying this larger room, fancy kitchen, and new fireplace. The sanctuary would be termite dust. Our congregation and community extend thanks and a heartfelt welcome."

Did they expect a response? His mouth was too dry to form words. He trembled as he forced himself to look at the audience.

Applause on his behalf? No way.

Noah lifted his head from Benjamin's chest to plant a kiss on his cheek. Why did the child have to call attention to his scars? "They're clapping, Grandpa. They love you too."

Sarah grasped Benjamin's hand under the table and whispered, "Just smile and nod."

The rest of the pastor's words became a blur. Pastor Morrison must have blessed the food at some point since Noah climbed down and skipped off toward the food tables with Becky.

Sarah captured Benjamin's attention. "Let's get in line. I'm starving."

He searched the faces around him. Smiling citizens carried heaping plates. Laughter rippled around the room. These people had applauded him. Unbelievable.

Then he spied Mrs. Hardin and her cohorts whispering up a conspiracy near the beverages. Planning some rumor about him and Sarah, most likely. He swallowed over the lump in his throat. Had she seen them in the parking lot? No, she'd been inside. Just insecurity kicking in.

Mrs. Hardin must have felt his gaze on her. She paused in mid-sentence and looked him in the eye. Benjamin's heart fell to his stomach. Her fingers twitched a tiny wave but those treacherous lips remained fixed in their permanent scowl. No such thing as a lasting truce; Mrs. Hardin carried a snake up her sleeve.

Emily and Thomas sat near the middle of the room with a lovely raven-haired teen. No doubt her daughter, Karla. Since they weren't with Mrs. Hardin, he might find the nerve to apologize.

Sarah grabbed his arm. "Benjamin! I've been talking to you. Are you okay?" She touched the back of her hand to his forehead. "You're pale and cold."

"I'm trying to convince my body to move from terrified to nervous."

A grin twitched her perfect lips. Little lines crinkled around her eyes. Golden strands in her hair gleamed in the firelight. Did someone so lovely actually care about him? Could he ever meet her expectations?

She slipped her arm through his. "Relax. Can you follow my lead?"

"Those words got us in trouble yesterday."

"Not tonight. You're among friends."

He reluctantly rose to follow her, keeping a hand lightly on her elbow.

"Remember, I'm proud of you." They took their place at the end of the line. Hands grabbed him. Friendly backslaps ... handshakes ... thank you ... so glad you came. His head spun. Dread surged up into his throat choking off words.

The crowd swept him forward. Sarah slipped from his grasp. He twisted, reaching for her arm. Gone. Caught in the surge of hungry people he became as helpless as a stick caught in a swift mountain stream. Desperate, but unable to escape, he gave in to the flow.

Near the sweet potatoes a "You're welcome" croaked from his throat. "Thank you," squeaked out when a woman forked turkey onto his plate. By the time someone handed him a glass of sweet iced tea, a little smile surfaced.

Unharmed and carrying a mound of food on his plate, he

headed toward his seat. A man he'd seen at the hardware store tugged his sleeve and said, "Come sit with us if you'd like."

Benjamin nodded and smiled. At least that part came readily. "No, thank you. Sarah and some other friends saved me a seat." Social niceties might not be so hard after all.

The song "Some Enchanted Evening" popped into his head as he scanned the room for Sarah. He heard her laughter and headed in that direction with the song rolling through his mind.

He found her, rooted to the spot where they'd parted. Sarah's gaze reached out to him and captured something deep inside his soul. A radiant smile; tears brimmed in her eyes—no need to ask. He understood.

CHAPTER EIGHTEEN

Arthritis plus aging equaled pain when cold December rain stalled in the distant mountains. Hot chocolate and a warm bed sounded good. Both would have to wait until they completed repairs on Emily's house.

Surprising how apologies for mutual offenses fostered quick reconciliation. With that accomplished, they'd met with Emily to plan repairs and scheduled a workday. The youth group became enthusiastic once Sarah offered Mosey Inn's sitting area and media room for their Christmas party.

Sarah crossed Emily's yard to sit in the sunny spot on the tailgate of Benjamin's truck. The sun warmed her face, but a brisk wind chilled her bones. She wrapped her coat around her knees. A gust of wind sent discarded shingles flying toward the woodshed.

The bank of clouds rolling in from the west stole her feeble spot of sunshine. Sarah shoved her hands deeper into her pockets and slid left to catch the remaining rays. The weatherman said rain on Monday. Sarah's joints preferred Sunday, since she normally improved once the barometer stopped fluctuating. Thank God for medicines. They'd made a huge difference. Not long ago, agony would have prevented her assistance today.

Another blast of wind almost sent her running to the house. No, she wasn't ready to face the boys again. Besides, as the project organizer she should observe the group's progress a bit longer.

Building chair-and-quilt houses with two rowdy boys hadn't helped her. In retrospect, sitting on the floor beneath their makeshift dwellings begged for trouble, but she'd laughed until her face hurt. Her assignment on the work crew gave Karla the freedom to empty the kitchen cabinets in preparation for a fresh coat of sea blue paint—a task that would fall on Emily and Karla later in the day.

Sarah watched Benjamin moving among their crew and marveled at God's timing. The encounter in the Food Lion set Benjamin on a path to build friendships and overcome his inferiority. It allowed him to use his training to help not only Emily and Karla but also other church members who would acquire carpentry and maintenance skills today.

Benjamin tightened screws on the sagging screen door hinge. At a nearby window, Todd squeezed fresh caulking around new panes of glass. Pastor Morrison wielded a hammer like a pro as he pounded nails into new siding. Other church members scrambled around the roof replacing loose or missing shingles. Becky helped the youth group stroke white paint on weathered porch railings.

In August, Sarah would have considered it impossible that Benjamin's mellow laugh would ever mingle with the hoots and groans of the church youth. Today, Benjamin jested and roughhoused with the younger crowd as if it were a common occurrence.

A dose of God's love, via His people, had certainly fostered changes in Benjamin's life. Since Thanksgiving, Benjamin had attended church services twice—a huge accomplishment, in her opinion. The terror he battled on Thanksgiving seemed to have abated. Sarah prayed absolute acceptance by her friends would melt all the ice around his heart.

Focusing on Emily's needs brought her a special kind of joy too. Sarah had spent too many years cooped up in her house, missing this part of life. Sure, she'd concentrated on her mother's needs. Doing this felt different ... exciting ... joyful. Surely, others needed repairs or other forms of assistance she and this group could provide.

Karla appeared in the doorway, wearing Thomas on her hip. "Mom called. The food is ready when you want to take a break." The screen door creaked before it slammed. Sarah added oiling the hinges to her mental list.

Work ceased at the mention of food. The teens rinsed paintbrushes under the outside faucet and tossed them in a bucket. The young people piled into the bed of the pastor's truck amidst whoops and shouts about lunch. Dust kicked up behind the wheels when Pastor Morrison rounded the corner on the dirt road leading toward the church.

Benjamin joined Sarah on her perch. "How you holding up?"

"Not bad. A little achy, but I'll make it."

"I shouldn't have taken you riding."

She shook her head. "It wasn't the ride or anything since then. It's simply part of my illness. Some days are worse than others." She inclined her head toward the storm clouds. "Blame the weather today."

"You should go home and rest since there's a practice for the children's Christmas program tonight."

"I'll rest after lunch. Karla's finished cleaning so she can watch Thomas and Noah. Not much more I can do here."

The screen door banged. Noah stalked across the yard, arms crossed, his lips stuck out in a pout. "It's not fair," he yelled over his shoulder.

Becky intercepted Noah near the truck. "Watch your tone young man. What's going on?"

"Karla says I can't help you. I have to play with the kid."

"She's right. Your job is to keep Thomas inside so he isn't in danger."

Noah huffed and stomped his foot. "Thomas is a baby. Let Karla watch him. I'm a big boy. I want to help Grandpa."

Benjamin sighed and lifted Noah onto the tailgate. A warning stare at Becky seemed to say he'd try to handle this the easy way. He wrapped Noah in a hug. "We need to get these repairs done before rain comes. I promised you a day in the woods when the work is finished."

"It'll be raining or too cold by then." Noah jerked away from Benjamin.

"There are plenty of nice days during December. I'll keep my promise, Noah. Thomas needs you to teach him big boy stuff."

"I'd rather help you and Daddy."

Becky threw her brush in the bucket of water. "Enough. Stop arguing, Noah." Her hands grasped his shoulders. "I expect you to cooperate. Emily and Karla need help fixing their house. If you can't handle your part then I'll take you home for a nap."

"I don't need a nap. Big boys don't nap."

"Then act like a big boy." Becky took his hand. "Jump down so we can go to the church. I'm hungry."

"I still say it's not fair." He hit the ground running.

Becky clenched her teeth and let out a low growl. "Some days he drives me crazy."

Benjamin said, "You're a good mother. He's tired and a bit jealous. I haven't spent much time with him lately."

"I hope that's all this is. He's usually a sweet kid." She hustled around the truck to catch up with Noah.

The remaining workers tumbled into a vehicle across the yard. Todd crossed the expanse of dried grass and wrapped his arms around Becky. "Our crew's heading out unless you need help with Noah."

"I can handle him." She rubbed a smudge of caulking from Todd's cheek and kissed him.

"Are you sure? I don't like it when he spouts off at you."

"Go on. He's hungry and tired. We're right behind you."

Todd stuck his head in Becky's car window. "Behave, young man. I can take away your pony riding privileges. Remember, Mom's in charge."

Noah stuck out his lower lip. Rebellion smoldered in his normally playful eyes.

Todd retraced his steps, waved goodbye, and joined the car full of roofers.

Food called Sarah's gnawing stomach. If Noah's tummy felt like hers, no wonder he was grouchy. Was it her imagination or did the scent of hotdogs and hamburgers waft from the church across the valley?

Karla settled Thomas in his car seat and adjusted the straps. "Thanks for the ride, Becky. I hope Thomas takes a long nap after lunch. He's worn out."

Noah fumbled with his seat belt. When Becky reached in to help, Noah snarled, "I can do it." With a sneering grin, he buckled it. "See!"

"You are asking for it." Becky slammed the door then rested her hand on the roof. "Sorry folks, I'm not setting a good example of motherhood today."

Karla said, "Sounds pretty normal to me. My mom would have tanned my backside." She gasped and several fingers covered her mouth. "Just saying."

Becky shook her head and groaned. "You're not out of line. I'm considering it."

As a Sunday school teacher, Sarah knew a change in circumstances didn't always sit well with children. "He'll be better come Monday. He's used to your full attention. Maybe we all need a nap after lunch."

Becky cranked the engine. "Sounds great to me. See you two at church."

Once Becky's car disappeared around the corner, Benjamin stood. He faced Sarah, resting his hands lightly on her thighs. "Sure you don't want to go home? I saw you limping."

"Nope. Emily and other church women worked hard making lunch. I need to make an appearance. You can drop me off on your way back."

Benjamin circled his hands around her waist to lift her from the tailgate. He engulfed her in an embrace after setting her on her feet. The smell of sawdust and paint, with a hint of aftershave, quickened her heart. His kiss weakened her aching joints.

He eased away from her lips but didn't release her. A slow grin spread across his face. She could get lost in those dark eyes that expressed words and emotions he wasn't bold enough to speak. Sarah didn't think her heart could beat any faster, but it did.

Was she foolish to act like a giddy teenager? Each day, and every kiss, took them into a deeper relationship. How would she reply if Benjamin said he loved her? Could she truthfully say she loved him too? They weren't kids who could call it quits and move on to another person next week. Marriage became an option as she saw Benjamin growing. Marriage ... the idea of such a drastic change in their status added confusion, and more than a hint of fear.

To avoid another kiss she turned her head to survey the work the crew had completed. "They've done a great job this morning."

"I'd say we made good progress." A sigh, and the slant of his lips, said he didn't want the change of subject.

Bringing up the topic of a future together wasn't the woman's role in a relationship. At least that's what Sarah had always believed. Maybe this attraction stemmed from her years without companionship. Dating had advantages, at least for now. Eventually Benjamin would broach the bigger subject. If not, did she have the courage to bring marriage, and all the complications it would foster, into a discussion? Not today. Maybe never.

She stepped out of his arms and moved toward the truck door. "They're waiting. People might talk if we stay too long."

His eyes lost their glow. "Right. Wouldn't want gossip, would we?"

༄ ༰ ༃

The sudden flash of overhead lights jerked Sarah awake. The stack of envelopes at her elbow scattered across the floor. Struggling to reorient, she blinked against the glare and focused on Ella. "You surprised me. I can't believe I fell asleep at my desk." Sarah rubbed the kink in her neck.

Ella nodded at the tray she carried. "I thought you could use some dinner. Daybed, desk, or recliner?"

Sarah rubbed sleep from her eyes. "Dinner? What time is it?"

Ella selected the daybed. Balancing the tray, she sat. "Six."

Sarah's heart bolted. "No! My four-o-clock guests." She jumped up and fumbled with the alarm clock on the bedside table. "I can't believe I slept through the alarm. I set it so I wouldn't lose track of time."

"Whoa, take it easy. I turned off your alarm. They settled into

Pine Tree and headed out for the evening."

Sarah glared at Ella then strode to the closet. "Ella! You let me sleep too long. I don't have time to eat. I need to be at the church by six-thirty."

"Nope. I saw you limping in after lunch. No practice for you tonight. Is your knee swollen?"

"Just aching. I can't stay home. Becky can't—"

Ella held up a hand to silence her. "Becky went to the church to prepare while the crews finished at Emily's house. Benjamin called about three to check on you. And don't ask, I turned your phone off too."

Sarah stomped to the desk and flipped the phone back on. "I had bills to pay. Now I'll have to stay up late. Wake me next time."

"As I was saying, Noah and Thomas fell asleep in some tent they made. Benjamin said you needed the rest. He's taking the boys over to the church and plans to help Becky with practice."

Sarah's jaw dropped, and her eyebrows jerked up. "Benjamin?"

"You heard right. I say it's a good thing. Let him stretch his wings a bit."

Ella patted the seat beside her. "Pick your jaw up off the floor and sit."

When Sarah sank to the daybed, Ella eased the tray onto her lap. Sarah lifted the water glass and took a sip. "Benjamin actually said he was going to the practice?"

"Yep, he seemed worried about you. Must think you're pushing too hard." Ella lowered her voice to a whisper. "I happen to agree."

"I've been doing well. The weather is the problem."

"Uh-huh, not to mention riding a horse, making meals, organizing a work crew, running this inn, planning programs and Christmas parties, and herding two boys this morning."

She didn't need to hear Ella tick off a list of her over-commitments. The consequences already throbbed through her body. Sarah compressed her lips, trying to check the mounting agitation. Benjamin and Ella would not control her activities. "I'll slow down after Christmas."

Sarah forked a chunk of chicken into her mouth and washed it down with a gulp of water. Indigestion might add to her misery, but she wouldn't be late for the practice.

Ella arranged pillows, kicked off her shoes, and settled into a comfortable position against the railing. "Don't eat so fast. You'll choke. You are not going to church tonight."

"Becky needs me. We planned this program. Benjamin doesn't know these songs. The children don't know him either."

"We've prayed Benjamin would change his attitude toward God. After two Sundays at church he's ready to handle the questions and stares of inquisitive children."

"I'm not so sure. He's making progress, but he hasn't been there without me."

"Sounded like he was ready to go without you tonight. Besides, you're forgetting Noah and Becky will be there."

"If I don't go support him—"

"You might as well tell Benjamin he's a useless coward. You've done the job God gave you. Get out of God's way."

Ella's words stung worse than a slap in the face. Sarah paused, her fork in midair. "That was harsh and unfounded." She'd invested energy and time into helping Benjamin. Was Ella suggesting she remove herself from Benjamin's life? "I thought we'd agreed I was part of God's plan. Benjamin needs me." A sense of loss rose in her heart. Uncertainty stirred a mixture of grief and dread. "Doesn't he?"

"He needs Sarah Campbell—not her control. God knows more about what Benjamin needs than you do." Ella leaned forward to place a hand on Sarah's shoulder. "Sweetheart, we all want to control our lives and the lives of those we love. You've done that most of your life. You thought you had to do it. Tell me, would God have taken care of your mom if you hadn't been around?"

Anger clouded Sarah's mind, and confusion followed close behind. "My answer should be yes." Sarah chucked the tray onto the floor, rattling dishes. She shook a finger at Ella. "I don't like where this is going. You're suggesting I did things my own way, not God's way."

"Turning it over to God isn't easy, Sarah."

Sarah moved back from her perch on the edge of the daybed to slump against the quilt-covered rail. "Nurturing is a gift from God. I used it to handle a difficult situation. God placed me in a position where I had to take charge of Mosey Inn, care for everyone, and ignore my own plans."

"Benjamin is not here to take your mother's place."

Ella's soft, gentle tone didn't ease the shock. Indignation churned Sarah's gut. Fists clenched the quilt beneath her. "Take her place? You make me sound like some sort of mental case. Do you think I can't exist without mothering someone? I have a life. Mother wasn't my total existence."

"Are you sure?"

The question hit like another blow. Had she forgotten how to live outside the realm of caregiver? Sarah chewed on a fingernail and forced a calming breath. Too much truth at once cut deep trenches into her soul.

Looking back, every aspect of her life had centered on her mother's care. A simple trip to the store required arrangements for her mom or an arduous day if she took her along. Cleaning, cooking, even taking a shower—every detail revolved around her mother. She'd told Benjamin her mother became her child. Pain tore across her heart. Ella was right. With her mother's death, Sarah faced an empty nest. Had she tried to fill it with Benjamin?

"I'm sorry I yelled." Fighting tears, Sarah's lips trembled. "Life did center on Mother. Maybe I can't live without taking care of someone. It seems odd I never saw the blatant truth before now."

She couldn't meet Ella's tender gaze, but she needed comfort. Sarah curled up into a ball and laid her head in Ella's lap. Anguish and loss flowed out with her tears. "Never alone. Always lonely," she choked out between sobs.

Reassuring fingers combed through Sarah's hair. "People can be lonely even when they're surrounded by a crowd. Adjusting to a totally different way of life takes time."

Gradually, Sarah's sobs lessened. "I miss Mom and Dad so much; but I have to admit, I enjoy the freedom it's given me."

"And then Benjamin comes along needing TLC and nurture."

"You're wrong about him replacing Mom. I gave him friendship and loving concern because he needed someone to listen and be his friend."

"Has that relationship changed?"

Sarah sat and stared at the hands she folded in her lap. Confession time. "I think I've crossed the line between friendship and love. We haven't talked about it, but I think he has too."

"I thought so. I'm not suggesting there's anything wrong with it. You're never too old to find love."

"Then why this talk about getting out of the way?"

"I'm speaking figuratively. Both of you need to follow God's plan. Benjamin needs spiritual maturity ... a deep personal relationship with Christ. Don't smother him."

"We're enjoying outings and conversations. Since I'm confessing, we've shared some intimate kisses. I think the term is dating."

"Benjamin has never invited a woman to get so close. Like you, loneliness is all he's known. He has friends now. His focus is on others, not himself."

"Those are good things. How am I hindering his spiritual progress?"

"Think about the custom of binding women's feet. What happened?"

"It deformed their feet and hampered walking."

"So it goes with the lives of men and women. You've helped Benjamin find the right path. As a fixer and caregiver, it would be easy for you to bind him too tightly. You want him to depend on God, not you."

"I'm afraid it would break my heart to let him go now."

"It was a chance you were willing to take. If it happens, you'll deal with the loss. Give Benjamin some time and space. I doubt that'll be the outcome."

"Should we stop dating?"

"No. Benjamin would see that as rejection."

"Ella, is he going to church to please me?"

"It's a question you should consider."

CHAPTER NINETEEN

Sarah turned the gas on under the eggs. She flipped on the porch light to check the thermometer. Ice crystals shimmered on the kitchen windowpane. Thirty-five degrees at seven thirty. Mist hung over the gnarled trees in the orchard. The sky wouldn't lighten much. The forecasted winter mix of snow, sleet, and rain might arrive if the temperature held all day. Cold air seeped under the back door. She wedged a towel along the crack and wrote a note to ask Benjamin about weather stripping.

Sarah sat, elbows on the table, and sipped her coffee while waiting for the eggs to boil. She had constantly griped about the weekend-long rest Ella and Benjamin enforced. Having less pain this morning made her thankful they'd insisted she obey. She should learn to listen to her body's needs. An apology and an expression of thanks were probably due.

Helping Emily and Karla decorate the inn for the youth party would be easier without aching joints. Sarah hadn't chosen to abdicate the decorating, but Emily insisted they help as payment for the house repairs. They would come this afternoon after school if bad weather held off.

Emily and Karla would not handle her cherished mementos. She would spend the morning separating those from the decorations used around the inn. Tomorrow, she'd decorate her private quarters. If Benjamin and Ella wanted to decorate their rooms, she had plenty for them.

It seemed pointless to decorate the guest rooms. Her two guests had ridden the trails and departed on Sunday. After they'd left, Sarah closed the heating vents in the vacant rooms—no sense wasting money. They'd remain empty for the next two weeks, unless a miracle occurred. Only two couples were booked for the town's New Year's Eve party. Barely enough money to buy groceries.

Bills still waited on her desk. All she had to do was decide which held priority. Medications and therapy had eaten most of the reserve cash. Would this be her final year at Mosey Inn? She couldn't think about it—too depressing this close to Christmas.

Her desire to travel the world didn't seem so wonderful today.

She should enjoy the festive spirit of Christmas. On Sunday afternoon, Benjamin had hauled boxes of decorations from the storage shed. Sarah obediently lounged on the couch and supervised their placement in appropriate locations around the inn.

Her two handlers had permitted church attendance, and then imposed their restrictions again. She'd guardedly observed Benjamin during the service. His mellow baritone sounded sincere when he joined the congregational singing. It occurred to her, as the timer dinged for the eggs, that he knew the tunes. That indicated more than a passive church-going background. He'd been attentive during the sermon and followed along in a Bible he brought with him. Was it his or had it come from the library?

She couldn't shake the question about his motives. She wanted to believe Benjamin went to church to worship. She wasn't usually a bad judge of character. If he'd stood beside her, simply to please her, the man was a magnificent con artist. He couldn't have pulled it off back in August ... unless his whole life was an act. That didn't seem plausible.

She should back off and see how things progressed. Right. Tell her wildly vacillating heart to obey. Why had love hit her so late in life? It must be love, or she wouldn't care what he did. He certainly was not a project she'd acquired to replace her mother. She'd at least decided that much since Ella confronted her with the terrible possibility.

"Morning." Benjamin's cheery voice echoed in the empty dining room.

"Coffee's in here." She moved to the counter to pour him a cup. "Eggs are done. Want one?"

He came up behind her and wrapped warm arms around her waist. "I'd prefer a kiss first."

Her mood brightened. She twisted around to face him and placed her arms around his neck.

He bent his head to cover her lips. "You taste like coffee."

"There are better ways to obtain your caffeine quota for the day."

A smile curled the corner of his lip. "Maybe, but I could get used to having my first taste this way every morning."

The kitchen door swung open. "Okay, you two. Stop necking in the kitchen."

Sarah dropped her hands and cleared her throat. "Morning, Ella."

"Trying to heat this place that way won't work. It's freezing in here."

Sarah squirmed, but Benjamin kept her pinned against the cabinet. His strong arms barred her escape to either side. He grinned down at her, unperturbed by Ella's presence.

"There's a crack under the kitchen door." Sarah fished behind her with one hand to retrieve the paper, which she waved at Ella. "I was showing Benjamin a note I wrote so he could check on it."

"After the appetizer or the dessert?"

Ella poured a cup of coffee and winked. "I'll sit beside the fire. Don't mind me. Carry on." The door squeaked, signaling Ella's departure.

Sarah swatted Benjamin on the chest. "It would have been less awkward if you'd allowed me to move."

"She caught us. I figured there wasn't any reason to pretend."

A quick peck on her cheek ended the encounter. He backed away. Why couldn't she admit what she felt? Moments ago, she'd questioned his motives. She'd just welcomed his embrace. It had to be love. This was not normal behavior.

Benjamin squatted in front of the door to check out the source of the draft. "Needs weather stripping. I have an errand to run. I'll pick it up while I'm out."

Sarah asked, "Could you get some groceries while you're in Statesville?"

"Sure, make a list. I'll be in the sitting room. I want to read over that passage pastor Morrison read in church last night. It prompted some questions."

"Mind if I join you?"

"Of course not. Reading the Bible with you sounds like a great way to begin the day."

It certainly sounded better than the questions she'd pondered earlier. She took her plate and followed him to a warmer spot on the couch.

By ten, Sarah had sorted several boxes of dusty Christmas decorations. Christmas music played. Tiny white lights twinkled against the green fir tree.

She and Benjamin had borrowed Todd's horses and ridden to the top of the ridge in search of the perfect tree. Today it would receive its complement of handmade and store bought ornaments if Sarah could keep the tears at bay long enough to select them.

She stretched and glanced up from her work to check the weather. The dull gray sky didn't help her melancholy. Snow might bring out her holiday spirit.

Sarah reached into the ornament box. Her childhood handprint, painted red and green, and dusted with glitter, set off a bout of tears. Why cry over a silly third grade art project? She'd given it to her father for Christmas, and it graced their tree every year. Each object seemed a reminder of the days and loved ones she'd lost. Nostalgia tugged at her emotions.

She couldn't go back to those days when her mother was normal and they were a happy family. Grief. Was sorting through the remnants of old Christmas memories part of the process Ella suggested she needed? Perhaps. Stepping out in a new direction took courage. Could she sell Mosey Inn, close the book on that phase of her life, and embark on a new adventure?

The jangle of the phone broke her reverie. She picked up the portable in the sitting area. "Mosey Inn."

Becky's frantic outburst sparked fear. "Is Noah there with Benjamin?"

"No. Benjamin left around nine thirty. Why would you think Noah was here? What's wrong, Becky?"

"I can't find Noah! I was hoping..." Gasping sobs consumed several seconds. "Benjamin was my last hope."

"Are you sure Noah hasn't gone somewhere with Todd? Maybe he's in the barn."

"I'm with the group decorating the church. Todd's at home. Noah was playing on the breezeway. He's gone! We've looked everywhere, we've called him—"

"Hang on. Ella needs to hear this." Covering the phone, Sarah yelled, "Ella, come down. Now."

Ella's door slammed. Sarah met her at the bottom of the stairs. She thrust the phone at Ella. "Noah's missing."

Ella's eyes widened, and her breathing quickened. Ella didn't wait to hear the story. "Becky, call the sheriff. Stop searching. You'll ruin any tracks Noah might have left."

A millisecond of pause to listen. "No. Becky, listen. Do exactly what I said. We're on our way."

༒ ❈ ༓

Sarah and Ella trudged up the hill from the rodeo arena to the church. Ella's stream of phone conversations during their ride from Mosey Inn opened Sarah's eyes to Ella's world. For the first time Sarah truly understood Ella. Noah was missing—not an unknown face on a milk carton. For Ella, those faces were just as real. They had families, expectations, and value. They compelled her to look long after others gave up. Today, that knowledge brought an odd sense of peace.

Sarah paused to catch her breath and look across the valley behind her. In a matter of minutes, dog handlers, the sheriff, deputies, search teams, emergency medical services—the list seemed endless—would converge in the arena parking area.

Ella relayed data to the sheriff with authority and skills Sarah envied. "Yeah, I asked the pastor to secure the immediate scene and keep witnesses there. Beth and Charlie Nance blocked off the roads leading to the church ... Right. They handle the rodeo arena. She's the town manager. I'm praying we preserved some tracks people didn't destroy in the initial panic. Beth and Charlie will route incoming traffic to rendezvous at the arena. I can talk to the parents while you look at the physical evidence around the church."

Ella paused at the top of the stone steps. "Hang on, Sheriff." She covered the phone with a hand. "Don't walk across the grass, Sarah." Ella waved at the pastor who stood on the breezeway between the fellowship area and the sanctuary. "Stay there. We'll be over in a second, Pastor. I'm talking with the sheriff."

Sarah glanced at the sky and prayed for Noah's safety. Threatening clouds hung low on the hills. Rain, snow, or sleet seemed inevitable. The temperature hadn't risen since daybreak. The damp air carried a bite. She draped the edge of her scarf across her face and turned her back to the wind. Did Noah have a coat, hat, or gloves?

"Sorry, Sheriff. I'm back." Ella paused, listening. "Ten minutes? Good. The search and rescue volunteers should arrive about that time too. The woman who helped with our search back in August agreed to bring her dog."

Sarah scanned the churchyard. A red plastic pail and a yellow toy dump truck lay beneath the magnolia tree. Seedpods spilled from the discarded toys. Sarah could imagine Noah driving the truck around the lawn, collecting fallen magnolia pods and dumping them into the bucket. She half expected him to bounce across the lawn to greet her.

"The Silver Spur will make a good command post ... yes, we'll need radios. I'll have Charlie send people up to the Spur for team assignments. Beth can arrange transportation to and from the search area. The kid left some toys in the churchyard. Want me to ask the mom what kind of shoes he has on and scout the area for tracks? ... No. I won't compromise your scene. You know me better than that."

A cruiser sped into the arena parking area, lights flashing, and siren blaring. "One of your deputies just arrived. I'll have a look at the front lawn while you radio him the plans ... Good, see you soon."

Ella fastened the special satellite phone she used during searches onto its belt clip. "Pastor," she called across the expanse of damp brown grass. "Could you ask Becky what kind of shoes Noah is wearing? I'll look for tracks before we walk across the yard."

Pastor Morrison said, "Be right back."

Sarah nodded toward the toys. "Noah was playing here today."

Pastor Morrison returned. "Cowboy boots with pointed toes. Becky saw him under the magnolia about nine-fifteen."

Sarah checked the time. Ten-thirty. Becky called the inn shortly after ten. How long had it been since someone saw Noah?

Ella said, "Walk in my tracks, Sarah. Look for boot prints leading away from the tree. Don't touch anything."

Sarah stepped in Ella's boot tracks and scanned the ground. She said, "The grass is matted down near the toys."

"Yep, see his knee prints and wheel tracks?"

"He drove the truck in the damp grass picking up pods." Sarah pointed. "Look! Is this a boot print in the dirt?"

Ella squatted to examine the depression. "Yeah. He stopped his playing and faced the church." She glanced toward the building. Stooping, Ella moved a few feet up the hill toward the church. "His tracks lead toward the building. He's still collecting pods." She tapped her chin and studied the yard. "Where did you go when you got tired of this, Noah?"

Ella and Sarah searched the front lawn a few minutes and found more footprints close to the breezeway connecting the two buildings. Ella said, "I'd say he came up to the church at some point." She scanned the gravel near them. "He may have gone into the parking area. Let's talk to the people and find out when they last saw him. Knowing when and where will help."

Inside, the fire invited them over. Huddled around a table, Pastor Morrison and a group of church members spoke in whispers. Sarah and Ella acknowledged them and headed toward the fireplace where Becky and Todd sat knee to knee with their foreheads together.

Todd's head came up as they approached. "Ella, I'm so glad you're around to help."

Becky's red-rimmed eyes searched their faces. "What is taking so long? If you had let us search, we might have found him by now."

Ella pulled a chair beside Becky and sat. "I didn't mean to sound harsh on the phone. There's a proper way to search. Untrained people walking around can destroy footprints and interfere with Noah's scent trail."

"But Noah can't be far away. The longer we wait—"

Ella placed an arm around Becky's shoulder. "He knows to stay put if he's lost. Benjamin and I taught him what to do. Remember? Noah probably left us a trail to follow."

Becky nodded and brushed away tears. "Will he remember? I mean," she shrugged, "a game is one thing, reality is..."

Todd hugged Becky. "He's a Love Valley kid. He's grown up riding the trails." Todd's little smile didn't hide the fear in his eyes. "Ella, I brought his pillowcase. Handled it like you said." He nodded toward a plastic bag on a nearby table.

"Thanks, Todd. That's perfect. Our search dog should be here soon. Now," she leaned forward, forcing Becky to make eye contact, "so you understand what's happening, the sheriff's deputies are setting up a command post at the Silver Spur. They'll send search teams out soon."

Todd placed a hand on Becky's bouncing leg. "We need to let the experts handle this, hon."

"I'm so afraid I'll never see him again." Sobs overtook her. She covered her face and leaned into Sarah's arms. "Oh, Sarah. He's my baby. I can't believe I let this happen."

Sarah wiped Becky's tears with a tissue she pulled from a box on the table. "This is not your fault."

"I never imagined Noah needing to use the skills Benjamin and Ella taught him. It's going to snow. He'll freeze."

Ella placed a calming hand on Becky's arm. "Noah knows more than most kids his age. We made survival skills fun for him. We'll do our best to find him before bad weather comes. Right now, the search teams need information. Can you answer some questions?"

Assured that Sarah would take care of Becky while she reported to the sheriff, Ella joined him at a table in the middle of the room.

Of all the law enforcement people she worked with, Marcus Bruster topped her list of favorites. With his six-foot-four, muscular frame, intimidation came easily. If you were on the proper side of law, the Robert Redford look-alike was a softy at heart. Ella's empathy for victims and attention to details made them a good team, in her opinion.

Ella handed each page to him after reporting the information she'd completed on her search and rescue forms. "Becky says Noah's wearing jeans, a red sweater, and a blue denim jacket lined with fake wool. He had blue gloves in his pocket. When Becky last saw him, he still had a blue and white striped scarf and a cowboy hat. You saw the pointed-toe boot tracks."

Marcus nodded. "Let's hope he hangs on to the warm clothes. He'll need them when sleet and snow comes."

Ella jotted interview questions while Marcus radioed the incident commander. "The parents say he'll answer to Noah. Ella's taught him some survival and trail skills. I'm releasing the incident area for a search. Assemble on the front lawn. Ella found tracks there. Keep vehicles away from the scene for now."

He rifled through his pages and leaned close to Ella. "That parking lot contains so many tire marks and footprints, it's impossible to tell who came and went. I did notice tire tracks with dual rear wheels that seem to cover other vehicle treads."

"Suggesting that truck arrived last."

He glanced around and whispered. "There isn't a truck with double rear wheels in the lot. Noah's boot prints are close to that set of tire treads." He shrugged and slumped back in his chair. "May or may not mean a thing."

"You think Noah talked to the driver?"

"Maybe." His pen tapped a constant rhythm on the table. "We'll ask about the truck in interviews."

"Right." Ella noted it on the appropriate page. "Horse trailers and campers are heavy. Lots of residents and visitors drive dual-wheeled rigs."

"And one of them drove into the lot today. Someone knows who."

Ella nodded and continued with her report. "Becky saw Noah playing in the gravel with his truck. That could explain his tracks in the parking lot. She told him not to leave the church grounds. I know this kid. Unless he was forced, he's not likely to leave with someone."

"I'd agree." Marcus pointed his pen at her. "But he is five. If something caught his eye, his mom's orders don't count. I'm not suggesting this driver took him. That would have attracted attention. I think Noah wandered off into the woods. Problem is I didn't see his entry point."

"So we let the dog find it." Ella cleared her throat and lifted her chin to indicate someone approaching.

Mrs. Hardin strode through the doorway into the fellowship hall. Her bulk, coupled with her labored breathing, made Ella want to call the paramedics.

She stopped at the table, hands firmly planted on her hips. "I can't believe you're sitting here talking when that precious child is missing."

The sheriff turned the stack of papers upside down. "We're planning the best way to locate him."

Ella shoved her pen into the hair above the barrette holding her ponytail. "Teams are starting a search now. We're ready to get details from the decoration committee."

"Well, it's about time, considering I have information you need to know."

The sheriff shot Ella an exasperated look, then nailed Mrs. Hardin with a glare. "If you had information, why didn't you approach me when I arrived?" He shoved a chair out with his foot. "Sit."

No gentleman-like chair holding? He obviously recalled his last encounter with the woman. Ella held back a frown as Mrs. Hardin clunked around the table and sank into the chair with an exaggerated sigh. What gossip was she cooking up now? Might as well listen to her story before conducting the first interview.

The whole group could hear Mrs. Hardin's not-so-hushed whisper. "I came back about nine-forty. Forgot the lights for the alter railing, so I went back to my house. That ugly carpenter was in the church lot. He was standing beside his truck talking to Noah."

Ella's mouth went dry. She'd love to slap the woman. "Benjamin was talking to Noah at nine-forty?" Ella asked.

"That's what I said. He didn't so much as wave. I'll bet he took the kid off somewhere just like he did that teenager. I told you the man was no good."

Out of the corner of her eye, Ella saw Noah's parents perk up their ears.

The sheriff clenched his teeth and ground the tip of his pen into the paper stack. "Benjamin had nothing to do with that teenager's disappearance. Don't lead me astray again today. Did you see Noah leave with Benjamin?"

"I didn't see it, but I'm certain he took the poor child."

Anger flared in the sheriff's eyes. Marcus wouldn't tolerate idle gossip. With no solid proof, Mrs. Hardin entered a one-way street the wrong way. Heedless of her precarious position, the woman blundered on. "I went to work in the sanctuary. Heard the truck pull away a few minutes later. Must have been about nine forty-five."

Todd Spangler lunged against the table. Supporting his weight on his hands, his red face stopped inches from Mrs. Hardin. "I won't listen to your gossip. Benjamin would never hurt Noah. If he came here, there was a good reason. The sheriff came to find my son, not hear your lies."

"Well, close your eyes if you want. Mr. Pruitt is the big lie. He only pretends to love your child. Men like him do that to gain their trust, you know. I see right through his phony attempts to make us think he wants to be a part of this community and congregation."

"Enough!" The sheriff's shout made everyone jump. Dead silence. Soft murmurs gradually rose from the group sitting across the room.

Marcus stood and clamped a warning hand on Todd's shoulder. Todd backed off, allowing Marcus to move into Mrs. Hardin's personal space instead. "You wasted my valuable time once with your insinuations, Mrs. Hardin. Benjamin had an alibi in the previous case, and I'd wager he does now."

Becky took Todd's arm and tugged him away. "You don't think he'd hurt Noah?" Her eyes begged her husband to say no.

Todd pulled Becky to his chest. "No. Benjamin is family. He wouldn't take Noah anywhere without asking us."

Marcus shoved his chair so it grated across the floor. "Calm down, people." His voice rose, bringing everyone into the conversation. "You heard this information. Give me some clarification. Benjamin Pruitt may be the last person to see Noah. Did anyone else see him today? And I don't want any guesses or conjectures. I want solid facts."

Emily Pierce said, "We were taking turns going to the door to check on Noah and keeping an eye on him through the windows. I saw Benjamin drive into the lot when I got holly sprigs from the plastic bag I left on the parking lot side of the building. Didn't think anything of it when Benjamin drove up. He's close to the boy. Noah calls him Grandpa. I saw Mrs. Hardin park beside Benjamin."

"Did anyone see Noah leave with Benjamin?" he asked.

Questioning looks with shaking heads. Everyone seemed to release a collective breath.

Emily continued. "We wouldn't have seen Benjamin leave. I think we moved over to the arena side to decorate the tables when I brought the holly."

Mrs. Wexler said, "Emily's right." She pointed to the side of the room opposite the parking area. "We went to decorate those tables. Mrs. Hardin stuck her head in the door to say she was back. I glanced at the clock. It was nine forty-two."

Marcus noted times on the data forms. "Ella, what kind of

truck does Benjamin drive?"

"A Ford F-350. Your dual rear wheels. Like you said, it just means he came here."

Marcus nodded and reached for his radio. His finger stopped before he keyed the switch. Good. No dispatch to Statesville for Benjamin's apprehension. Marcus wasn't buying Mrs. Hardin's accusations any more than she was. Perhaps Todd and Becky's parental instincts held sway over any possible culpability.

He placed the radio on the table beside his hat. "After Benjamin left, did anyone see Noah or go check on him again?"

Nervous glances. Pastor Morrison said, "I went to the sanctuary to help with the lights. It sounds like we got preoccupied and didn't check on Noah for almost ten minutes."

Becky covered her mouth to muffle a sob. "After we put the holly out, I went outside. He was gone." Becky studied Todd's face. "Can you forgive me for losing our son?"

"Shh, you didn't lose Noah." Todd held her in a bear hug and stroked her back with loving hands. "Noah plays outside at home too. He wandered off. We'll find him."

Emily said, "We heard panic in Becky's voice when she was calling Noah. We rushed outside. It was almost ten. We spent several minutes looking. That's when Becky called Sarah."

Sarah! Ella had forgotten about her. Sarah sat motionless, hands hanging limply in her lap. Pale lips quivered as if holding back tears.

Ella moved to squat in front of Sarah's chair. "Where was Benjamin headed today?"

Sarah whispered so only Ella could hear. "Why does she do this to him? Benjamin loves Noah."

Ella patted Sarah's knee. "Benjamin is likely the last person to see Noah. His statement could tell us a great deal. When did he leave and where was he going, Sarah?"

"Statesville. He left the house about nine-thirty. You went upstairs after breakfast. I was sorting decorations when Becky called." Sarah turned a shade whiter, and a tear ran down her cheek. "Benjamin wouldn't drive past the church on his way to Statesville. Why did he come?"

Ella grabbed a tissue and squatted again. "Stop crying. Don't let Mrs. Hardin see you ruffled. Did you notice Marcus didn't send police to bring Benjamin? If he didn't think Benjamin was innocent, he would have them looking for him. Marcus trusts him. You need to believe in Benjamin and trust him too." Ella returned to Marcus' side to report Sarah's comments.

Damp coldness sliced through Sarah's coat and into her bones. Drizzle fell and froze on the grass and trees. With just enough accumulation to make footing uncertain, Sarah grasped the pastor's arm. Jerking it back, she said, "I'm sorry. I should have asked."

He tucked her hand into the crook of his elbow and placed a gloved hand over it. "It's fine. Neither of us wants to fall." They took several steps on the ice-coated lawn. After a glance at the sky, he said, "Snow would be preferable. Freezing rain won't help Noah or the searchers—much more treacherous." They moved cautiously across the lawn toward the steps. "You're walking better than you were at Emily's on Saturday."

"Benjamin and Ella forced me to rest. I don't understand why Mrs. Hardin treats him so harshly. Benjamin's a good man, Pastor."

"Yes, he is. Once Marcus asks him some questions, he'll be cleared. Mrs. Hardin craves attention. I believe she has another reason as well. A topic to discuss another time."

On the opposite side of the church, voices called for Noah and then paused to listen. Through the breezeway, Sarah watched them search along the dense kudzu and rhododendron thicket beside the parking area. They must be looking for Noah's boot prints.

The four people gathered on the front lawn waited beside a tall, dark-haired woman and her sleek German shepherd. Heavy coats, gloves, and scarves obscured the identities of the searchers. The dog strained against a blue nylon leash as if anxious to begin.

Sarah and the pastor paused at the top of the steps.

The team seemed wound up like tops awaiting permission to spin. The woman squatted, stroked the dog, and spoke softly to her. She unclipped the leash. Ella opened the bag. The dog sniffed its contents, raised her nose, and lunged toward the magnolia tree. After sniffing the toys and the lawn where they'd found footprints, the dog raced toward the gravestones at the edge of the church property.

Nose to the ground, the animal plunged into the undergrowth with the handler close behind. "Over here. Sophie found Noah's scent. I see boot tracks! Good dog. Find our boy before the rain washes away his trail."

The team fanned out to follow the tracks Sophie's handler indicated. Sophie sniffed the shrubs and weeds a few yards downwind. Within moments, the rhododendron swallowed up the searchers.

Pastor Morrison took a tentative step on the icy steps. "We'd better move on. We have a job to perform as well."

Five minutes later Sarah and Pastor Morrison swung open the batwing doors at the Silver Spur, then closed the wooden door behind them to keep out the cold. She was grateful a patrol car had saved them the long trek across the meadow and up the icy trail to town. Once her eyes adjusted, Sarah slid onto a tractor seat mounted atop a wagon wheel at the bar. The seats always fascinated her as a child when her family came for Friday evening square dances or a soft drink after a rodeo. The place hadn't changed much over the years. The same wood stove belched smoky heat across the dance floor. The two carved carousel-like horses, perched on the brick mantel, surveyed the woodpile. They, along with two Indian head statues, flanked the stovepipe that disappeared through the ceiling. Metal folding chairs lined pedestal style dining tables. It took her back to carefree days when she might have slipped away into the woods exploring.

Today was not a carefree day. Noah wasn't old enough to explore alone, especially when sleet pelted the tin roof overhead. At the tables, men and women bent over maps and forms. Everyone seemed to talk simultaneously. How could they comprehend what was happening when confusion seemed to rule? A few moments of observation showed each person knew their role and performed it with practiced precision—a normal day in Ella's work world.

Pastor Morrison touched Sarah's shoulder. "Are you okay?"

A little smile graced her lips. "Got lost reminiscing."

"I'll find the portable phone and be right back. Do you want some coffee or a sandwich?"

"Not now, thanks."

Jars of pickled eggs and kosher dills glared at Sarah from their spots on the wooden bar. They seemed to say this wasn't supposed to be a command post where police and volunteers gathered to search for lost boys. Sarah snagged an extra cushion from the adjacent tractor seat. She shoved its horse-and-cowboy-hat motif between her backside and the biting metal seat. How did a farmer sit in one of these contraptions all day?

Pastor Morrison returned with the phone. "The incident commander said Sophie's on Noah's trail, but the woods are dense and make for slow going." He laid a hand on her shoulder. "Call Benjamin. I'll give you some privacy. My wife and some other women are making sandwiches." He indicated another room where people normally gathered to shoot pool or listen to the band. "I'm in there."

Benjamin answered the second ring. Somehow, his prompt answer assured his innocence. Why had she let that sliver of doubt prick her?

With a shaky voice, Sarah relayed the basic story of Noah's disappearance and asked Benjamin to return. She disconnected. No discussion about why he'd come to the church. Not her role. Her task was prayer and trusting God.

Backlit by the light from the soft drink cooler, the jar of eggs glowed red. Unnatural—like the idea Benjamin would harm Noah. Guilt nibbled at her. She had momentarily considered Mrs. Hardin's accusations. Circumstantial. Benjamin must never know she'd doubted him.

Grandpas loved. Noah had chosen Benjamin and basked in the man's attention. Noah had opened Benjamin's heart so God could heal the deep emotional scars. Acceptance and love did that. Would the accusations and questions raised today damage that fragile balance and plunge him back into seclusion?

CHAPTER TWENTY

Benjamin barreled through the swinging doors. The controlled chaos around the tables brought him to a halt. He'd imagined coming in to hear Noah was fine, merely playing hide-and-seek, stubbornly refusing to come out of his perfect hiding place. Not going to happen.

Sarah rose from her seat at the bar—another reality that didn't fit. Was she rehashing painful memories of Bryce's drinking bouts? Did that, coupled with Noah's disappearance, twist her stomach into knots too? He crossed the creaking wooden floor to stand beside her.

Her face contorted as she held back emotions, but she turned to him, opening her arms. Benjamin enveloped her. "Any news?"

"Ella's working with a search team and a dog handler. They're following Noah's scent." Sarah lifted her head to capture his gaze. "Mrs. Hardin's telling lies again. She's saying you took Noah. I'm so sorry."

The sheriff appeared in the doorway to the back room. "Benjamin, come on in and sit."

Benjamin said, "Her malicious tongue isn't a surprise. I'll clear things up with the sheriff." He let Sarah go, trailing his hand along her arm until his fingertips met only air.

Marcus popped the tops on two soda cans and passed one across the table to Benjamin. "The search team says they're finding broken branches. Sophie, our dog, has a good scent trail. We're racing the weather."

"Did Ella tell you we've taught Noah some trail and survival skills?"

"She did. Good thing too. If the weather gets worse, Noah may need them."

"The boy means the world to me." Benjamin took a swallow of his drink and almost choked. Showing emotions in front of a virtual stranger—not a problem today. Noah mattered more. "I didn't harm him."

"I believe you. We need to talk because you're probably the last person who saw Noah. The rest," he shrugged one shoulder, "is following up on a lead from a witness for my records. You had an alibi the last time Mrs. Hardin accused you; I'm sure you do now."

Benjamin's eyes widened. The soda can stopped half way to his mouth. "No one ever told me I'd been cleared in that other case."

"Hmm, Ella knew. Must have forgotten to pass it on."

Benjamin recalled the day after his bee stings. They'd talked about his alibi. "She started to tell me and got distracted by a phone call."

Marcus said, "The clerk at the Statesville hardware store recognized your picture. The credit card records and his statement confirmed the time you were at the store. That girl went missing when you were shopping. Hard to be in two places at the same time. I always believed you were a reputable business owner who stopped for supplies. Mrs. Gossip wasted valuable time with her accusation. The way I see it, today's no different."

"Why do people always believe her?"

"They don't. Can't figure out what to do to keep her quiet."

"They could stop listening to her."

Marcus shot him a satisfied smirk. "I plan to have a little chat with the esteemed woman. Maybe she'll shut up after today."

"Don't count on it." Benjamin took a bite of a sandwich. Not that he wanted it with Noah out there hungry and cold. The day might be long. He needed strength. "I tried to avoid Mrs. Hardin's accusation the first time. Sarah made me follow through. At least the few people who really matter will know I'm not a kidnapper."

"The wise people of Love Valley knew that all along. They wouldn't have hired you for more jobs if they believed Mrs. Hardin. By the way, we closed that case yesterday. The girl came home."

"That's good news."

"Ran off with her boyfriend. She found out the party scene she wanted wasn't much fun. Hunger and living in the car changed her attitude. Maybe she'll appreciate her parents more now."

"Does Ella know?"

"I planned to call her to thank her for the help. Didn't know I'd be working a case with her."

Benjamin set the can on the table. "Time to get down to the real reason we're talking. I didn't take Noah."

"Sarah said you were on your way to Statesville. People saw you at the church. Why'd you drive out of your way to see the boy?"

"We often take walks or ride a trail. A group from church

made repairs on Emily's house on Saturday. Noah didn't like me giving attention to her grandson, Thomas. Noah played with the boy, but he wanted to work with his dad and me. He said Thomas was a baby."

"A little jealous, huh?"

"Very. He got rude and acted out at Emily's house. I knew he wanted attention, so I promised him a special day in the woods when the repairs were finished. Becky heard us making plans. Ask her."

Marcus nodded, jotted a note, and motioned for Benjamin to continue.

"Noah isn't old enough to have a concept of time. Later means in a few minutes to him."

"Was he angry enough to run away when you left today?"

Benjamin rubbed his chin. "Not happy, but I don't see Noah running away. He's a good kid. Obeys his folks. Curious though. If something caught his attention—"

"My thoughts too. Sophie picked up his scent near the graves."

"Harvey."

"Who?"

"A rabbit. We call him Harvey. When I worked at the church this summer, he'd come every day to nibble clover. Sarah packed carrots in my lunches. Noah had him eating out of his hand."

"So the kid's upset, sees Harvey, and takes off after him."

"Those woods around the church are covered in kudzu and poison itchy." He choked up again. "That's what Noah calls it. I can't see him going too deep following Harvey. He'd lose the rabbit as soon as he went in."

"Something else around there that would tempt him to go deeper?"

"We saw a six-point buck on a trail near the stable. That trail comes out near the pond below the church."

"So Noah follows the rabbit and decides to look for the deer?"

"Or the deer comes looking for food closer to the church."

"Sounding reasonable. Our curious boy knows a bit about the woods. He's mad. Wants to prove he's growing up. Add a rabbit or a deer, and we've got us one lost kid."

Benjamin rested his head in his hands. "If I'd only realized how upset he was. I should have taken him inside to Becky before I left."

"You had no idea he'd leave. Mind you, we're speculating, but it makes good sense. Show me the trail on the map. We'll send a second team in that way."

They entered the main part of the saloon. Sarah had moved from her seat at the bar and seemed to be following the progress of the search as radio reports arrived.

Benjamin leaned over the map table and located the trail. "Here." Tracing it with his finger he said, "It winds around for a couple miles and ends at the pond."

Sarah eyed the place he indicated. "That's the trail where we saw the moss beds."

"And the place where I saw the deer I mentioned to you. I think he may have followed that deer."

Marcus briefed the incident commander. People scrambled to gather appropriate clothing. Chatter over the radios increased. Within minutes, two men left to secure horses and several others prepared to search the trail on foot.

Marcus said, "I have a few more questions, Benjamin. Let's go back where it's quieter."

Pastor Morrison approached. "I'm taking food for the group at church, Sarah. Do you want to go with me or wait for Benjamin?"

"I'll wait. Go take care of Becky, Pastor."

Benjamin leaned close to Sarah's ear. "No worries."

Marcus and Benjamin returned to their seats in the poolroom. "I need to check your alibi, Benjamin. For the report, you understand. Where'd you go in Statesville?"

"A jewelry store. It's a surprise, so I'd appreciate it if you don't spread around this detail."

"Doing some Christmas shopping?"

Benjamin checked to see that Sarah remained out of earshot. "I went to buy something for Sarah."

"Shopping for a lady at the jewelry store sounds serious."

Benjamin pulled a small ring of construction paper from his pocket. "It's silly, but you should know the whole story so I'm safely off the hook. This is the reason I went to the church this morning."

"This?" Marcus' eyebrows shot up, confusion obvious on his face.

"I helped Becky and Sarah during Sunday school yesterday. The children made paper chains for their Christmas trees. I planned to ask Becky how I could find out Sarah's ring size. I was afraid to go snooping in Sarah's jewelry box."

Marcus took the paper and grinned. "How is Noah involved in this little adventure?"

"Sarah put some glitter glue on that strip of paper and wrapped it around her finger. We laughed and admired her ring.

She wore it during church. Later, at the inn, I noticed it was gone. Figured she'd tossed it in the trash. I planned to take a look in the garbage cans."

"Sounds worse than raiding her jewelry box."

"I know. It's a cockamamie story. Thought I'd offer to take the trash to the dump on my way out of town. When I saw Noah this morning, I asked him if Miss Sarah still had the ring she made. Noah had it in his pocket. She'd taken it off and left it on the pew. Noah picked it up. That kid always has junk in his pockets."

Benjamin blinked away tears and swallowed over the sudden lump in his throat. "Anyway, I told him I'd give it to her when I came back from Statesville since she wasn't going to be at the church decorating."

"So I'm going to call the jewelry store and ask them about a paper ring?" Marcus' smile widened as if he were enjoying this a bit too much.

"It isn't paper now."

CHAPTER TWENTY-ONE

Noah searched every pocket for his gloves—only one. He pulled it on and jammed the other hand into his coat pocket. "Mommy!" No answer again. How far had he walked?

He sniffed and wiped his nose on his sleeve. Crying didn't help, but he sure was scared. Something rustled in the leaves on the right. His heart thumped louder in his ears. "Mommy? Miss Ella?" Thinking about creepy crawlies or animals in the bushes made him more afraid. He ignored the sound, bent a branch to mark his trail, and took a few more steps.

Cold rain dripped off his cowboy hat and ran down the back of his neck. He scrunched his hat, turned up the collar on his jacket, and pulled the scarf over most of his face.

Noah turned in a circle one more time. No signs of a real trail. Lost. Why had he followed that deer? He'd been too excited to think about marking a trail. Too late. Nothing to follow back. What had Grandpa taught him?

"Find shelter."

All he saw was dead kudzu, leafless trees, and dead poison itchy vines. Could he get poison itchy in the winter?

He'd begged Grandpa to take him along to Statesville. Playing alone at the church was boring. Grandpa said they'd go riding later when the rain and snow melted. With grownups, everything happened later. Later took too long to get here. When later came, would he still be lost in the woods?

Noah spied a tall green tree ahead. Maybe it would give shelter. He pushed aside the kudzu vines, broke branches on bushes he passed, and headed for the tree.

Real icicles hung from the huge pine tree. They didn't glow like the ones on his Christmas tree. Maybe they would when the sun came out. Branches sticking out from the trunk almost touched the ground. He squatted and found a cave-like place. Noah walked around the tree and broke limbs to mark his hiding place.

On his hands and knees, he crawled under the drooping limbs. The pine needles under his knees made a thick, prickly layer. Close to the trunk, they were dry. Under the tree the wind and icy rain didn't sting his face.

He remembered the day he'd helped Daddy rake leaves. Thinking about that made him want to cry, so he stopped thinking about his daddy and heaped pine needles into a pile.

"Stay put."

Leaning against the trunk, he scooped dry needles over him. His stomach growled. It must be lunchtime, but he didn't have any food. Maybe Mommy would remember that Miss Ella and Grandpa were good trackers and send them to look for him. If he'd remembered what they had taught him, he wouldn't be lost.

At least he'd remembered after the deer disappeared into the thick briars. Had he stomped his feet in the wet ground enough times to mark a path? Were there enough broken limbs to lead them to the tree? If he'd walked too far before he remembered, would they ever find his path? What would he do if no one came?

Noah shivered and sank deeper into his pile of pine needles. He sat still and listened. The wind howled through the branches above him. More icicles stuck to the limbs and made the branches droop lower.

"Find shelter and stay put." That was hard. He whimpered and thought about running home to Mommy. Crying made it hard to hear if a voice called him or footsteps passed the tree. He held his breath to listen. Only his heart beat. No voices called his name. Soon—they'd call him soon.

CHAPTER TWENTY-TWO

Presumed innocent after one phone call to Statesville. No one had seen Noah after Benjamin drove away. The circumstances and timeframe still allowed room for his guilt. Trust. A welcome experience. Would the others see the truth as well?

Benjamin assisted Sarah from the truck. He slipped an arm around her waist as they navigated the skating rink that had once been the church parking area.

An inch of frozen rain and sleet had fallen since he came back from Statesville. One look at the sky told him the weather wouldn't change. If the temperature dropped, they'd likely have snow. Put snow over ice—that dog had better have a good nose.

They entered the fellowship hall with its welcoming fire. Tight groups sat around the tables. Some bowed in prayer while others ate.

Becky and Todd huddled beside the hearth. Benjamin's mouth went dry. What if they rejected him or believed he'd harmed their son? Benjamin lagged behind Sarah, who wove around chairs to join them.

"Benjamin." Todd clapped him on the back. "I trust you got things cleared up with the sheriff."

"He's satisfied I'm innocent. I promise you, it's true."

Becky stood to hug him. "We didn't really believe her. We know how special Noah is to you."

It seemed impossible. Relief warmed him. Benjamin sighed, closed his eyes, and wrapped his arms around Becky. "They'll find him, Becky. We won't lose our boy."

Sheriff Bruster blew in with a gust of wind. He announced to the group, "Ella reported they've found a trail of broken branches and boot prints. Benjamin, you were right. Noah probably followed a deer. Deer tracks preceded the boot tracks for a while. Then the deer branched off into briars. Now Noah's marking a trail the way you taught him. They're closing in."

Becky gasped, and a smile flitted across her face. "Oh, thank God. I hope he isn't hurt." Tears coursed down her cheeks. She intercepted Todd, who paced from one side of the room to the other.

Todd engulfed her in an embrace. "If Noah's marking trail, he's going to be fine." Benjamin clapped Todd on the back. Todd nodded and tried to smile through the uncertain expression on his face. The deep sigh and quivering lips said he wanted to believe the words of comfort he offered his wife.

A sensation of excitement and hopefulness descended over the room. People glanced at Benjamin. As animated conversation resumed, Benjamin heard his name dart around in non-derisive, almost complimentary tones. From suspect to hero in one statement. Fickle people—swayed by the words of a pained, power-hungry woman. How could anyone feel at ease in a social situation involving her?

His gaze traveled to Mrs. Hardin who appeared acutely uncomfortable. Embarrassed or ashamed? Not likely.

"Mrs. Hardin," Marcus boomed. He strode to the table where she sat. Once there, he met the snake she hid up her sleeve nose to nose. "If you ever approach me with another lie, I'll make you wish you had never met me. I will personally see that your slanderous statements come before the courts. Is that clear enough for you to comprehend?"

She inched back in her chair. Beads of sweat popped out on her forehead. "Yes, sir. My apologies."

"Your apology belongs elsewhere. You can leave. I don't need to hear from you again." Marcus backed away and calmly crossed to sit in the chair beside Benjamin.

Silence fell like the calm in the eye of a treacherous storm.

Mrs. Hardin shoved out of her chair, smoothed her dress, and stuck out her chin—or did she stick her nose in the air? Either way, she exited as if she were the queen of the world. He'd never hear her apology, and he doubted the sheriff's words would take away her control over the residents. The snake merely slithered back up her sleeve.

After her departure, chatter resumed. The heaviness lightened with the news Marcus brought.

In their little corner, Todd said, "Noah must have followed that big buck we've seen around."

Marcus nodded. "Benjamin told me about the deer and a rabbit."

"Harvey." Todd snapped his fingers. "Of course. I should have thought of him. He's in the graveyard almost every time we come to church. If Harvey came out, Noah would have gone over there."

Sheriff Bruster said, "That's what Benjamin and I decided. I'm encouraged by the report that Sophie's following Noah's scent."

Benjamin said, "I hope he remembers I taught him to find shelter and stay put."

Marcus tossed his hat on a nearby table. "The weather's getting worse. I hope you're right. On a positive note, there are no signs he's injured. Sophie's a great dog. Ella's about the best search team leader on the east coast. They'll locate Noah."

Emily Pierce approached. "Have you folks eaten?"

"I did, thank you." Benjamin looked at Sarah. Pale, tired, and probably hurting. "You should eat something."

"I'll get a bite soon."

Emily touched Benjamin's arm and glanced at the sheriff. "I wanted to tell you how sorry I am about Mrs. Hardin. She, well, let's just say she has a way of blowing things out of proportion. I'm afraid I tend toward following her at times. This isn't one of them. You went out of your way to help me, Benjamin. You are not the sort of man who hurts little boys."

He should say something, but the lump in his throat prevented words. Instead, he smiled and nodded. Placing an arm around Emily's shoulder, he gave her a half hug. If he read her smile correctly, it sufficed.

Sarah asked Becky, "Have you and Todd eaten?"

Becky pulled a tissue apart, dropping the shreds in her lap. "Todd ate. I'm not hungry."

"Well that doesn't matter. Benjamin's right. We need to eat. Come with Emily and me. Want to join us, Benjamin?"

"No thanks. I need to be alone for a while. I'll be in the sanctuary if there's news."

Sarah raised her eyebrows. A satisfied smile curled Todd's lips. Benjamin said, "Why are you so surprised? You taught me that church is the place to be when life gets tough."

Outside, a man Benjamin recognized from the Thanksgiving dinner scattered salt on the breezeway. They exchanged nods of greeting. Benjamin paused and let his gaze travel to Kudzu Territory.

He'd shared his fanciful flights of imagination with Noah. He could almost believe the Kudzu soldiers had captured the child. During their times of pretending, they'd treated Harvey as a friend. Perhaps he was a foe—a spy on a mission to determine how the soldiers could rip out Benjamin's heart. The fire hadn't been enough. Taking Noah might complete the task. He'd told that rabbit the details of his sorry life. No doubt, Harvey's commander had received a full report and sent the most destructive warriors. Stupid thoughts. A rabbit and imaginary soldiers had nothing to do with the situation. Still, it made Benjamin think about his life.

He'd never experienced the sort of love Noah gave him. Now circumstances might snatch it away. The slander didn't hurt nearly as much as the idea that the Kudzu soldiers had found the way to crush him. Only one thing would hurt more—losing Sarah.

He watched the man toss one last handful of salt on the cement, put his bucket down, and enter the fellowship hall. Benjamin crossed the melting ice to step inside the dimly lit church. He hesitated while his eyes adjusted.

Garlands of green pine twined the alter railing. Tiny white lights twinkled against the deep green. Poinsettia plants lined the kneeling bench below. Daylight filtered through the stained glass windows to illuminate the otherwise dark church. Benjamin made his way to the second row and knelt.

Worship and prayer—things he'd never planned to do after the fire. Sarah set that change in motion on the first day he arrived as her tender spirit led him toward loving people.

He focused on the stained glass window located behind the altar. A magnificent depiction of Jesus praying in the Garden of Gethsemane. It moved him to reflect on the deep valley he'd created between himself and God. Todd and Pastor Morrison had patiently shown him verses that convinced him he needed forgiveness. They'd told him how much God loved him, even during the torturous days following the fire. They were right. God hadn't left him to suffer alone.

He'd never thought of himself as self-righteous, never considered that his actions bordered on self-pity. He'd always believed he had a good reason to be angry with God. He should be thankful for life, not mad because he'd survived. Sarah had shown him that truth.

How did he go about making amends? Approaching God to ask for favors after years of rebellion seemed wrong. Would God forgive him? He certainly didn't deserve it. His pride was like a tangle of kudzu, separating him from God.

He'd treated all people as evil because some of them mistreated him. He wouldn't allow them to get close enough to see how much he hurt, how lost he was deep in the darkness of his soul. That was sin, and he knew it.

There wasn't sin in asking honest questions. Sarah understood God's forgiveness even as she pondered the bad events of her life. She'd find answers or simply trust that God knew best. Could he?

Time to meet this head on. He needed to reconcile the past and get on with a future—a future he hoped would include Sarah, Noah, and the others who believed in him and were making efforts to love and accept him.

How should he begin? "I'm wrong, and I need forgiveness." It didn't sound like enough, but Todd said that was all it took.

Benjamin bowed his head, tears running down his cheeks. "Father God, thank you for the acceptance Todd and Becky have shown me. They could be accusing me. Instead, they love me. Please don't take Noah or his family from me. And my Sarah. She understands me. You know I love her. Help me find the courage to tell her what I feel. I'm so sorry for the years I neglected you. I was wrong. I'd like to come home. Would you consider taking me back?"

The door creaked open, letting a sliver of light slip in. Pastor Morrison knelt on Benjamin's right. Sarah rested her hand on his left shoulder and eased onto the pew. The sanctuary gradually filled as more community members came to pray for Noah. Some prayed in silence, others murmured their requests aloud.

Many of them paused to place a hand on Benjamin's shoulder before finding a seat or a place to kneel.

CHAPTER TWENTY-THREE

Noah watched fluffy snowflakes fall outside the tree. If he were at home, he'd make a snowman and then have hot chocolate. Mommy might let the mother cat come inside the house. Since it was so cold, he'd cuddle her close so they'd both be warm. They could curl up under his fuzzy blanket and watch cartoons. The cat would take a nap, but not him. Big boys didn't need naps.

The snow pulled the branches closer to the ground so he had to lie down now to see if someone was coming. The wind seldom blew under the tree anymore. That was good. Wet jeans felt very cold when the wind blew. His pine needle blanket wasn't so warm anymore.

He shouted, "Miss Ella. Grandpa." No answer. A yawn—too hard to hold his eyes open. If he fell asleep, would he hear them calling?

Noah jerked awake. He held his breath to listen. Nothing. It must be the wind again. The tree creaked like the old rocking chair on Miss Sarah's porch.

The sound again. Something in the bushes. Maybe Harvey or the deer. He called again. "Miss Ella!"

A dog barking?

"Grandpa!"

Another bark.

"Noah, can you hear me?"

He sat up, bumping his head on a tree limb. He rubbed the knot and yelled, "Miss Ella! Over here!"

Voices and barking. Closer. "We're coming Noah. Don't move."

"Miss Ella, I hear you. I'm here under the Christmas tree."

"Stay, Noah. We're coming."

They'd found his trail. He could see boots now. "I'm under here. I see you."

A big dog crawled under the branches on its belly. It whined a hello. A warm wet tongue licked his cold face. The dog wagged all over, barking and then licking Noah again. If dogs could smile, this one did.

Miss Ella and a lady peeped under the branches. "Noah. Hey,

buddy," Ella said, "Come out, Sophie. I need some room."

The lady called, "Come, Sophie." The dog backed off. The woman knelt in the snow to rub the dog behind its ears. "Yes, I know. You're a happy dog. You did a wonderful job. We're glad to see him too."

Noah could see other feet outside the tree now. Miss Ella crept toward him on her stomach. "You sure found a great place to wait. Are you hurt?"

He shook his head. "Just cold and hungry." He reached his stiff hands toward Ella. She grasped them and pulled him out.

Sitting in the snow beside the huge Christmas tree, her arms felt warm like the tears that stung his cold cheeks. A man wrapped them in a blanket. She tucked it around Noah, hugged him against her, and rocked back and forth. "Don't cry, sweetie. You're safe. We'll carry you home."

"I want Mommy. Where's my mommy?"

CHAPTER TWENTY-FOUR

Sarah hung back, observing the bustle of activity when the search team returned with Noah. Nothing she could do. Plus it made watching Benjamin easier. His interactions with the community, searchers, law officials, and reporters amazed her. Weeks ago, he would have disappeared or panicked due to the public attention. More recently, he would have relied on her to sustain him as he conversed. Today he talked openly. He even stood up bravely against Mrs. Hardin's allegations.

Sarah understood his refusal of photographs with Noah and the rescue team. The rest of his actions? She should overflow with happiness. With Benjamin's newfound self-esteem, everything changed. Where did she fit?

After the paramedics declared that Noah didn't need hospital treatment, the Spangler family decided the rest of the team should meet Noah and join their celebration. Sarah climbed into Benjamin's truck for another trip uptown. Weary church members said their good-byes and wandered home to wait out the rare winter storm.

At the saloon, backslaps, handshakes, and "job well done" floated around the command post. It enlivened Sarah to see Ella's volunteers and the local deputies rejoice over their successful search. Another glimpse into Ella's world.

When Todd brought sandwiches and hot chocolate, Noah pushed the blanket off his arms and propped his elbows on the table. "Can I look at the map and the radios after I eat?"

"Maybe. I need to hold you for a while." Becky probably wanted to hold and protect her child forever. Unfortunately, life didn't provide mothers with that ability.

Sheriff Bruster took a seat beside the family. "You gave us a big scare, son."

"I'm sorry." Noah twisted in Becky's lap and clung to her shirt. "Will you put me in jail?"

A smile creased Marcus' tired face. "No. Boys who wander off don't go to jail." He leaned back and laced his fingers behind his head. "You can learn a lesson from what happened, though."

"What's that?" Noah relaxed and faced Marcus.

"Did your mommy tell you to stay at the church?"

Noah nodded and hung his head. "I didn't obey."

"That's right. She wanted to keep you safe. When you get older, she may tell you other things to keep you safe. Moms and dads usually know what's best for their children. Obey them."

"I'll try."

"Here." Marcus pinned a metal badge on Noah's shirt. "This special deputy badge is for you. Brave boys who learn from their mistakes get these."

Noah beamed, studying the trinket. "Thanks."

Ella walked up behind Marcus, plopped a stack of papers in front of him, and placed a hand on his shoulder. "My paper work, sir. We made a good team again today."

He touched her hand and smiled up at her. "Yes we did. I keep telling the other sheriffs who shun your efforts that you're the best."

As the pair chatted on their walk toward the command area, Sarah caught the demure grin Ella sent Marcus. Obviously more to that look than Ella cared to admit. Maybe it was time for some girl talk about Sheriff Bruster.

Noah tossed off the blanket, apparently warm and revived by the food. He slithered off Becky's lap and joined the deputies and searchers packing equipment. The CLUES sweatshirt that brushed against his ankles and a pair of men's socks pulled up to his knees dwarfed him. Noah wandered among the crew collecting hugs. For the next fifteen minutes, he held their attention as he chattered about his adventure.

Becky said, "Maybe I better rescue them. If I don't intervene, he could talk forever. Noah, come back over here. We need to leave."

Team members patted Noah on the head and moved off to complete paper work, pack equipment, or venture home. Sarah longed for her recliner.

Noah wove his way around tables until he stood in front of Benjamin. "I'm sorry, Grandpa."

Benjamin gathered Noah onto his lap and pressed him tightly against his chest. "It's okay, Noah. I'm glad you're safe."

"Miss Ella said I left a good trail." Tears brimmed in Noah's eyes. "I didn't start soon enough."

"You started when you realized you were lost. That was smart."

"I tried to do what you told me. I didn't mean to cause trouble."

"I'm proud of you. Ella says you found a good place to get out of the weather."

Noah lifted his head and gazed into Benjamin's eyes. "Do you still love me?"

Tears pooled in Benjamin's dark eyes. He kissed the top of Noah's head. "Of course I do. Getting lost doesn't change the way I feel about you."

Noah settled deeper into Benjamin's embrace. He'd fall asleep if the conversation lulled. "I love you too, Grandpa." His eyelids grew heavier. "I wish you could have seen the big Christmas tree. It was covered with icicles." A yawn escaped.

"I still owe you a special day. If it stays cold, we'll go see it. You could show me the trail you left for Miss Ella."

Noah perked up. "Would you come to my house and help me build a snowman?"

"Sure. We'll do whatever you want. Tomorrow." Benjamin rumpled Noah's hair. "I'm tired, kid. You need to go home." He handed Noah off to Todd.

Todd said, "We'll make plans later." He hugged Sarah and clapped Benjamin on the back. "You two get some rest. We've all had a traumatic day."

Marcus called to Benjamin from across the room. "If you don't mind staying a few more minutes I want to talk with you about a carpentry project at my house."

Sarah said, "Go ahead. I'll walk them out."

She waved as the Spanglers' truck pulled away from the saloon. The wind whistled around the corner of the building. The windmill at the end of Main Street creaked and moaned. She should go inside. No. Easier to think out here.

The search, and Mrs. Hardin's false accusations, brought Benjamin to the forefront. When the evening news aired, Iredell County would know how Benjamin and Ella's training had probably saved Noah's life.

Sarah sank to a bench on the boardwalk, hugging her knees to her chest. She watched more snow accumulate on the miry mixture of ice, mud, and snow. Quarter-sized flakes collected on the drier surfaces along Main Street. Muddy shoeprints led in and out of the command post and trailed down the weathered boardwalk. Across the street, icicles hung from the tin roofs. The hitching rails wore white caps rather than the usual reins. On the opposite corner, a few lights blinked on at Miss Kitty's Bed and Bath. Some searchers must have opted to rent rooms rather than travel home on icy roads. Too bad Mosey Inn wasn't closer to town. She could use the income.

Approaching footsteps drew her out of her contemplation. Pastor Morrison held two steaming cups. "It's too cold to sit out here. Come inside. Or do you want a ride home?"

"I'll wait for Benjamin." She stood, took a cup of cocoa, and followed him back inside the saloon.

Sophie had the right idea. She'd stretched out before the stove to roast her belly. Sarah bent to scratch the dog's ear. Sophie whined, yawned, and rolled over to toast her other side. "You deserve a long rest by a warm fire, girl."

Sarah followed Pastor Morrison to a vacant table in the back room. The din of people discussing details from the search faded.

He sat, shredding his empty foam cup into tiny pieces. "I'm not sure how to approach this subject."

"What?"

"The topic of Mrs. Hardin." He stared at the table.

"That's over," Sarah said. "The sheriff hushed Mrs. Hardin for the time being."

"As her pastor, I shouldn't allow such gossip. However, I fear that many people would get hurt if I tried to control her tongue. She puts me in a difficult position. The woman knows way too much about people in this town."

Sarah wrinkled her forehead and shook her head. "I don't understand."

"Pastors receive confidential information from their congregants. Mrs. Hardin makes it her business to obtain details from other sources."

"You keep things private. That's where the difference lies."

"True." He brushed the cup remnants aside and drummed his fingers on the table. "Some of her gossip is true. Most is exaggerated or downright lies." The sadness in his eyes showed his distaste for the behavior. "I've kept a secret that shouldn't stay private any longer."

Sarah had never seen her pastor so flustered. She stilled his fingers. "Don't betray some confidence."

"It affects you directly."

"Forget it. Mrs. Hardin's treated me as an outcast for years. I'll survive."

He folded his hands, resting them on the table. Fresh resolve seemed to transform his demeanor. "You questioned why she treats Benjamin so harshly. It's has little to do with Benjamin. She resents your family."

"My family?"

"Something happened years ago. Telling you the truth will benefit you. It won't change her ways. She hated your father because of his integrity. She's a lonely, bitter woman seeking revenge."

Sarah tilted her head to one side. "What did my father do?"

"Your father came to me about a year after the accident. He confided that Mrs. Hardin had made overtures and wanted a relationship. He asked me to help him protect your family and Mosey Inn. He begged me to speak with Mrs. Hardin and remove her from the list of church volunteers who came to help at the boarding house. Your father stood by your mother the rest of his life. I confronted Mrs. Hardin. That's when she changed."

"Mrs. Hardin ... wanted my father?"

Sarah gaped. How had she missed something like this? She closed her mouth as pieces of old memories fell into place. Sarah recalled the vibrant and beautiful Mrs. Hardin from thirty-something years ago. Mrs. Hardin, along with other local women, brought meals and helped with cleaning. Incidents Sarah now viewed as flirtations darted through her head. Snatches of the woman's laughter ... touches too intimate to be mere condolences ... arriving at inappropriate hours ... staying longer than necessary to assist with chores. Sarah had been too busy caring for her mother and the boarders to notice her father's attempts to rebuff Mrs. Hardin's advances.

Sarah's mother was incapable of a romantic relationship. Did Mr. Hardin, traveling as an engineering consultant, provide Mrs. Hardin with abundant money and zero affection? If so, she must have seen the Campbell family tragedy as a perfect opportunity for two hurting people to rectify their lonely existences. An impropriety could have remained secret if Sarah's father had chosen to relent.

Great respect for her father swelled within Sarah. He'd spurned the seduction of an attractive, wealthy woman, to remain faithful to his invalid wife. No wonder Mrs. Hardin hated them.

The scenario jelled in Sarah's mind. Destroying the reputation of Mosey Inn and its owners became the jilted woman's lifelong goal. Family responsibilities fell on Sarah as her father worked long hours to pay for her mother's medical care. As age crept up on Mrs. Hardin and Sarah's father, the bitterness crossed over to Sarah. Motives hadn't changed, merely the recipients.

"I assumed the Hardins were happily married," she said, her voice husky as if his story sucked the air out of her. "They've never indicated otherwise. I thought her actions were due to her wealth and a desire for power."

Pastor Morrison said, "People cover a multitude of pain. Given her recent actions, I thought you deserved the truth. I won't divulge what I know about her marriage."

Sarah held up her hands. "You've said enough. So many things are clear to me now."

The pastor lowered his voice and leaned forward. "You must never tell anyone, Sarah."

She picked up his mutilated cup and dumped the pieces into hers. "I promise to keep it confidential. If necessary, may I tell Benjamin?"

He nodded. "It affects him, so I'll trust your judgment. It can't become town knowledge."

"Thank you for sharing. I always had great respect for my father because he was loyal to my mother all those years. I wish I could tell him how proud he just made me."

Pastor Morrison glanced over his shoulder as if insuring their privacy. "There's another reason I told you. Benjamin and I have regular Bible studies. His faith is growing. So is his self-confidence. Before long he'll find the nerve to tell you he loves you."

Surprise almost choked her. "Has he told you he loves me?"

"No, but his actions speak loudly. You share that attraction, if I'm not mistaken."

Sarah nodded. Her heart slipped into a fast gallop, the warmth of a blush flooded her cheeks. "I've never loved a man. I'm afraid to admit my feelings for Benjamin."

"Don't be. Tell Benjamin about the fears. Share the joy he brings you. In my opinion, God planned to bring you two together many years ago."

"That's a Christian concept Benjamin might have a hard time accepting. That fire damaged more than his body."

"He isn't the same man we met back in August, Sarah. God's love, and the love of a fine woman, can work miracles."

He held up a finger. "One last thought. Mrs. Hardin will be very upset about the reprimand she received today."

"That sounds like a warning."

"It is. Renters dwindle during the winter. She'll spread lies if Benjamin is your only guest. God has ultimate control, but He expects us to behave wisely. Don't give Mrs. Hardin a reason to exact revenge. You've waited many years to find love."

CHAPTER TWENTY-FIVE

Benjamin slipped his arm into the suit jacket—not his normal attire. One of many atypical things lately. The box in his left pocket seemed to create an obvious bulge. A glance in the mirror showed it was his imagination.

He rehearsed the plan in his head one last time. His Tuesday night booking meant fewer diners. The manager had reserved the table in the back corner behind the piano ... out of sight and intimate. Quiet music, romantic candlelight, beautiful Christmas décor, and Sarah. A real date.

His image in the mirror didn't seem too repulsive this evening. He looked downright decent considering what he had to work with. The navy turtleneck hid the scars on his neck. He ran the comb through his hair to cover the missing part of his ear. Not bad, even if there were more gray hairs than he'd noticed back in August. He could handle a dinner date in the dimly lit setting where other couples would focus on each other and not him. The rest of his plan brought fear to the edge. "You can do it. You have to."

He stepped into the hallway and latched his door. At the bottom of the stairs, his breath caught. Sarah stood before the mirror in the foyer, fumbling with a necklace clasp. The form fitting red velvet dress cascaded over her slender hips, slid down her long legs, and skimmed her delicate ankles. Moonlight, peeping through the window, caught the intricate beadwork on the bodice. It shimmered with every breath.

Sarah jumped. "I didn't hear you coming."

"You're absolutely gorgeous."

She slipped on her shoes and turned a slow pirouette. "I hoped you'd like it."

He relished her slow appraisal of him.

"You look very handsome yourself." She held out the necklace. "I can't fasten this. Would you mind?"

Benjamin put on his reading glasses and stood behind her at the mirror. He slipped the silver strand around her neck. A large oval ruby, in an intricate setting, came to rest above the modestly scooped neckline. Costume jewelry. Sarah could never afford such a stone. The result was still alluring. He focused on the clasp to avoid looking at the soft pale skin below the pendant. He managed to insert the dainty earrings into her pierced ears and attach the backs without shaking. The rubies, dangling against her silky hair, caught the sparkle in her eyes.

Amazing. Two middle-aged anomalies behaving like teens getting ready for the prom. No. This was better. He hadn't appreciated the value of a woman like Sarah back then.

She reached up to caress his hand.

Perfection caught his eye in the mirror and smiled.

༄ ✵ ༅

After dinner, Benjamin thanked the waiter who removed their dessert plates. The pianist segued into a rendition of "Winter Wonderland."

Benjamin reached across the table and took Sarah's hand. "Thank you."

A puzzled look crossed her face. "For what?"

"Helping me reach a point where I can take you out to a fancy restaurant."

"You're welcome. I'm proud to be here with you."

Her smile tripped the fast forward in his heart. "I've wanted to tell you something for a long time." He stared at their hands, trying to get out the words he'd practiced saying. Raising his head to meet her gentle gaze, he found his courage. "I've been afraid to say ... I love you."

It sounded odd as the words fell off his tongue. Correct, yet odd. He'd seldom used them.

Sarah leaned closer and stroked his hand. "I think I love you too. We need to talk about some problems with that."

"That's not what I expected to hear. You have doubts about us?"

"Concerns. My health is fragile. I have debts to pay. We should talk about these issues. I have to decide if it's right to pull you into such an uncertain future."

"I don't see those as major concerns. I think God meant for us to find each other."

"I want to believe that too. I'm scared, Benjamin. I've never loved a man. I don't know where to go from here."

Benjamin pulled the box from his pocket and opened the lid. "You could say you'll marry me."

The diamond gleamed in the candlelight. Sarah's sharp intake of breath pulled his focus to her face. He didn't find an expression of joy.

"Oh, Benjamin. It's beautiful." Tears welled in her eyes. "I'm not ready." She touched the ring and looked away. "I need more time."

He hid the crushing disappointment. Rejection. Back to normal life. Maybe Sarah wasn't so different. He snapped the lid and pocketed the box. "It's me. I interpreted your signals wrong. I don't know how to go about this dating thing."

"No. It isn't you." She caressed his cheek.

Her touch seemed to brand him. Perhaps she didn't overlook the scars.

Sarah took a sip of water and glared into the candle flame. "It's me. You didn't read things wrong. You're making friends. Finding your place in the world. I don't want to hinder that by putting you in a care-giving position. Enjoy life. I'll hold you back."

"That's not true. Look at you. You're better. You're beautiful. The medicines are working. And even if they don't keep you healthy, I need you."

"That's a problem. You should stand on your own. Needing me is wrong. I've spent my life taking care of someone. You don't require a caretaker."

"I need your love. There is a difference."

She propped her chin on a fist and stared into her water glass. "Are you going to church because you want me in your life?"

His jaw dropped. "Is that what you think? Do you honestly believe I would fake reconciliation with God to gain your approval?"

"It crossed my mind. You have to admit the changes are drastic."

"Trusting God brings changes. What's happened to your faith, Sarah? Can't you believe God is good enough to give us joy in our old age?"

Shame crossed her face. "Yes. But I'm floundering in a valley of self-pity and fear. I can't control the circumstances this illness has created. Sarah Campbell has always handled the problems. It isn't easy to place my trust totally in God."

"You have to. It's the only way."

She sighed, closed her eyes briefly, and chuckled. Her hand found his again, and her eyes lit up. "You have grown."

"I have wise teachers."

"I didn't expect this, Benjamin. The marriage part, I mean. I knew you loved me."

"Then what are you saying?"

"Bad timing. Thursday is the anniversary of my mom's death. I'm depressed and remembering the bad things about my life. I may look and act fine, but I'm not. I'm terrified that I'll lose my ability to function. I'm struggling to find peace with that possibility."

"I'd still love you. The same way your dad loved your mom. In sickness and in health. It's part of the agreement."

"There's something else. I didn't want to tell you, but honesty seems important. Talking about marriage is a big step." She tugged on her lower lip with her teeth. "I doubted your innocence yesterday."

He propped an elbow on the table and rested his chin in the palm of his hand. "Ouch. That one stings. Mrs. Hardin does have a way of driving wedges between people."

Sarah nodded. "I almost believed her. That's how confused I am." She grabbed a napkin to swipe away the mascara running down her blotchy face. "It was only a second, but she made me wonder."

"It doesn't change anything. She almost convinced me I'd taken Noah."

There. He'd made her smile. He could joke about Sarah's doubt? A month ago, it would have spelled devastation. Him understanding and forgiving? The difference astounded him. When had he changed so much?

Sarah nibbled on her thumbnail.

A subtle change captured his attention. The knuckles of several fingers twisted slightly to the left. Valid reasons for her concerns.

He dipped his head to catch her gaze, and nearly choked on his words. "Do you want me to leave? Go back to Charlotte?"

Her head wagged. Fear sprang into her eyes. "No. You need to help me sort out these emotions. We're together for a reason. I'm just not certain we're supposed to marry."

Desperate, he grappled for ideas. "We'll talk. Get counseling. Pray." She had to comprehend his sincerity. "My spiritual changes are real. So is my love. You held me up when I couldn't stand alone. I'll do that for you."

Her sigh reflected profound fatigue.

He hadn't seen such dullness in her eyes for several weeks. "You're exhausted. Let's get you home. This date was a bad idea."

Sarah grasped his hand again. "No it wasn't. I've enjoyed our evening. Getting the worries out in the open helps. Now we can talk freely about who we are and where we should go."

"I thought we had. Guess I missed some important information. Like I said, this dating stuff baffles me."

"Please don't view this as rejection. The changes I see in you are real. I'm the one asking tough questions about the future."

They'd work through this. Fears weren't new to him. "I understand. Too busy. Tough week. Details we haven't discussed. I've never talked much. Always trying to cope with my bitterness. Life's different now. I'll learn to listen."

"You already listen. That's one reason to keep you around."

Much better. There was hope in that attitude.

"You're decorating tomorrow for Friday's youth party, right?"

"That's the plan since Noah changed the agenda yesterday." She leaned back in the chair, letting her arms flop to her sides as she glared at the ceiling. "My energy and my holiday spirit are lagging. I haven't been this tired in weeks."

"Let Emily and Karla decorate. You need to rest after the ordeal with Noah. I'm taking him riding tomorrow."

"He didn't get to show you his icicle-coated tree today. The ice melted too quickly."

"I'll go see the trail he made and the place he found for shelter. That's the important part of this trip."

A tiny smile curved her lips. "He'll talk your ears off."

Benjamin grinned. "That's okay. I've already lost most of one."

She squeezed her eyes shut and scrunched up her face. "Oh, that was rude of me."

"Nah. It proves you look past my flaws."

A genuine smile. Progress.

"After Christmas, when things settle down, we'll have a quiet evening. Discuss your concerns."

She gathered her purse and coat. "You're a very special man. I should say yes. Will you ask me again?"

"It's an open-ended proposal. I've waited a long time for you."

CHAPTER TWENTY-SIX

Sarah would need her coat, scarf, and gloves later if the predicted snow arrived. Currently, the temperature in the packed church hovered near eighty. Someone should turn down the heat. She slipped her feet out of her shoes and propped them on the pile of outerwear stuffed beneath the pew in front of her. Forget concentrating on the service. Her head bobbed again. She needed two toothpicks so she could prop her eyelids open like a silly cartoon character. Wedged between Ella and Benjamin, the temptation to lean her head against a shoulder and snooze almost won.

It couldn't be Sunday evening already. The days since their Tuesday dinner date had rushed by in a dizzying whirl. Decorating, shopping for gifts, one last children's program practice, and a joyous evening with the community youth during their party at Mosey Inn. Good thing her medicines had controlled her pain. Fatigue dragged her toward the bed at every possible chance. If she could make it through tonight...

Benjamin rested his hand on her leg, palm up. An invitation for handholding in church? Something she'd never done. It seemed right. Other couples, sharing the joy of children or grandchildren performing, were probably doing the same. She complied, giving his hand a little squeeze.

He whispered, "Becky's lining the kids up for their part. You awake?"

"Barely. I'm about to roast."

"Me too." He fanned them with his program.

Becky knelt in the center aisle. The children moved forward from their spots on the front pew. Becky had insisted one leader would be less distracting. Hopefully she was right.

An angel stumbled on her robe and overturned a poinsettia on the kneeling rail. Her wing caught a shepherd's staff. The shepherd toppled a wise man while yanking his staff from the angel's wing. A sheep, overwhelmed by the blunders, lost its nerve and fled to his human mother. A chain reaction of childish calamities. No one cared. A Christmas program wasn't complete without them. Precious children in God's sight, and in the eyes of each parent. When the giggles died, Becky reorganized the children one last time.

Benjamin's expression—grandfatherly pride. Any nervousness on his part was for Noah. Unshed tears reflected his love for the boy. Sarah tightened her grip on his hand.

Angelic voices, slightly off key, sang several Christmas songs. They ended with "Away in a Manger." One by one, they stepped out to recite their part of the Christmas story found in Luke. Noah, his wise man crown askew to the left, quoted his verses perfectly. Benjamin exhaled a breath Sarah hadn't realized he held.

Ella's satellite phone vibrated against Sarah's leg. Ella whispered, "Sorry. Catch up in the fellowship hall."

The congregation stood for the candlelight service. Ella tiptoed out the front door.

Singing "Silent Night," the group moved en masse across the breezeway. The rush of cold air revived Sarah. Perhaps a glass of punch would sustain her energy until she completed her job on the cleaning committee.

Ella paced beneath the magnolia tree. A sinking sensation hit the bottom of Sarah's stomach. If Ella left, she would be alone at Mosey Inn with Benjamin. "Something's happened. We may have to make alternative plans."

He steered her toward the refreshment line. "What do you mean?"

"Ella got a call this morning about an old case. If she leaves—"

"She'll do everything she can to get back for Christmas."

"That's not what I had in mind." Sarah tilted her head toward Mrs. Hardin. "Nothing would please her more than knowing we're alone in my house."

"You're right. It would look bad. I'm sorry, Sarah, but you'll have to move out."

She chuckled, scrunched up her nose, and swatted his arm. "Very funny. I'll help you pack, Mr. Wise Guy."

"Noah's motioning for us. We'll figure this out later."

They took the seats Noah saved for them. While Sarah was deep in conversation with Becky, Ella grabbed Sarah's arm. "I have to run. I can catch a plane in Charlotte if I hustle."

"To where?" Sarah's brow wrinkled, dreading what was coming.

"Norfolk, Virginia. Huge lead on an old case. Call you later." Ella sliced through the crowd and flew out the door.

Mrs. Hardin eyed Sarah from her spot on the opposite side of the room. Sarah dropped Benjamin's hand. Caught like a kid sneaking cookies. Surely she hadn't held it all the way through the line. She must have released it to carry her candle and fill her plate. Why worry? Mrs. Hardin couldn't see under the table. Others wouldn't think it was wrong. They were dating after all. She had to ignore the paranoia Mrs. Hardin created.

Benjamin's words drew her back to the conversation. "Ella's left Sarah with no other renters. I need to stay somewhere else."

"Come sleep with me, Grandpa."

"Do you steal the covers?" He poked Noah in the ribs.

Becky grinned. "Your bed isn't big enough for two. Grandpa would be more comfortable in the extra bedroom. It's our office but it has a pullout couch."

"I'd be imposing. I'll find a hotel in Statesville. I'm going over there to remodel a bath at Sheriff Bruster's house anyway."

Todd said, "You're always welcome, but I don't get why you need to leave. It's not the first time Sarah's had only one guest."

Becky laid a hand over Todd's and whispered, "People talk." She lifted her eyebrows as if trying to make him comprehend without saying a name in front of Noah.

"Oh, yeah ... I see." He shook his head. "It won't work. Your sister's coming tomorrow."

"Benjamin can at least stay in the office tonight."

Todd polished off his punch. "What about the shed we converted into a bunk house? It's empty until spring."

Becky said, "It's air conditioned but not heated. Would a space heater keep it warm?"

Benjamin wiped chocolate from his fingers. "It should. I added insulation so the pipes won't freeze. It'll do for a few days. Sarah has a closet full of quilts. I'll stay warm."

Noah said, "Miss Sarah's bed is warm and big enough for two people."

Sarah choked on her punch. She sputtered into a napkin, coughing so hard her eyes watered.

Becky clamped a hand over Noah's mouth, her eyes wide, chagrin obvious.

Noah glowered at Becky and pried her hand loose. "Why'd you do that? When old people get married, don't they sleep in the same bed like you and Daddy?"

Becky's face turned a brighter shade of red. "Yes, Noah. It just wasn't a good thing to say."

Benjamin pounded on Sarah's back. He leaned forward to catch her gaze. "You okay?"

She nodded. Still coughing, she looked up at him. That face.

He wasn't the least bit embarrassed. His eyes were sparkling. He'd clamped his lips together to hold back a smile.

She kicked him under the table. It only made his jaw drop and his eyes go wide. He stifled a laugh behind his hand.

She should clobber him when they left.

"Why wasn't it nice, Mommy?"

"Because Miss Sarah and Benjamin are not old. And children don't suggest people get married. Come with me. We'll find our cookie plate and go home. You can help me get the bunk house ready for Grandpa." She mouthed over her shoulder. "Sorry."

Todd looked as if he would burst out laughing.

Sarah growled, "Look at you two. I could kill you."

"Aw, come on, Sarah," Todd said. "It's funny. You have to agree, the kid had a better plan."

Sarah opened her mouth to lecture them. The lights flickered. Gasps, then the scuffing of chairs and the jostling of people.

Pastor Morrison stepped to the microphone. "I hate to break up the fun. It's snowing again." Murmurs around the room. Yips and laughter from the children. "Perhaps we'd be wise to get home. You know our routine for trash disposal. We'll remove the table decorations another day. Have a wonderful Christmas. Drive safely. See you next Sunday."

People offered hasty goodbyes. "Merry Christmas" floated around with the rustle of napkins and paper plates. Dishes clattered.

"I'll take Sarah home and pack a few things," Benjamin said.

Noah bounced and tugged on Benjamin's arm. "Let's go build a snowman, Grandpa."

"Tomorrow. It'll be bedtime when I get to your house."

"From roasting to freezing." Sarah slipped her gloves on. "I hope Ella doesn't have snow on her way to Charlotte."

Benjamin and Sarah stomped snow off their shoes in the foyer at Mosey Inn. Benjamin went to gather essentials for several days. Sarah chose three quilts from the closet. They met again at the bottom of the steps.

Benjamin dropped his bag, titled her chin up, and kissed her. "Hold my room a few days?"

"Yes. But I won't let you pay for it."

"We'll see about that. Money will be one of those concerns we eventually discuss."

She fiddled with a button on his shirt, and remained in the circle of his arms. "It shouldn't have to be this way. Mrs. Hardin doesn't dictate who stays at my inn."

"In this case, she does. If I stayed, she'd have a motive to ruin our future. Especially after what you told me on the way home. I'm thankful Pastor Morrison shared Mrs. Hardin's secret with you. Even if we forget her desire for revenge, I shouldn't stay while Ella's away. People know we're dating. They would assume the worst."

"Maybe Ella won't be gone long. I'll know more when she calls."

"Is it Ella or me you'll miss?"

His crooked smile, and another kiss, made her knees go weak. She wasn't behaving like a woman who was unsure about her love.

"You. I said I needed time to work out details. I didn't turn your proposal down. I sort of like having you around."

"We'll talk." He took the quilts she'd placed on the railing. "I'd better go. Do not drive in this snow."

"I know how to drive in bad weather."

"I'm sure you do. Just don't. I heard you telling Emily you'd help clean tomorrow. You feel obligated to help since you're on the committee."

"I do. Other women did the decorating. It's my turn to clean. Besides, we'll have church mice if we leave crumbs too long."

"Then I'll pick you up. I won't be going to Statesville if the roads are bad."

"You have a snowman to build." She took a couple steps toward the door.

"About Noah ... I'm sorry I laughed. The boy's right. Why does everyone but you see marriage as a good idea?"

"There isn't time to talk. Don't push the issue tonight."

He picked up his bag and moved to the porch steps. Sarah watched from the open door. Total silence—nothing moved except the snowflakes tumbling from the sky.

"I'll call when I get to Todd and Becky's." With one foot in the truck cab and one on the ground, he turned. "I love you."

She didn't respond. Simply waved goodbye.

The truck door slammed.

Why did I love you stick in her throat every time she had a chance to say the words?

It wouldn't look bad if they lingered to talk at the church tomorrow. Maybe they could speak with Pastor Morrison about counseling. She had to decide what her heart wanted. Benjamin deserved an answer. Soon.

Her kitchen was too quiet. Benjamin wouldn't come to share breakfast or sneak a kiss this morning. They wouldn't linger at the table or snuggle under a quilt on the couch to read. No sitting on the porch swing talking while the sun rose. They wouldn't share the beauty of fresh snow on bare apple trees and pendulous green cedars. Alone. How long had it been since she'd been alone?

Sarah threw open the drapes, raised the mini-blinds, and climbed back in bed. With the quilts pulled over her legs, she sipped a second cup of coffee and stared at the winter wonderland.

Still snowing. At least six inches during the night. Rare to have this much snow in Love Valley. It was the sort of snow with incredible beauty but disastrous potential. Heavy and wet—it weighted the electrical wires and clung to every twig and branch. Silently deceptive, it fell in great round flakes. It didn't dance and swirl. Nothing encouraged it to frolic. Peaceful and calm. Unlike the turbulence churning in Sarah's heart.

The ringing phone made her jump. "Mosey Inn."

"I'd like to, but I can't right now." Benjamin's voice played sweet notes that seemed to set the snow dancing. She could hear Noah's laughter in the background. "Sarah, have you looked outside?"

"The orchard's amazing. Every twig is white."

A limb breaking on the maple near her room echoed like a shotgun blast across the valley. The branch crashed to the ground and rattled the windows. A geyser of white exploded into the air. Sarah startled, a hand flying to her chest. "Did you hear that?"

More squeals and shouts from Noah. "Hear what? ... Settle down, Noah. I can't hear what Sarah's saying."

"Never mind. Sounds like you two are having fun."

"It's gorgeous over here. We're building a snowman to guard my bunk house."

"Glad you're finally getting around to that. He's waited a whole week. Were you warm last night?"

"It's nothing like Carpenter's Wheel, but it'll suffice. The heater knocked the chill off. The quilts made it cozy. It'll work until Ella comes back."

A dull thud sounded in her ear. "Hey, no fair, kid. I'm defenseless." Benjamin panted as if running.

Laughter in the background and laughter from Benjamin. The snowflakes seemed to perk up and swirl around the apple trees.

"The roads should be slushy. No more ice under the snow. I'll come get you about ten."

A louder thump. "Ouch! Have to run. I'm getting bombarded with snowballs."

"I miss—"

The dial tone hummed.

She did miss him. His smile, his laugh, his touch. More than anything, she missed his presence. Companionship. Was marriage about the simple pleasures they weren't sharing this morning? Maybe it was the things he did to make life easier. Like making coffee, opening a jar, mopping a floor, or tugging on a sheet corner. It sounded better than alone.

Were those reasons to say yes to a lifetime together? Well, the remaining years of their lifetime—they'd spent over half of life alone. With her financial issues and uncertain health, perhaps it would be better to spend the rest alone as well.

৪০ ✠ ୧୪

"I think it was eighty in here last night. It's freezing this morning." Benjamin tossed a log on the fire in the fellowship hall. "That should knock the chill off. Are you sure you want to work since the power is off?"

Emily said, "It won't take long to store these decorations and clear the tables. We'll need this room Sunday. We have enough light from the windows to see what we're doing. You game, Sarah?"

Sarah extended her hands to the warm fire. "We can at least sweep up the crumbs. They'll attract mice. Nothing important planned for a snowy Monday afternoon."

Emily grabbed a broom from the corner. "Sounds fine. Sarah, you bag decorations. Benjamin can carry them to the attic. We'll toss the paper tablecloths and call it quits. If those who stayed at home want to do more, they can come later in the week."

Benjamin stuffed a miniature Christmas tree into a plastic bag. "Sounds like a plan. Do you bag each item separately?"

"Yeah." Sarah situated a fake poinsettia in a bag Benjamin held. "We should label them. It'll make decorating easier next year. Grab a marker off the shelf where the Sunday school supplies are stored."

Benjamin labeled the bags, laid them beside the door, and returned for another one. "Getting these up the folding attic stairs in the sanctuary is the challenge. I'll rig up a flashlight at the top of the steps so I don't fall and break my neck."

Emily stilled her broom. "Don't take any chances. Getting the tables cleared is the important thing."

"Understood."

Sarah spent the next fifteen minutes bagging and tagging. Emily chatted about Thomas' delight over Christmas. It put a little crimp in Sarah's joy. If Ella didn't return, she might spend Christmas alone. She needed to talk with Benjamin. They could invite other single church members over for the day. Did she dare consider spending the day at Mosey Inn with just Benjamin?

Benjamin bustled in and headed straight to the fireplace. "Man, it is cold in that attic." He rubbed his hands together and held them out toward the fire. Dirt smudged his left cheek and cobwebs clung to his red stocking cap. Wayward curls peeped out around his forehead and neck. "There isn't much sunlight coming through the stained glass windows. I've rigged a flashlight so I can see the stairs."

Emily said, "We're almost finished with the decorations. I'll help carry the bags over and hand them to you so you don't have to climb up and down." She propped the broom against a table, grabbed two bags, and departed.

Sarah twisted the tie on one last bag of decorations. A little smile touched her lips when Benjamin purposely grasped her hand instead of the neck of the bag. "A better way to warm my hands." He winked, took the bag, and headed out the door.

The dwindling fire didn't reach far into the room. Almost done anyway. She'd go home and have a hot cup of tea. Sarah zipped the old ski jacket she'd dug out of the closet.

A large log smoldered on underlying coals. It needed air to burst back into flame. If she adjusted its position, the log would catch and provide heat so she could comfortably remove the tablecloths and wipe the tables.

She picked up the fireplace tongs and grasped the log. Heavier than she expected. Pain shot up her wrist. The log slipped loose. Her stomach did a flip-flop. She jabbed the tongs forward to brace the log.

In what seemed like slow motion, yet too fast to prevent disaster, it rolled off the flaming coals.

Terror soared. The log teetered on the edge of the hearth before falling with a thud. Sparks flew. It rolled beneath the nearest table. Flames darted up the overhanging paper and raced along the table.

"Help! Benjamin. Emily. Fire!"

Bits of burning paper floated on unseen currents and landed

on adjacent tables. Her screams for help disrupted the quiet. Fires whooshed to life on several tables. Black smoke billowed across the room.

She ran toward the fire extinguisher hanging on the wall. A chair leg caught her right foot. Pitching forward, her left knee crashed against the floor. Pain ripped across her chest when the floor stopped her forward momentum.

Don't lay here. Roll away from the fire. A tangle of chair and table legs greeted her. Which way led to the door?

"Benjamin!" The smoke detector's beeps swallowed her cries.

Through the maze, she saw light. Felt cool air. The door. "Sarah! Where are you? Sarah! Can you hear me?"

Impossible to answer. Smoke stole each breath. Acrid smells strangled her. Coughing and gagging, she rose on her knees to crawl toward his voice. Agonizing pain. She dropped to her belly.

Emily shouted. "I'll bring help."

Another alarm with a different pitch. Benjamin had punched the fire alert on the security alarm. He coughed and called her again. A blast from a fire extinguisher cleared a path in the smoke.

Sarah caught a glimpse of his red stocking cap, close to the floor beneath a table. Her exit. She grabbed a table leg and dragged herself forward.

"I hear you coughing. This way, Sarah." Another sweep of white from the extinguisher.

Chairs crashed, tables scraped across the floor on her right. The red hat. Closer to her.

"I see you. Roll left."

She obeyed. An aisle opened between chair legs. Clawing her way from chair leg to chair leg, every inch became a struggle. Her lungs filled with smoke and complained with fits of coughing that stopped her progress.

Outside, a car horn ripped through the roar of the flames and alarms. Emily. Volunteer firemen and other valley residents would come. The deafening sounds would beckon everyone. Maybe they could save the sanctuary.

Smoke stung her eyes. Coughing from the spot near the door.

A table collapsed behind her. Flames licked out toward her legs. Was she screaming? Fire jumped toward the ceiling. Another blast of the fire extinguisher.

She swiped at her watering eyes. Can't give up. Focus on that spot of red near the floor. Harder to pull her way along the endless line of chairs.

Benjamin's strong hands grabbed her arms. For an instant,

they were almost eye-to-eye. Terror and relief surged between them.

He rose to his knees, tugging her toward the breezeway. Away from the flames. Away to safety.

Cold. Wet snow on her face. Benjamin rolled her several times. She hadn't felt the flames. Was she burning?

Arms scooped her up. He stumbled in the snow. They dropped to the ground somewhere near the road. Alarms faded with the distance.

Benjamin pulled her into a sitting position against his chest. His heart pounded in her ear. Coughing and sobs shook his body. "You'll be okay. Breathe. Oh, Sarah, I thought I'd lost you. Take another breath. Good. Stay awake. Breathe."

She couldn't speak. Coughs hampered each effort. Adrenaline died. Pain took control.

༺ ⚜ ༻

Benjamin paced the length of the emergency room waiting area, halted, and checked his watch. Two hours—with one report that Sarah was stable. He'd go crazy waiting. He retraced his path.

Shaking enough without the aid of bad tasting caffeine, his cup of cold coffee went in the trash. A silent prayer came with every breath, punctuated by a cough now and then. He sank into a chair and let his head fall into his hands. If screaming would help, he'd resort to it.

A hand on his shoulder brought his head up. "Todd. Becky." He stood to accept Todd's manly hug. His strength and morale improved with their arrival.

Benjamin hugged Becky. "Tell me you didn't bring Noah. He doesn't need to be here."

She took the seat beside Benjamin and Todd sat in the row across from them. Becky said, "Noah's with my sister. How's Sarah?"

Benjamin swallowed over the lump in his throat. "I wish I knew."

Becky laid a hand on his arm. "I don't know how to ask this without sounding insensitive. Was Sarah burned?"

Benjamin squeezed his eyes shut. Tears threatened to erupt again. "I don't know. Her coat was smoldering. I rolled her in the snow. Coughing kept her from speaking." He leaned his head against the wall and forced some shuddering breaths. "I didn't see any obvious burns."

Becky squeezed his arm. "Sounds like good news."

Todd inched closer. "You look rough, man. Are you hurt?"

"No. The paramedics insisted I needed oxygen. I used it in the ambulance on the way." If he admitted his chest ached when he took a deep breath, they'd stick him in some treatment room where he'd never hear about Sarah. Knowing she was safe would fix him.

"The church?" he asked. "What happened to the church?"

"The fire's out," Todd said. "Mostly smoke damage. We lost some tables and other equipment. Both buildings are standing. Nothing we can't replace."

"Sounds right from what I saw. There were flames but mostly thick smoke. I could barely see Sarah."

Benjamin leaned forward, bracing his elbows on his knees. Sarah's terrified screams and her coughing rang in his ears. Horrid images of her inching toward him, one chair at a time, flashed before him. He'd hesitated, too terrified to enter the smoke and flames, until he could see a way to safely reach her. If he'd gone to her earlier ... no ... they'd both be dead. The past hadn't held him back. He'd acted appropriately, kept his wits when she needed him. Pushing the alarm, using the fire extinguisher, and following her coughs saved her.

"Was she conscious on the way here?" Becky asked.

"Sort of. Her oxygen levels were low. Lungs irritated by the smoke. On oxygen of course. They put a tube down her throat in case her airway swelled and she needed a ventilator. She was breathing on her own through the tube."

He couldn't hold it together any longer. Sobs broke free. Comforting, supporting arms held him. Words wouldn't help. What could they say? Sarah's struggle to breathe filled his ears anyway.

Todd took him by the elbow. "You're covered with soot. Come wash up. Becky brought you a change of clothes." He held up a plastic bag.

Benjamin studied the filth on his hands. A closer look showed his clothes looked the same. "I hadn't noticed. If I leave, they might—"

Todd stood, tugging Benjamin to a standing position. "Don't argue. Sarah shouldn't see you this way. The restroom is on the other side of the waiting area. Becky's here."

Benjamin shot her an uncertain glance.

"Go on. I'll knock if there's news."

Benjamin splashed water on his face again. When he ran

warm water over his hair, black water poured into the sink. The makeshift bath eased some tension in his neck. He toweled his face and hair while watching dirty water swirl down the drain.

Todd punched the button to activate the hand dryer. "Here. Dry your hair." He shouldn't need help with this. Emotional shock? Weird. He'd have stood there wondering what to do next. "You smell less smoky."

Benjamin stuck his head under the dryer. Todd stuffed the dirty clothes into the bag with the towel and washcloth Becky had brought. The blower turned off. Benjamin finger combed his hair. Presentable at least. "Thanks, Todd."

"You need food."

"It wouldn't stay down."

"Then at least drink something. I'll buy you a Coke. Do you even realize you're coughing? You could use more oxygen."

"Drop it. It's minor." Benjamin pushed open the door. "Right now, all I care about is Sarah."

The cold drink stung his throat with the first few sips, and then it eased the rawness he hadn't noticed. The pack of crackers settled his stomach.

A woman dressed in blue scrubs and a white lab coat came to the waiting room door. "Benjamin Pruitt?"

He stood. "Yes."

"I'm Dr. Mitchell." She offered a hand to shake. "Sorry to keep you waiting. Come with me."

"Sarah's friends?" He gestured toward Becky and Todd.

Dr. Mitchell addressed them. "She's improving. I'll send a nurse to give you an update."

The door closed behind them. Man, he'd forgotten how much he hated the smell of a hospital. The doctor stopped outside the third room on the left. "Sarah was hysterical when she became fully conscious. Apparently, she dropped a log that started the fire. I gave her medication to calm her and ease the pain. Don't upset her if she wakes up and wants to talk."

"No ventilator?"

"Not necessary. She has some minor airway irritation but doesn't need assistance breathing. I removed the tube. She's fine with an oxygen mask. Things are looking good."

"You said pain. What's hurting?"

"She fell. Bruised her left knee and some ribs. Nothing's broken. Her labs and x-rays look better. If she continues to improve, I'll release her tomorrow morning. She can recover at home."

"Sarah has RA. Will this knee injury affect that?"

Dr. Mitchell nodded. "I spoke with her rheumatologist. He adjusted her medicines. He'll follow up on the knee injury."

"No burns?"

"None. Her ski jacket had melted areas in the fabric. Probably some embers. If she hadn't been wearing several layers of clothes, we'd have a different story. She asked for you. Sit with her. Give her some juice. A familiar face will help."

"What about Becky and Todd?"

"One visitor at a time. Don't overexert her. Push the call button if you need a nurse. We'll move her upstairs to a room soon." She touched his arm and headed toward another room.

He'd expected to hear much worse. Benjamin cracked open the treatment room door. Sarah looked fragile against the white sheets. The hospital gown swallowed her. IV fluids, heart, and oxygen monitors. Routine hospital equipment. His heart settled into a better rate. He pulled the plastic chair close to the gurney.

She looked pale beneath the oxygen mask covering most of her face. Lips slightly parted, her breathing indicated sleep. A few wheezing breaths started some coughing. Her eyes moved beneath her eyelids. She didn't awaken. Her chest must feel like it had an elephant sitting on it. His did. He couldn't be sure if irritated lungs or emotions cut off his air.

He took her hand, kissed her fingers, and settled back in the chair.

She stirred. Her eyes fluttered open. "Benjamin?" The hoarse, raspy whisper sounded painful.

He bent over her. "I'm here." Gentle fingertips stroked hair away from her sooty brow.

Her face twisted beneath the mask. Tears slid down her dirty cheeks. "The church. I burned—"

"Shh, don't cry. It'll make it harder to breathe. Look at me." Her bloodshot eyes met his gaze. "The church did not burn. Smoke damage. Nothing we can't fix."

She pressed her lips together and searched his face. "Don't lie."

"It's the truth. You're improving. The church is standing."

"Honest?"

"Absolutely." He wiped her tears and helped her blow her nose.

She swallowed then moaned. "Thirsty."

Benjamin slid the oxygen mask up to her forehead and brought the straw to her lips. "Slowly. Don't choke. Bet your throat's sore."

She nodded. Took a few sips. "Feels better."

He slipped the oxygen mask back over her nose and mouth. "The doctor says you'll go home in the morning."

"I can't stay. How will I pay for this?"

"We'll figure that out later."

"I don't want you paying—" A fit of coughing stole her breath. She sank deeper into the pillow.

"Don't talk. Breathe." Keeping her eyes open seemed to require more strength than she had. He brushed a finger along her cheek. "Rest."

"My knee hurts."

He pushed the blanket off her leg. A dark bruise indicated where she'd fallen. He adjusted the ice pack and pillow. "Bad bruise. No breaks. No burns. You'll be back to normal in a few days."

"Running for the extinguisher. Tripped on a chair." She coughed, grimacing.

Her throat had to feel raw. "Stop talking. It's making you hurt."

"Eyes sting. Awful headache."

"Need more medicine?" He picked up the call button.

"Not yet." She closed her eyes, drifting off for a few moments. "Are you hurt?"

Forget rest until he'd satisfied her that all was well. "Slight cough. I'm fine."

Another bout of coughing caused her to gag and gasp. She fished for his hand. Once the spasm and wheezing subsided, she asked, "Emily?"

"At home. Every one's fine. Becky and Todd came. Want to see them?"

She shook her head. "Chest hurts. Can't focus."

Her eyes closed, but her expression showed pain. He plucked a washcloth from the supply cart, ran water over it, and returned. Lifting the mask, he washed her dirty face. "Feel good?"

A little grunt and a nod.

He wrung out the cloth under warm water and bathed her smutty hands, then tucked them under the blanket.

A new cloth, with fresh cool water, covered her eyes and forehead. "Sleep. We'll talk later."

"Later."

An hour passed. Nurses moved her to an inpatient room. She drifted in and out of sleep, asking the same questions each time she awoke. His reassurances satisfied her for a while. Becky and Todd visited briefly, and then departed. Benjamin dozed, his head resting on his arms, propped on the edge of the bed.

Sarah's hand rarely left his.

The doctor and nurses came and went. Blood draws, x-rays, vital signs. Constant attentive care. They changed the oxygen from a mask to nasal prongs. Reduced the oxygen flow. Administered medicines.

Through the night, Benjamin kept a constant vigil. He pushed aside the memories from years ago. Sarah wouldn't face this ordeal alone and afraid.

CHAPTER TWENTY-SEVEN

Needing help with a shower ... how demeaning. At least the hot water eased the ache in her ribs. Becky lathered Sarah's hair again. Strength spiraled away with the filthy water. Depression she'd held at bay for days settled over her like a pall. Benjamin said she hadn't burned the church, but she'd created inconveniences for her fellow congregants. They shouldn't have to take care of her or meet somewhere else until repairs were complete on the church. If she thought about the issues, she'd never survive the day.

She pulled the quilts up and appreciated the comfort of her bed. Sleeping all afternoon might be a great avoidance technique. Sunlight bathed her bedroom, and the world outside, with warmth. The melting snow dripped from every twig and turned the yard into mud. Winter. A fickle season in the Brushy Mountains.

Becky emerged from the bathroom with an armload of towels. She dumped them beside the bag of dirty clothes they'd brought from the hospital. "Got to run. My sister's making cookies with Noah. I'd better rescue her." She scooted the walker away from the bed, out of Sarah's reach.

Sarah frowned at it as if some alien being had invaded her territory.

"I see that look. Behave. Don't get up alone." Becky gave her a peck on the cheek.

Benjamin rose from the recliner and crossed to stand beside the bed. "Becky's right. You're too unsteady to walk alone. Ask the sitters to help you. Need Becky to do anything else before she leaves?"

Sarah shook her head. If she spoke, her frustration with the entire ordeal might pop out in words she didn't want to use.

Benjamin walked beside Becky to the bedroom door. "Thanks for helping this morning."

"Not a problem. Be back at bedtime."

Sarah fretted about the sitters scheduled to care for her and the home health nurses coming to teach them about breathing treatments. What a disaster.

Benjamin held up the plastic bag of sooty clothes. "Want these washed or tossed?"

"Toss them. They're old and useless." Tears sprang to her eyes. She turned over to keep him from seeing them. Perhaps he'd believe she was watching Becky leave.

Benjamin dropped the bag and sat on the edge of the bed. He cupped her chin. "Stop the negative thoughts. You'll be back to normal soon."

She couldn't look into those warm brown eyes. She turned her head, dislodging his hand. Better to glare out the window. "I wasn't … okay, I was. I hate being dependent." She pounded a fist into the mattress. "You're supposed to be working for Sheriff Bruster, not taking care of me."

"Marcus understands. Besides, tomorrow is Christmas Eve. I'll start the job after the holidays."

"It's not only him. Church friends have changed holiday plans to stay with me." She fought to control her tears. A stuffy nose wouldn't help matters.

"You're more important right now. Most of the volunteers don't have families. They'd rather help you than be at home alone. You're overreacting."

Oh, it would never do to let her wallow in self-pity one day. She understood his snap out of it and appreciate the fact you're alive rationale. She should. But life wasn't good right now. God had tossed her a curve she didn't want to accept. Plus, Benjamin had an answer for every complaint. He'd been here not long ago—debased, angry, and bitter. Couldn't he back off a bit—let her enjoy her guilt and depression?

She pointed to the walker beside her bed. "I hate that thing. Makes me feel like a decrepit old woman."

"Then use the cane. Either one keeps pressure off your bruised knee."

She crossed her arms over her chest and studied the knots in the paneling on the wall. Another easy answer. Her scowl deepened. "My knee might swell if I put weight on it."

"Okay, Sarah. If you want to be curt with me, I can handle it. At least be nice to helpers who come. We agreed to avoid gossip by not staying alone at your house. Pastor Morrison set up volunteers so we can do that. Since you can't manage by yourself, accept their gracious gifts. And understand this, I'll love you no matter what you say or do."

Anger simmered. She fought to prevent an eruption into a huge tantrum. "What happens if I reach a point in the future where I am in bed forever?"

"Nope. Not going there. You are not in the proper frame of mind to make decisions about our future."

"Fine. We'll ignore your marriage proposal today. I doubt you want a future with an old woman anyway." She turned her back to him and concentrated on water dripping from an icicle on the porch railing.

"Stop it. I won't become involved in an argument when you're not thinking clearly. Rest. It shouldn't take Mrs. Wexler long to drive from her place."

Silence. Sarah rolled over to find the room empty. How dare he walk out when ... okay, he was right. Ignoring a child pitching a fit usually worked best. Benjamin seemed to see through her to the painful core—to the fear she couldn't face. This went way past a few days in bed.

By mid-afternoon, she craved a nap. Coughing fits brought agony to her ribs and tears to her eyes. Exhaustion tugged at her eyelids, and her knee ached. Mrs. Wexler wouldn't be content to sit in the recliner and read. She'd droned on about everything from cooking to horses.

Sarah cleared her sore throat, took a sip of hot tea, and said, "Sorry ... can't talk ... hurts."

Her wizened older friend looked much like Yoda. "Oh, me, I have babbled on and on." Mrs. Wexler tapped a finger against her lips and chuckled. "I don't get to visit often. Lonely, you know." She grabbed her cane, hobbled over to Sarah's bed, and adjusted the covers. Her friend shook two pills from the bottle into the cap. "Take those, dear. They'll help you rest." Sarah held out a hand to accept them. Mrs. Wexler caressed Sarah's cheek, and then handed her a glass of water. "Sleep for a while. I'll go watch a game show on that nice TV of yours. Home health will be here in about an hour. Don't let me forget to wake Benjamin." She limped off, mumbling about checking the cake in the oven.

Why should she need babysitters at her age? Two words kept rolling in her brain—old and useless. They fit her attitude. Some of her helpers were in worse shape than she was. If coming over to chat or bring a meal made them feel needed, maybe it wasn't an inconvenience. Mrs. Wexler had enjoyed talking and mothering her this afternoon. Still, requiring help galled her. Sarah tried to wrap her mind around an idea, but it kept floating away. Later, when she felt stronger, she'd grasp the concept. It seemed important.

A breathing treatment opened her lungs. If only the relief would last more than a few hours. Benjamin had better understand the nurse's explanations. Those details sailed over Sarah's fuzzy brain. Staying awake, much less focused, wasn't happening today.

Several hours later, a horrific coughing bout jerked her awake. She sat up in bed and scanned the room. Empty. Breaths became gasps. Searing pain tore across her ribs. Every particle of smoke debris seemed to dislodge from the crevices in her lungs. Disgusting gunk came up with each cough.

Benjamin rushed in from the library.

Sarah waved toward the door. "Don't let her—"

Benjamin closed the door and hurried over. "Mrs. Wexler's icing a cake in the kitchen. Lean on me." He wrapped Sarah in a hug and held her upright. Tissues appeared when she needed them.

A pillow braced against her chest did little to help her sore ribs. It seemed like forever before she could take a decent breath between the coughs. She collapsed against his chest. She'd swear she'd coughed up her toenails. A whiff of oxygen would be nice. Maybe she should have stayed in the hospital another day like the doctor suggested. Eventually, Benjamin lowered her to pillows.

Too weak to move; too weak to complain. Humiliated didn't begin to describe her emotions. Benjamin shouldn't have to watch this. Shouldn't have to clean up after her. She'd apologize when she found the strength.

He disposed of the tissues. He didn't seem the least bit perturbed by the revolting phlegm. Taking care of her didn't faze him. The cool cloth he stroked across her face took away some of her headache. Her head must be full of black soot as well.

Concern etched lines in his forehead. "You sure you're okay?" Loving fingers combed through her hair.

"Exhausted. Not sure I want to live." She attempted a smile.

"I can relate."

"Experienced it?"

"Missed the smoke inhalation part. Sedated and on a ventilator. Debridement was my undoing."

The idea of such pain prickled her skin. She shouldn't feel so sorry for herself. She hurt, though—a different sort of hurt. Lost plans and a changed life due to circumstances she couldn't control. Life-changing decisions she didn't know how to make. Too much at once. Too weary to think.

Benjamin prepared a breathing treatment that calmed the remaining spasms. Leaning against him, she drifted toward sleep.

The glare of the overhead lights teased her awake. Dark outside. She'd lost all perception of time. Had Mrs. Wexler left? Benjamin dozed in the recliner. Events seemed jumbled. He remained the constant that held her day together. Always there. Always comforting. Always ... loving. If her arthritis made days like this a permanent fixture, would it be fair to ask this of him?

An elderly couple brought dinner. Sarah couldn't recall their names tonight. Strange. They attended church, lived near the newest campground. Who were they? If this odd confusion lasted, she'd have to admit it. Fear tugged at a corner in her head. Should she go back to the hospital? Maybe she wasn't okay.

The spoon shook when Sarah brought it to her mouth. The lady with the gentle smile said, "Let me help." Sarah creased her brow, searching again for the lady's name.

"Oh, don't look so upset. You've had a terrible shock to your system. Tomorrow will be much better."

Total mortification. Mrs. No Name fed her a bowl of chicken soup. Even in her worst arthritis flares, she'd managed to shower and feed herself. The warm salty liquid soothed the rawness in her throat. Now she wanted more sleep.

"Thank you. I hadn't realized I was hungry."

"Good. You're getting stronger. I'll join the men in the library so you can rest. Call if you need me."

This fussing over her had to stop. Too tired to socialize, she dozed, aware of their muted voices, soft laughter, and an occasional snippet of the conversation.

The woman loomed over the bed again. "We'll come back and visit when you recover. Please, call on us if you need anything. We've enjoyed our evening with Benjamin. Go back to sleep, dear." She'd have to ask him who they were. Later.

Becky and her sister bustled in shortly after the couple left. That dreadful walker. She had to use it for the trip to the bathroom. At least she could brush her own teeth.

Becky settled her in bed then grabbed the CD player and an overnight bag. "We're having a girly sleepover. Sorry you're sick, but staying here lets us giggle all night. We're in North Carolina Lily. Call on us for help, Benjamin." They scurried off like two teens at a pajama party.

Sarah patted the bed beside her. "Come sit."

Benjamin joined her, smoothing stray hairs away from her forehead.

"I'm feeling more alert. You haven't slept much. Go up to bed."

"You think I'd sleep with them across the hall?" Benjamin's engaging grin tugged at her heart. "I'll sleep on the couch in the library." His gentle kiss took her by surprise. "I wouldn't hear you upstairs. You look better. Rough day."

"Totally disgusting for you. Sorry you had to stomach my coughing fits."

He sighed, trailed kisses from her forehead to her cheeks, and finally to her lips. "Why can't you understand? Love doesn't care."

The intensity of his gaze and the gentleness of his caresses brought a twinge of guilt. "I do understand. I did it for years. That's what makes it so hard. I'm afraid to get old. I do not want you taking care of me."

"I'd do it with love. You did."

≈ ✠ ≈

Sarah stared at the ceiling. The middle of the night harbored thoughts that hid from the daylight. The house creaked and popped. Music and snatches of laughter floated down from the happy sisters. Sounded like way too much fun. Chaperones. The idea rankled, though propriety made sense even if Mrs. Hardin didn't seek ways for revenge. Benjamin couldn't care for her alone under their current circumstances.

Benjamin coughed in his sleep. Preoccupied with her troubles, she'd ignored his coughing. His chest and throat must hurt too. After all, he'd breathed almost as much smoke as she had. Should she check on him? He'd never hinted that he was ill. He shouldn't sacrifice his health for her.

Her health. What a joke. Now she had more medical bills she couldn't pay. The future looked as dark as the sky outside. This injury was temporary. If she didn't have a life-altering illness, she wouldn't be lying here wondering about the future. The doctor said her RA was under control. Overall, it was true. She functioned close to normal. Minor aches and pains, fatigue if she overexerted—decent for a woman her age.

One thing didn't need contemplation. Friends and church family would not take care of her the way they had today. Meals and visits were one thing. Basic hygiene was a different story. Becky had gone beyond what Sarah could handle on a regular basis. She wouldn't belittle friends or herself that way.

The "what ifs" held Sarah by the throat tonight. Wrestling with them got her nowhere. She couldn't predict the future. She might never have crippling from the RA. Her crooked fingers might not worsen. She might never develop deformed knees or twisted useless feet. It could happen. Benjamin deserved better options.

His love was obvious. A man didn't act this way unless he loved someone. She'd watched her father exhibit the same gentle care toward her mother. She had never asked him if he regretted his decision to keep his wife at home rather than place her in a facility. It wasn't something a daughter asked. Sarah's life could have taken on a very different meaning if he had chosen that route. Life would have meant a job, probably a husband, and maybe a family. She'd receive none of those ... except the husband if she wanted to change her entire existence. She didn't begrudge her role as caregiver, but facts were facts. She had given up many things. Would it be right to require such sacrifices of Benjamin if she became an invalid?

He'd found deliverance from his solitary life. Self-confidence had come with his return to faith. She'd fulfilled the task God had given her. He needed space to grow. Would marriage help or hinder?

The clock in the library bonged three times. Benjamin coughed again. The leather couch creaked as he moved. She willed him to remain asleep. She should ask about his cough, but she wasn't ready for a long discussion.

His rhythmic tones of sleep continued.

She longed to seek Ella's sage advice. Not happening. Ella wasn't coming home for Christmas. She'd confirmed that on the phone sometime during Sarah's jumbled day. Ella's missing person took precedence. Someone always seemed to come before Sarah. Her self-pity was getting out of hand. It wasn't fair to force those around her to endure her ill temper. Prayer usually dissolved the blues. Not this time.

In her head, she understood that God had her ultimate good in mind. Letting her heart trust Him was her battle. It wasn't simply her future. It was Benjamin's future too. Would his love hold up under pressure? If it did, should she take away his freedom?

CHAPTER TWENTY-EIGHT

Where had the last two days gone? It couldn't be Christmas. More stuffed than the turkey, Sarah retreated to a comfortable chair in the Spanglers' living room. Her plan to host friends at Mosey Inn changed due to her accident. Just as well. Most of them had cared for her during her convalescence. They deserved a break from her. She propped her sore knee on an ottoman. Each day brought her closer to normal. She could walk without the aid of devices and had no coughing fits today. Progress.

The blue sky and moderate temperature should lift her spirits. Sunlight streamed in the window. The foil paper that littered the floor sparkled. Dust motes danced to the Christmas music playing on the CD. A full stomach and the warm sun encouraged a nap.

Noah flitted from one new toy to the next. He glowed brighter than the lights on the tree. Watching a child on Christmas Day should bring immense joy. Simple gifts, loyal friends ... why did her heart feel heavy?

Benjamin placed her mug of coffee on the adjacent table. "Need anything else?"

"No, thanks. I'm fine. Go enjoy the afternoon with Noah."

Todd stepped over the toy train that chugged lazy figure eights in the middle of the floor.

"Careful, Daddy. Don't step on the track."

"Turn it off, son. Time to go." He handed Sarah the portable phone and hefted Noah's new saddle. "We'll be on the trail several hours. Pastor and Mrs. Morrison said to call if you need help."

"I'm perfectly capable of taking care of myself. Go. You're driving me crazy."

She'd convinced Benjamin she could stay alone since it was Christmas. Her parade of caregivers would end tonight. The prospect struck a note of fear that sent a shiver down her spine. She had no renters coming until New Year's Eve. Physically she could do it. Emotionally? She wasn't certain she could face the changes.

The day after Christmas might not be the best time, but she saw no point in delaying the inevitable. Sarah spread her financial accounts and bills on the coffee table so Benjamin could peruse them. Becky and her sister had volunteered to chaperone for a couple hours. A chick-flick blared from the TV. Their laughter trickled in from the media room. But tonight anything short of a wake would feel wrong.

Sarah leaned against the arm of the couch, legs stretched out under the quilt. Benjamin settled on the opposite end, cradled her feet in his lap, and covered them. When had they developed routine sitting positions and behavioral patterns? Thinking about couple-like actions wasn't smart tonight.

She stifled the urge to jiggle her foot, a habit Benjamin had pointed out when nerves got the best of her. Not wanting to distract, she stared at the twinkling lights on the Christmas tree. He hunched over the ledgers and punched numbers into the calculator. Maybe he'd find some error in her calculations.

Fifteen minutes later, Benjamin turned a grim face in her direction. "It's worse than you said." He pressed his lips together and pinched the bridge of his nose.

Sarah tugged at her lip with her teeth. "I told you I couldn't see a solution."

She shifted to scoot closer to him. "There isn't enough to pay the utilities, buy food, and pay the medical bills. I juggle them by overdue dates."

Benjamin tapped the pencil against the ledger. "Is this the first year you've faced this?"

"I've squeaked by in the past when things were slow. I had Mom's disability money. Once she was old enough for Medicare, that helped. The doctor says my arthritis is almost in remission. I'm thrilled, but my medical costs outweigh the income."

He tossed the legal pad on the table and placed his arm around her shoulders. "I thought you'd worked out discounts with the doctor and the pharmaceutical company."

"I did. I pay part of the cost. The last medication change achieved the desired results. It also pushed me over the financial cliff. There isn't any reserve. The hospital expenses from the fire episode haven't arrived yet. Dropping that log will bury me."

"What about disability? You should qualify."

She fidgeted with the hem on the quilt. The idea she needed disability benefits placed her in the aged and infirm category. It curdled her stomach. "We started the process last month. I have no idea when it might kick in. I won't have a house full of renters until late spring."

"There is a solution." He stroked a hand along her arm, then caressed her cheek. "I have money, Sarah."

She jerked away and raised both hands, palms out. "I don't want a marriage of convenience."

He sighed, worked his tight jaw from side to side, and scrubbed a hand over his face. "I've told you over and over how much I love you. I'd think my actions show it too. I want to be a husband who provides for his wife."

"No." She shook her head and waved her hands. "I can't take the money you've saved for retirement. It isn't the answer."

A cold hand grasped hers and nervously squeezed. Fervent pleas leapt from his dark eyes. "I don't care about the money. I want a life with you."

Her fingers laced with his. "Money is an issue for me. I can't place my financial burden on your shoulders." Tempted to yield to the sadness in his eyes, she focused on the flames in the fireplace.

"As your husband I'd want that. I weighed all of this before I proposed."

"If we were younger, it might be different. My debts are my responsibility if we combine two households."

"I disagree." Benjamin bolted off the couch, shoved his hands in his pockets, and paced in front of the hearth. "If you insist on using your money to pay, you'll have to sell Mosey Inn."

She'd decided that already. Hearing him confirm the need hurt more than she'd anticipated. She studied a loose cuticle on her thumb. "A realtor is coming Monday. It won't be an easy sale. I own a huge isolated house. If the person who buys it wants a B&B, they would need another income or money to live on in the off seasons."

His gaze took in the features of the room as if visualizing it redecorated and occupied by other people. "A couple with a large family would love this house. It's a perfect location for a ranch."

"I don't care what they do with it." She pointed to the seat beside her. "Sit. You're wearing a hole in the floor."

He joined her again and captured her hands between his. "We can keep dating until you sell Mosey Inn. We aren't getting any younger. I'd prefer to marry you before I'm ancient, but I can wait." His lips curved into a weary smile that would normally trip her heart into a flutter. The look twisted it into a knot instead.

"It will take all the money I get from Mosey Inn to cover my expenses until I'm old enough for Medicare. We're back to depending on you for normal living expenses." She shot him a glance. Ouch. Not a happy face. His smile had faded. With narrowed eyes and sternly set lips, he struggled to control anger.

"One of the reasons I love you is your stubborn determination but this is downright ridiculous. I have rented a room and helped buy groceries. That wouldn't be the case if we married." His face reddened. Patches of white stood out along the lines of grafted skin. He glared at her and raised his voice. "You're talking like we'd be roommates who split expenses. Couples share."

Anger wasn't the way to approach this. She softened her tone. "That's why marriage can't work. I've always controlled my money and paid my way. I don't think I'd ever be able to let you pay for everything."

He paled, and his lips trembled. Hurting him seemed to be the only thing she was accomplishing. How could she explain this in a better way? He combed his fingers through the hair over his ear. His nervous gesture. She stopped tapping her foot and turned sideways on the couch.

He bent forward and let his head sink into his hands. "Another option." He took several deep breaths that quavered when he exhaled. Assuming a cross-legged position beside her, he rested his hands on her thighs. Calmer. This was better. "I don't want to live in Charlotte. It's too big. I'll sell my house. It's marketable. We can buy a small house in a location we like. Doing that, along with my retirement money, would give us adequate income to cover your healthcare costs and keep us going a long time. When you sell Mosey Inn, we'll have your money for expenses too. You wouldn't be depending on me for support."

"It takes away your freedom. You should use the money you've saved for your pleasure, not my problems."

"I came to Love Valley looking for solitude. Selling my house was always part of my plan. Meeting you changed things. Sharing the rest of life with you would be my greatest pleasure."

Meeting and dating Benjamin had brought her more joy than she'd ever believed possible. Changing their relationship would jeopardize his future happiness. She couldn't waver. "I've never depended on anyone. We're talking about a huge change in lifestyle for both of us."

"Marriage is a big change regardless of age. This is a trust issue, Sarah. You pointed me back to God. This money fixation isn't normal. God's given us what we need. Can't you accept His plan?"

She held up her hands. She couldn't keep her tone calm. "Look at my fingers. They're crooked. In time, you may be taking care of a crippled old woman. I won't do that to you. I couldn't handle it."

"Oh, I see. This isn't about money. It's fear of the unknown." He held out his deformed hand and shoved up his sleeve to reveal his shriveled arm. "Look at this. I've managed to work my entire adult life with this arm. You've improved. New medicines come along regularly. You might never require constant care. If you do, we'll enjoy the time we have."

"You've spent your life avoiding people. You're able to face them again. Go find a woman who can offer you something more. I won't tie you to a tiny house and a wife who can't satisfy your physical needs."

His eyes went wide, and his mouth fell open. "You're worried about the intimate aspects of our relationship?"

"If the medicines don't work and deformities become too bad, I might not be able to—"

He laid his fingers on her lips. "If that's a concern, forget it. That is not why I want a wife."

"I've never ... been with a man." She closed her eyes and touched the hand resting on her quivering lips.

"Look at me, Sarah."

Tears brimmed in her eyes as she met his gaze. She didn't know how to talk about this.

He cupped her chin. His eyes clouded as if he didn't want to express his thought. "I was intimate with a girlfriend in college. She refused to live with a reclusive burned man. I regret that relationship—not because she left—because it was wrong. I knew I should wait for the woman God meant for me to marry. I learned that growing up. The physical part ... it's not why I want you."

"But it's important. And I'm no gorgeous college girl."

"I didn't tell you about it to make you feel like a competitor. It happened years ago. You saw a portion of my scars when the bees stung me. I'm not exactly Mr. Universe."

She traced a ropey tendon on the back of his hand. "I may become a wife like the one my father had."

"We are not there. Swollen joints and crooked fingers will not make you a brain-damaged woman. Even if something that drastic happened, I'd love you. Your father loved your mother until the day he died. I'll be here for you too. Let me finally be a man."

She turned, set her feet on the floor, and flopped against the back of the couch. "I'm not willing to take the chance. You already take care of me more than I'd like." His unshed tears and anguished expression were killing her. It shouldn't be so hard to say no.

He dropped to his knees in front of her and took both hands.

"There is no guarantee I won't develop some illness. You could end up caring for me long before I have to take care of you. If we'd married years ago, we would still face aging and perhaps becoming invalids. We simply skipped the younger years of marriage. I want a partner, a companion who loves me. Someone to share coffee in the swing and a sunset on the porch no matter what happens. Grow old with me, Sarah."

She freed her hands, laced his hair through her fingers, and kissed his misshapen ear. Why had she done that? Did she need one last moment of tenderness to give her the courage to stand firm when he left. "I've made up my mind. Stop trying. I can't marry you."

Benjamin returned to his seat and rested a hand on her arm. "Please, Sarah. Don't do this to me. Let's get some counseling. You brought up some valid concerns. We can work this out. You were depressed last week and overextended because of the holidays. You're upset about the church fire. You've been sick. Don't make a rash decision."

If he continued, her heart might explode. He could probably hear it pounding in her chest. "It isn't rash. It's practical. Please, Benjamin. We are not supposed to marry. God used me to help you. Accept that and forget about a life together."

"Say it."

"What?"

"Tell me you don't love me."

Her voice became a whisper. "I can't." She looked away from his sad face. "It would be a lie. I do love you, but marriage isn't right for me."

His moan of deep despair hit like a blow. He dropped his head into a palm. Eyes closed, he sat working his jaw from side to side for a good minute. Would he accept her choice and end the torment that strangled her?

"Where will you live, Sarah? What will you do?"

Looking at him was impossible. She rose, crossed to the hearth, and stared at the glowing coals. "There are assisted living places in Statesville. I'll move there. My disability income, with the sale of the inn, will cover the costs. When I need nursing care I'll go to a nursing home."

"You don't need to make that sort of sacrifice. This is not practical or wise."

Squaring her shoulders, she brushed away the tears and faced him. "You need to leave. Clean out your room and don't come back. I couldn't say goodbye to you again."

"This is wrong." His raised voice cracked. Anger and grief

seemed to flow out with his tears. "I can't believe you're doing this. We love each other. It can work, Sarah. I want it to work."

A simple shake of her head. A touch might compel her to cave in. "No. We spent some happy months sharing a dream that can't last. These past few days changed my perspective. I'd be miserable if I put you in a full time care-giving position. Find someone who isn't sick."

Squatting at the table, she gathered the bills, stacked them, and closed the ledgers. If she looked at his dejected face, she'd cry. She would not end it with tears and hugs. Her moments of weakness were over.

He squatted beside her and placed his four-fingered hand on the back of her neck. It might as well be a branding iron. "You need to listen to the lectures you gave me. I'll leave so you can wallow in your stubborn self-pity for a while."

The fiery anger had scorched her. The change to a gentle imploring tone burned more deeply.

"Maybe Becky or Ella can talk some sense into you. I'll come back when you decide to trust God and me. God sent me here to find your love. You're the woman He made for me. I've waited years for you."

She stood to force away his hand. It didn't work as expected. It trailed down her back and stopped for an endless moment at the small of her back. The final caress seemed to travel up her spine with intense heat and unbearable pain.

Why did he have to force her to look at his face? He shouldn't have bent his head so she saw the torment, his clenched teeth holding back sorrow and wrath.

"You know how to find me when you change your mind."

He stormed up the stairs. His door slammed in the distance.

Becky appeared in the doorway. "Sarah?"

"Don't ask." She fled to her room. If she watched him leave...

༄ ☒ ༅

For several hours he'd wound along country roads searching for peace, searching for reasons. Not certain how he'd ended up there, Benjamin paused on Pastor Morrison's sidewalk. The house was dark except for a single light in the office area. Was he awake?

Somewhere deep in Kudzu Territory, a screech owl sounded its mournful call. Appropriate for his mood and location. The Kudzu soldiers had won. They'd taken Sarah and Noah in one fell swoop.

Down by the arena, a horse nickered. The sound brought a pang of remembrance—lazy afternoons, lounging on the grass with Noah, Todd, and their mounts—gone. Memories were all he'd have of those hot days when they'd spun tales about Harvey and the Kudzu soldiers. He'd never repeat the times he'd shared picnics with Sarah in the shade of the magnolia tree.

He stepped onto the small stoop, ready to rap on the door. The porch light flicked on.

Pastor Morrison cracked open the door. "Benjamin. I thought I heard someone drive up."

"I need to talk. Hope I didn't wake you."

"No. Please, come in. We were watching the news."

A woman's voice called from the back of the house. "Do you need me, dear?"

"It's Benjamin. Don't wait up. We're talking for a while."

After a cup of hot cider and fifteen minutes of relating the events, Benjamin expected his hands to stop shaking. He still needed both hands to hold the cup steady. "I never anticipated Sarah would tell me to leave. I thought we'd resolve her fears and work out details."

Pastor Morrison poured him another cup of cider. "I'm shocked, and truly sorry. How can I help?"

"Would Sarah talk with you?"

"Perhaps. I'll attempt, but my guess is that Becky or Ella might accomplish more. A woman's perspective, you know."

Benjamin nodded and slouched against the cushions. "I called Ella. She's coming back tomorrow. Tying up loose ends. The woman isn't happy with Sarah right now. I'd love to be there when she hits the porch."

A bit of laughter and talk about Ella eased Benjamin's tension. Pastor Morrison placed an empty cup on the table. "Ella may be exactly what Sarah needs. Will Becky stay with Sarah tonight?"

"It wasn't part of the plan. Her sister leaves tomorrow. They were going home after chaperoning. By the way, thanks for lining up help the past few days. Sarah needed me. Well, I thought she did. Maybe I hovered too much."

"Sarah's too independent for her own good. That's the main reason you're here tonight. Don't kick yourself."

"The church fire seems to have pushed her over the edge. I knew she had reservations about growing old and needing care. It's extreme now. And she's overwhelmed by this money problem."

"Things may look different in a few days. Give her some space.

Will you stay or go to Charlotte?"

"I suppose I'll go home. The man who delivered my materials from the hardware store needed a place to stay. He's taken care of the house since I left. He went to visit relatives during Christmas. I'll go back. Check on things. Decide how to proceed."

"I'd hoped you'd organize a team to repair the church. Insurance would pay; but if we handle some work ourselves, we'll get more for our money. Guess that would be too much to ask."

"I'll consider it. I need to come back to Statesville for a few days to work on a job for the sheriff. Love Valley has become home. Don't see how I can stay, though. I'd see Sarah too often. It'd kill me." He laid the back of an arm across his forehead.

"Where are you staying tonight?"

"Don't know. I have to go back to the Spanglers' eventually. I have to tell Noah…" He choked on the name. How could he say goodbye? Noah wouldn't understand. "I'm losing the two people who mean the most to me."

Pastor Morrison crossed to the couch and took a seat beside Benjamin. The pastor's hand of comfort on his shoulder was all it took for fresh tears to well in his eyes. "Sorry. I hate to act like a weakling."

"You aren't. You have reasons for tears and anger. A wedding seemed inevitable."

"My thoughts too. I didn't anticipate ending up alone again."

"You're never alone."

Benjamin rubbed his palms together. "I won't give up my faith. The anger with God … that's over. I'm still struggling with image issues."

"I am concerned that Sarah's rejection will change things. Don't want you to take up your old lifestyle again."

"I won't. I know where to go for strength."

The pastor clapped him on the back. "It's nearly midnight. Stay here tonight. I'll call Todd so he knows where you are."

Benjamin nodded, too numb to argue. He wouldn't sleep wherever he laid his head. Speaking with Becky or Todd could start an all-night talk. He wasn't ready for that. Emotional weariness sapped his energy.

The pastor eased to the edge of the couch. "Let's pray before we sleep. We'll talk more tomorrow." Pastor Morrison's hand resting on his shoulder lightened Benjamin's crushing despair. The pastor's prayer for wisdom, emotional healing, and possible restoration gave some consolation.

After the Amen, he chucked Benjamin on the shoulder. "Don't give up hope. Sarah's upset, confused, and scared. In a week…"

"I'm thankful I met her even if we can't make a life together. If it weren't for her, I wouldn't have a relationship with God again."

The pastor rose and turned off the porch light. He stopped in front of the couch. "Extra bedroom's on the right. Bath's across the hall. You a morning coffee drinker?"

"Yes, but I won't bother you with breakfast."

"I'll ask my wife to add some extra cups to the pot. We can talk while we gather fresh eggs. There's a toothbrush or anything else you might need in a basket on the nightstand. She keeps it stocked in case things like this come up. Get some rest."

CHAPTER TWENTY-NINE

Sarah placed her cereal bowl in the dishwasher. The gray sky of a winter morning added to the loneliness in the kitchen. Becky had offered to spend the night. She'd refused. It would have meant telling her about the confrontation. More than she could handle last night. Becky and her sister probably heard some of the exchange despite their supposed interest in the movie.

Sarah poured a second cup of coffee then contemplated how she would explain Benjamin's absence at church tonight. Ending their relationship should be between them and them alone. Didn't work that way in a small town. By nightfall, everyone would know he'd left. In fact, she'd kicked him out on Saturday night before ten. She checked her watch ... nine o'clock on Sunday morning. Already old news.

She wiped the kitchen table and wandered into her room. She should call Pastor Morrison and get the list of volunteers who'd assisted her. No. Calling him would require talking with someone who might ask about Benjamin.

So many questions. Had Benjamin gone back to the bunkhouse? Was he still in town? Would he return to Charlotte and resume work there? Noah. What would he tell Noah? She'd not considered those consequences. The poor child would be devastated.

Benjamin's accusation of stubborn self-pity stung more with Noah woven into the picture. In many ways, it was true. But she couldn't burden Benjamin with her bills, her care, her illness, her need to control, her ... all about her. She'd ignored Benjamin's need for love and companionship. His desire to love her no matter what happened. His relationship with Noah.

Second-guessing wouldn't help. She'd made the choice. The right choice. If that were true, why did her heart sink like a helium-depleted balloon when she thought about him? One reason. She loved and missed him. That didn't make her choice wrong. Plenty of people loved each other but didn't belong together. A "Forgive me; I love you" would bring him back. The phone beckoned to her from the desk.

The unmistakable sound of Ella's Pathfinder sent her heart on a marathon. Sarah bit her lip and peeped out the window. Ella wasn't due back until Monday. Explaining to her why it was necessary to stomp Benjamin into the mire on Main Street might be harder than telling him to leave.

Sarah inhaled a calming breath and opened the door. "Welcome home. I wasn't expecting you."

"No? I got a phone call about ten last night. Guess you didn't talk to him again after that. What have you done, girl?"

"He called you?" She gasped, trying to guess what he might have said.

"Why not? He was upset." Ella shoved past her and into the foyer.

Sarah rested her hands on her hips. "The nerve. He had no right to—"

"We're friends. He had every right to call me. Thing is, he wasn't calling because you turned him down and he was hurting. He was concerned about you. Wanted to know if I could come home early."

Ella tossed her keys in the bowl beside the door, peeled off her coat, and dumped her suitcase at the bottom of the stairs. She cast a weary look in Sarah's direction. "I need a cup of coffee before we get into this. Late night flight and a drive from Charlotte. Got any breakfast left?"

Ten minutes later, Ella plunked the mug on the table in the kitchen. "Okay, I'm ready. First, are you still sick?" Sarah hung her head and stared at the floral pattern on the coffee mug. "I'll always be sick. The issues caused by the fire are better. Walking fine and the cough's gone."

"You don't look better."

Sarah's eyes went wide and a huff snuck out. "Wow. Thanks. I love you too. You could use a nap, Miss Cheerful."

"Nap comes later. We talk about you first." Ella rested her chin on a fist and studied her. "Dull, sad eyes, stooped shoulders, wrinkled brow. It could be pain. I'm thinking more along the lines of remorse."

Sarah's lips formed a thin line. Fingers fidgeted with her napkin. "What I did was not easy. It was right; but yes, it hurts."

Ella stilled Sarah's hand. "Why? I thought you loved each other. When I left last Sunday you were holding hands like a couple of teens."

Sarah looked away from the questioning eyes boring a hole in her. "Monday happened. I set fire to the church and almost killed us."

Ella closed her eyes and took a deep breath. She seemed less irate and rubbed the back of Sarah's hand. "It was an accident. Anyone could have dropped that log."

Sarah's voice rose. "But I'm the one who did." Yelling wouldn't cut it with Ella. She had to keep the nervous tension under control.

Ella leaned back in her chair and crossed her arms. "How did saving you from that blaze make Benjamin feel? What sort of trauma did he experience?"

The question sent shock waves coursing through Sarah. "I don't understand." Oh, she understood all right. Answering was the problem. She didn't know.

"Did you ask him? Was he scared to go in that burning room? Did he relive the horrible fire and the pain he went through? Did he mourn the death of his friend again?"

Sarah hung her head. "I didn't ask. I was too busy coughing and being angry because people had to take care of me."

"He called from the hospital after you were in a room. Said he was terrified to plunge in there to save you. That wasn't what frightened him most. He was afraid he'd lose you, or he'd find you burned and have to watch you suffer like he did."

Sarah covered her mouth with a hand. "I'm ashamed. The hospital stay and my first day at home are a blur. Benjamin was always there when I woke up. People came and went. His gentleness and love filtered through the haze. The things you asked ... did he experience them?"

"Every one of them. And you missed a chance to show him your love. Too worried about you."

Ella's sober statement jabbed at Sarah's guilt. It grew worse as she kept nailing the lid down with even more revelations. "Benjamin called again during your first night at home. He'd had a nightmare. You were with him when the propane tanks blew. You were the one who died instead of his friend."

Sarah recalled his night on the couch. Tossing when the clock struck. Coughing in his sleep. It never occurred to her to question his emotional state. She'd been too proud to look past self and see he'd experienced a huge trauma too. "All I saw was what a burden I was to my friends and to him. Pretty selfish, huh?"

"Didn't sound like you were a burden. I talked with Pastor. He said people were happy to come over. Some of them were lonely and wanted company."

"Mrs. Wexler said that. Actually, I was humiliated by my need for total care. It made me feel like Mother. I can't be a burden like that in the future."

"Ah. The growing old and not wanting care thing surfaces again. Everyone gets old. Some of us may face bad outcomes. You have to get over this idea that you can't accept help. Especially from Benjamin."

"I won't become a burden for Benjamin. I won't make him live a life like I did now that he can make friends."

"Resenting your past a little?"

"Regret sounds better. I missed so much in life. I loved her, Ella, but it cost me a great deal. Is it fair to ask that of him?"

"He wouldn't have proposed if he didn't want to accept the responsibility."

No need to lie or hedge on the details. "I can't pay my bills, Ella. I have to sell the inn. We'd need to live on his savings."

Ella pointed a finger at her. "You promised me you wouldn't go without medicine."

Sarah raised her hand in a Girl Scout sign. "I haven't skimped on meds. I've neglected other bills. Life is crashing in on me. There's a realtor coming on Monday to price the place."

"We'll discuss that in a minute. You need to take a closer look at what you're turning down. The man adores you. Why can't you grow old with a man who loves you?"

"He shouldn't have to use his money, take care of me, or sacrifice his new self-assurance."

"Hogwash. Your words or his?"

Regret nudged the base of her neck and singed the spot on her back where he'd left his final touch. "Mine."

"You need to do some serious thinking, Sarah. None of us has assurance of a long easy life. Benjamin needs love and so do you. Trust God for the money, and let Benjamin develop his role as a husband and a man."

She'd struggled all night with her decision. It looked different in daylight. Especially when her friend asked virtually the same questions Benjamin had. She'd botched her chance at companionship because of self-centered pride. Hard to admit being selfish would cost her years of happiness.

Sitting still under Ella's scrutinizing gaze became uncomfortable. She shoved her chair back and paced around the room, arms crossed tightly across her chest to keep her trembling hands under control. "I'm afraid, Ella. I'm scared he'll regret it. I'm scared to make a commitment and end up tying him to a little house with a sick wife."

"You know how to solve that problem. Practice what you teach the kids at church. Tell God about your fears. Jesus walked this earth. He understands."

Sarah paused at the table but didn't sit. "It's hard to do that. My heart tells me I can't be in control. It tells me to trust. I'm not sure I can. Now that I've sent Benjamin away, I'm ashamed. You're right. I was only thinking about me. Despite the fact he's spent years away from God, Benjamin has more faith and trust than I do."

"You helped him get to this point. Since you've looked past you and thought about him a little more, you're heading in the right direction. Did you make such a mess of it that he won't come back?"

Sarah sank into a chair and twirled the coffee mug so her hands would have something to do besides shake. "I don't want him to come back."

"That's a lie if I ever heard one. You messed up. Ask him to forgive you for your selfishness. Talk about the emotional trauma you've caused him. Stop living a bleak future that might not come. There can be a lot of happiness in merely holding hands."

Sarah had to smile at that one. "Since when did you become the voice of marital counsel? I'm not seeing you heading down the aisle."

"No. But I'm off in a new direction." Zeal leapt into Ella's eyes. "It includes you. Benjamin too, if you correct the mess you've made."

Ella's enthusiasm aroused Sarah's curiosity. The change of subject didn't stop the guilt nibbling away at her insides.

Ella grinned and waggled her eyebrows. "I have news that will astonish you."

୮୦ ✠ ෆ

A single ray of feeble sunshine peeped from behind a cloud. Sarah turned toward the church. While Ella napped, Sarah would assess the damage to the church and consider Benjamin's proposal. The bleakness of the afternoon added to her grim expectations. She couldn't find the courage to attend services tonight—too close to the day of the fire. Too embarrassed to face inquisitive members was more accurate. They'd try to discuss her health, the fire, and Benjamin. Her extensive talk with Ella had raised some possibilities, but her emotions vacillated more than the winter weather.

Becky had called to say she wouldn't need her to help teach for a couple weeks. The pastor had decided the congregation should skip dinner and Sunday school during the repairs. They'd still convene in the undamaged sanctuary for a worship service. Sarah couldn't ask if Benjamin had left or was at the bunkhouse. If he showed up at church ... she didn't want to consider that awkward possibility. Becky's hesitation to offer further information plucked strings of fear in her. If the Spanglers blamed her for Noah's loss of his Grandpa, mending the broken link with her friends might prove difficult.

Yellow caution tape barred the entrance to the fellowship hall. From the parking lot, Sarah couldn't discern that anything had occurred. She'd expected a gutted ruin of charred timbers and glass. She walked around the building to the side near the arena. Two broken windows. Black stains marked the areas above them where smoke had licked the brown siding.

She steeled her nerves and ducked under the tape to peer in a window. Blackened ceiling tiles indicated where the flames had leapt upward in their walk across the tables. Close to the hearth, charred remains of wooden tables and twisted metal chairs formed the tangle she'd escaped. Soggy Sunday school booklets littered the floor where shelving had collapsed. Several puddles remained from the firefighters' hoses. Overturned chairs lay scattered between skewed tables—evidence of Benjamin's efforts to create an escape route. The path where she'd crawled and the trail where he'd dragged her stood out in the chaos. He'd gone almost halfway into the blazing room. How had she failed to question the terror this must have brought him? He'd made a huge sacrifice. His courage, fueled by love, had saved her. Benjamin might have lost his life or, worse, been burned again. Guilt, darker than the soot that covered everything, chipped away at her pride.

The sun broke through the clouds as Sarah crossed the breezeway and slipped into the sanctuary. The early afternoon light streamed through the stained glass window behind the pulpit. Vivid hues of red, brown, green, and blue cast a glow on the dark paneled walls. Sarah slid into the pew where they'd sat the day Noah disappeared. She studied the window depicting Christ praying in Gethsemane. Jesus knelt before a rock, gazing up at a purplish-blue sky. The city of Jerusalem nestled against a distant hill. He'd crossed a valley to pray. Lush green trees and shrubs surrounded Him. A single thorny bush occupied the foreground. The sunlight through His red robe spread a crimson streak across the church's kneeling rail.

The magnitude of His sacrifice wrenched her soul. In that garden, the Son of God wrestled with painful choices, burdens far greater than any she'd ever face. He'd chosen to become the escape for mankind from the bondage of sin. Certainly, she could trust Him to meet her meager needs. She could trust Him to forgive her pride and selfishness. Time to come out of the dark valley she'd created. Time to cling to the hand of God that had guided her life for years.

Benjamin was a gift she should welcome. He'd promised to love her and care for her. Why had that been so hard to accept? Believing they could experience good health with years of happiness seemed easier this afternoon. She'd let money stand between them. Preposterous behavior. She had to ask for Benjamin's forgiveness and tell him how deeply she loved him. And it wasn't because he'd saved her life. He'd shown her human love, as she'd never known it, many weeks ago.

Sarah hurried to her car. The clouds lifted by the time she was on the road to the Spanglers' stable. The sun warmed the car and brightened her attitude. Perhaps Benjamin hadn't left. Maybe he'd stayed to see if she came to her senses. If only he would forgive her and extend his proposal of marriage again.

CHAPTER THIRTY

A white truck pulling a horse trailer blocked the dirt road to the barn and corral, so Sarah parked in front of the Spanglers' house. Just as well. Walking would give her an excuse for her shortness of breath and pounding heart. Voices led her toward the riding ring around back.

Nearing the rear of the house, an unmistakable laugh put a lump in Sarah's throat. Benjamin. She paused. So he hadn't left. Was she ready to face him? Putting off the apology would delay the chance of restoration. Her heart skipped a few beats, then settled into a rapid rhythm. She took a calming breath. Ready. Go. She rounded the corner beside the deck.

Perched on the edge of a picnic bench, Benjamin dangled a string above a cat. Hard to believe the gray kitten had grown so much since the day Benjamin pulled away the boards of the shed and uncovered the beehive. Benjamin yanked the string up just as it sprang. The cat twisted in the air and landed on its feet. Noah grabbed his sides, rolling with laughter. Sarah smiled. Nice to see their joy. It wouldn't last if she let dread force a retreat. She couldn't let him leave Noah. Somehow, she had to convince Benjamin to stay, even if he couldn't forgive her and become a part of her future.

Becky, Todd, and a thirty-something man stood along the white metal fence railing at the riding ring.

"Sarah!" Becky rushed toward her. "I'm glad to see you." Her friend embraced her. So much for fearing rejection. "We could use your help." Becky grabbed her arm, tugging her along.

"But ... I came—"

"Whatever it is, it can wait. Todd's trying to sell Topper. Come talk with these people."

The laughter on the deck had ceased. Sarah shot a backwards glance at Benjamin, locking with his gaze for an instant. His lips tipped up into his characteristic smile. "Afternoon, Sarah." Did that smile say he knew why she'd come?

Sarah felt Benjamin and Noah fall into step behind them. "Let's go see what happens out there, Noah. Behave, the way we discussed."

Becky gushed out the story as they almost ran to the ring. "Mr. Henley promised his daughter a barrel racing horse for Christmas. We've been negotiating for several weeks. She's not sure Topper's the horse she wants."

"So what does this have to do with me?"

"You were a champion. Give her some tips. Compliment her. Something. Anything!"

"I haven't raced in decades. My words won't help. If she doesn't like ..."

A sharp breath slid past Sarah's open mouth. Sarah came to a standstill. Topper charged across the open pasture, his young rider's auburn hair trailing behind her. What a sight. Topper's hooves threw up clumps of grass. In a full gallop, he was magnificent, with the speed and frame of a winner. If she'd possessed a horse like him in her day ... "Has the girl trained for barrels?"

"She's trained with someone in Wilkesboro." Becky whispered, "Her father's rich. We could use a chunk of his cash. Todd says Topper's ready."

The attractive pre-teen slowed Topper and walked him over to the ring, arriving as the group from the house sidled up to the fence. "He's fast, Daddy, but I'm not sure I can get him to make the turns."

"Afternoon, Todd." Sarah clapped him on the back. "Topper's a fine horse. Better suited for barrels than the trail."

"Yeah, I learned that from experience. Sarah Campbell, meet Mr. Henley and his daughter, Brianna." They exchanged greetings and handshakes.

Todd turned to Sarah. "Your former trainer's daughter has worked with Topper on the barrels for weeks. She says he has the makings of a champion." Todd placed an arm around Sarah's shoulder. "Sarah won barrel racing awards as a teen. She probably has some tips for you, Brianna."

Sarah stroked a hand along Topper's neck. She smiled up at the girl, sitting tall in the saddle. "His mane and tail are the same color as your lovely hair, Brianna. You're his perfect match." Round green eyes smiled back at Sarah's compliment. "Have you given him a try around the barrels?"

"Yes, ma'am. He's fast but hesitates in the turns."

"If Judy's daughter is training Topper, I'm sure she uses the technique I learned. It's all about body language. When you and Topper learn to ride as one, you'll be a wonderful team. Mind showing me your style?"

"Okay. I'll give him another go." Brianna maneuvered Topper

into their starting position. With precision and grace, Topper flew through the gate, dead on target for the first barrel. Sarah scrutinized the girl's form as she led him around the three barrels and sped back to the finish. Bingo! Easy to see the flaw in Brianna's turns. How could Sarah correct her form and guide her to see that Topper would make a perfect choice?

Brianna walked the horse around the stable yard to cool him. Sarah rehearsed the proper moves in her head until Brianna returned to the group beside the fence and dismounted.

Sarah said, "With your permission, I'd like to take him through some moves, get the feel of his stride. I think I can help you gain some valuable seconds. I see a couple reasons why he's slowing on the turns."

Mr. Henley nodded. "We'd be honored, Miss Campbell."

"I could use a pair of boots, Becky." She held up a sneaker-clad foot. "I didn't expect to barrel race."

"Sure. I have a pair in the barn that should fit. Be right back." Becky trotted off, Noah hot on her heels.

Sarah took a seat on a nearby bench to remove her shoes. Benjamin eased down beside her and took her hand. "Stop shaking. The moves are still in you. I see the look in your eyes. You're rehearsing every step."

She gave his hand a squeeze. The reaction seemed as normal as breathing. "I came to talk with you, not give a barrel racing lesson."

"So, we'll talk after you sell this horse. Todd needs you. Trust your instincts. Show her what a winner looks like." The confidence and tenderness in his gaze should calm her jitters.

"I'm afraid."

"Are you hurting? Afraid you'll cause a flare?"

"Neither. I don't want to make a fool of myself."

"You won't. Topper knows his role. I saw him several days ago. He was perfection." He kissed the top of her head and trailed a finger along her cheek. "So are you."

Forgiveness before she asked? Could it be as simple as making an appearance? It might not be easy to express her regret, but she would muddle through.

Confidence replaced doubt as she slid her feet into the boots. Sarah addressed the group. "I'll show Topper how I want it done. Then I'll make a run."

Over the next fifteen minutes, Sarah walked Topper through the routine multiple times. He responded as she'd expected once the familiar pattern emerged from his training.

Could she match or produce a better time than Brianna's?

Topper pranced at the starting point. "Okay, Todd. See if we shave off any seconds. We're ready."

"Timer's set."

"Yah!" Topper never faltered. They flew through the pattern as if glued together. The rush of wind as he loped toward the finish took Sarah's breath. Her heart hammered. The perfect ride pumped ecstasy through her veins. She'd bank on a time several seconds more than her rodeo days. Sarah eased Topper into a walk and headed back to the group.

Todd checked the timer. "Two seconds less than Brianna."

The freckles across the girl's nose danced as she bounced up and down and clapped. "You were splendid. He didn't hesitate at all. What'd you do? Show me."

"Gladly." Sarah leaned forward to run her hands through Topper's mane. "You flew, boy. Hold that head up with pride."

Benjamin rushed over to assist with her dismount. His eyes asked if she was okay. She stood in the stirrup and slid down into his outstretched arms. His hand lingered at the small of her back when she turned to face him. Its touch didn't burn guilt into her. It conveyed assurance and respect.

She cradled his cheek with her hand. "Not bad for an old lady, huh? I'd forgotten how spectacular that surge of adrenaline feels."

"You looked as young as Brianna. I wish I'd had a video camera." His brow furrowed. "Anything hurt?"

"No." She leaned close to his ear. "Wouldn't let her know if it did." Her lips grazed his cheek. Had she really done that? Her heart said it was right. The rest of her body wanted to share the joy of her victory with Benjamin in an everlasting embrace. Sarah smiled up at his optimistic eyes. She winked. "Gotta sell this horse."

Unbelievable. She'd pounded around the barrels on a bolt of lightning. Her joints had withstood the ultimate test. And she wouldn't regret her jaunt tomorrow.

Sarah spent thirty minutes walking Brianna and Topper through the moves and correcting Brianna's positions in the saddle. The other adults sipped coffee on the deck. Noah settled onto Benjamin's lap and dozed in the pale winter sun. A cool breeze ruffled Sarah's hair. If the rest of the day went so well...

Brianna trotted back to the entrance. "I'm ready to try another run."

"When the horse and rider understand their roles, you achieve mutual trust and success on the rodeo circuit. It'll take time for Topper to bond with you. Don't be upset if every ride isn't perfect. Relax and have fun."

Twenty minutes later, Sarah beamed as Topper entered the horse trailer for his departure. Mr. Henley placed an arm around Brianna's shoulder. "I'll contact Judy about some lessons." He flipped the business card with a finger. "Your style seems to work, Miss Campbell. Sure you don't want to be her trainer?"

"I have other plans during the next few months. We'll stay in touch." Sarah tweaked Brianna's nose. "You'll be a winner, friend."

"Thanks for your help, Sarah. He is a good match." She flipped her hair over a shoulder and giggled.

Becky said, "Let us know when you'll be riding in a rodeo. We'll come and watch you win."

Before the dust settled behind the departing truck, Todd scooped Becky off her feet and twirled her around. They whooped and ended the exchange with a loving kiss.

Todd set Becky on her feet and lifted Noah for a hug. "You were a good boy this afternoon."

"Grandpa said it was important to stay quiet. Do I get a treat?"

"You bet. We'll talk about it in a minute. Run on and play." Todd popped him on the rear, sending him off toward the house.

"Thanks, Sarah. I'm not sure they would have bought him if you hadn't come along. His money will buy another trail horse and hold us through the winter. If Zelda produces another Topper, I'll be sure you come help me sell her offspring. Sorry to tie you up all afternoon. Why'd you stop by?"

Sarah took Benjamin's hand. "I came to ask Benjamin if he would come to Mosey Inn for the evening. Ella's home and has something we need to discuss as a threesome."

೮ ✠ ೦

After a quick shower, Sarah joined Benjamin on the couch in the main sitting area. "Sorry to keep you waiting. Didn't want to smell like a horse all evening."

Ella tossed a magazine on the coffee table and took a seat across from them. She cleared her throat and locked her steely gaze on Benjamin. "Sarah tells me there are problems between you." She held up her hands as his mouth opened. "Don't want to hear them. I have something you need to consider if you're here to talk."

Benjamin slanted a gaze toward Sarah. "I'm assuming you came to the Spanglers' to discuss things again."

She dropped her gaze to the hands shaking in her lap. "I did. You were very kind this afternoon. I didn't deserve that after the way I acted last night." She looked into his dark chocolate eyes and found the respect she'd seen before. "We'll talk about us in a few minutes. I want you to hear Ella's idea first."

He brushed a hand along Sarah's arm. "Okay, Ella. We're listening."

"This case I just closed involved a very wealthy man. We're talking billions. His eighteen-year-old son rebelled three years ago. Ran away. Various agencies, including CLUES, looked for him without success. Short version, my volunteers found the son this week and helped them reconcile. Mr. Moneybags wants to reward CLUES since we never gave up."

Benjamin leaned forward, absorbed by her story. "You checked on leads for three years?"

"We regularly go over old cases to see if anything new is happening. People get careless when the heat dies, or in this case, after time passes. That's often when we locate them."

"So he wants to give you money?"

"Precisely. Right now, my company is disjointed. We waste time bringing key volunteers together. I need a headquarters where my key staff can be together—my computer tech, search coordinator, the psychologist who works with families, and others who play daily roles. We keep in touch via e-mail and phone, but we should be in one location. Sarah needs to revamp Mosey Inn. It's a perfect location for CLUES. We'd have private living quarters. There's room for parking our new command post vehicle, areas for conferences and equipment storage, and the house is available immediately."

Sarah twisted to face Benjamin. "Ella and I talked last night. We're discussing a partnership. I'd keep my room and convert the library into a private area to give a bit more space. Ella's team occupies the rest of the house. We share the kitchen. Her benefactor pays the bills and upkeep. I'm still the owner."

Ella eyed them as if anticipating agreement. "It'll make CLUES run more smoothly and solves a problem for you two. You'll have a comfortable home, and so will we as long as my benefactor wants to fund us."

"Sarah sent me packing. Why include me in this decision?"

"I want your help with the remodeling. The marriage questions are between you and Sarah. I'm offering a solution to one issue. If you two solve the rest..." She shrugged, slapped her knees, and rose. "Well, I'll leave you alone to talk. I'm in North Carolina Lily if you have questions. Goodnight."

Tension hung between them like an August morning fog. Sarah took Benjamin's hands. She stroked her thumbs across them rather than look into his face. "I came to say I was wrong." Would he hear the sincerity in her voice? "I had no idea if you were even there."

"I spent last night at Pastor Morrison's. Todd asked me to watch Noah so he could devote his attention to selling Topper. I didn't want to tell the kid I was leaving. It bought me some time."

She gathered her courage and looked him in the eye. "You were right. It is a matter of trust. I wasn't able to trust God or you with my life. I spent last night and this morning thinking and praying. I found peace with God. Can you forgive me too?"

He sighed as if her request reached his soul. "My love for you never changed. Of course, I can forgive you." He cradled her face in his hands, his eyes searching hers. "Do you honestly want to make a marriage work?"

She nodded. The gentleness of his hands and his eagerness to forgive caressed areas in her soul she'd never allowed love to reach.

He held her head with a finger beneath her chin. "This arrangement with Ella will let you keep Mosey Inn, but you'll still have to depend on me for daily living if I understand Ella right."

"You do. We'd need money for food and other expenses. I can't believe I let money come between us." She moved to settle against his chest. His arms enfolded her. They seemed to welcome her. "What we have is worth more than all the money in the world." She glanced up at his face. "I'm not doing this because Ella can save Mosey Inn and pay for its upkeep."

He combed loving fingers through her hair. "You'd accept my role as provider and live on what I have?"

"I'd be a fool not to."

"Then we'll be fine. I'll take on some small jobs if necessary, but I want to spend my time enjoying you."

"Sounds wonderful."

The dread of asking about his emotional state tied her stomach into a knot. He had to hear that she knew about his nightmares and admit that she'd caused him unimaginable pain. Putting it off wouldn't erase what she'd done. Confession might ease her conscience.

"I need to ask something." She took a deep breath. "I've spent this week looking at my own selfish desires. I never asked how you've handled the trauma of the church fire. I went over there and saw—"

He stiffened. "Ella told you."

There was an edge to his voice. Shame? Anger? Sarah moved out of his arms to observe his face. Had she overstepped her bounds and hurt him again?

"Ella thought I needed to look at things through your eyes. A smart choice. If you think she betrayed a trust, it wasn't—"

"Feeling sorry for me isn't a reason for marriage either."

She laced her fingers in the curls above his ear. "I'm not doing this because of pity. You loved me enough to risk your life for me. At the church this morning, I saw evidence of what you did."

He closed his eyes. A long slow breath hissed out of his lungs. "Fear almost kept me from coming in after you. Losing you would have been..."

His sad eyes almost let guilt grab her. No. She'd accept the forgiveness she'd received and press on. "Are you still having nightmares?"

He shook his head. "I'm back to normal. The first couple of days were rough. Watching you recover took away the fear. Last night ... your rejection hurt more than the trauma of either fire." He chewed on his lower lip and traced circles on her back. "I love you. I don't want to live without you."

She wouldn't cry. They'd shed enough tears. Deciding if the future could allow marriage required level heads, not emotions. "I can't change what I did, but I am sorry. I rejected other people's love too. I complained because people cared enough to come help me. My heart should have overflowed with gratitude. It didn't. That's wrong. I see both things differently today."

He pulled her close again, his breath whispering against her cheek. "I understand why. I'll pray that you'll never need that sort of care again. It wouldn't be easy to see you like that every day."

"I don't want to go there. I want to feel the way I did riding Topper. I wish moments like that could go on forever. They won't. We'll both get old. And I'll trust you to give me love and physical care."

"I'd stay with you and find the best people possible to keep you from feeling like an invalid."

"You've already shown you'd do that. Requiring total care taught me a valuable lesson. Some people enjoy helping." She sat, glad for the chance to lighten the subject matter. "I'd like to form a group of volunteers to visit shut-ins, make meals, and sit with people. Give caregivers a break. I got meals occasionally when Mom was at her worst, but what I needed was a way to have a normal life. I want to help others in those situations get the type of help they need."

"It's a good idea. You'd be good at it. Pastor Morrison asked me to form a team to repair the church. If we add some projects like the one at Emily's house, we'd both have a way to help others."

She grinned and nestled against him again. "We're getting better at solving problems. Think we'll learn to communicate as we spend time together?"

"I'd say we're on a roll."

She grinned, and he returned the smile. "Another item then. I'm in decent health. There are things I could never do because of my commitments. If I don't have to worry about running Mosey Inn, we could travel. Could you do that?"

Silence spoke for a few seconds. She wanted to look at him but didn't move. She'd asked him to jump a big hurdle.

"You're talking about cruises and seeing the world. Things you read about in your travel magazines."

She looked up to find his brows knitted together and uncertainty in his eyes. "Yes. But we can stay here and enjoy life without—"

He touched his fingers to her lips. "I can do it. I'm changing. My heart still pounds when I meet someone new, but it's getting easier. If we're together, I could handle some traveling. I was contemplating the money."

"We'll plan wisely. I'll be content to take local trips if it won't work."

"We're venturing into areas where we'll have to stretch. I can face people if you can let me be the kind of husband who loves his wife and takes good care of her."

"Being the leader is important to you, isn't it?"

"Yes. But I don't want to squelch your independence. It's one of the things I love about you. I need you to see me as a man who doesn't take his responsibilities as a husband lightly."

"I can handle that. It'll force me to change my focus. You came to love me, not control me. I'll concentrate on returning your love."

"So we're ready to share a house with CLUES and each other?"

"If your proposal is still open. I'd say we are."

He pulled the ring box from his pocket. "I hoped I might need this." A broad smile accented his facial scars—scars she now viewed as a sign of valor.

She held out her left hand. For some reason, her fingers didn't seem so twisted today. He slid the ring over the knuckle and kissed her hand.

"How did you know my size? It's a perfect fit."

He grinned. "I'll explain later. Right now, I need you to answer a question. Will you grow old with me, Sarah?"

CHAPTER THIRTY-ONE

Sarah brushed a finger over Benjamin's picture in the photo album. Hard to believe she'd been Mrs. Pruitt two months. She'd managed to coax Benjamin into a few snapshots. He'd understood the value of having pictures to remember their wedding day. He'd bravely posed, knowing only their closest friends might view them. His smile reflected the joy they'd shared on the rainy February day when Love Valley residents gathered to witness their union and celebrate in the refurbished fellowship hall.

Sarah placed the photo album on the shelf between the cookbooks. She crossed to the stove, lifted the lid from the simmering beef stew, and gave it a stir. The rich aroma of beef, spices, and vegetables permeated the kitchen. Her mouth watered, and her stomach growled. If Benjamin stayed late at the church work project, she'd have to eat without him. A church member's moldy bathroom wall had turned into a larger-than-anticipated repair. His volunteers were gaining valuable experience despite the long hours. Benjamin enjoyed their company and teaching them. He'd come a long way.

His truck pulled into the back drive. Not late after all. The back door slammed. Benjamin stuck his head around the corner of the kitchen door. "Hey. Didn't expect to find you in the kitchen. Smells good. I thought it was Ella's turn to cook."

Sarah buttered the tops of the dinner rolls while relating her story. "We switched days. Ella's monitoring some volunteers conducting a search in Asheville. They're testing their new computer equipment in the mobile command post vehicle. They've oohed and aahed in the conference room all day."

"Must be working well." Benjamin's work boots thudded in the bin beside the door. Familiar sounds. Habits and routines that came with married life. Much better than loneliness.

She ambled out to the laundry and bathroom area. He held his arms open, but the grin on his face said he didn't expect a hug. His hair was white with sheetrock dust, each fold and wrinkle of skin ashen. He beckoned her.

"No way, mister. You look like a piece of floured and seasoned chicken."

His laughter tickled her heart. "Aw, come on. You know you want a kiss."

"After you shower. I'll bring you some clean clothes." The rumble of thunder grabbed her attention. "A big storm's coming."

She hurried to their bedroom and peered out a window. Dark clouds rolled across the hill toward the orchard. Gusts of wind sent apple blossoms swirling from the trees like pale pink rain. She gathered Benjamin's clean clothes, pausing a second to run a finger over the lace-covered bodice of her white satin wedding gown. She should store it properly, but having it in the back of the closet served as a daily reminder of their love. Might as well enjoy it. She wouldn't pass it on to a daughter.

Thunder boomed again. She scurried back to the laundry room and picked up the dusty clothes he'd tossed outside the bathroom. She stepped onto the porch to give them a shake. The wind yanked the screen door from her hand. Fat drops of rain spattered on the porch. No moonlight kisses in the swing tonight. They'd snuggle on their couch this evening. She tossed the dirty clothes in the washer. Her mind drifted to a quiet evening with Benjamin. How had she ever considered that living alone would be better?

Steam curled underneath the bathroom door. It billowed out when she entered. She fanned the fog and found the cabinet through the haze. "Your clothes are beside the sink. Rain's started."

"Almost done."

"We could use an exhaust fan in this bathroom. I'd forgotten it's like a steam room."

He laughed. "Feels good to me. Add it to your 'honey do list.' I'll fix it some day. How's Mrs. Wexler?"

"Better. Her broken hip is mending well. Emily helped her today. Mrs. Wexler likes it when Thomas comes. They watch game shows while Emily cleans." Sarah swiped a sponge over the faucets since she was standing there doing nothing. "The new lady in church wants to join my food preparation team. I'll add her to the rotation next week. We gained a family who needs a break from their caregiver routine. Speaking of cooking, I need to finish dinner. I'm gone."

Sarah slid the bread into the oven and set the timer. She'd planned a simple meal, knowing Ella's team might eat in shifts. With Ella's fancy new toys, she seldom left Mosey Inn for extended trips. Oops. It would take time to remember they now called this place CLUES. Ella's benefactor had provided a wonderful arrangement for everyone. What a relief to have freedom to come and go as she pleased. Closing the inn and canceling future reservations had lifted a weight from her shoulders.

Returning to the utility area, she stood outside the bathroom door and spoke to Benjamin. "The quilt barn painter loved the colors in the Bear Paws pattern. She'll paint it on the square they're hanging on a barn in Hiddenite. I took her two more patterns today for a fabric store owner to consider."

"Glad you joined that project. I've seen several people taking pictures of the quilt square she painted for the Spanglers' barn. Good for tourism."

"The owners love Mom's quilts. Good inspiration. Our crew has three squares to paint this spring. Guess I'll join them again when we return from our trip."

If she still ran Mosey Inn, she couldn't have taken a long honeymoon cruise. She wouldn't be planning a trip along the Quilt Barn Trail through Tennessee, or attending spring festivals.

Their decision to rent Benjamin's house to its current occupant gave them one less item for concern, and a guaranteed income. Benjamin trusted his grateful friend to take care of his house as he'd done since August.

Water stopped flowing in the bathroom.

Sarah put the spoons on the kitchen counter and met Benjamin at the door. Sliding her arms beneath his shirt, she leaned against his bare chest. The scent of her husband set off ripples of pleasure. She waggled her eyebrows. "Maybe we'll leave this shirt unbuttoned."

"Someone might come in and catch us."

"They're too busy to care what we do."

He pulled her close for a passionate kiss. Lifting his head, he whispered softly against her ear. "Let's dine in our private quarters tonight."

"A splendid idea." She ran her hands along his bare back, memorizing the pattern of the scars.

After they'd eaten, Sarah reclined against Benjamin, listening to the cadence of his voice as he read aloud. Thunder rolled across the valley, and rain pelted the windows. Firelight danced on the hearth in the redecorated library. Sarah treasured these moments spent in their private retreat—a place where they could forget the cares of the world and savor each other.

Whoops echoed through the house. Benjamin laid aside the book and kissed the top of Sarah's head. "Sounds like success."

She turned to look at him. "Want to get the scoop tonight?"

He nuzzled her cheek and trailed kisses down her neck. "Not

particularly. I'd rather spend the night enjoying my wife."

"Good plan. We'll hear about the search tomorrow at breakfast. Which snippet of fabric in the Double Wedding Ring quilt do you want to learn about tonight?"

"Let's go discuss it." He pulled her to her feet and led her toward the bedroom.

Later, Benjamin spooned her to him. She settled into his embrace and basked in the afterglow of intimacy. "Will you stay awake to hear my story?"

"Until they stop celebrating. That's the only thing I hate about sharing this house."

"So I'll bore you until you fall asleep. Which piece?"

He rose up on an elbow. "Tell me about this one." He indicated a piece of blue cotton near the top of the quilt, nestled closer, and draped his arm across her again.

Sarah giggled. "That was back in the early seventies. A piece of a very short mini-skirt."

"Too bad I missed seeing that."

"It wasn't a pretty sight. I had chubby legs and acne."

The mellow rumble of his laugh shook the bed. "Some things get better with age, huh?"

She swatted his arm. "Forget about the mini-skirt. Go to sleep. I love you."

He answered with a mumbled, "I love you."

The deep breaths of contented sleep carried him away. She listened to the patter of rain on the porch roof and relished the comfort of Benjamin's arms.

The patterns of life seemed to move along so fast. Before she knew it, they'd be old. The inevitable didn't hold the dread she'd experienced when she'd faced the prospect alone. God had planned it perfectly. An old maid and a misfit sharing love in their waning years. Life couldn't be better.